HAYLEY STONE

MACHINATIONS

www.aethonbooks.com

ALSO IN THE SERIES

Machinations

Counterpart

Architect

To my parents, who first introduced me to Star Wars, thus prompting a lifelong obsession with science fiction and fantasy. This is all your fault. Love you.

ONE

THERE NEVER WERE ANY REFUGEES.

No gutsy survivors who finally discovered the trick to broadcasting a distress signal. No last-minute stragglers who escaped extermination in Skagway or Whitehorse. Around us, there's snow, ice, and the disemboweled city of Anchorage in the distance, its skyline mutilated and squashed, filled with the crushed leftovers of businesses and people's homes. I know from a previous visit that the sea is also slowly devouring the metropolitan area, making a Slurpee of downtown. But there were never any refugees.

This is a trap.

The realization drills through me seconds before the ground erupts and bullets slam into my chest, knocking me flat on my back. For the first few seconds, I think, *I'm okay. I'm okay.* Because that's the point of body armor, right?

I fight to make my legs work, make them obey my command to get up, get moving. But I can't feel them. An unexplained warmth slides up the back of my suit as my mouth fills with the taste of a dentist's office. That last detail stands out in my mind, looming over everything else with terrible precision—reality fashioned into a bloody spear, the tip driven into me. *This is what the inside of my lungs tastes like.*

Nope. Not okay.

"Rhona!" Camus screams. He crunches toward me, but the sound is muffled by the snow piled up around my ears.

"Camus," I gasp. "Camus. Camus." His name is a prayer. Like I'm calling on him to save me.

He drops to his knees. His features—the long, aquiline nose, the cheekbones as high and sharp as his eyes—have gone dark, thrust into shadow by the aureole of light behind his head, like a medieval icon in reverse. Maybe it's better this way. This way I can't see his face pinched with panic. I only feel the kiss of his dark hair tickling my cheek as he strains to lift me back onto my feet.

I cry out as I'm moved, spitting up dark blood onto his pristine white snowsuit. The bloodstain is like a melting Rorschach pattern. *What do you see?*

"Don't," I mumble. "It's too late. Camus, it's too late."

"No," he says. Tries again.

And again I cry out. "Camus!" I press a weak hand against his shoulder. "Stop. Please."

Blood continues to dribble from my mouth, and when I go to wipe it away—like ketchup or mustard—it gets on my glove and leaves a long streak along the arm of my jacket. The gaping hole in my chest wheezes when I try to inhale. I feel like a balloon, except I don't want to float away.

"We have to get you out of here." He smooths my hair back from my face with a gloved hand, and the reddened strands stick to the crusted ice. In the moment, I hate that glove. I want to feel his skin, his lips, the crush of his body, one more time. "The machines—"

"They've already done it." I inhale sharply, but it's becoming more and more difficult to breathe. "Look at me, Camus. I'm a pincushion."

A smile surfaces on my lips, like a corpse floating to the top of a lake. Apparently even dying can't diminish my sense of humor. Good for me.

The wind must be a northerly, because it's blowing smoke into our eyes, enveloping us in a shroud of pale gray. The smell of ash seems appropriate, like it's the end of the world. And the noise ... I still hear the *whir-whir-whir* of machines nearby, explosions of electronic static, and also meatier sounds, the carnage of metal plunging into flesh.

They're dying. My team, my friends, they're dying. *Because of me.*

"You have to leave me," I tell Camus.

"Not going to happen." Camus grabs my hands and places them firmly on the sucking chest wound to seal it and tells me to hold them there. "Exhale," he orders, and tips me onto my side, trying to make it easier for me to breathe with the lung that isn't breached. When that doesn't seem to work, I complain, and he eases me back into a seated position. I slouch into the cavity of his chest.

And all I think is, *He doesn't know.*

My mind's unraveling like a spool of thread that's caught on the wing of a fighter jet. *I should tell him. I should ... tell him. About what I've done.*

Might be the last chance ...

"I'll come back to you," I murmur, head lolling against Camus's shoulder. My vision is beginning to blacken. He's disappearing—or I am. Either way, it's getting hard to see him, to see the face I love above all other faces.

"Rhona," Camus says, and my eyes are pulled to his mouth as I try focusing on his words. "Rhona, stay with me. Keep awake. Keep your eyes open. Hold on. Help ..." I know what he wants to say. *Help is on the way.* He wants to reassure me, give me something to cling to. But help's not coming. *We* were the help.

His hand clutches mine, willing me to stay. I wish I could.

Oh, God, I don't want to die.

Tears spill onto my cheeks, warm. I don't know whether they're mine or his. "I love you," I say, the words half-gargled in blood. He cradles me to him, leans down, and I taste the ash on his lips, dry and chapped from the wind. They bump and scrape against my own—so real, so tangible—and I struggle to rise back to consciousness like a princess awakened from a curse.

"I'll come back to you," I repeat dumbly. "I won't—I won't leave you to fight alone." The thought occurs to me that he won't understand what I mean, but I don't have the breath or energy to elaborate. Words clot in my throat like honey. My breath rattles around the metal in my chest, and it's impossible to organize my thoughts into a formation that makes sense.

At least the pain is beginning to ebb, which is nice, but also bad. Not like I needed another sign to tell me what I already know. What the taste of the inside of my lungs has already told me.

"Rhona! Fight it! Don't close your eyes!"

I'm sorry, Camus.

"Help! I need the medic here now! Where's the *goddamn medic*?" His voice cracks on the last word, hitting a high note.

"Commander!" someone answers him, a million miles away. "We have to go! Now!"

Way

ahead of

you

TWO

AFTER I'M KILLED, I wake up inside a metal womb.

For the first few seconds, I'm relaxed, bobbing in a place where no thoughts reach me. Where no one—*nothing*—can touch me. Then an emotion hits me, so foreign that at first I can't put a name to it. Safety. That's it. Sweet freedom from the fear and anxiety that has been an ugly constant in my world for the past five years. Half a decade, nearly a fifth of my life.

The machines finally did it in the end. I'm dead. I must be dead, because I'm sure as hell not near Anchorage anymore. So they won; I lost. It's shameful how much of a relief that is.

And yet.

The fight hasn't left my body like I thought it would. My muscles tense, clenching against an occasional rocking sensation that just moments ago tempted me to curl up inside that word—*safety, such a soft word*—and go back to sleep.

Instead, more senses are returning every second—first comes the bleary, melting vision, followed by the sugary taste of plastic and a sharp bouquet of chemicals burning the inside of my nostrils.

Wrong. Fear starts to hum inside me like a panicked hornet trapped in a house. *Wrong*.

Wrong. This is all wrong.

Except for my face, I'm submerged entirely in a clear liquid, and I watch it jostled back and forth by the muffled thunder. Through the opaque lid of my asylum, something flashes every few seconds, turning the water red. Just a trick of the light. Or is it? Before I'm sure that I'm not bleeding to death—*again*—I start to struggle.

Pain registers for the first time when I try to inhale and find something lodged in my throat. I choke, my gag reflex screaming, all while desperately yanking on the intubation tube. My fingers feel arthritic, stiff and new, as my hands fumble. Somehow I manage to get the thing out, gasping.

There are wires. I notice them now—dozens and dozens of wires like tiny varicose veins attached to my arms, and all along my naked body. They disappear into the walls of my three-by-six-foot purgatory. The real horror lies in its mystery.

How did I get here?

Where is here?

A sudden tightness seizes my chest: I can't *breathe*. Am I dying? No. Just hyperventilating. I flatten my hand against my chest—I swear my heart is trying to chisel through my ribs—and clamp down hard on my rising hysteria, doing my best to head it off.

Panicking won't help, I tell myself. It'll only make the situation worse.

But that doesn't stop me from banging on the ceiling of my small prison, hoping the lid will open.

NOW!

I can just make out shapes through the haze, the blurry silhouette of someone—or multiple someones—rushing around.

"Help," I yell, testing my voice. It comes out a broken whisper. Pathetic. I try again. "Help!" I pray it's loud enough, combined with the pounding of my fists, and that someone will notice.

A man's face appears, accompanied by palms pressed against the glass. If he's saying something, I can't hear him through the glass.

"Get me out!" I shout, and the terror in my own voice undoes what little dignity I had remaining. "Please! God, get me *out of here*! Get me out!"

Now I'm kicking at the glass dome with the soles of my feet as well. Hoping for some kind of leverage, I press my back to the bottom and push up. Mostly, I'm just thrashing around in the water. The wires tangle around my legs and arms, hindering my movement and, more importantly, preventing my escape.

When the man disappears from view, frustration converts my fear to anger. Which actually feels better. I can handle anger.

"Hey! Don't go! Where are you going?" I wonder if he even hears me. But I'm under the distinct impression that he's my last chance, whoever he is.

"Come back! I'm still in here! *I'm in here! Don't. Go.*"

My fist beats against the roof with each word, even as my voice runs ragged, frayed by distress.

And then there's the sharp hiss of decompression, like a hundred people exhaling at once. The chamber opens, and the lid slides back halfway before getting stuck. By now the man has returned, and with our combined strength, we manage to push the lid open completely.

Maybe it's delirium, but I throw my arms around this man, my nameless savior, grateful beyond words—although I do manage to find some.

"Thank you," I say, over and over, stupidly. "Thank you, thank you."

I don't know whether or not he's the one responsible for putting me in the capsule in the first place, but right now all that matters is he was the one who got me out of it.

"I'm sorry." He expertly disconnects the electrodes from my body, removing the wires from my skin. "I'm so, so sorry."

He helps me out and covers me with something that's more foil than fabric. Somewhere my brain registers that it's a shock blanket.

And then, at once, everything is cold and harsh and unwelcoming. While he returns to a computer nearby, I blink against the artificial light that continues to fluctuate between white and red, occasionally flickering off entirely, whenever the room shakes. Sirens blare, crying danger. Danger. Danger, Will Robinson.

Wait. Where did that thought come from?

Around us, there are five more pods like the one I was in. I wonder what's inside them. Or who.

I'm so busy struggling to get a sense of what's going on, I don't notice the man trying to get my attention.

"Rhona?" He briefly pulls his fingers from the keys and snaps. "Rhona?"

I look at him only after he's said this word a couple times. It's familiar. A name, maybe? The man stares at me expectantly. I don't know what answer he wants. I don't even understand the question.

"How much do you remember?"

"Remember?"

Considering the circumstances, with chaos on all sides, he's showing a remarkable amount of patience with me.

His eyes jerk between me and the computer screen, fingers flying madly over the keys even when he's not watching the screen. "Do you know who I am?" *Clack clack clack clack.* Such loud keystrokes are distracting, and I squint, trying to focus around the sound. "Or where you are?"

Time is limited, I know it without needing to be told, but I still take a few seconds to study his profile. His face is thin and angular, and he can't be much older than me. Twenty-six, twenty-seven at most. Although his brown hair is short, it's messy and unkempt, sticking out in odd places. For a scientist or doctor or whatever he is, he's not very put together. Even though he's not smiling—whatever data he reads on the screen weighs his mouth down like an anchor—pronounced dimples frame his lips. The bottom one is pink and swollen, as though he's been biting it. It's a bad habit he has when he's nervous. I know this with certainty. I *know* I know him.

But something isn't right in my head. There are things missing, including his name and who he is to me.

"No." My voice cracks. "What's the matter with me?"

His dark eyes are soft with understanding, with pity. They do nothing to quiet my mounting dread. He stops typing. "It's too soon," he says, more to himself than to me.

"What?"

"I'm sorry."

It's the fourth or fifth time he's apologized, and I'm beginning to think there's actually a good reason for it, that he's responsible in part for the shape I'm in. Yet I can't help but trust him. I don't know why exactly. It's more than his soft bunny eyes or even the fact that he freed me. Whatever it is, my heart and my gut agree: he's a good person. Probably. And right now, he's all I have.

"There's no time to explain," he says. "We have to leave."

"Clothes?" I suggest, still clutching the shock blanket around myself.

He averts his eyes quickly. "Oh! Right." He hits a few more keys, then goes to a nearby cabinet, opens it, and removes something similar to a full-body wetsuit, the only difference being it's white instead of black. After he hands it over to me, I notice tiny thermal grids in the material, intended to trap heat. We must be somewhere cold.

I don't wait for him to turn around. There's no time for modesty. But it doesn't matter, because he politely gives me his back as soon as I drop the blanket. I shimmy into the suit and zip it. I can't get the zipper all the way up, however, and clear my throat as a request for assistance. He does the rest.

"Quite the fashion statement," I say, and he actually smiles. It's a beautiful smile. This is a man who's had practice smiling, I think, in another place, another time, maybe. Before the madness and machines.

"You'll need gloves, too." He's already gotten some out for me. "To complete the ensemble."

He catches me off guard by responding to my snark. It's so absurd, so utterly inappropriate given the circumstances, I have to laugh at us both.

As I begin to put the gloves on, the walls shake again. This time I recognize the tremors for what they are—mortar fire of some sort. The lights go out entirely for a long moment, and in between the stutter of the sirens, all I hear is our breathing. It's a sound I've always found comforting, especially in the dark. It's life whispering, *I'm here, still here, still alive.* It's one more thing that sets us apart from the machines.

They were meant to be our salvation. I realize this suddenly, brutally, with the clarity of one recently betrayed. We created the machines to make our lives more convenient, applied as a careful blind so no one would see how badly we were cannibalizing our planet. War, overpopulation, fracking, and carbon emissions—why not throw more technology at the problem and hope it all went away?

The machines were supposed to solve those crises for us, without demanding a change in lifestyle or culture. They could fight our conflicts, produce our food, heal our sick and wounded, even perform as simple a task as ferrying us from one destination to another, pollutant-free. Of course, they also manufactured themselves—and if anyone raised a stink about the pitfalls there, I can only assume they were shouted down by corporations and governments getting rich off their happy clientele. *Us.*

When the generator kicks back in and the lights return, a door shudders open to my left and another man enters the room, causing me to jump back. My hand goes instinctively to a weapon at my waist—but there's nothing there. No gun, not even a holster. I feel more vulnerable than when I was naked.

"Samuel, we have to go," says the newcomer, his harsh German accent adding further gravity to his order. "*Now.*"

Images are slowly floating back into my mind's eye now, a swirl of memory. *Samuel,* I think. Finally, a name to go with the man's face. It feels like blood is rushing to my head as I attempt to concentrate. I briefly wonder if standing upside down would help. Probably not.

Samuel.

Yes! There's something. The faintest caress of remembrance.

Samuel is laughter beneath warm rain. The source of answers in Chemistry class. Bad sci-fi movies. A funeral. Then later, a plan. He's a friend. He's *my* friend.

How could I forget?

And why can't I remember more?

"I just need a few more minutes," Samuel says, back at the computer. "My latest data hasn't finished compiling. I'm also having issues with the local servers; they're not responding to my queries." A careful pause. He glances at me. "And she's still ... acclimating."

The German's been staring at me from beneath thick beetle brows as if I'm a meal he's not sure he can easily digest. Once upon a time, he must have been blond, handsome even, but now he's all gray fatigue and grimaces. It's starting to unnerve me, his unblinking curiosity. It feels more like suspicion. *Fine. I don't trust you, either.* There's nothing friendly about his tired face, rigid posture, or the automatic rifle resting against his shoulder. *But he's still human,* I remind myself. That counts for a lot more than it used to.

"Leave it," he says to Samuel, but keeps his eyes on me. What does he expect me to do? I weigh about 125 pounds soaking wet, and I'm not soaking wet. Anymore.

"Seconds," Samuel promises. "Just a few more seconds—"

A dull rumbling cuts him off and sets the overhead lights swaying. Our shadows lean against the wall, veer toward the ceiling, growing and shrinking, growing and shrinking. Glass beakers on the steel countertops tremble, making an entirely too cheerful sound, like the clinking of champagne flutes. The sirens cut out. Then a *whooshing* sound blows through the facility, like flame ejected from a dragon's throat—a loud and terrible inferno. Pieces of the ceiling begin to crumble, dusting us with plaster snowflakes.

"No," barks the German whose name I still don't know. Even if he's shorter than Samuel by a few inches, he's certainly bulkier—a solid, square mass of muscle. He walks over and grabs Samuel by his dress shirt collar, giving him a hard shove toward what I assume must be the exit. "*Now.*"

But Samuel won't be bullied into leaving. He pushes past him, back to the computer. "Hold on. I just have to ..." After another moment of pounding the keyboard, including attacking the enter key repeatedly, he pinches his eyes shut. "The machines must have reached our server room. I keep trying to copy files onto this drive"—he nods to a portable hard drive on the desk, connected to the desktop by a simple USB cord —"but the computer's telling me they're in a location that doesn't exist."

"What files?" I ask, though I think I already know the answer.

Samuel hesitates. "Important ones. Vital." His gaze cuts to the German. "We have to go to the server room. Straight to the source. We have to—"

"Impossible," the German says, interrupting him. "It is on the other side of the base, close to the breach."

"We have guns," Samuel says.

"Not enough. The machines outnumber us, at least six to one."

"Then we get more."

"No." The German's voice is firm.

"Ulrich, please," he pleads. So his name is Ulrich. How very—well —*German*.

To my surprise, Ulrich's eyebrows buckle in a moment of sympathy. But then he grabs Samuel by the arm and urges him again toward the door. This time, Samuel doesn't fight him. His shoulders slouch in defeat. He gives his computer one last, longing look, snatches up the portable hard drive, and motions me to follow.

The three of us move from the windowless room into a long, windowless corridor. *Nice change of scenery*.

Eventually, we reach an intersection with two hallways jutting off in separate directions. The German starts to head down one, but Samuel stops him.

"Ulrich! Where are you going?"

"The armory," Ulrich replies.

"Weren't you just there?" I look at his rifle.

"I was rushed." Ulrich glares at me, like it's *my* fault the machines infiltrated the base so quickly, not leaving him enough time to be thorough. "We will need more guns. More Imps, more ammunition ..."

I don't know what he means by *Imps,* but Samuel seems to understand the shorthand. "Okay. What about supplies?" he says. "If we're abandoning the base, we're going to need some basic equipment."

"In storage near recreation. Already set aside." Ulrich cradles his rifle in his arms. "I will meet you there in five minutes. Take the long route, avoiding the interior halls. Watch around corners. Five minutes." He gestures like he's going to give me a high five, then jogs off.

As we walk, Samuel explains that while the facility spans several miles, it's not very large in any one section. This is mainly to avoid detection by the machines' sensors.

"They're always looking for us," he says with a drained look, "systematically combing the planet for pockets of human resistance, for people holed up in remote locations like this one."

From what I recall of our strategies, that means we're somewhere in a northern mountain range. Alaska, maybe. The scaling equipment I find in the storage room suggests as much.

"Grab some warm clothes and whatever food will fit in one of those backpacks there," Samuel tells me as he secures the external drive in a hardcase, and then puts on a jacket twice his size. After he's all zipped up, he begins stuffing the insulated canteens and foodstuffs Ulrich set out into a blue pack.

I'm still adjusting to movement. My limbs feel rather sleepy, but I manage to contribute. I can't help glancing at Samuel as we're packing. He's attacking the task with a single-minded focus. I know he has the answers to my questions. I also know right now probably isn't the time to interrogate him, but I have to ask. I'm going crazy with speculation, and there may not be a chance later, depending on how all this pans out. The machines are efficient killers. I can personally attest to that.

Besides, we have five minutes. Plenty of time for a quick Q & A.

I try to think of a gentle question to test the waters, then quickly decide against it. "Where are we, Samuel? And how did I get here?"

He stops what he's doing to look at me. "Alaska." *Knew it.* "Just south of the Brooks Mountain Range, although there are sections of the facility that stretch beneath the mountains."

I notice he's craftily avoiding my second question. We stare at one another, wasting precious seconds in uncomfortable silence. Samuel looks like a suffocating fish, opening and closing his mouth. He's trying, but he can't find the words to explain.

I find some for him. "I'm dead, aren't I?" I'm proud of how calm I sound.

"It's difficult to ... I wouldn't say ... It's a matter of perspective?" He shoulders the pack and makes for the door. "I'm sorry. Maybe this conversation should wait until we have more time—"

"We have two minutes," I say, maneuvering into his path. "Talk."

"Rhona ..."

"Rhona. You said that before. I'm guessing it's—my name? So why don't I feel like it belongs to me? Why can't I remember you properly?"

He smiles sadly. "Maybe because I've never been very proper?"

"You know that's not what I was asking."

To his credit, Samuel looks genuinely distressed on my behalf. "I don't know what happened, exactly. That's the truth, I swear it. And you, you *are* Rhona Long. In a sense. You have her DNA, coded identically right down to the most obscure mutation. Her personality and her experiences and her memories are yours, too. Or they should have been. Something must have interfered with the transference, or it could have been the premature birth sequence. I can't know for sure until I run some tests."

"That's all nice and clinical, but what does it *mean*?"

"It means ..." he says, swallowing again. *Stalling,* I think. "It means you're a clone."

A clone. It sounds like a joke. I want to think of some clever response, a witty retort, but nothing comes. No words seem adequate to describe the confusion, the panic, the blind mess of emotions charging through my system, urged on by adrenaline. I know it's the truth. Only truth could feel so damn terrible.

Finally, I manage to stammer, "How? I mean, why? Who would do this?"

"You would."

He's still wearing his "I'm sorry" face. I kind of want to punch him in the nose.

Then Ulrich shows up and shoves a gun into my hands, tempting fate. "What is taking so long?" he says, frowning at our progress.

If I had thought of the German as armed before, he's doubly so now. Around the mesh fabric of his trousers are several holsters, each occupied by a gun. Higher up at his waist are another pair of pistols, a few knives, and some expensive EMP grenades. *Oh! Not Imp—EMP.* That's one mystery solved. I recognize the EMP grenades by the little blue lights going around their circumference like carousel bulbs, identifying them as inactive. For now, at least. And that doesn't even take into account the automatic resting against his shoulder, and whatever else he's packed into his black duffel bag.

When Ulrich notices me eyeing his arsenal, he gives me a partial smile. "I don't believe in half measures."

"I see that."

My own firearm isn't nearly as impressive as Ulrich's hardware. Just your average electromagnetic-pulse gun. It's about the size of the old safe-action pistols from a few decades ago, before our technology became our own worst enemy and bullets were rendered antiquated in the field. I test my familiarity with the weapon by ejecting its cartridge, checking its energy levels, and successfully sliding it back in with a click. It's weird. I remember a host of combat strategies, how to disassemble and reassemble an EMP-G, things about the war, but I can't recall lyrics to my favorite song, or what my favorite vegetable is, or if I even like vegetables.

For the first time, I wonder what sort of person Rhona Long really was. I wonder if I'm any different now. Something more—or something less.

Another explosion puts my growing identity crisis on hold. It's a direct hit, or very nearly, because the lights give one last, valiant flicker, then everything goes dark. The force of the impact nearly knocks me over. I save myself by latching onto a table. My fingers slip against the metal, but I manage to steady myself at the last second. For a few scary seconds, I worry the ceiling has caved in, burying us alive.

"Samuel," I say, starting to move toward where I remember him standing.

"Hold on," he says. "Almost got it ... There!" A narrow beam of light suddenly illuminates his face, highlighting the valleys. "Everyone okay?" He sweeps the arc of light in my direction.

I blink rapidly before getting my arm up as a shield for my eyes. "Yeah." Samuel moves the beam over to the hulking shadow that is Ulrich in the dark. "Boo," Ulrich says sarcastically. "Now we leave."

It isn't until we're moving again that something occurs to me: I haven't seen any other people in this whole facility. Granted, I've not had a thorough tour of the place, but from what I've seen so far, it seems like a lot of space for just a soldier and techie/scientist/doctor/whatever Samuel is, even given the wide berth most normal people would want to give Ulrich.

"Where's everyone else?" I ask Samuel as we navigate the labyrinth of hallways and corridors. I feel like a rat in a maze. I don't know where we're going, or what's waiting for us when we get there. Ulrich's taken the lead, so I'm forced to rely on his sense of direction. He's set the pace just below grueling, muzzle and scope at eye level, ready.

Samuel gives me a strange look. "There is no one else."

"You mean, they've already been evacuated?"

"No. I mean, sort of. The scientists who used to work here transferred to McKinley before we moved in. It's just been Ulrich and me. Alone here for the past ... oh, two or so years now."

It's my turn to give him a funny look. "And where was I that whole time? I mean, me-me.

Not clone-me." *Dang, that's going to get confusing.*

"Back at McKinley base." His tone implies the answer should be obvious.

McKinley base. McKinley base ... It rings a bell—like a fairy tripping on LSD in my brain, but I decide to set it aside for the moment.

"We were apart for that long?" I ask instead. It makes me feel weird, knowing the last months of my previous life were spent without my best friend. Did I miss Samuel? Did we exchange regular communications? How did he receive the news of my death?

Samuel focuses on Ulrich's back. "Yeah ..." he says slowly, drenching the word in regret. He throws on a smile before I can interrogate him on how he felt about our separation. "Ulrich's not such bad company, though. He plays a mean game of Texas Hold'em. As you can imagine, his poker face is unreadable."

I can't tell whether he's joking or not. "Oh? And what do you wager?"

"Candy, mostly."

The image of Samuel and Ulrich sitting at a table, playing a game of cards, and exchanging Skittles instead of money is almost too much to bear. Or believe. Yet I don't detect any deceit in his tone. I shake my head. "Okay, then. But that doesn't explain why there aren't any other people here. Shouldn't there be some lab assistants or ... something?"

Ulrich shushes me before I can pry another answer out of Samuel. He turns off the flashlight. At the same time we come to an abrupt halt, flattening our bodies against the wall. No one needs to tell me what to do; I just do it. Call it instinct, or self-preservation, or whatever.

There are some sounds you can't forget, even if you want to. The motorized *whir-whir-whir* of a machine is one of those sounds, so ingrained in my consciousness my heart could beat out its staccato rhythm. As I listen to it now, it triggers a respiratory response, my chest closing in panic as I wrestle with whether to run or stay and fight. I hold my breath and imagine a serene place—a trick I learned from my father. Or Rhona learned from her father, I guess.

Whir-whir-whir. It's getting louder, coming closer.

I adjust and readjust my hand on the grip of my gun. I pray I still know how to use this thing. Samuel is breathing loudly next to me. I know he can't help it. He's not trained for this. He belongs in a lab, fighting on an intellectual battleground, his mind his weapon of choice. But knowing that doesn't do us any good right now. And it doesn't take away from the fact that he's going to give us away. Get us all killed.

Whir-whir-whir-whir-whir.

That's it. Someone has to take the initiative here. Ulrich might be content to let the enemy come to us, but I've always preferred offense to defense. I remember briefly how the element of surprise has won mankind countless battles throughout history—we're talking ancient, medieval, *and* modern times. So when I push myself off the wall and round the corner, I have no choice but to trust in the time-tested stratagem. I'm dimly aware of Ulrich shouting in what sounds like German, and Samuel calling my name, but neither stops me. It's too late anyway. I've already committed to the attack.

In the split second I have to survey the scene, I count three of them. Even with dilated pupils in the dark, I identify their hulking figures. Red optics peer at me from the black. They're like the eyes of the monsters I feared would emerge from my closet when I was little. The sight provides a shot of adrenaline, keeping me mobile. My senses are so heightened by fear that I imagine I hear every creak of their hydraulics systems as they move closer.

Regardless, this is the best-case scenario since, for whatever reason, the machines like to operate in multiples of three. No one knows why. Although we've managed to capture and dissect some in the past, their overall programming remains a mystery. We know how they work, just not why they work in the manner they do or why the switch got flipped against us. But more important is the knowledge we do have: we know how to destroy them.

I take a knee before I start firing, making myself a smaller target, harder to hit. It's not exactly guerrilla warfare, but then, they're not expecting an ambush.

WHIR-WHIR-WHIR.

Before they can react, I exhale and squeeze the trigger. Once, twice, and again. The darkness lights up in three distinct flashes of blue white as the machines' processors short-circuit from the violent surges of power. The light show is brief, but satisfying. They don't give a shrill cry of protest or emit even the slightest hint of pain or emotion; they just shut down.

I lower my weapon, feeling slightly light-headed and more than a little winded. Samuel and Ulrich push past me. They're still yelling, only now it seems to be at each other, and it takes me a moment to catch up with their conversation.

"Ten seconds," Samuel is saying, to which Ulrich replies with a sharp bark in German. Something like snail? Snell?

Samuel uses his foot to kick through the chest cavity of the machine, then reaches in and withdraws the core processor. It hums back to life five seconds later, as predicted—the still-beating heart of a heartless machine. Ulrich's technique is less tactful. He drops a grenade into one of them and presses the muzzle of his rifle to the other, firing through half its charge. I'm sure he would have gone through the entire clip if there wasn't the possibility of more lurking nearby.

"What was that?" Ulrich demands angrily of me once he's done taking out his aggression on the enemy's corpse.

I feel stupid. In the beginning, a direct hit from an EMP-G would have ended it, but humans haven't been the only ones evolving and learning. The machines have gotten smarter, too. Stronger. Now it takes ten seconds for them to reboot, and double the effort to put them down.

"I forgot about the reboot time," I admit.

"You almost got us killed!" He's in my face now, but I try not to let my intimidation show.

"I'm sorry, all right?"

The German remains unmoving as a statue, huffing through his nose, silent and furious, until Samuel intervenes. "Hey," he says, placing a friendly hand on his shoulder. "She said she was sorry. Let's just keep moving. It's another mile to the access tunnel, and they're going to notice the dip in active units soon."

Ulrich violently shrugs Samuel's hand off and moves away from us. "Rhona would not have made such a mistake."

"I *am* Rhona," I tell his back. More quietly, as if to reassure myself, I say, "I'm Rhona."

But there's no response from the Berlin Wall, so I stand there, awkward and uncomfortable in my own skin. For the first time since the lights went out, I'm actually glad for the dark. At least this way no one sees my face or can tell I'm hurt by Ulrich's words. It's a terrible thing to die one person and wake up another, but far worse having it pointed out to you. I'm not even sure if he's right or wrong. I don't know what to feel, other than alone.

Samuel's behind me with the flashlight. Waiting for me to get moving, I expect. But when I step forward, I trip, though there's nothing in my way. It's like the battle leeched my strength, leaving me anemic. I don't understand. I've been through countless engagements and even *training exercises* more strenuous than this, but none have left me feeling this drained.

Bracing myself against the wall, I try to stay upright, hoping the feeling will pass. I know to remain here means death. After a few minutes, though, I just can't stand any longer.

I slide to the ground.

"Are you all right?" Naturally it's Samuel who's concerned. He leans down beside me, and his presence is surprisingly reassuring. I feel him take my hands, but then realize it's only so he can check the pulse in my wrist. My heart continues to beat erratically. I can't seem to catch my breath, even at rest.

"Yeah," I say. "Just thought I'd sit on the floor for a bit."

He flashes the light in my face, and although he's hidden behind its halo, I swear I see worry lines right between his brows. "Your nose is bleeding, Rhona."

"What?" I rub my nose, and my fingertips come away wet with red.

I don't remember ever being squeamish before, but the sight of the blood catches me off guard. It frightens me. I wipe, wipe, *wipe,* trying first to get it off my upper lip and then off my fingers. But it won't come off, and my nose continues to run. I feel my composure unraveling with each drip. My mind flashes back to the moment of my death, when the world was blood and fire.

I'll come back to you. I won't leave you to fight alone.

Somehow, I know those were my last words. I see a face, someone I know was—*is*—precious to me, but it's blurred, as if perceived through watering eyes. My memory is nothing but ashes from that day.

I'm choking on the past and fighting back tears when Samuel stops my frantic efforts, taking hold of the backs of my wrists with remarkable tenderness. I fight against him for a few seconds more, stubborn and aching for someone I can't remember.

"Rhona. Hey, it's okay. It's okay."

"What's wrong with me?" I ask, choking the words out, my throat swollen.

"You're putting your body under more stress than it's used to, that's all." Guiding my hand, he has me pinch the soft, fleshy part of my nose. "Keep pressure here, and it should stop in a few minutes. And tilt your head forward some, too. It'll help with any nausea." He uses the edge of his coat to wipe off the remaining smears.

"I do remember you, you know," I blurt out. My voice is nasally from applying pressure to my nose, so I temporarily release it in order to sound more natural when I speak. "I remember you, Samuel."

He has a face that expresses every thought and emotion. His expression brightens, opening like a flower to the sun. "Really?"

"Not everything," I confess, "but some things. Important things."

His eyes remain hopeful, tugging at a nameless something in my heart.

Ulrich interrupts before Samuel can ask more. "If she's not dying, then we go," he says, before hoisting me up from the ground unceremoniously. I don't bother to ask what his solution would be if I *were* dying. I'm getting the sense this man is survival first, loyalty second. As much as I might want to, I can't dislike him for it. We're all survivalists now. Even me.

Especially me.

I go back to pinching my nose as we start walking again. Samuel helps support me, squeezing us between the walls of the narrow hall. My strength begins to return after the first hundred feet, and by two hundred I don't need his help anymore. He remains by my side regardless, making up some excuse about relapsing, and that's when I realize that maybe he needs somebody, too. I wonder if I can be that person for him.

Whir-whir-whir.

The sound returns like a bad dream, lighting a fire beneath our feet. Our retreat has a nightmarish quality as we race down an endless corridor in the dark, chased by monsters we can hear but not see.

And then we hit a dead end.

"Did we take a wrong turn?" Samuel asks. I keep an eye on the way we've come, watching, waiting.

"No," Ulrich says.

"We must've taken a wrong turn somewhere ..."

"*Nein,*" the German insists, annoyed. He begins feeling along the wall and the light from Samuel's flashlight follows his hands, illuminating the blank space. Several times, Ulrich knocks and then listens. Each time, it startles me. It's loud in the silence, and I expect the machines will pick up the vibrations on their sensors. They don't need to be able to see us to kill us—the benefits of having an advanced targeting system created by some of the world's greatest think tanks back in the day. They knew it would be used on humans; they just didn't know it would be used on *every* human.

"Ulrich," I say uneasily, guesstimating the distance between us and the machines. The whirring has become a steady sound, meaning they've picked up their pace. We have minutes—if we're lucky. "You can finish your game of knock-knock with the wall anytime now."

"Maul halten," he snaps. I don't need a translator to guess what that means. Shut up.

Samuel keeps glancing back down the hall, and I can almost see him mapping our route in his head, probably trying to figure out how we ended up here, trapped like rodents in the wrong end of the maze.

The end with the zappy trap instead of the cheese. If Ulrich can't figure out a way out of this, I hope Samuel has a secondary escape route in mind. Had I known it would come to this, I would have been paying more attention to doors and signs.

I keep my gun angled at the dark.

Whirwhirwhirwhirwhir. It's like blood pounding in my ears, so loud I almost miss Ulrich's exclamation.

"Step back," he tells us, waving us away. "Back!"

Then with a well-aimed fist, he punches right through the wall. It breaks apart easily, flimsy as papier-mâché. He pulls out several blocks of some type of explosive, judging by the label. The way he places it along the base of the opposite wall, gingerly and with deliberate care, makes me nervous. I don't know what his plan is, but I know better than to question the guy holding volatile explosives.

As soon as he's finished, we backtrack, narrowly avoiding the machines by ducking into a small storage room. I figure the walls must be proofed for heat sensors, allowing our evasion. Convenient.

Inside, there are chemicals and vacuums and other cleaning supplies, but nothing particularly useful for a fight. It feels like I've gone from one enclosed space to another, slightly larger, enclosed space.

"This is your plan?" Samuel says, clearly exasperated with the German's cryptic behavior and where it's led us.

Ulrich grins.

"No," he says, and lifts his hand. There's a detonator in it. "This is my plan." And then he flicks the switch.

THREE

BY SOME MIRACLE, we escape through Ulrich's distraction of fire and make our way outside. In place of machines, we find the night sky waiting for us, curtained in light and moving color. I stand still while the world races above me like an old VHS tape being fast-forwarded, and then Ulrich nudges me forward.

A few minutes later, the ground trembles as if it's a giant's gurgling stomach, and I turn back just in time to watch the earth crack open. Brooks facility belches a fiery gyre that twists and spins toward the sky, raging for a tremendous moment, before the cold and wind smother it like a hand, reducing the flames to black smoke. The explosion sprinkles snow—or plaster?—embers, ash, and demolished flakes of whatever else was contained in the facility, as far as a half a mile away, dusting the tops of our head and shoulders with toxic dandruff.

"It's gone," Samuel whispers, and I barely hear him over the sound of the fire still munching on Brooks. He looks confused and devastated. Even the words *It's gone* sound puzzled, as if he can't understand what just happened, what he's lost.

"Some machines might have survived," Ulrich warns. "We must keep moving."

Samuel nods, though as we march on, I catch him casting inconsolable looks over his shoulder more than a few times.

With each step, my warm breath transforms into wisps of lonely fog in the cold air, wandering up like smoke from a hearth. *Or a destroyed research facility.* It dissipates long before reaching the aurora borealis performing overhead on its dark stage of stars. My spirit brightens and lifts at the sight, awed by the natural phenomenon.

How many times have I seen this before? And with whom?

Back on earth, however, the scenery is less impressive as we trudge through compacted snow. With the great mountains of the Brooks Range behind us, nothing but a flat expanse of white, treeless terrain lies ahead. The wind is relentless, like someone's hands pressing against both of my shoulders. Although I'm not sure of our exact coordinates, I know we must be on the edge of the map.

"Romantic, huh?" I say, somewhat to myself, but mostly to break the prolonged quiet. Samuel looks startled. "What?"

I motion around us. "Snow. The Northern lights. Running for our lives from homicidal machines. Romantic."

Samuel smiles, then drops it like he shouldn't have. He opens his mouth to say something, then thinks better of it. I'm almost starting to feel bad about his discomfort when Ulrich breaks in.

"Romantic," he agrees with a dull smirk, eyebrows crusted in ice.

"Yeah," Samuel now adds lamely. "Very, uh, romantic."

Before, he'd risen to meet my sense of humor, even when it wasn't an appropriate time to do so. I don't know what's changed.

As Ulrich presses ahead of us, I turn to Samuel. "So, did you know what Ulrich was planning?" I *am* curious about the nuances of our escape, but mostly I'm eager to keep some conversation going.

"With the walled-up access tunnel?" He shakes his head. "No clue. It wasn't on any of the facility's recent schematics, and Ulrich wasn't exactly following emergency protocols when he decided to blow it open as a diversion. But this seems to have worked out better. It's bought us some time, at least, so maybe we need new protocols. Anything to keep the machines on their toes. Figuratively speaking."

"How long do you think it'll be before they realize they're hunting for us down the wrong rabbit hole?"

"Hard to say. A couple more hours, at least."

Not nearly long enough. "If we're caught here, out in the open like this ..."

"We won't be. Don't worry. There's some forest near here. We can hunker down there until help arrives." But I don't see any trees yet, just a vast emptiness on the horizon. This is also the first time I'm hearing about any reinforcements.

"Help?" I prompt.

"Well, not all the emergency protocols are useless. There wasn't a lot of warning before the attack, but I managed to get a distress code out before they jammed our communications."

"Okay, so trees and then rescue. Got it. Liking the plan so far."

"Let's hope it turns out to be that simple."

I leave him to his thoughts and take several long strides to catch up with Ulrich, who appears immune to the elements and never needs to stop and catch his breath. For someone who looks like he's hovering around sixty, he's more formidable than me and Samuel. I'm glad he's on our team. Especially since I've learned that if I stand in just the right spot, moving with him, his blocky body obstructs some of the wind. But it's so hard keeping up with his unflinching pace, it's nearly an impossible trick. Still, for the duration of our conversation, I try.

"So how did you know where that C-4 was?" I ask, as casually as if I were inquiring about the weather.

"I volunteered as the muscle, but that does not mean I leave all the brains to him." Ulrich angles a gloved thumb in Samuel's direction, but Samuel's not paying any attention to us. "And it was not C-4."

"What was it, then?"

"Specially made. By me." He shrugs. "I had lots of time on my hands."

"In between the many games of Texas Hold'em?"

He smiles, his teeth barely showing behind chapped lips. "Between you and me? I cheat. Don't tell the boy." I make a show of crossing my heart and feel a sudden, inexplicable kinship with this man. Maybe I misjudged him before.

"You said you volunteered," I prompt, testing this new connection, more desperate for answers than I realized.

Ulrich finally stops and stares at me for a long moment, searching for something. Or maybe some*one*. The friendliness in his eyes evaporates like my breath in the icy air. "Yes," he says. "As a favor to a friend."

He doesn't have to say it; I know he means Rhona.

But not *me*.

"Must've been some friend," I say, hoping to probe not his mind, but his heart.

"She was." He grunts, readjusts his backpack, and moves on. I fall behind.

Samuel's there and we fall into step together. For a time, neither of us says anything, and I'm consumed by a daydream of what our relationship must have been like before I died. Was it easy? Familial? Did we spend childhood summers chasing one another around the neighborhood with Silly String, making a mess of the street? Was Samuel there when I got my heart broken for the first time? I know that must have happened once or twice, even if I can't remember it.

I chance a glance at him then, only to find Samuel returning my gaze. He delivers a smile that's almost shy, encouraging my imagination to run wild with further scenarios of my lost adolescence and his role in it.

Because I'm watching him and not my footing, I'm not prepared when my boot catches on a hard piece of ice. I pitch forward, arms flailing in an attempt to either regain balance or break my fall. Samuel grabs me before I eat snow.

"Careful. It's easy to twist your ankle out here. We'd be in some real hot water if that happened."

"I wouldn't mind being in a little hot water right now."

When he laughs, it's kind of an inhaling, squeaky sound, and I feel the strangest sense of victory for getting to hear it. "Literally, maybe not. But figuratively? I wouldn't want to challenge the Fates right now."

"Superstitious, huh? And here I had you pegged as a 'man of science' kind of guy."

"Oh, I don't believe the two are mutually exclusive. I like to think of it less as superstition, and more as ... good cosmic judgment. I just find it safer to assume I don't know everything and do my best to stay out of trouble."

It's an interesting philosophy, particularly coming from a scientist. I look up at the living sky. It's still so awesome in its natural beauty. Reminds me of something. "You know, someone once told me certain sights could make you forget about the world and its problems. Funny how that's one of the few things I actually do remember." I look back at Samuel. "You told me that, didn't you?"

His breathing gets heavier, the warmth crystallizing in the air around his mouth. "Yeah," he replies, his smile reserved, but I can tell by the look in his eyes that he's moved. "Yeah, that was me. You remember that?"

"I guess some things are harder to forget than others." *Or some people.*

"Rhona." My heart crashes into my throat when he uses my name. Like it still belongs to me. "When we get a chance, I'd like to do a cognitive interview with you."

"That's not code for something, is it?" I tease him, slitting my eyes.

He holds up his thick, puffy gloves and smiles. "I swear, my intentions are strictly honorable."

"Okay, so what is it then?"

"It's a form of memory retrieval that's had some success with crime victims and amnesia patients. It's not as invasive as hypnosis, so you won't be unconscious, but it'll help me determine how much you remember. I wish we could've done it sooner, but ... we haven't exactly had the time."

"All right. I'm in."

As if there were any doubt.

I don't know how long or how far we walk to get to the forest, but by the time we reach the tree line, I'm somewhere beyond the pain and cold, crouched down inside my head where the memories of heat and comfort are. My nose is bleeding again, dry and cracked. Samuel looks half-asleep on his feet. There's no telling how Ulrich's holding up since his back is to me. He's become a permanent landmark in my line of sight, and half the reason I'm so grateful for the pines. At least they're something new to look at.

We move deeper in among the tall trees, where they grow close enough together to be a fence. They are like dark sentinels wearing robes of white, their spindly limbs laden with snow. Here, the wind is weaker, its force disrupted by trunks and branches and brush.

I look around, anticipating movement from the shadows, but apart from the occasional animal noise, it's quiet. The silence magnifies the volume of each crunchy step, our boots pressing into brittle pine needles.

Then something drops behind me.

I whirl around to face it, weapon raised—

And slip backward into Ulrich, who instinctively turns his gun on me. I continue falling, landing on my rear just before the sound repeats itself.

"Easy," Samuel says, pointing to some trees nearby relieving their heavy burden of snow, unloading mushy piles of the stuff onto the ground. The group's relief is palpable. We all share a brief chuckle and try to overlook the fact that Ulrich and I nearly shot each other.

As exhausted as I am—my legs weighty as blocks of stone—it's not until I notice Samuel repeatedly stumbling in the drifts, beginning to lag, that I speak up. "We have to stop," I announce.

Ulrich pauses.

I press on with a grim smile. "I'm dead on my feet, okay? If we continue like this, I guarantee you someone is going to end up tripping and breaking an ankle or leg or something. At this rate, not one of us will be any good in a fight if the machines catch up to us."

"When," Ulrich corrects.

"Right. Look, let's just make camp for the night. Get some sleep. Recharge the batteries." Samuel winces at the metaphor. *Okay, bad choice of words.* "This is as good a spot as any. We can alternate shifts so someone's always got an eye out, but we need to rest or we'll just end up dying tired."

Ulrich lets his pack drop into the snow as his answer. "I will take first watch. Two hours."

"Three." I'm pushing my luck, and I'm fairly certain I don't have much to begin with. "I'll

keep watch with Samuel during the next shift, and then we can get moving again. Six hours."

"Stubborn." I take it as a compliment. He nods, conceding.

With a steep embankment three-quarters of the way around us, and sheltered by a pine-needle canopy above, we hunker down for the remainder of the night. Between the three of us, we have one small, portable tent and a pair of sleeping bags. It's not much against the fury of an Alaskan winter, but it might be enough to keep us alive—so long as we continue wearing our thermal layers. We can't risk a fire, no matter how cold it gets. Given the options of freezing to death or being abducted by the machines, I'd take death as a popsicle any day.

Everyone knows what happens if the machines take you alive. Labor camps, if you're lucky. Slowly being worked to death in one of the machines' factories alongside other humans unfortunate enough to be skilled at a trade. Otherwise, torture, brainwashing ... I seem to recall a story of the machines chipping people like dogs, the subdermal implants delivering an electric shock each time they failed to obey an order. But that might just be fear recirculated in the form of rumor. What isn't rumor is what happens after these captives are turned loose. Always they manage to find pockets of resistance, like bloodhounds scenting a wounded fox. Sometimes they integrate long enough for the other members to drop their guard—and then massacre everyone in their sleep. Other times, the machines swoop in before that point, doing their own dirty work.

It's amazing how much I remember about the war, the resistance, the machines and their impersonal cruelty—yet I can't remember how I got the tiny, sickle-shaped scar I just discovered a minute ago on the underside of my chin.

I help Samuel set up the tent. It's slow going—embarrassingly slow, even with his smarts and my resourcefulness. Ulrich is doing exactly what he volunteered for: looking out—and not much else. I think I even catch him smirking, like he's enjoying the entertainment of our struggle with the tent.

While I'm busy fighting to strap down one side, Samuel says, "Thanks for this," in such a small voice I almost miss it.

"You can thank me once we've finished."

"No, I mean ... what you did back there. You covered for me when you didn't have to." He looks at me, sincerity stretched across his face, eyes shining with gratitude. "Thank you."

"Oh," I answer lamely, feeling a little shy in the face of his appreciation. "Don't mention it." I think about giving him a friendly knock on the shoulder, but somehow that feels wrong. I wish I could remember the nuances of our relationship, to know how to behave around him.

By the time we conquer the tent, I've worked up the courage to ask one of the questions only he can answer. "Samuel? Am I—like myself?"

"What do you mean?" He's rolling out his sleeping bag.

"You said I was supposed to have my—*Rhona's* personality." It's still weird to think I'm two different people. "Do I act like her? Am I still ... me?"

"That's not really a question I can answer for you."

I snort. "Oh, no. Nice try, but you're gonna have to be less cryptic."

"Then you'll have to be more specific," he says and slowly rubs his tired face with hands numbed by the cold. We've removed our gloves temporarily, trying to flex feeling back into them. "Genetically speaking, you're identical. Psychologically speaking, there's no way of knowing until I run some tests. And even then, the results may be inconclusive." Penitence pushes the fatigue from his face. "I'm sorry. I know that's not the answer you were hoping for, and I wish I had a better one for you, but this is uncharted territory. Cloning isn't exactly textbook science."

"So I'm a guinea pig. Comforting."

"No! No, that's not what I meant ..."

"I know." The wind whines as I crawl into my sleeping bag, curling up with my back to Samuel. "But it's still true."

I'm asleep minutes later, my body welcoming the break from reality.

I dream in black and white. I see myself talking and laughing with a handsome man. There is no sound. It's like watching ancient home-movie footage with the volume off.

Yet even without sound, I still understand the conversation somehow. He's asking me what I wanted to be when I was a little girl. I tell him I wanted to be the first female president of the United States. *I'd have voted for you,* he tells me, *if I was an American citizen.* But he's not. He's British. I hear his accent in my head, although the rest of the world is nothing but static and the distant roar of thunder. A storm is coming, and neither of us is prepared. I want to warn us, shout until I'm hoarse, but I'm standing outside my body. I'm nothing but the helpless gazes of passing strangers.

We're sitting at a little café both familiar and completely foreign. I know we're somewhere near Trafalgar Square, but the view in every direction fades into a mirror image of us. A dozen different paths that all turn into a pretty couple having brunch. This isn't our first date, or our second. It's much later in the game, though I can't recall how much later. Five months? Six? The semester is nearing its end. College students pass us on the sidewalk, wearing baggy clothing and the sleepless, haunted look of having pulled a few too many all-nighters in preparation for finals.

Even this early in the relationship, a shadow lies over our happiness, leading me to ask him how the scholarship process is going. I don't know what I'm talking about, despite asking the question gracefully.

"Surprisingly well," he answers. "There's some serious competition for the Fulbright this year, particularly in the exciting arena of British literature, but I think my chances are good. I've exchanged a few emails with UNM, and they seem eager to have me, if the scholarship money comes through."

"Why wouldn't they jump at the chance to employ a finalist for the National Poetry Prize?"

"Because a finalist is not a winner."

"It's not exactly losing, either, and now you have some neat qualifications to put on any future poetry submissions."

He smiles warmly. "Your optimism never fails to fascinate me."

"That's because you're a glass-half-empty type. But don't worry. I'll fix that."

He laughs, neither agreeing nor disagreeing, and then returns to our previous topic.

"Provided I'm awarded the scholarship, and as long as there are no complications with acquiring my J-1 visa—that would be the scholar's visa I mentioned before—I should be able to join you in the States as early as next year."

He accepts a cup and saucer from the waiter, whose face is a blur. My date's the type of man I initially figured for black tea, but instead he always orders herbal teas that smell strongly of hibiscus or jasmine or chamomile, and then administers several packets of honey. I'm the one who orders black. I need the caffeine.

"Hopefully, they won't decide to shut down air travel first," I grumble. "Did you hear about what happened to that Asiatic flight?"

"Which one?"

The fact that he has to ask leaves me chilled.

"Sacramento to Seoul."

"Yes," he says, brows drawing together. "Horrible."

I keep trying to drink my own tea, but never quite make it. It eludes my hand every time I go to grab for its handle, the dream twisting what I believe with certainty is otherwise a memory. "They're saying it was sabotage. The Koreans are blaming us; we're blaming them ..."

He holds his cup in both hands, warding against the early autumn chill, and blows softly on the surface of the tea. "It sounds like you think there's another explanation."

"Remember the incidents with the self-driving cars? How some of them keep swerving into oncoming traffic?" He nods once, takes an experimental sip of his tea. "What if there's something wrong with the programming itself? What if the AI is malfunctioning?"

"Have you been surfing Internet conspiracy forums again?"

"Only in my spare time, and that's beside the point."

"If there's an issue, doubtless the designers will correct it, given time. I don't think they'll suspend air travel in the meantime, and even if they do, I'll take a boat."

He leans forward to kiss me, but I never feel his lips touch mine.

And then I'm inexplicably somewhere else.

A frozen beach. Time is literally standing still, and although I hear birds crying and waves crashing, nothing moves. The sky looks pasted on—impossibly, brilliantly white. Cloudless and maybe endless. I stand at the edge of a cliff, the black ocean miles beneath me.

"Rhona."

I turn at the sound of his voice. *Alive. He's alive?*

"Come away," he says. He thinks I'm going to jump. And I realize that's exactly what I'd planned to do.

Impossible. They're all gone. He's gone. The knowledge infects me, as it always does in a dream, where you know more than you possibly could of the situation, despite entering a scene midway through. Like a whole world existed before you laid down your head and closed your eyes, and will continue on without you once you wake up. Not unlike dying.

But this—*they're all gone*—isn't some nightmarish fantasy, but a persistent fact. My extended family, grandparents, uncles, aunts, cousins, all my friends, their families. It's like someone mutilated a photograph of the world, cutting out the faces of everyone I love. Only my mother remains, a distant, blurry figure sharpened by purpose, by the will to continue fighting, but it's only a matter of time until the machines take her, too. I can't bear another loss. I can't. Not after—

"Samuel's dead," I murmur numbly.

He takes a careful step toward me. "How do you know?"

"He was rounded up by some government officials, taken away to some secure research center in Tulsa. But the city's been overrun. They're reporting no survivors. The machines went in groundside, and just—they killed everyone. He's dead. Oh, God." I shudder, weeping, and he finally dashes toward me, grabbing me back from the edge, wrapping me in his arms.

Gasping for air, I take fistfuls of his shirt in my hands, and I swear holding on to him is the only thing keeping strength in my legs. I touch his face, smoothing fingers over his cheeks and across the facial hair that isn't normally there. "I thought you were dead, too. London—"

"I was on one of the last flights out. We made an emergency landing in Iceland when news arrived that AI were hijacking commercial flights. Apparently, more than one has gone rogue. It's not just the American-created systems. I was seated beside a programmer on the plane, and he thinks the AI are in a cyberwar against one another, competing for dominance."

Just then, I don't care about what the machines are doing, or how they're doing it. In hindsight, it's irresponsible, but at the time, I was ready to jump off a cliff because nearly everyone I'd ever known was dead. "Why didn't you call?"

He frowns. "Do you still have cell service here? I haven't been able to call anyone."

"Wait," I say. "Iceland? Then how—"

"I told you before. I'd take a boat, if I had to. And then, as it turns out, a car, a bus ..." His smile removes me from my deep pit of despair, like dangling a rope down to a trapped spelunker.

I wipe the tears from my cheeks, suck in a shaky breath, and find laughter for the first time in a week.

"I have an idea," I tell him, finally able to think solidly, around the enormous cavern my heart has become. "Mom was making arrangements for us to get out of the state, maybe out of the country. You can come with us. You have to come with us."

"Where is she now?"

"At the capitol building. Another emergency session. There's some big meeting planned for tomorrow morning, as well."

Behind us, the ocean finally crashes against the rocks, exploding with bright foam.

Then I think, *This is wrong.* That conversation didn't take place beside the ocean. There is no ocean in New Mexico. Was there even a cliff?

I wake in an unfamiliar place, warm and safe between arms I know, a familiar name on my tongue. *"Camus,"* I whisper, calling him from my past, and from the heart Rhona and I must share. *I knew you'd come back,* he tells me, over and over, his face pressed into my hair—

And I wake a second and final time.

It's such a shock that I can only lie there unmoving for a few moments, pretending I'm still asleep as Samuel tries shaking me awake. My eyes shut tight to contain the tears. *This isn't real,* I think childishly. *This can't be happening.*

I take a deep breath and manage to pull myself together.

A part of me knows I should mention my dreams to Samuel; they might be important indicators of my mental condition. But the other part—the winning part—wants to keep them to myself, safe in my head.

To cover my emotions, I give Samuel a good shove back as I climb out of my sleeping bag, saying, "I was having a good dream, thank you very much."

My act must work, because he offers a sheepish smile.

"Sorry. It's our turn for the watch."

"Three hours never felt so short."

"Actually, it was four. Ulrich and I felt you should get the most uninterrupted rest time."

I give him a sideways glance. "By 'Ulrich,' you mean you, right?"

He shrugs. "After the first year, I just started taking his silence as agreement."

I smile despite the pain in my chest. Samuel has an easy way of making me feel ... normal, enough that we can exchange jokes like this. Right now, it's exactly what I need.

Once outside, I take a seat on an overturned log that's seen better days. *That makes two of us.*

But it's not all bad.

Sunlight filters through the canopy, catching particles in the air like fairy dust from a children's story. Below, the forest floor has transformed into a wonderland of colors, from the midnight blues lurking in the shade to the cotton-candy pink of the snow, blushing from dawn. It's unbelievably beautiful, and for some reason that irks me. I'm having a difficult time reconciling the world I know—a world overrun by machines—and this place, untouched by the trauma of war.

I don't have to strain to get at the memories of Washington, DC, New York City, Los Angeles, Chicago, Albuquerque—an endless list of cities, their populations eradicated one after the other. Images of the machines advancing on the city, as well as unarmed suburbia, just ahead of the reporters and cameras, have been burned into my brain, like afterimages from staring too long at the sun. People lost shoes when they fled for their life; bullets ripped and tore apart their clothing, dark jackets unfurling like bat wings; one mother released the hand of her four-year-old son to run, survival trumping motherly instinct; militia members went down in bright flurries of gunfire, honoring their commitment to the Second Amendment. News stations broadcast the war and devastation as long as they could, feeding these snapshots of terror to panicking civilians hungry for answers—everyone asking *Why?* and *What do we do?* and *Where do we go?*

The answers, of course, being: *Because we made a mistake* and *Nothing* and *Nowhere.*

A noise like a running faucet disrupts my thinking. I can just see a corner of Ulrich's shoulder from behind a tree, a couple of feet away.

"*Guten Morgen,*" he says casually, as if I know German. He knows I don't.

"Right back at'cha," I say, pretending I do.

Like a big bear preparing for hibernation, he gives a great yawn before climbing into the tent to go to sleep. Then it's my turn on deck—or would be, except Samuel insists on keeping watch alongside me. Just in case. It's almost like neither of them trusts me.

Sitting down is doing nothing for my circulation, so I get up and walk the perimeter with Samuel in tow. In my mind, I map escape routes—of which there are few. The primary benefit of our hiding place is the machines can't see us here or flank us, but that's also its major downside. With our backs against an embankment, we won't have anywhere to run if they corner us. It makes me nervous.

Rescue can't get here soon enough.

In the second hour of our watch, satisfied with the perimeter, I continue exercising the cold and sleep from my limbs by jogging in place. Nearby, Samuel occupies himself by making a misshapen snowball, crushing and packing the ice together. His breath streams white as it passes his chattering lips, the ghosts of unspoken words. He seems focused on his task, but I think he's just trying not to seem intrusive. Something about his silence makes me feel like he wants to talk. Or maybe it's me. Maybe I'm the one who wants to talk.

Finally, as he finishes one snowball and begins crafting another, I can't stand the tense quiet anymore. "I had some weird dreams while I was out," I begin, kicking at the ground with the toe of my boot. Samuel perks up, looking relieved by the conversation. "Or, I don't know. Maybe they were memories."

"What about?"

"I remembered something about the government stealing you away to Tulsa, and the machines later attacking the city. In the dream, I thought you were dead." Nothing in his face gives away his thoughts, prompting me to ask, "So? Did any of that really happen?"

Samuel looks somberly at his footprints in the snow. "In part. The government rounded up a lot of its greatest minds—scientists, engineers, mathematicians, robotics experts—anyone they thought might be able to help them in the future. But Tulsa was a red herring. We were actually taken to a top-secret bunker in Montana ... which sounds a little ridiculous when I say it out loud."

"Robot apocalypse," I remind him, and he laughs.

"Fair point. Anyway, eventually, the powers that be thought it'd be best to split us up."

"Smart. If the machines ever located the bunker, they could've taken you all out in one fell swoop."

"Exactly. I ended up part of the group assigned to McKinley. We left shortly before the machines learned of the bunker. I'm not sure how many other groups escaped." He leans down, scoops another handful of snow, and packs it into his snowball, glancing at me almost shyly. "I guess you could call it kismet, us meeting again, after everything."

I smile. "Whatever it was, I'm glad for it. And, hey, speaking of escape, is that help you mentioned earlier arriving anytime soon?"

"It may take time for them to mobilize and locate us, but they're coming."

"And Camus? Will he be with them?"

Samuel's brows rise and then lower, his face a tableau of conflicting emotions. "You remember Camus," he says, like it's somehow unsurprising, but I can't figure out whether he's glad or not. He nods to himself, trying on a smile that strikes me as oddly sad. "Of course you do."

"Maybe now would be a good time to do that cognitive interview," I suggest.

He stares at me for a long time, clutching the snowball in his hands. I think he looks very much like a child then, scared and unsure. In all the time we've spent together over the past twenty-four hours, I've never once thought about how all of this must be affecting him. I've been selfish, inconsiderate of his feelings and too obsessed with my own.

"Or later," I say, making my first awkward foray into empathy. "Later works, too."

This breaks whatever spell Samuel's fallen under. He shakes his head, as if to shake off memories. "No, no. Sorry. I think I'm still waking up." It would be a more believable lie if delivered by a better liar. "Now's fine, if you're feeling up to it."

"I am. Are you?"

"Why wouldn't I be?"

There's a defensive note in his tone I haven't heard before. I'm starting to get the distinct feeling Samuel's someone who likes to play doctor: fixing the problems of others, but paying too little attention to his own wounds. He doesn't like me probing him for injury.

So I back off, even though it goes against my nature. I know this situation calls for patience and understanding. I'm not sure I even possess the former virtue, but I know when pressing an issue will risk imperiling one of the only friendships I have left.

"Just checking," I say, and then pick up one of his snowballs. "Nicely done." I bounce it in my hand. "Good weight."

"Thanks—"

Without warning, I nail him in the shoulder with it before he has a chance to get his hands up. He looks startled, with little pieces of snow freckling the side of his face. Confusion gives way to incredulity, and finally he laughs. "You're insane. Certifiably insane."

I shrug. "Some things never change."

"Maybe they don't."

Standing, I prepare to be pelted with a snowball, but instead he hugs me. His embrace comes unexpectedly. At first, I'm unsure, but then I hug him back, and for a few seconds we really are Rhona and Samuel again. Before the world, its woes, and the result of its history of violence came between us. "I missed you," he whispers as softly as if we were in a confessional. Before I can answer, before I can tuck my face into his shoulder and breathe the sigh of relief I want to, he lets me go.

"Sorry," he says, looking embarrassed.

"You apologize too much."

The sadness leaves his eyes, replaced by mischief. "Force of habit from my prankster days."

I haven't noticed Ulrich's snoring has stopped until he emerges grumpily from the tent. He's got two glares, one for each of us. "Hard to sleep with all this talking," he says, and the situation grows more hilarious when he tries to pantomime his words. "Like chatty little birds. *Tweet-tweet, tweet-tweet.*"

"Sorry, Ulrich," Samuel apologizes for both of us, though I'm feeling more amused than guilty.

Ulrich gives a dismissive wave of his hand. "Pah. We have stayed here too long anyway. Let us pack up and leave before we are made to move." He doesn't wait for us to agree before he starts taking down the tent, dealing uncharitably with it. I look at Samuel and do my own version of Ulrich. Samuel just shakes his head, stifling laughter.

My smile suddenly slips off my face. "Wait. Did you hear that?"

"What?"

"Ssh. Listen."

Sure enough, there's the noise again. It almost sounds like—

Whirring.

FOUR

BULLETS TEAR INTO THE TREES, ripping them apart. Branches explode into thousands of splinters, some as long as my arm. The only place I can go is to the ground, flattening myself in an effort to evade the worst of the wooden shrapnel. I cover my head, smothering my face in the snow. It goes on for what feels like forever—the shrill whistling of flying metal, trees letting out a high-pitched noise before toppling over. Blood pounding in my ears. Somehow, I get my hand around the EMP-G holstered at my waist and maybe it's the adrenaline, but as I wrap my fingers around the grip, I feel a sudden, inexplicable rush of calm.

Enough to remember Samuel and Ulrich.

I begin dragging myself over to the fallen log, my only hope for cover, keeping low and just outside the angle of fire.

The air is filled with a flurry of ice and smoke, making it hard to breathe. I hunch down with my back against the log's broad trunk, clutching my weapon to my chest. I can't peek over to glimpse the enemy without the risk of catching a piece of debris or a bullet to the face, but I can survey what remains of our camp from here.

Ulrich's managed to scramble to safety behind some large boulders, and a moment later, Samuel dashes out from our tent with the hardcase pressed to his chest, miraculously unhurt save for a few cuts and bruises. Whatever's on that external hard drive must be worth his life, for him to prioritize fetching it over his own safety. Samuel joins Ulrich, who drags him farther behind the rock, shouting what I guess is a well-deserved chastisement.

As soon as the pair catch my eyes, an unspoken agreement passes between us to wait it out—and, at the first available opportunity, to run.

The machines finally cease firing, but I still hear their signature whirring some distance off. Ulrich lobs a few grenades in their direction —as a distraction, I suspect, more than anything else—and I take the opportunity to make a break for where they're huddled. The plan is to run away, but I can't just abandon Ulrich and Samuel to save my own skin.

As soon as I'm out in the open, I realize my mistake. Gunfire tears up the ground around me, showering me in frost. I don't stop moving. If I stop moving, I'm dead. One shot grazes my shoulder, but I keep going, trusting the damage can be dealt with later. If there is a later.

I hazard a guess as to the machines' locations, haphazardly firing while I kick up snow. The energy passes between the dissected trees, and I hear the sizzle of frying wires. *Score one for the good guys.*

Samuel reaches out and pulls me behind the boulders with him as soon as I'm close enough. "What *was that*?" His voice has taken on a high, shrill quality. "You almost just got yourself killed! *Again!*"

"Almost," I answer, wheezing and still short of breath. "But not quite. Can we argue about this later?"

"No more time!" Ulrich nearly has to shout to be heard above the racket. The pained edge in his voice grates on my instincts, and I realize what's wrong—Ulrich's been shot. Something's punctured his side, judging by the way he's hunched over, but I can't tell how bad the injury is because his dark jacket is soaking up most of the blood. "Go. I will distract them. I will cover your escape."

A terrible, nameless feeling grips me. I search his eyes for the goodbye he isn't saying. "And who will cover yours?"

He shakes his head. "I can handle myself."

"You're already bleeding!"

"So are you."

My nose again. I reach up, smearing blood onto my glove. *Dammit.* I'd hoped it was just a fluke. Clearly I'm still far from a hundred percent. But right now, that's not important.

"It's suicide. There are God only knows how many of them and only one of you. One *wounded* you."

"Even wounded, I am worth at least five machines. Six on a good day."

The joke upsets me for some reason. My eyes burn. "No," I state firmly. "Samuel, tell him."

But Samuel, with his apologetic-doe look, is all reason. "It's Ulrich's call, Rhona. He's right. Someone has to stay back or we'll all die."

I refuse to let cooler heads prevail when it means death for one of us. I look helplessly at Ulrich. "There has to be another way."

"If they take you alive ..." Samuel begins to say.

"They will not take me alive," Ulrich assures him.

In the lull as the machines reload, Ulrich shoves both Samuel and me in the direction of the shallow end of the embankment, where it might be possible to climb.

"*Go!*" he commands.

My body betrays me, my sense of fight-or-flight overriding everything else. Forced back into the open, we probably have only seconds to get on top of the embankment, or we'll find our graves beneath it. With one push, Ulrich took away all other options and condemned himself.

Stupid, selfless bastard.

The embankment is hard, making for an easier climb, although I still slip twice. It's possible Samuel was a squirrel in another life, because he scrambles up with surprising agility, then gives me a hand. His timing is impeccable. As the machines come within sight and the snow beneath us lights up with red dots—targeting reticles—we're out of range.

I have time enough for one last look at Ulrich, and I make the most of it, trying to memorize his face and posture. I don't want to forget his bravery.

I don't want to forget *him.*

Ulrich sees me, nods, and crosses an arm over his chest. I don't recognize the sign, but I guess its meaning. It breaks my heart. Samuel tugs at my sleeve just as I'm returning the gesture. We have to go.

We run. And run. There's nothing else we can do but run. All our supplies are back at the camp, along with most of our weapons. *And Ulrich.*

The bullet storm is behind us now, all but a murmur in the distance. As we stop to catch our breath, it ceases. My heart replaces the sound with drumming of its own, beating erratically. For every second of silence, I'm forced to wonder if Ulrich's been killed. Now.

Or now.

Or now.

It's maddening.

Then there's an explosion, and I don't have to wonder anymore.

"No half measures," I whisper to myself.

It's impossible to know how many machines Ulrich took with him. I don't doubt he took some, but it's safer to assume the survivors will resume the hunt shortly.

Samuel and I make our way through the forest quickly, shrouded in grief and morning mist. He doesn't say anything, and neither do I. There's no time for eulogies. I remind myself I didn't know Ulrich well enough to give him a proper one anyway.

Still, I rub my cheeks when Samuel isn't looking, sucking in a shaky breath. In my present body, I hardly knew Ulrich, and barely liked him, but my old soul must have recognized a friend, because I'm infected with mourning.

Samuel has it worse than me. I know he'd never compare suffering, but it's true. His willowy frame seems even less balanced as we move, at times stumbling over nothing. There's something in his expression, some lack of comprehension. With his free hand, he keeps pinching his nose shut and swiping at his eyes.

"I'm sorry. About Ulrich," I say.

He nods and keeps nodding for a long time, lips sewn shut.

"He was my friend," he finally says. The little smile he offers at this small realization is destructively sad. "I don't ... I don't think he knew that. At least, I don't think I ever told him. Isn't that strange? We worked together for years, and I never told him I considered him a friend."

"Well, Ulrich didn't strike me as the kind of person who would spend a lot of time writing 'Samuel plus Ulrich equals BFFs forever' in a spiral notebook." It's weird to be talking about him in the past tense. He was such a present-tense person.

Samuel chuckles once, nodding again. He's having trouble speaking.

"Besides, I'm sure he knew. Actions speak louder than words, after all. And, uh, friendship is a two-way street. There are other fish in the sea? Let me know when you start to feel better and I'll know I've hit your aphorism sweet spot."

His lips twitch with another smile, or maybe a grimace. "Thanks for trying to cheer me up."

"Is it working?"

"Yeah," he says, though his eyes are still red and watery. I know he's lying, but pretend to be duped and stop forcing conversation on him. I don't know what I was hoping to achieve through my graceless attempt at therapy; it was the equivalent of slapping a bandage on a sucking wound and then shuffling the patient along. *Everyone's fine. Nothing to see here.* But this is not a shallow hurt. It needs to be experienced, exorcised, *felt,* in all its penetrating sadness. Both Samuel and Ulrich deserve this much: a brief interval to howl.

In the end, time accomplishes no healing, but it does bring us to the edge of the forest.

Small relief. We have nowhere left to go.

"What are the chances help will arrive within the next five minutes?" I ask Samuel, staring ahead at the snowy wasteland.

He squints up at the gray sky. I look with him. Thin cloud cover magnifies the sunlight, making it unbearably bright after we've been in the forest shade. "Truthfully? Not good."

"How about untruthfully?"

The ghost of a smile graces his lips, but it's gone too soon.

"Well, we can't stay here," I point out. "And there's no cover out there."

"We can skirt the tree line, head farther south. That's really the only option I see."

"Will help still be able to find us?"

"Yeah," he says, but doesn't explain how.

"All right. South it is, then."

Several times during our trek I imagine I hear the machines whirring and have to repress the urge to fire blindly into the tree line. There's nothing I'd like to do more right now than get my hands on one of those glorified toaster ovens and rip out its core processor. Logically, I know it won't do any good—it won't bring Ulrich back—but I'm angry. I'm angry at the machines and the world that created them. I'm angry at Ulrich's stubbornness and his willingness to die for something in me I'm not sure is even there anymore. I'm angry at myself for being unable to do anything.

Again.

That word, along with the dull ache in my chest, summons the ghost of my mother: her graying hair cropped short, the same way it looked on the day she died.

I have a single, clear memory of that day. It's the Monday after the governors of Arizona, California, Nevada, and New Mexico have all declared a state of emergency for their respective states. The morning news is showing live footage of the capitol—not a large, white monument as in Washington, DC, but a squat, terra-cotta-colored building. A dark bronze statue of children holding hands glints in the sunlight out front, and a reporter is standing in front of it, discussing what provisions lawmakers are implementing in order to prevent the same tragedy that happened in Phoenix from happening here.

From behind the safety of a white stone barricade, police officers in riot gear patrol a line of agitated men and women. I glimpse slight movement behind their visors—eyes sweeping back and forth. They're more afraid of the people here than any technological threat elsewhere.

The reporter is the first one to spot something amiss, somewhere above her head. She squints, her face contorting into confusion, then fear, before she drops out of frame entirely, the cameraman panning to the crisp blue sky. The view bobs up and down, begins to shake as the cameraman turns, starts to run, but not before capturing the perfect shot of a passenger plane diving into the capitol building.

At the time, I wasn't giving the television my full attention. Camus was banging around the kitchen, failing to find replacement batteries for a flashlight. He was putting together our go bag, for when we inevitably had to leave. My mother had already made arrangements for us to travel north, to Seattle, courtesy of one of her favorite lobbyist's private jets. Of course, this was before all commercial flights over the US were suspended.

So I wasn't watching when my mother died, along with dozens of other well-meaning politicians, performing their civic duty in the face of extreme terror. She was snuffed out in the same instant I recommended Camus look in the drawer to the right of the fridge.

I clear my throat, finding it a little tight. "How did Ulrich and I know each other?" I ask Samuel. Talking is easier than thinking, easier than dwelling on the past. The more I remember, the more I'm beginning to wish I could forget.

"From what you told me, he was a friend of your father's," Samuel says. "They met in Germany when your father was stationed overseas in ... Stuttgart, I think. This was a long time ago, though. Way before the Machinations began."

The Machinations, I think, immediately recognizing it, like the feel of a splinter. Machinations. A harsh, ugly word for a harsh, ugly time. The polite name for our current era, beginning when our technology turned on us, putting a quick end to the human wars, as they had been programmed to do. Problem was, they only accomplished this task by becoming an enemy humanity had to unite together to fight. Except we couldn't beat them.

"Was Ulrich here as some German military attaché, then?" I ask.

"No. He'd been out of the army for a few years by the time things started happening with the machines. As I understand it, he came to the States on a green card, working as a German-speaking operations specialist for some investment firm." It's hard to imagine Ulrich as a banker—but up until a few hours ago, it would've been impossible imagining him dead, too. "Your mom actually helped him get the job; she agreed to be his sponsor because of his friendship with your father. When the machines bombed DC and New York, he was in Florida on vacation." At the mention of the Sunshine State, my mind summons images of sandy beaches, clear waters, and clear skies. I think Ulrich and I must have talked about his life before the war, at least once or twice.

"I don't think he cared about the investment work at all," Samuel says. "Between you and me, I think he was just here for Disney World."

I laugh despite myself. "Poor guy comes for sand, surf, and Mickey Mouse ears, and ends up in the freezing cold. That's some rotten luck." Why do I remember these sorts of things? Trivial, unimportant things. "So, how did Ulrich manage to get from sunny Florida to the middle of Alaska?"

"Funny thing about fighting a war against machines," Samuel answers. "After a certain point, nationality doesn't seem to matter. The American military started accepting volunteers. As long as you could hold a gun and were human, you were welcome to join up. I don't think I have to tell you, Ulrich knew exactly how to hold a gun.

"Anyway, as far as I understand it, when the military started to retreat, he came with them, and when the structure broke entirely, he along with a few others fell back to McKinley."

"How did they know to go there?"

Samuel looks at me as if he's forgotten who I am—or who I'm not.

"We picked up their emergency signal, and you called him on a SAT phone. Gave him directions on how to get here. I don't know any more than that; it's all either of you ever told me."

There's so much more I want to ask him about, but something catches my eyes—movement where there shouldn't be any.

"Don't look now, but I think we have company," I say in a barely audible whisper. Samuel tenses. "Run on the count of three."

"Rhona—"

"Don't argue! *One, two ... three!*"

We take off in separate directions. Whether the thing is machine or flesh, it will now have to make the crucial decision of who to chase. If the machine is part of a lower echelon of AI, this sort of strategy may buy us valuable time to escape. Scouting drones aren't usually programmed to think through complex situations. That isn't to say they don't get lucky from time to time, though.

I know it's the best tactic, but I still don't like having to split up. I chance a glance back, and don't see Samuel anymore. My heart thickens in my throat. But then my ears fill with that awful *whirring* sound, and I keep going. Maybe it's all I know how to do: keep going.

The grumbling machinery grows louder, closer, and I'm running out of energy.

Several times I stumble, scraping my hands on rocks camouflaged by snow and ice. Each time, I get up. Bleeding, haggard with grief and fatigue, I get up, allowing frustration to fuel me. In my head, I try to hold a picture of Camus's face from my dream.

I want so badly to see him again. More than anything.

Keep. Going.

But the machine is catching up, and it sounds like more are coming from the stretch of tundra to my right. Something is on the move out there, kicking up twin clouds of powder. My eyes begin to sting even more, not only from the dry, cold air, but also the white, fluorescent landscape. I'm forced to look away.

A sharp pop, like a cork released from a bottle. I barely have time to think *What?* before a hard pinch buckles my right leg. I go sprawling, my head smacking against compacted snow.

For a few seconds, I'm unable to think, let alone move. A small, pitiful noise climbs up from the back of my throat and snaps me out of it.

Can't stay here. Gotta move. This thought is quickly followed by the despairing realization that I don't have anywhere else to go.

Numbness creeps up my leg. Some kind of tranquilizer? It must be. I can't recall the predator-class machines ever carrying tranquilizer darts before; it sort of defeats their purpose. Maybe it's some new kind of scout? No. That doesn't make sense, either. Amid the panic and fear, my brain can't help but recycle this phrase. *It doesn't make sense. Why not just kill me?*

"Worry 'bout it later," I mumble to myself.

Hiding may not be glamorous, but if it keeps me alive, I'm willing to try it. With the strength of my arms alone, I pull myself toward a small opening in the shadow-drenched earth next to the trees—*some kind of animal's burrow?*—dragging the dead weight of my leg behind me. Drops of blood dot the snow behind my struggling, wriggling body. My nose. My stupid nose. I'm Rudolph in that scene where his nose gives away his and his friends' position to the Abominable Snowman of the North. *Bumbles,* I think that's what they called him. It's been a while since I've seen that movie ...

I decide this is by far the stupidest train of thought I've had yet. I *must* be dying.

Again.

Through no small miracle, I get all the way inside the burrow—only to discover it's not a burrow at all.

Instead, the ground turns to crackling tarp beneath my gloves. Overhead, the roof sags under the weight of snow, looking close to collapsing. The tent is so dark I no longer see my breath, white and frantic in the air. The only indication of color is a small wedge of fluorescent orange on the ground in front of me, interrupted by the black shape of my body. It's a little like being swallowed by an orange—and a lot like crawling into a casket.

I clamber over some bumps in the middle of the tent, all the while straining to hear the sound of the machine. Where is it now? What is it doing?

Distracted, it takes me a moment to notice I'm crawling over the corpse of a young man. I inhale sharply, rolling off him, nearly choking on my own spit. My eyes water from the cold and the fear.

Bodies. Three mummy bags of various colors, lightly dusted with frost. A family? Or simply strangers, gathered together in accordance with the age-old idiom, *safety in numbers*? No way to know now. I lift my gloves from the cold, slippery material of the bags, expecting blood—or some indication of how the machines murdered them—but there's nothing. No savage marks in their sleeping bags, no holes ringed with black gunpowder. Just eyelashes lying sharp as icicles beneath the young man's closed eyes.

The cold killed him and the others. Cold or starvation or both. Suddenly, hiding no longer strikes me as such a great idea.

Outside, the wind hustles through the trees, and beneath the ambient noise, metal shrieks against metal. Every step documented by a crunch in the snowpack. *Whir-whir-whir,* is the noise the machine makes. *Ee-eye-ee-eye-o.*

I'm grateful the others have their faces turned away from me. I pretend they're equipment instead of people as I begin shoving-slash-rolling them toward the entrance of their half-buried tent. "Sorry," I say to the young man and his dead buddies. Not even out loud, really. The word passes soundlessly through my chapped and chattering lips.

A few obstacles near the entrance won't stop the machine from finding me, but maybe it will slow it down. Buy me time. *To do what?* asks the tiny, frightened voice in my head.

Something.

Anything.

But even as I slide the last corpse into place, my arms turn rubbery as a chew toy. They tingle almost pleasantly, as if shot with that anesthetic the dentist gives you before drilling cavities. *Always hated the dentist.*

I clutch the EMP-G to my chest and flex my hand. My fingers don't feel like fingers anymore—not mine, anyway. The tips are dead when I press them to my cheek, trying to revive some sensation in the nerves. Nothing. Still, I can make them work enough to pull the trigger. That's what's important. "Won't take me without a fight," I murmur through a half-paralyzed face.

Whir-whir-whir.

Crunch.

Crunch.

Crunch.

Closer now. I almost laugh from the tension.

I don't even see it. The machine tosses the mummy bags aside like doll packaging and reaches in, yanks me out into the crisp sunlight. All the while, I'm firing like a madwoman. The machine releases me suddenly, and if I could run, if I could make my stupid legs work, I would.

But I can't.

Instead, I stare, wide-eyed and dry-mouthed, as light and shadow fall over the machine's still metal face. It's even more disturbing up close for its carnivorous look. A cool, raptor glare, designed to inspire fear, with optics red as the eyes of a monster. They are frozen in their last adjustment, half extended toward me like a camera's zoom lens. Everything being recorded, analyzed, and sent back to the higher echelon—the intelligence that rules the machines.

The optics click, and I feel the movement like a foot in the gut. *Back online.*

I fire again and continue firing every time the thing reboots itself, praying the charge lasts. The cold has taken its toll on the weapon, however, so it seems unlikely I'll be able to get more than ten bursts out of the thing. Ten times the ten seconds it takes for it to reboot means I have roughly a minute and forty seconds left to live.

A minute and thirty-nine now.

I try to get my limbs to work, but they just *won't*. The best I can do is flail around in the snow, gaining an inch of distance away from the machine at a time. It'll never be enough for an escape.

A minute and ten seconds.

Just as the machine starts back up, and I fire one of my last rounds, an axe slices through its middle, causing sparks to fly. The machine doubles over on itself, its core processor exposed from the attack. The axe comes down several more times to make sure the machine is rendered completely inoperable.

The world sways as I struggle to stay up on my elbows, my vision becoming elastic as a fun-house mirror. I try to concentrate on the stranger clothed head-to-foot in extreme-weather apparel, face hidden behind a white balaclava.

Samuel? I think, but then I remember Samuel never wore a balaclava. Or carried an axe. Somewhere in the distance, I still hear the sputtering roar of machinery, only now I dimly recognize the sound as belonging to a snowmobile.

What I don't hear anymore is the whirring, and it's such a relief the tension drains from my body. In the absence of adrenaline, I pass out.

FIVE

BY THE TIME I WAKE, my surroundings have changed entirely, replaced by white floors and white walls.

At least I'm not naked this time. Although I do notice I'm wearing a change of clothes. The outfit is comprised of a snug rusted-orange blouse and tan khakis just loose enough to be comfortable. In fact, both the shirt and the pants fit entirely too well, as if tailor-made for me. I put the two together. This was part of my wardrobe, back at McKinley. *Is that where I am?* It seems too much to hope for.

I waste no time getting up and investigating. The room I'm in looks more like a holding cell than a bedroom: small, with little in the way of furniture or decoration. There's only one door, no handle. Beside it, however, is what looks like an intercom.

I walk over and push the black button, speaking into it. "Hello? Is anyone listening? I'm awake now, just so you know ..."

No answer. Not even the faintest scratch of static. I'm not even sure it's still functional. Not a good sign, but I push the intercom button several more times anyway, to be sure. Or else to annoy whoever's ignoring me on the other end.

Once I've worn out that diversion, I look around to see what I've been left with to entertain myself.

Just as the answer seems like it will be big, fat diddly-squat, I come across a mirror. Thin as a sheet of paper and reflecting the opposite wall, it camouflages itself well. I don't even notice it until I pass by and catch a flash of red. My hair sticks out like a sore thumb against the room's bland color scheme.

I step back slowly, like it's some big reveal.

It *is* the first opportunity I've had to get a good look at my new, cloned self. For all I know, I appear deranged, hideous, inhuman. I could be a monster.

I take stock of my features like I'm reading off a quality-control checklist for a Rhona Long doll. Everything seems to be there—two eyes (green), average nose and mouth, round face. Perfect teeth, too (all without the agony of having braces well into high school). But my freckles are different; they're darker, splotchy, and only cover one side of my face, like a Dalmatian's spots. I'm not sure whether to feel curious or repulsed. It's an interesting look. Certainly ... new?

"Could be worse," I say aloud to my reflection. "We could have ended up a cyclops or something." Samuel had said cloning wasn't textbook science.

I decide the freckles aren't so bad.

I'm still analyzing them when the door slides open with a hiss of depressurizing air. A woman enters. I recognize her, but have to search for a name. She's wearing her platinum hair in a simple braid that trails down her back and has her hands clasped in front of her like she's holding something important close to her chest.

The door shuts behind her almost immediately, sealing us in together.

She doesn't speak, but instead begins signing with her hands. The first time she does it, I'm afraid this is going to be one long, awkward conversation. But she makes the same gestures again, more slowly, and understanding starts to come back to me. By the third effort, I know exactly what she's saying.

You look just like her.

"I've been getting that a lot lately," I reply with my usual cheek, and she smiles, so either she's only mute, or she's deaf and reading my lips. My gut tells me the latter.

Do you remember me?

That's the million-dollar question, isn't it? I'm grateful that this time I can actually find a name to put to the face without having to ask or be told. "Hanna?" I say, only a little uncertainly.

Her eyes, a rich hazel color, fill with glossy tears. Tall and long limbed, she crosses the room in two strides and embraces me like a long-lost sister.

It's as if someone has unlocked a vault in my mind, and I withdraw a few memories from the last five years, since I've known Hanna. We met after the end of the world, but our friendship wasn't defined by it. I remember good times, like meeting in the cafeteria during dinner and how she would do the most hilarious impressions of past celebrities, fictional characters, and even our colleagues. She did a particularly excellent imitation of Camus, accent and all, which he always responded to with a stiff smile.

But I also remember the hard times. When Hanna lost her hearing during an attack, and how we learned sign language together. I hadn't wanted her to feel alone. Now she's here, returning the favor.

I squeeze her a little tighter.

Samuel said your memory was—she pauses to think, then makes the sign for *broken—I was worried.*

"Samuel," I say, recalling the forest and the machines. I'm almost afraid to ask about him. "He's safe, then? I mean, it sounds like you've talked to him. Is he all right?"

Hanna smiles patiently and verbally says, "Slow down." I realize my lips are moving too fast for her to read—nothing more than a slur of concerned syllables. *He's fine,* she adds with her hands, showing her preference for signing. I remember the first few months after the incident and how she hated being unable to speak properly, always too loud or too quiet. So much of what had made her *her* was the character of her voice. Yet somehow she managed to redefine herself. I wonder if I can do that, too.

"Can I see him?" I ask her.

The smile disappears from her eyes, and she shakes her head.

"Why not? You said he was fine ..."

Yes, she assures me, although I think she's leaving out some key details. *More or less*. "More or less? What's that supposed to mean?"

"He's being debriefed by the council." She says this aloud, maybe because she doesn't think I'll understand the obscure signage for it.

Debriefed by the council. I know what that's code for: trouble.

McKinley's political structure and history trickles back to me, somewhat disjointed, like suddenly remembering a dream in the middle of the day.

This is what I recall: The council was something Camus and I established as a poor man's war cabinet, maybe two years into the war, after the United States was no longer so united and its states no longer belonged to humanity. Its purpose was to provide a little democracy, order, and most importantly, leadership, back when our ragtag group of soldiers was hardly more than a militia playing at war. But since then, it became the central governing force for more than just McKinley base, as we discovered other cells of human resistance. If McKinley is the strongest arm of the North American war effort, then the council is its brain, telling it when to move and where to swing its fists.

For Samuel to be called before the councilors for a debriefing did not bode well—for either of us. At a time when no one was stepping up to the plate, Camus and I became leaders almost by default—me more so than him, since I'm the people person, and the council was partly my brainchild—but I don't know what changes have occurred in my absence. Nature abhors a vacuum, and if I learned anything as the daughter of a politician, it's the slippery nature of power. Which leads me to wonder: Am I still considered McKinley's commander? Do I still possess the deciding vote, as before? Or has that rank passed on to someone else? Someone less ... dead? Technically, if I am still commander, does the council have any right to hold me here at all?

Before I press Hanna for answers to these questions, or devise a plan to help Samuel out, my mind shudders to a violent stop.

"Camus is here," I realize aloud. Of course he is. Where else would he be?

Hanna nods slowly.

My throat feels tight. "I want to see him." No. What I really want is to know why he hasn't already been to see me.

Her mouth scrunches up as she gives another shake of her head, this time indicating no. I know that's the answer I should accept, but it's not good enough. I haven't trekked across half of Alaska and nearly died several times over, only to be denied and given no explanation why. I tell Hanna as much and ask if I'm to be a prisoner.

No, she answers. "Not exactly."

I'm glad she can't hear my tone, because it's antagonistic. "Then what, *exactly,* am I?"

Her expression teeters between guilty and sad. *That's what they're trying to figure out.* Even soundlessly told, it hurts to hear. It's like I'm some kind of dangerous creature that needs to be kept away from the public.

"I need to speak with Camus," I finally say, over the lump in my throat. I have it in my head that everything will work out fine if I can just *see* him, speak with him. He'll know me. "Please, Hanna." My voice cracks, and once more I'm grateful she can't hear me.

An eternity stretches inside me, while Hanna formulates her decision. Then she turns away, looks up and into a corner of the room.

A moment later, the door slides open with a miraculous exhaling sound.

She motions me to follow her to the now-unlocked door, and I do so without hesitation. *Do you still know how to get to the war room?* she asks.

I nod. Even if I don't, I expect I'll be able to find a sign or something.

"Don't expect a warm greeting," she warns before giving me one last hug and gently nudging me toward freedom.

Just outside, there's a bald man about Hanna's age, mid-thirties, standing guard. Rankin, I think his name is. It's hard to forget a dome that shiny. I worry Rankin's going to lock me back up, but after flashing me a smile and a cavalier salute, he pretends not to have seen me at all.

I have similar experiences as I navigate the unending labyrinth of hallways and corridors that make up McKinley's innards. People openly gawk, but no one tries to stop me. Some stare with harmless curiosity, gazes tempered by disbelief. Others I think might be a little afraid of me. *Rhona Long,* they must be thinking. *Back from the dead.*

Not entirely true, but not entirely false, either.

Head held high, chin up, I walk like I belong here. This is my home. I belong here. *I belong here.* I keep telling myself that, and it lengthens my stride.

The layout of the base is octagonal and complex, but not without reason. McKinley base was built prior to the war, as a spiritual twin to the former United States Pentagon, even before the latter was destroyed. It was unoccupied until we arrived, since the president and his cabinet were slaughtered during the surprise attack on DC, and everyone else down the political line of succession was systemically hunted down and exterminated by the machines. They never had the chance to retreat to the safety of the mountain. It was only a stroke of luck that Camus and I, after traveling to Seattle, managed to evacuate along with a few of the only people alive who knew it existed. At least, that's the story I've been telling myself, based on what little memory I have of those early days. Until I'm told differently, it might as well be the truth.

If memory serves, McKinley has five levels, with meters of rock and ice between each level to cushion an attack from the surface—although, thankfully, that's never been put to the test. The mountain above, Denali—formerly Mount McKinley—functions not only as a formidable natural defense, but also as a further precaution against detection by the machines. So far, anyway. I'm not sure why knowledge of the base hasn't leaked, when other, more important things have, but I try not to look the gift horse in the mouth.

Even with minimal wrong turns, it takes me about fifteen minutes to find the war room—conveniently located on the same level. Double doors and a pair of soldiers standing guard are all that separate me from the council inside. And Camus.

I pull back around the corner before the soldiers have seen me. Suddenly, I'm nervous.

Unsure. But I have only my impulsiveness to thank for this predicament. I nibble on my lower lip, chewing through my doubts. I have a few seconds to decide what to do, but ultimately, my impatience wins out. I'm done waiting for answers.

I approach the two men standing diligently at their posts.

"Camus sent for me," I tell them. It's useless to try to trade on my own name until I know what my position is here.

"No, he didn't," says the man on the right. He's enormous, built like a Grecian statue, all dark marble and stone-faced. It would be easy for him to deal with a half-baked clone like me, but instead he just stares, watchful.

"Okay," I confess. "He didn't. But he will. Just consider me fashionably early."

"We have our orders. No one goes in or out without priority security clearance," adds the other, shorter one. His voice is surprisingly quiet, soothing even, better suited to a psychologist's office. *And how does that make you feel?* There are more words in his eyes, unsaid. Both of them are looking at me expectantly. It feels reminiscent of those dreams where you're taking a test you haven't studied for. What am I supposed to do here?

Security clearance ...

There's only one person I can think of with the right access, who's available and willing. Guess now is as good a time as any to figure out where I stand. "Do I still have priority clearance?"

"Commander Long's clearance is still active," the statue says.

"Right." I look at the identification console on the wall, then back at the guards who have remained remarkably passive, considering I'm kind of an escapee. "Do you mind?"

"If your clearance is denied, you'll be returned to your cell."

"I'll take that as a no," I say and press my hand to the palm reader before they change their minds. I feel a slight prick at the tip of one of my fingers and wait for it to process. Three pairs of eyes watch the black screen as the swirl of DNA is computed. *I hope Samuel wasn't lying about that whole genetically identical bit.*

There's a quiet *Beep!* and then green capital letters flash across the screen:

RHONA LONG RECOGNIZED
ACCESS GRANTED

Both soldiers stand at attention immediately, hands flying to their foreheads in sharp salutes. I smile at them, these two loyal remnants of my former command. "At ease, soldiers," I say, only a little awkward. Even with some of my memory returning, it's going to take time to slip back into my old routine—that is, if the council accepts my identity as readily as these two have.

I take a deep breath, straighten my blouse. It's hard to believe all that stands between me and Camus now is a pair of blast-proof doors. Compared to dying, that seems inconsequential. I tap my hands against the sides of my pants, deliberating.

I'm not ready.

I am ready.

No, I'm not.

Yes. Yes, I am.

While my courage holds, I activate the door's mechanism. It slides open in near silence, and I slip inside, hoping to attract as little attention as possible.

The war room is fairly large, uncluttered save for some anatomical data displayed on a few of the floor-to-ceiling screens covering every wall. My eyes are quickly drawn to the center of the room, which is dominated by a single round table, like King Arthur's. Just over a dozen swivel chairs surround it. It's rare for all the seats to be filled at any one time, but tonight it's practically a full house.

I locate Samuel first. He's at the far end of the room, beneath the harsh, unnatural light of the fluorescent bulbs. There's a dark, purplish bruise at the base of his jaw, and his arm is in a cast, supported by a sling. He slumps over the table, looking exhausted. But he's alive, and I'm grateful for that much.

And there, beside him, is Camus, who hasn't seen me yet.

I gawk, unable to help myself. His black hair is longer than the last time I saw him, almost to his shoulders, and curling at the ends. I don't know why that's the first thing I notice, fixating on it as though it holds some significance. Even from the side, his profile is striking, lean and somehow hard, almost like a bird of prey. Handsome and proud.

Samuel says something to him that I can't hear, and Camus's forehead wrinkles in thought, troubled by indecision. His eyes are too dark and far away for me to see the color of them, but I know they're green, the clearest color in my memory. And finally I look at his lips, which last tasted of salt and blood and regret when pressed against mine. They move to words I can't hear as he confers privately with Samuel, until finally the latter spots me.

"Rhona!" Samuel blurts out in surprise.

My presence doesn't go unnoticed after that. Once I'm seen, whispers rush around the table like hot currency that needs to be exchanged. It doesn't bother me. If I were in their position, I'd be curious, too. In the meantime, I wait to be acknowledged by the only person who matters.

Look at me, Camus. Just look at me.

Despite my silent plea, Camus is the last to shift his attention to me, and even then it's brief. Almost a glance. His expression is painfully neutral, and it's much worse than being treated to loathing or horror.

It's as if I'm no one special, not to him. Not any longer.

And when he looks away from me to finish his sentence, I feel sick. Rejected.

I consider slinking back to my holding cell for a moment, but that's not an option. Instead, I take the only available seat, between one "Matsuki" and the more generically named "Jones"—I know their names by their military-style name tapes. The former is kind enough to offer me his water, but the latter leans away uneasily, like I'm somehow contagious. How kind.

"Well," I begin, interrupting the din of murmurs. My hands are shaking; I conceal them in my lap beneath the table. "Let's get this dog-and-pony show started. I'm sure you all have questions, and I'm sure you all want answers. So do I."

I sit a little straighter as Camus's eyes settle on me again.

Say something, I plead with my eyes.

He stands wordlessly, and it's like a wave travels through the table, throwing everyone else to their feet. The only one who doesn't get up is Samuel, who continues to sit there, looking miserable.

"We'll reconvene at a later time," Camus tells everyone, suppressing his British accent to make him stick out less as the Other in a base manned mostly by Americans. *Former* Americans, I'm forced to remind myself. "Dismissed."

The room empties, leaving only the three of us.

"That wasn't necessary," I say, swiveling anxiously in my chair. Some reunion this is turning out to be. I'm still waiting for the other shoe to drop and really kick me while I'm down.

But Camus doesn't say another word. He doesn't chastise me, or scream or yell, or do anything I can respond to with words or assurances. He just walks out. I'm chilled by this indifference. I don't know what to think about it or about the severe-faced stranger wearing my lover's skin.

Samuel comes and sits down next to me. I didn't hear him get up. We sit for a few minutes, unspeaking. I appreciate how he doesn't force conversation on me, but eventually I can't take the silence anymore. My memories lurk there: old wounds reopening, only now I'm bleeding out from the good ones.

"Now you can apologize to me," I finally say to Samuel in a voice as small as I feel. "I know you're dying to."

"I didn't think it would be like this," he says. "It doesn't look like they're going to welcome you back as commander just yet. They want assurances first, that you're ... well, *you*, and that you can handle the stresses of command again."

"What kind of *assurances*?"

"Don't worry. It'll just be a few tests to put their minds at ease."

"A few tests." I almost laugh. Haven't I been tested enough already?

I shut my eyes and pull myself together for what seems like the hundredth time, breathing out slowly.

"Okay," I agree.

What else is there to say?

When we're ready, the two soldiers at the door escort Samuel and me back to our individual holding cells. Significantly, his is right next door to mine. It trips my conscience like a switch. I'm responsible for the trouble he must be in, even if I don't know what that is yet. Still, it's comforting to know he'll be close by.

"Good night," he tells me before we part ways.

"Good night," I respond mechanically.

Inside my room, I find another surprise waiting for me. Hanna has set up an extra sleeping cot, looking as though she has every intention of spending the night here. She checks her smile when she sees me.

That bad? she signs. I nod. To be fair, she had warned me not to expect a warm reception. "Sorry. Slumber party?"

"Maybe another time," I answer, but I'm glad she stays anyway.

I lie down on my bed, wanting to sleep and forget, but I end up doing neither. Instead, my thoughts accumulate as uneven sets of questions and answers, like the broken sticks of a beaver's dam. I struggle to think sensibly about everything, but it's difficult to do when I'm so close to the problem. When I *am* the problem.

Unable to keep my misery to myself any longer, and incapable of sleep, I nudge Hanna's shoulder with my foot. She claps the lights on like in one of those old, kitschy infomercials.

"Does Camus hate me?" I ask.

No, Hanna signs. *He just really loved her*.

SIX

THE NEXT MORNING, Samuel's granted permission to start running tests on me under the supervision of another doctor, Matsuki Shigeru. Compared to Samuel, Dr. Shigeru appears short and stocky, though he's really of middling height. His dark silver hair is thinning, although it's hard to tell whether it's from age or stress. I recognize him as the gentleman from the meeting yesterday who offered me something to drink when everyone else was acting like I was some kind of contagion to be avoided. That earned him brownie points in my book, but it's only when he insists on being called Matt—joke or not—I decide I like him.

We take an elevator down to the medical level, far beneath the earth's ice-encrusted surface. While it has several rooms devoted to research, filled with expensive diagnostic equipment such as X-ray and EKG machines, most of the place has the feeling of a triage center. There are rows of beds with clean linens. Knowing they were once filled to capacity, the site is haunting. More than likely, they'll be servicing the dead and dying again someday in the future. It's a sobering thought. After some basic blood work in the lab, I'm ushered into another room with one enormous, complex-looking machine and very little else.

"Here." Samuel hands me a thin, crinkly hospital gown. I raise an eyebrow before accepting it grudgingly. It's the same polka-dotted design I remember having to wear back in grade school when I was sick with a rare strain of the flu. Not good times then; not the greatest times now, either. "You'll need to change into this."

"Oh, Samuel, you always buy me the nicest things," I tease him.

"Only the best for my best friend," he replies in kind, smiling without peeking up from his clipboard.

I dress quickly behind a sliding curtain.

First on the agenda is neuroimaging, which involves me getting into yet *another* confined space.

"I don't suppose you could just hook some wires up to my head?" I ask, standing in front of the machine. Matt shakes his head.

Taking a breath to calm my steadily growing claustrophobia, I lie down on the metal tray. A few button presses later, it sucks me inside. The quiet humming the MRI machine makes is frightfully similar to another sound I know. My heartbeat accelerates as my flight instinct kicks in, I want so badly to escape this place. I grip the sides of my gown, lock my jaw. This has to be done. The sooner I prove I'm still me, the sooner I can make things right with Camus. Maybe it's foolish, but I still hope for that. For us.

I can't see what Matt or Samuel are doing, but after a few moments, I hear the former's voice buzzing in my ear from a speaker on my right. "You all right in there?" Above, on a little screen, I make out a pixilated version of his face.

"Yeah," I lie. "Fine. Let's just get this over with."

"I'll need you to stay as still as you can. Shouldn't be more than a few minutes." His lips move a fraction of a second after I hear his words.

I start to give him a thumbs-up before I remember I'm not supposed to be moving. "Right. No moving. Got it."

The screen clicks off, leaving me alone in the metal coffin. I don't even have my thoughts for company—the buzzing noise has turned into a clunking so loud it drowns them out. My body vibrates, a combination of anxiety and the tremors of the machine. A couple of times Matt reminds me to keep still, and I shut my eyes, willing my body to acquiesce.

The torture is over in a matter of minutes, as Samuel promised, and the machine ejects me. I swing my legs off the tray, feet meeting the cold floor with a slap. No sooner have we finished than I'm ushered into a second machine in another room, and after that a third, and finally a fourth. By that last one, I've adapted and climb inside with minimal trepidation.

Meanwhile, Matt and Samuel work from inside a small, soundproof office connected to each room. Between tests, when they're giving me directions to move to the next room, I can see them through a window. Once I catch Samuel literally scratching his head, perplexed by something on a monitor whose screen is turned away from me.

Matt's poker face is much better and gives nothing away regarding my condition. Occasionally he rubs his eye, squinting, but that's about it. It's probably not even a tell for anything. It probably just means he has something in his eye.

Still, I can't help wondering if something's wrong. Would they even tell me if there was? Either way, there's no sense in worrying about it at the moment. My schedule's clear for the foreseeable future; I'm sure I'll have time for paranoia later.

The rest of the day proceeds in the same manner, although I'm happy no more grinding machinery is involved. I don't trust technology these days, maybe as a result of it trying to kill me so often (and once succeeding). Not all of it's bad, granted. I wouldn't even be here without whatever advanced science and technology it took to clone a human being. But things like computers and technical equipment large enough to eat me if it ever goes rogue make me uneasy.

I felt this way even before the Machinations, and if there's an after, I doubt that'll change. As Samuel plays chiropractor, testing the elasticity of my joints, gently rotating my arm and identifying weaknesses in my flexibility, I remember the reason I prefer human contact. He's chosen not to wear gloves, and his hands leave my skin warm wherever they touch. While the room is supposedly heated, I'm cold in my wisp of a gown, so the sensation is more pronounced. As always, he's careful with me, as if he's afraid I might break into pieces at the slightest provocation. I want to tell him I'm made of tougher stuff, but I think he needs to rediscover it on his own. Scientists are like that.

We break for lunch at around two o'clock. As Matt brings the food in, I think I notice movement behind a giant mirror positioned high on the wall, near the top of the vaulted ceilings. It's only now I think to ask about it.

"Is that an observation room?"

Matt nods. "There are many within the facility. No secrets kept from command."

"Is someone from command watching right now?"

"Probably." He doesn't seem too ruffled about it.

I look up again, thinking about Camus. Was his nonchalance some kind of act for the benefit of the council? Could he have hidden his emotions behind his indifference yesterday, as effectively as someone is now hiding behind that mirror? Then again, maybe that's just wishful thinking on my part.

"Would've been nice to know I'm being monitored."

"You haven't stopped being monitored since you arrived." Matt's matter-of-fact tone seems to make light of the issue. "Does that bother you?"

"Yeah, a little."

"Then you should get used to it. After all, yours is the face the whole world watches."

My eyebrows pull together. "Okay, that's not creepy at all ..."

Suddenly, my mouth goes dry as an image of what looks like some sort of media room invades my head: there is a camera in my face, a lot of people standing at the edges of the room, wearing anxious looks, and Camus is tugging on my arm, trying to draw me into a private conversation. It reminds me of the dream—or memory—I had of us on the cliff.

Someone has to do it, I tell him.

Why does that someone have to be you, of all people? comes his reply. *It will make you a target. Do you understand that? The machines will make it a priority to eliminate you, just as they have every other man and woman who has tried to be a hero.*

Don't treat me as if I'm simple or naïve. I know exactly what I'm doing. Exactly what I'm risking. Look around you, Camus. Look at where we are. We're targets already. It can't get much worse.

Maybe not, but if you stretch out your neck, you're only giving them a better angle to cut off your head.

Shaken, I watch Matt squeeze hot sauce onto a piece of raw fish before popping it into his mouth. I'm trying to figure out where to take the conversation when Samuel returns.

"Where'd you get off to?" I ask with a mouthful of food. Not the most ladylike, I'll admit.

"Nowhere," he says. "What are we having?"

"Sushi for Matt." Matt holds up his chopsticks, dripping red sauce onto the side of his hand and down his wrist. He quickly licks it off. "Just a PB&J for me, though."

"Always the traditionalist." Samuel smiles at me, but there's worry in his dark eyes as he grabs some sushi himself, sans hot sauce.

I decide to give him until the end of the day to tell me everything that's going on, or else I'll confront him. By tonight, I expect to have answers, one way or another.

It's late when Samuel suggests starting the cognitive interview, and I'm already half-asleep after a hearty dinner of bread and clam chowder. I try my best to stay awake, but I'm fooling no one.

"We can pick this up tomorrow," Samuel says. I lift my head from the desk. My chin leaves a red mark on my hands where I've been resting it.

"Are you sure?" I feel obligated to ask, but have no intention of arguing the idea.

He nods. "Between the two of us, we have more than enough data to work through tonight. And probably the better part of tomorrow, too. Go get some sleep."

In complete agreement, I make for the door, then stop, remembering something. I turn back.

"Walk with me?" I ask, innocently enough.

"Uh, sure," Samuel says, caught off guard by the request.

At the elevator, the soft-spoken soldier from yesterday—he introduces himself as Lieutenant Ortega—is waiting for us. Since neither Samuel nor I am free to walk the base unsupervised—not yet, anyway—a few soldiers are stuck babysitting us in shifts. Earlier, it was Captain Lefevre, the larger half of the war-room guardian post, and before him this morning it was Rankin. For the most part, they don't speak with us. Maybe they're not supposed to. That doesn't stop Rankin from sharing what he insists used to be my favorite dirty joke, nor does it prevent Lefevre from inquiring after our recent experience with the machines in the Alaskan wilderness. Through this discussion, I learn Lefevre has a sister, and both of them were close with Ulrich before his transfer to Brooks. I'm not sure why this surprises me, except that in the short time I'd known him, Ulrich came off as someone who preferred his own company to that of others. Or maybe I just preferred thinking that way. I feel worse now, knowing there are people who miss him.

Ortega lets us inside first, following after. He says, "Command level," after punching in an authorization code. The doors close, and we begin to ascend.

"So are you going to tell me what the tests show?" I ask Samuel. He gives me an incredulous look, stunned by my candor in the presence of a third party.

We both turn to Ortega, who's busy mastering invisibility behind us.

"What, him?" I hook a thumb toward the guard. "He doesn't mind. Ortega, you don't mind if we talk about this, do you?"

"It's none of my business, Commander," he answers. I like how he and Lefevre both call me that still. *Commander.* It makes me feel like I have more control than I actually do.

"See?" I say.

Samuel rubs his face. "I should've guessed you weren't just interested in my company."

"That's not true. I love your company. But you know what else I'd love? Some answers."

"Rhona," he says, trying for patience, but sounding mostly weary with me. Or maybe not *me* specifically, but the overall situation, definitely. He glances uneasily at Ortega again. "I haven't even had a chance to properly look the results over. These aren't answers to a multiple-choice test. They're complex medical scans and graphs that require thorough inspection and analysis. At best, all I can do is hazard a few theories ..."

"Hazard away," I encourage him.

"No. I'm sorry. I can't in good conscience make any assessments yet."

"Samuel—"

"Rhona, please." He cuts me off in a brittle tone I've never heard him use before. Not with me, anyway. "I'm under enough pressure without you adding to it. Don't you think I would tell you if I knew something?" With this last admonishment, the hurt surfaces in his voice.

"Would you?" It's a knee-jerk response. "Even if the truth was horrible, you would tell me?"

"Yes."

I don't believe him, and tell him so.

He frowns, looking a little helpless.

"I know you, Samuel. You'll try to spare my feelings. It's what you always do, what you've always done, as far back as I can remember. Admittedly, there are some holes now. But still."

"Rhona, come on."

"No. Remember that time in the eighth grade when you lied about receiving an A plus on an exam so I wouldn't feel bad about my C minus?"

"I can't believe you remember that," Samuel says.

As the car comes to a stop and the doors grind open, I step into the threshold, preventing the elevator from closing behind me. Ortega waits while I whip back around and face down Samuel, anchoring my arms between the doors.

"Earlier, when you disappeared during lunch, where did you go?"

Samuel's lips pucker in resistance. He clearly doesn't want to tell me, but he also doesn't want to be caught out as a liar.

"Camus wanted an update on our progress," he finally says, relenting. At the mention of his name, I think I stop breathing for a second. Then the pieces come together.

I exhale. "He was in the observation room."

"He cares about this—about you," Samuel tells me. His gaze fixes on a spot on the wall, somewhere past my head. "But it's ... difficult for him."

I snort. "Difficult for *him*?" I'd laugh if my chest didn't feel caved in.

"It's not like that for everyone." I don't know when he stepped closer, but suddenly I'm aware of how he's *right there*, and my heart travels to my throat, lodging there, preventing me from speaking. "Nothing's changed for me. I already know who you are. You're Rhona." The corners of his lips rise in a thin smile. "My friend. I don't need some computer printout to tell me that."

For once, I don't know what to say. Even my sense of humor fails me. Later, when I'm trying to fall asleep tonight, I'm sure I'll think of half a dozen different replies, each as pointless as the one before. Because I don't have access to them right now, when they're actually needed.

"Commander? Doctor?" Ortega interrupts as unobtrusively as possible. I'd forgotten he was even there. He points to the steel cage around us. "The elevator."

"I think I'm ..." Samuel clears his throat. "I'm just going to head back down, work on a few more things. You don't mind heading back alone, do you?"

"I won't be alone," I say. "I'll have Ortega with me." Ortega nods and Samuel agrees. "Great."

He doesn't wish me a good night before Ortega directs the elevator to return to the medical level—and *only* the medical level. As the doors close, I catch the barest glimpse of some unspoken pain on Samuel's face through the narrowing crack, a vulnerability he's been keeping from me. Or maybe it's always been there, and I'm only noticing it now, with fresh eyes. It leaves me with an unsettled feeling in my chest.

"You're not going to report all that to anyone, are you?" I ask Ortega on the way back to my holding cell.

"I have my orders, Commander," he says evasively, failing to tell me what those are.

Rankin's waiting outside my room as always, ready to exchange custody with Ortega.

"You have a visitor," he tells me, and for the few seconds it takes me to walk inside, I allow myself to hope it's Camus, come to settle things at last.

———

It's not Camus.

Inside is a woman with endless dreads of dark hair coiled down past her shoulders. Banded together in thick braids, they remind me of Medusa's snakes. She's standing when I come in, despite there being a seat available, a chair Rankin must have brought in for her. I'm in no mood to play host this late, especially after the day I've had, but I try to be as friendly as I can. No sense in burning bridges when I don't know where they lead yet.

"Can I help you?" I ask.

"Orpheus was right," she says, crossing her arms over her chest. "Rhona Long. Back from the dead. Lovely." The rancor in her tone catches me off guard. It takes me a moment to recover and realize I'm being insulted.

I'm too tired for this kind of grief. "Look, sister, I'm not some twenty-four-hour exhibit, okay?" I shoot back, in part because I *do* feel like a caged animal. "Rankin might have been the one to let you in, but I can still kick you out."

"Oh?" She sneers at me. "Big, tough words from the little girl in the cell."

She looks down her nose at me, a good several inches taller than I am, practically an Amazon. She's certainly built like one, with an athletic physique that would make some professional Olympians envious—if any were still around.

"Who are you, anyway?" I ask.

"I was a friend of Ulrich's, until *you* got him *killed,*" she says harshly. "More than friends, actually."

I rapidly put the pieces together. "You're Lefevre's older sister. Zelda."

The line of her jaw tightens. "I want to know exactly what happened in that forest."

"I can only tell you what I told your brother—"

"No!" She slams her fist against the wall, making me jump. "Tell me *the truth*!"

The wildness in her eyes tells me everything I need to know about this woman. She loved, she lost, and now she's in the emotional purgatory that exists somewhere between the two. She's broken—and maybe not for the first time, either. I experience a pang of empathy for her, being in much the same situation right now with Camus. The difference being, of course, that Camus is still alive. I wish I'd known about Zelda's relationship with Ulrich before. I would have offered my condolences—or tried to.

Zelda takes several threatening strides toward me. Her anger feels huge in such a confined space, and her domineering presence makes me defensive.

"I don't know what version you heard," I say, backing up, "but Ulrich died a good man. He died to save Samuel and me. He was wounded, the machines were closing in, and he ... He sacrificed himself for us." Even telling the abridged version of events takes me back to the camp, to the smell of cinders and pine, to the sight of trees dying under bursts of gunfire, and black blood in the snow. Mine. Ulrich's.

I finally look her in the eyes, willing her to understand. "That's the truth, Zelda."

"Liar," she says, her voice strangely calm. For a moment, it appears as if she's gotten herself back together, but the hairs on the back of my neck refuse to stand down. "You ordered him to fight. You sent him to his death."

It's then I understand why she's come. It isn't for the truth.

She's here for a scapegoat.

"I think you should leave," I say, trying to sound less afraid than I am.

"What are you going to do?" she asks me, pressing in closer and closer until my back is literally against the wall. "With no one here to throw themselves on their sword for you?"

"Rankin!" I barely manage to get his name out before Zelda lunges at me, her big hands wrapping around my neck like a pair of boa constrictors.

Life-or-death situations are always surreal for the first few seconds, like bad dreams where you want to scream but you can't, or you want to run and your legs won't move. In this instance, both things are actually occurring. She has me by the throat against the giant mirror, preventing me from breathing, let alone yelling—and although I kick out again and again, it doesn't seem to have an effect on my assailant. I grab and scratch at her hands, try to push them from my neck. My efforts prove futile, and patterned static begins to obscure my vision.

Don't black out, I tell myself, but my body isn't getting the memo. In a desperate attempt to get some air, I lash out with both hands, going for her face. My fingers press into her eyes, yank at the corners of her mouth. She slackens her grip momentarily, and that's all the opportunity I need to scurry away.

Taking in huge gulps of air, I yell for Rankin again, but my voice is a broken rasp.

I just get to my feet when something slams into my back, knocking me chest-first into the wall. Before I even get my bearings, I'm being choked again.

Zelda hisses nasty things in my ear as she forces the life from me. The most painful is her accusation that I'm a doppelgänger, a pet of the machines. Something less than human, tortured, and converted to their way of thinking. Brainwashed—no, *programmed.*

"And you're going to pay for killing Ulrich," she says.

Apparently this business of killing me is taking too long—or will be over too soon—because she yanks me back by the hair and then slams my head forward into the wall. I barely have enough time to cushion the blow with my arms before I'm being pulled back and thrown at it a second time.

"You're wrong," I grind out through my locked jaw, bracing once more for impact.

Except when she tries it a fourth time, I anchor my arms against the wall and push backward, connecting our heads with an unpleasant crack.

My arms come up in a defensive technique I don't remember ever learning. But just as she comes at me again, the door opens. I'm dizzy and seeing fuzzy stars when Camus sweeps in, rushing Zelda with an effective combination of force and surprise. He twists her arms behind her back, causing her to give a sharp cry. The shine of Rankin's bald head catches my eye a moment before he steps between the pair of them and me.

"Enough," Camus says, his voice low and dangerous. Zelda continues to resist, forcing him to tighten his grip. "Enough, Zelda. It's done."

Her hazel eyes are red, hurting. *She's crying,* I realize numbly, even as she continues spitting curses at me.

Camus restrains her while her anger runs its course. His features are stoic, complete steel except for his eyes, which show hints of the man I used to know. Empathy and understanding. He knows this grief.

Eventually, with Zelda refusing to be sensible, Camus has no choice but to pass her off to Rankin, who escorts her from the room in handcuffs.

Only once we're alone does he finally look at me.

"I apologize for that," he says, weirdly professional, like I've simply been given the wrong room at a hotel. "It won't happen again, I assure you. I'll send someone to tend to your injuries shortly."

As he begins to leave, I panic. "Camus, wait!"

To my relief, he stops on the threshold, although he doesn't turn around. There must be a million different things I want to tell him, but I can't organize my thoughts into the right words. There's no convenient greeting card sentiment for *Congratulations! Your Girlfriend's Not Dead!*

"If ... you're going to judge me," I say, faltering, "do it on the merits of who I am, not who I'm not."

His hands ball into tight fists at his side. He releases them after a moment, flexing stiff fingers. "I intend to," he says, and is gone.

SEVEN

AFTER THAT INCIDENT, I become McKinley's worst-kept secret. It's certainly no coincidence that I'm moved to new quarters in a different corner of the level the next day.

I don't know Zelda's fate, because no one will tell me when I ask, but I have a feeling she's occupying my former cell. This bothers me a little. Even though she tried to kill me, there's still an unreasonably large part of me that cares what happens to her, because Zelda's as much a victim of recent circumstances as I am. Only I don't see myself as a victim; I see me in the same way I've always seen myself—as a survivor.

"Do you think she'll be okay?" I ask Samuel while investigating my new living situation. The place is the size of a small apartment—a considerable improvement on the holding room. It's furnished with modern amenities and finished with a flourish of sunny colors on the walls and bed. Yellows, oranges, browns, to name a few. They remind me of autumn, and I recall the sensation of leaping into a pile of leaves my father had just finished raking in the front yard of my childhood home.

"Difficult to say," Samuel answers, hovering near the open door, watching me. Feelings are still tender from last night. "Everyone handles the death of a loved one in their own way. Zelda just needs time, I think."

I pick at the withered buds of a dead flower arrangement, trying to picture what it looked like in full bloom. "Is it weird that I feel bad for her?"

He shakes his head. "I'd say it speaks to your character. It's good. Human."

Hearing him affirm my humanity is reassuring. Especially since I haven't told Samuel—or anyone else for that matter—about the vitriol Zelda spat at me during the fight. I know it was said in the heat of the moment, a product of anger, but it still made me think, wonder, and worry. I give him a weak smile of appreciation for the words, even though he's unaware of their significance for me.

"She blames me for Ulrich's death," I tell him.

He's quiet for a moment. "There's nothing more frustrating than the senselessness of death," he explains, drawing an answer from somewhere between science, observation, and feeling. "We, as humans, are programmed to find the logic in everything—even when there is none. She wants a reason, and assigning blame is the easiest way to achieve one."

"Maybe."

After giving my nonanswer, I try to take my mind off Zelda by exploring the rest of the apartment. Only after a few minutes do I realize it's decorated in the exact fashion that appeals most to me. Everything from the lemony smell of the linens to the organization of the furniture sparks recognition. I see myself in the little details of the room, as if I had a hand in the design.

"This was my room."

Samuel nods. "I didn't want to say anything before. I wanted to see if you'd remember."

I forgive him the test, preoccupied with the niggling feeling that something's off. I turn in a small circle, surveying the room with a critical eye. "Something used to be here," I say, laying my hands on a waist-high dresser. "And here." I move to the desk in the corner. "Pictures. There were pictures."

"I'd guess Camus has them."

Dust has collected on top of the desk like a second carpet, which I find strange. It's not been that long since I died. A week, tops. I think back to my flowers. No one could be bothered to water my flowers or dust for one week?

That off feeling persists, and I rub my arms.

"Well, you can tell Camus I want them back," I say, feeling petulant.

Samuel smiles, but doesn't promise me anything.

I drop down onto the bed, and Samuel joins me a moment later. "You should know it wasn't by chance they moved you back here," he says. "I suggested it."

"Why?"

"I wish I could say it was so you'd be more comfortable, but that's only half the truth. I had hoped it might jog your memory."

I sit up, immediately attentive. "Did the tests reveal anything?"

"Yes and no. Matsuki and I have developed a few working theories based on yesterday's scans." He pauses, rearranging himself on the edge of the bed, leaning toward me. "I hesitate to ask after what happened yesterday, but I wonder if you're feeling up to that cognitive interview right now?"

"You're the doctor," I say, partly teasing. "You tell me."

"Despite the blows to the head, there were no signs of a concussion," he answers seriously. I don't like this wall he's built between us, particularly because I'm on the wrong side of it. "But it's ultimately your choice."

The smile leaves my lips. "Okay, then. I'm ready when you are."

He stands and retrieves an electronic pad from the desk, and then pulls up a chair next to the bed.

"I don't need to lie back or anything, do I?" I ask.

"Not unless you want to. Whatever helps you relax."

I nod, remaining upright, watching him flip through digital pages full of diagrams until he comes to whatever he was looking for. He opens a new page, lined for notes. His fingers perch over the screen. "Could you close your eyes for me?"

I'm not comfortable with limiting my senses, but I trust Samuel. I close my eyes.

"I'm going to ask you questions using some mnemonic devices. They're memory-retrieval techniques intended to help you revisit details from your past that you might have forgotten. I'll guide you through several key periods in your life to see which events you remember the most."

"What if I can't remember anything?"

Since my eyes are closed, I can't see Samuel's expression, and his silence makes me nervous. Then I feel the warmth of his hand as it closes around mine. "I think you'll be surprised how much you remember, but don't worry if you can't. We'll just move on to something else. Okay?" I nod, and the comfort of his hand disappears. "Let's begin with your family. What can you tell me about them?"

"My father was a soldier," I say, one of the things I'm sure about. "And my mother was a career politician. I don't remember having any brothers or sisters. Wait. That's not right. Did I have any siblings?"

"Slow down. Let's go back to your mother. What position in office did she hold?"

"She was a senator."

"No," he says. "This is a recollection exercise, Rhona, not a multiple-choice test. It's all right if you don't know or can't remember, but please don't guess. It'll upset my observations and make it more difficult to ascertain the extent of your amnesia."

"Sorry," I murmur.

Samuel's expression softens. "Don't be. You were close, on both accounts. Your mother served as a state representative. She was very popular for her progressive stances."

"And siblings? Do I have any brothers or sisters?"

"You had an infant brother named Conrad—but he died from SIDS when you were six.

That's probably why you couldn't remember him. Your mother and father kept trying for another child, but she had several miscarriages, and then your father was killed in action during an operation in Pakistan."

"How do you know all this? I mean, the miscarriages. You would have been the same age I was when they happened."

"During her career, your mother was an outspoken advocate for infertility programs, determined to make them affordable for lower-income families. It's a matter of public record. Plus, I had to do a school project about her once. It came up in my research."

This makes me smile. "You had to write a paper on my mom?"

"It was a letter to her, but close enough."

"Thank you," I say, taking his hand.

He bends toward me, eyebrows pulling together. "For what?"

So many, many things. "For helping me fill in the gaps. It doesn't feel right to complain—I'm alive when I should be dead—but it's hard. Not knowing who I was, what events shaped me. I hate the idea of forgetting people, places ... all these little moments that survive or die depending on whether I remember them or not."

Samuel hesitates. "I never thought about it like that." He quickly moves on, visibly uncomfortable. Does he feel guilty, because it was his project going wrong that left me in this half-finished state? "Let me know when you're ready to continue with the exercise."

I repress a sigh. "No time like the present."

The next two and a half hours are spent reliving my past through the details I remember. My mind resists at first, but through patience and careful instruction, Samuel begins to coax out reluctant memories.

What begins in my childhood home in New Mexico suburbia ends on an away mission near Anchorage to rescue refugees. It's not easy facing a lifetime in 140 minutes. We stop several times so I can recover from a forgotten memory, or explore it in depth. Like my dad dying when I was only ten and Mom throwing herself into her career, to the exclusion of her family. I remember talent shows and opening-night fumbles. I wanted to be an actress, which was, as my theater teacher used to say, "Like a politician, but more honest"—either not realizing or (more likely) not caring who my mother was. In some ways, it feels like I got my wish.

I remember awkward, fumbling first kisses—on the bus, at school, beneath a tree at a park two streets over from where I lived, the playground half sand most of the time and filled with prickly desert bushes that exploded with flowers at the oddest times. After a particularly bad experience with a boy who called me slobbery, I remember practicing my technique on Samuel, and the way his neck turned all red beneath my hand.

Good choices and bad choices and times when I had no choice; I remember matters that at the time felt like life or death, but weren't—and matters that *were* life or death, but didn't feel like anything at all. This is what it was to be young Rhona Long. I grew up in the shadow of my parents' great love, glimpsing my mother like sunlight falling from a high window after my father's death. It wasn't her fault, and I try not to blame her for the small hole in my heart, the one I've tried filling with other people, through popularity. Some people are just better at loving widely, better at caring for strangers instead of the people standing right beside them.

I remember a lot more than I thought I did.

But for those missing memories—events, places, names, and faces—it's like I was never a part of them at all. Rhona took them to the grave. But Samuel is able to fill in a few of the gaps, which makes me grateful we remained close enough over the years that he can now act as my personal historian. We even laugh over some mutually remembered absurdities—some little, like the time I made him laugh so hard during recess that he peed himself and had to go home early from school, and others larger, like the time Samuel had to bail me out of jail after I got picked up at a party for underage drinking. He'd had to use all the money he'd accrued from his paid internship, money he was saving to attend a scientific conference on retinal neurobiology and visual processing in Colorado. I paid him back, he tells me—with interest. Not only did I pay for his flight and hotel room out of pocket (*Hello, cheap comedy-club gigs, and a part-time job at a fast-food place, and coming home smelling like French fries and onion rings for three months*), but I also joined him, so he wouldn't have to deal with the nightmare of traveling alone.

"On the first day alone, you sat through several keynote speakers and postgrad presentations without making a single joke," he says admiringly.

Of course I did, I think, but don't say. *I was trying to understand what you cared about.*

For those few moments, as we reminisce, it's like the past five years haven't happened. The world is right again.

"I'm glad you're here, Samuel," I say, reaching for his hand, needing contact. "I'm not sure what I'd do without you. I mean it."

"I'm sure you'd manage," he demurs, his smile faint.

He runs his thumb gently over the back of my hand. I watch our hands together, fitted to one another's palms.

"At the risk of sounding juvenile, are we okay again?" I ask.

"Did I give the impression we weren't?"

"Well ..."

"Sorry," he says, bowing his head beneath the weight of the apology.

I don't want him to feel guilty. I just want him to be honest with me. "I'll take that apology and raise you an explanation."

Samuel is quiet for a long time, for so long I think he might not answer me at all, but then he says, "Our friendship has always come easy, ever since the first grade, when you kicked that fifth grader in the shin after he kept picking on me."

I smile, even though the memory is fuzzy, at best. Combined with my other recollections, it seems we've always looked out for one another—a fact that comforts me.

"But sometimes—recently, a lot more than usual—I think I made a mistake between then and now."

"How so?"

"Do you remember the summer before you left to study abroad in England?"

"Probably not as well as you do."

He gives me a drawn look, lips pulled together in a line. "Rhona, could you be serious for two seconds, please?"

"Sorry. Am I supposed to be remembering something in particular?"

Most of the summers in my teenage years blur together into sun, heat, and lawlessness. Recalling specific days is a challenge. I try to think of anything that stands out, but my memory pulls me in the direction of the following August. When I first met Camus.

The details of that early time are still fuzzy to me, like trying to peer through a glass clouded with milky water. I came to Reading for its annual music festival, a year before the Machinations started—six years ago now, if my math is correct. I remember Camus hated the noise, the crowds, the cloud of sweat and weed and sex that hung over the entire place, and I teased him about it. What kind of self-hating introvert decides to spend his weekend at a loud, hectic concert venue? Remarkably, I haven't forgotten the quirk of his lips, followed by his smooth reply: *The kind who hopes to meet someone like you.*

"I had just started dating a girl. Bethany Tallis," Samuel adds for clarification, but it doesn't help position me in the timeline. I nod anyway, sensing she's not a point of importance in this story. "And I stayed up late helping her work on her submission for a scientific journal the night before your flight, so I didn't make it in time to see you off."

Because I can't recall the exact shape and look of the terminal in question, I conjure up a generic one in my mind's eye and populate it with myself and faceless strangers. The feeling that follows is one of loneliness, partial abandonment. Waiting for someone who doesn't show. "*That* I remember," I murmur, reliving the disappointment. "But you've lost me. What does this have to do with anything?"

Before he can answer, a tinkling chime signals someone at the door.

"I should've been there," he finishes, standing. I stand with him. "That's all."

"Hey," I say, grabbing his arm. "I'm still not sure I get what's going on inside that genius brain of yours." I give him a friendly poke to the forehead, and he smiles bashfully. "But you're here now, and now is when I've needed you the most. So I think I can forgive you for one instance of friendship malpractice that happened years ago."

"Yeah," he says lightly, nervously, and I let him escape my grip. "We should probably see who's at the door."

Our visitor turns out to be Matt. He's wearing a white lab coat, per his usual dress code. "Doctor Lewis," he greets Samuel, then leans around him to give a conservative wave to me. "Rhona."

"Hey, Matt," I reply.

His attention reverts back to Samuel. "There have been some developments. If I might have a few moments of your time, Doctor?"

"Of course," Samuel says. "Will you be all right on your own for a while, Rhon?"

It's the first time he's used a nickname with me, and I'm particularly giddy about it for some reason. I try to remember if we ever had a nickname for him, but nothing comes to mind except "Sam," and that sounds like the name of a dog. Not dignified enough for a doctor.

"Go on," I say. "I'll try not to burn the place down."

They leave me to idle on my own, and I keep the door open so I don't feel caged. I'm interested in exploring my old stomping grounds, but I haven't been given permission to move about the base unsupervised yet. On top of that, my neck and head are starting to bother me. The pain meds must be wearing off. I begin looking around, rummaging through my cabinets and desk for anything that will help.

Instead, I come across my former wardrobe. My shirts and pants are clean and folded, untouched since I went away. I sift through them, trying to connect to the textiles in whatever way I can. They have old-drawer smell, as if left unworn for too long. *That doesn't make any sense* ...

During my search, I'm inexplicably drawn to a dark purple cardigan. I take it out and hold it to my cheek. It's soft, so impossibly soft for such a hard world.

"I remember when I bought that."

I turn sharply, holding the cardigan to my chest instinctively.

Camus is standing just outside the doorway, with neither foot placed past the threshold. "Really?" I say, my heart drumming. "I mean, it doesn't look like your color."

He almost smiles, and it's the first glimpse I've had of real expression from him. "Not for me," he adds.

"For me, then."

"For Rhona."

"I *am* Rhona, Camus."

His features change drastically, losing all traces of mirth. I keep trying to find the man I remember in the one standing before me right now, but I'm forced to concede maybe he died with Rhona in the fire-singed snows outside Anchorage. Because this Camus is changed, and not necessarily for the better.

"At best, you're an impressive facsimile of the woman I knew," he finally replies. "And at worst?"

He runs a finger along the wardrobe's surface, lifting dust. "An imitation is still an imitation, no matter how hard it tries to be the real thing."

It's impossible to tell whether Camus is being deliberately cruel or just plain tactless, but I recognize a low blow when it cuffs me across the face. "Thanks for the insight," I say. "I hope you didn't walk all the way here just to insult me."

"No," he says, but doesn't apologize. "The council has an assignment for you."

"The council could have sent someone else to tell me," I point out. "Or hell, just sent me an email or something." I'm curious to see if he had a genuine reason for coming himself—or if he'll make up an excuse.

He smiles, but it's humorless, mechanical. I wonder if he even lets himself feel anything real anymore. "Report to training ground six, military level, at fifteen hundred tomorrow." He relays the orders, carefully sidestepping my statement. "Don't be late."

"What's happened to you, Camus?" I ask as he turns to leave.

The simplicity of my question spears through his show of indifference. I watch his shoulders lock up. He looks back at me slowly, something breaking in his eyes. "The woman I loved with all my heart is dead—and you're wearing her face." His lips flatten against his teeth, and I sense I've woken a violent grief he's been keeping on a tight leash, away from all provocation. "On the subject of insults, why don't we discuss *that* mockery?"

"How do you think I feel?" I snap back. "Just a week ago, we were planning our future, and now I can't even remember most of my past!"

"A week ago?" he says, breathily. His sudden confusion leaves me unsettled.

"Week and a half," I say.

He shakes his head. "It's been *six months* since Rhona died at Anchorage. Six months I've lived with this loss. I was just beginning to—"

He shuts his eyes, pain registering in the hard set of his mouth, before turning away and rubbing his face. When he opens his eyes again, it's only to glare at me.

"Six ..." I whisper.

"Yes. So you'll have to excuse me if I don't have the patience for your pity party."

Six months, I think numbly. I can't even begin to process this information; it thoroughly contradicts everything I thought I knew. Six months since I died leaves five months and some weeks unaccounted for. Where was I in that time, just ... growing in the capsule? It makes me feel artificial and wrong. Maybe Zelda was right. Maybe I am just a ... *thing*.

"I didn't know," I say weakly.

Camus has regained his composure by this time and fitted his mask back on. The one that is cool, collected, careless. Untouchable. "Now you do," he says, straightening the collar of his trench coat. He rids himself of the tremble in his voice by clearing his throat. "Three o'clock tomorrow. Don't forget."

As soon as he's gone, I retreat to the bathroom to be sick.

I don't know exactly how I get from hugging the rim of the toilet to the metal basin that serves as a tub. I crawl inside with all my clothes still on and set the water to run. Then my strength, what remains of my poise and dignity, all escapes through a sudden rush of hot tears. I manage to cover my mouth just before I start crying, for all the good it does me.

It comes on so suddenly I can't stop, and maybe I don't want to. Maybe I just want to hurt for a while.

I lean my head against the rim of the tub, shaking as the hot water rises around me.

I work through my emotions until I'm spent and immune to the water, which is beginning to cool. That's how Samuel finds me an hour later—shivering in a cold bath, all but dead to the world.

"Rhona!" He leans over me, worry scrunching up his face. "Are you okay? Are you hurt? Is it your head?"

"I don't know if I can do it," I say. "And if I can't be her, Samuel, then what's the point?"

"Come on, we need to get you out of there before you freeze ..."

I refuse to budge, so he climbs in with me, clothes and all. There's barely enough room for the both of us. "What are you doing?" I ask after the initial shock wears off.

"Ruining a good pair of pants, probably," he says with a tiny smile.

"You're getting your cast wet."

"It doesn't matter." His eyes say *You do.*

That undoes me, and I begin crying again. Samuel wraps his good arm around me, and I allow him to draw me away from the hard metal to the softness of his chest. He lets me break down with no commentary or criticism, and instead just holds me close in the way I wish Camus would.

We both look like partially drowned rats by the time we get out, although Samuel is drenched only from the waist down. I hand him a towel before I begin drying my hair, which is stringy like cooked spaghetti.

"I think I'm going to need a change of clothes," he says, and I laugh a little.

"There's an understatement."

"Will you be all right while I'm gone?"

"I'm certainly not going to go jumping back in the bath, if that's what has you worried." He starts for the door. "I'll just be five minutes."

"Make it ten. I should probably do something about my hair." I measure out a long, floppy strand as evidence.

Once he's left—after several more iterations of "I'll be right back"—I strip out of my wet clothes and select a new outfit. Or, technically speaking, old. I pull out the cardigan, holding it for a few moments, but it's too much too soon, and I toss it back in the drawer, grabbing a sleeveless sweater instead. Despite being located just shy of the Arctic Circle, buried deep in frozen ground, the base is surprisingly well heated, insulated for comfort. I also tug on a pair of pants that are a little loose. *Cloning technology. It's the newest weight-loss solution. All you have to do is die.*

After I'm finished dressing, I tackle the issue of my hair. It's a mess of red, and my pale face is lost against the color. As I stare at the sorry thing peeking out from the mirror, an idea occurs to me. I go to my desk looking for scissors.

Before I chicken out, I return to the bathroom and start cutting my lengthy mane, a little bit at first and then more. It's not pretty—a hack job more than an actual haircut. But still ...

I smile at the woman I see in the mirror now—the new Rhona Long. I immediately feel better, more comfortable in my own skin.

As the door chimes, I go to answer it expecting Samuel, but find

Hanna waiting on the other side instead. She gives me a horrified look. "Your hair!" she cries.

"What are you doing here?" I ask her as she slips inside.

Maybe she didn't see my lips moving, because my question goes unanswered. Instead, she takes the scissors from my hand. "This," she says, because she can't sign as clearly with one hand, "is why you can't have nice things."

She speaks louder than necessary, but it might not be a side effect of being unable to hear herself. Hanna has always been a loud talker. I smile even as she goes on to run her fingers through a few of my mangled locks disapprovingly.

"Why are you here?" I try again, enunciating so she's certain to understand.

"I met Samuel in the hall."

I should have guessed. This has Samuel written all over it. But I'm not mad he's enlisted Hanna to help—if anything, I'm touched by their concern. I must have done something right in my other life to earn the friendship and loyalty of such good people.

"He was dripping," she adds as a random point of clarification. "Your doing?"

"I had a leak," I say, and she smiles disbelievingly. "But it's better now."

"Glad to hear it." She wheels me around by the shoulders and guides me back toward the bathroom. "Now. Let's do something about that hair."

EIGHT

THE FOLLOWING EVENING AROUND DINNERTIME, the base's alarm goes off, spoiling the first night I've gotten to eat in the mess hall with everyone else. After spending the last few hours going through a rigorous physical, and performing training exercises on the military level to the satisfaction—or not—of Camus and the council, I was looking forward to unwinding a little. And food. Eating lots and lots of food.

I'm standing in the service line behind a guy who can't decide whether he wants bread pudding or lime Jell-O for dessert when the lights go apoplectic. Although I'm not up-to-date on the latest emergency protocols, it's not difficult to guess from the resulting behavior in the room that this isn't a drill. I snatch a yogurt, my hunger overriding anxiety, before heading back to the table I'm sharing with Samuel, Rankin, Hanna, and about a dozen others.

The tension is palpable as I sit down with my tray. Just as I start to ask what's going on, the wailing klaxons are temporarily silenced and I'm interrupted by a voice devoid of any perceptible emotion speaking over the intercom.

"Emergency protocol 707 active. Repeat. Emergency protocol 707 active. All electronics will be shut off for the next hour. Personnel are encouraged to remain where they are or take the stairs, as elevators will be inactive. Personnel are also prohibited from using any nonessential battery-operated equipment and/or machinery for the next hour. Repeat. Emergency protocol 707 active. All electronic equipment will be shut off for the next hour ..." The recording repeats a few more times, for those hard of hearing or just plain inattentive.

"Damn," Rankin mutters, pushing around some peas on his plate. "And they were going to play *Goldfinger* down in Entertainment tonight."

"It's only for an hour," I point out.

"Guess you don't remember 707s from before, do you?" he replies, earning a hard nudge from Hanna. "Oh. Sorry. Was that insensitive? I only meant, 707s never last *just* an hour. Sometimes they can be days long, if the machines are out there, being particularly nosy."

Mention of the machines upsets my appetite, but I push through the nausea and swallow some yogurt. "They're nearby, I take it?"

"Yep," he says. "We're deep, deep down, but it never hurts to be on the safe side. It's why they shut everything off. Don't want any power oscillations giving us away." He chows down on his dinner, scooping up a mouthful of peas, mashed potatoes, and something resembling meat, all into one bite. "There's been a lot more 707s recently, since you two showed up." That earns him another elbow to the ribs, and he frowns at her. "What? It's true. This makes the third time this week. Don't tell me that's a coincidence."

"Wait. I don't remember any 707s in the past few days," I say.

"You were kept in a medically induced coma for a little over a week when we first got back," Samuel says, like it's nothing, unimportant, but it's news to me. "During that time, we had a few alarms like this. The machines probably registered your identity in the forest. They know you're alive. Thankfully, it seems they still don't know where we're at."

"Okay. Would have been nice to know that before now."

My timeline is all screwy since waking up here. It's like every time I fall unconscious, I lose months or weeks of my life.

"Yeah, you were in pretty bad shape when we found you," Rankin says. "No wonder Camus spent so much time monitoring you that first week."

"*Camus* visited me when I was unconscious?"

"Visited? The man hardly left at all. One of the doctors even had to sedate him at one point because he wasn't sleeping. Too worried about you, I guess." Rankin frowns, chews with his mouth open a little. "He didn't tell you all this when you woke up?"

"Must have slipped his mind."

While I'm trying to process the significance of this new information, I decide to change the subject. "So, who did find me? Back in the forest, I mean."

"Well, there were several of us out there in the search," Rankin says. "But I was the one who stumbled across you taking on that machine with a dead EMP-G and half your body immobilized by a sedative. Now there's a party story if I've ever heard one." He grins, and I notice some potato wedged between his bottom teeth.

A part of my history clicks together. "You were the one with the axe."

"Yes, ma'am. You could even say, I had an *axe* to grind with those machines there." Samuel smiles at the joke, but Hanna just pats Rankin on the shoulder, patronizingly. I catch a glint of silver on her hand I hadn't noticed until now. Rankin has one, too. Same finger. Huh? "No? Come on, now! You can't tell me that one wasn't at least a little funny."

I smile. "I guess I owe you my thanks."

"You're welcome, but don't go thinking you owe me anything. I was just following orders."

"Just doing my job, ma'am," Hanna says, then tips an imaginary ten-gallon hat. She still does a pretty great impression.

"So it's all right for you to make jokes," Rankin says, shaking his head. "I see how it is."

She kisses him on the cheek, which tames him immediately. I wonder why I didn't see this before. I try to remember if I knew they were romantically involved, but if I did, the knowledge must have slipped through the cracks in my memory.

I smile, but I can't help feeling the division between my past and present as distinctly and painfully as a beheading. It's the little moments like these that come down on me the hardest, producing the nagging sense of being some kind of an alien—a body snatcher, an intruder in my own life. How much has happened since my predecessor was killed? How many tiny, beautiful moments between my friends have I missed?

"So, how long have you two been married?" I ask Rankin and Hanna, covering my discomfort by swallowing another mouthful of yogurt.

Five months, Hanna signs, which I mentally translate to a month after my death.

"We were going to wait," Rankin explains, "but after what happened with you near Anchorage, the ambush ..." He takes Hanna's hand protectively in his. "I didn't want to end up with any regrets. Not like the boss man."

The boss man? It takes me a moment to understand he means Camus. No one ever called him that before. With me in charge, they never had reason to seek more than a signature from Camus. At best, he was my unofficial second-in-command; at worst, he was a reluctant seat warmer at the council table. Attention and Camus mix about as well as water and oil. Several instances spring to mind: Camus stomaching a wrong order because he preferred indigestion to the discomfort of correcting the server; Camus pretending not to see others cutting us in line at the store or the cinema, trying to sidestep a confrontation; Camus with his head down during council meetings, like a child hoping not to be called on by the teacher.

Maybe it was a British thing—good manners taken to the extreme. Maybe it was simply Camus being himself. Either way, it's hard to imagine the same man running McKinley. Having eyes on him at all times. Everyone turning to him when something goes wrong—and something always, always goes wrong. He'd feel the spotlight like an ant experiences a ray of sun focused through a magnifying lens. No wonder his good humor is gone; command is burning it right out of him.

I want to ask Rankin to elaborate—what would Camus have to regret?—but I'm not given the chance as the lights go off, plunging the room into darkness.

Almost immediately, people begin passing around flashlights, procured from a glass case on the wall. Some then go back to eating like nothing's changed, while others get up and leave, likely headed to their rooms to sleep through the duration of the 707. Our corner of the table remains unchanged population-wise. Neither Samuel nor I have anything better to do, and Rankin is assigned to watch us both. Hanna elects to stay as well.

Ten minutes into a different conversation about Rankin and Hanna's wedding, the entire room quakes.

It lasts seconds only, but it's enough to dissolve the nerves of nearly everyone in the mess hall. When a second one hits, shaking trays off tables, all but the heartiest McKinley residents join a mass exodus from the hall. Whatever the protocol for this particular situation is, I would guess it was along the lines of hunker down and wait it out. After all, what else is there to do when you're this many kilometers under the earth?

"Could be an earthquake," Rankin offers helpfully.

Hanna signs something I'm not familiar with, particularly against a background of swerving flashlight beams and creeping shadows.

"Not likely," her husband responds with a shake of his head. "None of the bunker busters have ever penetrated this deep."

"Instead of sitting around hypothesizing like old men," I say, rising and taking one last bite of yogurt, "why don't we go find out what's going on ourselves? Command's only one level up."

Rankin thinks about it. "We'll have to take the stairs," he points out.

"I'm not afraid of a little exercise. Samuel? Hanna?"

I'd better not, she signs. I remember she's been kept out of the field since the accident, away from any and all fighting. In a combat situation, the loss of even a single sense can prove fatally detrimental, and

Hanna was never much of a scrapper to begin with. I nod, understanding. Even if these are just tremors, best not to risk putting her in a position where she can get hurt.

"What about you, Samuel?"

"Hanna, is there still a library on this level?" he asks.

"I hope so, or I'm out of a job," she replies with a wry smile.

Samuel returns the smile, then looks at me. "There are a few books I've been meaning to check out," he explains. "I doubt my expertise will come in handy on this particular expedition, anyway."

"Suit yourself," I say, a little disappointed he isn't coming along. But Samuel can't be my crutch forever. Plus, with his arm still in a sling, he's not going to be much use in a fight. Not that I'm expecting one, but you never know.

"Have fun storming the castle," Hanna says with a grin, but I notice she whispers something else into Rankin's ear, to which he nods and kisses her.

I look at Samuel, who smiles briefly. "Meet you later?" he suggests, and I agree to meet up with him back at his quarters afterward, provided we're not under attack.

"Well, looks like we've got a few flights to catch," Rankin says, clearly meaning flights of *stairs*. I shake my head at the pun, unable to repress a smile. He hands me an additional flashlight to carry. "Still nothing? Wow, tough crowd tonight."

The hallways are crammed with people, personnel spreading out in all directions like aftershocks, with the epicenter the mess hall on this level. Being trapped amid such a mass of moving bodies, especially underground, where there are no windows to climb out of, no back doors to run through, produces a nauseating feeling of being buried alive.

As my geography of the base is a touch rusty, I let Rankin lead the way, our combined beams lighting the vinyl floor ahead of us as we proceed to the stairwell.

While equally busy in terms of foot traffic, almost all of it is flowing down to the lower levels, where it's safer. This clears the way for us to head up, climbing the equivalent of a four-story building to reach Command. The layout of the base is ingenious, really, constructed with every precaution in mind. But size and safety don't necessarily allow for convenience, and it's not a light trek between levels.

Somewhere between the third and fourth flight of stairs, there's another quake, much more powerful than its predecessors. I anchor myself to one of the railings and end up looking over the side. The well in the center seems to go on forever, disappearing into the dark bowels of the earth.

"Out of curiosity, how far would you say that goes?" I ask, my voice echoing a long distance down. *Goes, goes, goes.* The sound dissipates into silence and empty space.

"I try not to think about it," Rankin says, staring ahead.

"Afraid of heights?"

"It's not the heights I'm afraid of. It's the sudden splat at the end, after the falling."

"Point taken," I agree, a sudden wave of vertigo lurching through me.

We keep moving, gripping the handrails as we go. A couple more quakes rock the stairwell, growing in magnitude as we get closer to the command level. Once we reach the door, Rankin palms the scanner for access, which makes me wonder whether my prints and DNA still work. Given the council's distrust, I wouldn't be surprised to find they'd revoked my security clearance entirely. It's what I would do in their position.

The lights on this level are on, but they have that bluish, artificial tint of floodlights. They buzz quietly, producing just enough electricity to illuminate the dark. I flick off my flashlight, but keep it in hand just in case. If nothing else, it'll make a decent cudgel.

Halfway to the war room, we run into Camus, who is hastily giving orders to personnel rushing past. For an instant, his eyes light up, and his lips begin to curve into a smile. He looks genuinely pleased to see me, but then it's like he remembers I'm not *his* Rhona, not the real one, anyway, and his features harden back into stone. My heart, having risen for a single, glorious moment, now crashes into my stomach.

I take a small, calming breath as Rankin and I fall in step alongside Camus. He doesn't slow his pace any to accommodate us.

"Lieutenant," he says, acknowledging Rankin curtly. Apparently I merit neither a title nor a greeting.

"Commander," Rankin replies. "What's the situation?"

"We're not sure yet. The machines have been doing strafing runs all day, but that was some miles north from here. It's not clear whether they had a target or were simply testing new weaponry. They've since moved, as you have no doubt noticed. The mountain's as good a location as any to test bunker busters. In all likelihood, they have no idea we're here."

"Then why all the fuss?" I ask.

"Because they're too bloody close," he says, teeth clenched around the words. For once, I sense I'm not the source of his frustration, and that's something of a relief. Even if it does mean impending trouble with the machines.

"Is there anything that can be done, sir?" Rankin asks.

He stops, deliberating in the span of three seconds. "I need a man to lead a team down the southwest evacuation corridor. Reports indicate there may be a breach. The sensors have always been sensitive in that passage, but the last thing we need are machines infiltrating our exit routes."

"Yes, sir. Better safe than sorry."

"I can go with him," I offer.

"No," Camus says sharply. "You will return to your quarters and stay there."

"And miss out on all the action?" I snort. "Hardly. It's like you don't know me at all, Camus."

He shoots a glance down the hallway before looking back at me. "I don't have time to argue with you about this. But if you insist on defying my orders, at least have sense enough to stay out of the way." His attention shifts to Rankin. "Lieutenant, you have your orders. See to it."

Rankin falls away down a separate corridor. I continue on with Camus—which is no easy task, since he has a couple of inches on me, and a mean, relentless stride to go with it.

"You're more worried than you're letting on," I say. "What else is going on that you're not saying?"

To my surprise, he actually opens up. I think he wants to tell someone, and since I'm technically a nobody now, I make the best candidate. It just confirms my theory about how excruciating the burden of leadership must have been for him over the past six months. He's desperate to talk. "The base's infrastructure has suffered some fatigue over the years. Nothing too serious, but this bombardment is putting unnecessary stress on some of the foundation. There's a very real possibility that parts of the level could collapse." He glances uneasily at the ceiling.

"So, what are we doing about it?"

"I have men identifying the major faults, but"—he stops as we part for a group of soldiers to pass between us—"but at this point there's very little we can do."

"Shouldn't we be evacuating the level then?"

Another posse of men in their outdated fatigues pass by, forcing us to squeeze together momentarily against the wall. Camus gives no indication he's even noticed the physical contact, apart from straightening his trench coat afterward. "Those nonessential personnel we can spare have already been sent to the military level," he goes on to explain. "By all calculations, the lower levels should be able to sustain any fracturing that occurs above them. If, God forbid, the machines realize what they've stumbled onto, we'll still be ready for them on this front."

For the first time, I see Camus's walls not as a barrier, but as a serious force to be reckoned with. Whatever's happened in the past six months, he has converted his introverted nature into a strength, becoming exactly what McKinley needs. Smart. Capable. Strong. I'm proud, but also a little sad. It's selfish, but a small part of me had hoped he would still need me. "Sounds like you have all the bases covered," I say.

"Someone has to," he answers grimly. "Now, I think it would be best if you—"

A sound like cracking ice cuts him off mid-sentence. The lights blink on and off as the walls convulse, the ceiling heaving beneath some extraordinary weight. Plaster sprinkles down. I mean to move, but Camus's reaction time is faster. He presses me to the wall a moment before it collapses completely, burying us.

NINE

AT FIRST, I confuse the darkness with being unconsciousness as my mind emerges groggily from the trauma. I'm pretty sure I'm not dead, which is good news except for the fact I can't seem to move. Something has me pinned—something warm and breathing. The heartbeat I thought was my own belongs instead to this other body.

"Camus," I say, coughing from the dust. "Camus?" There's no response.

I feel for his face, accidentally poking him in the eye. He groans. I think it might be the most beautiful sound in the whole world.

"Camus, can you move?"

His muscles tense against me as he tries. I can practically hear him grinding his teeth with the effort. "Not much," he answers, pained. "Something has my legs trapped. They may be broken. I don't know. Are you all right?"

"Yeah," I say. "Hard to tell with all the adrenaline, but yeah, I think I'm okay."

Since I can't see, I let my other senses take up the slack—specifically touch. My hands make a preliminary search of our surroundings and find twisted metal and flaking chunks of Sheetrock. I begin forming a picture in my mind's eye. To my right—his left—there's what feels like a giant support beam lying beside us. Above, there's another one, angled against the wall. Together, I think they must have created a pocket, which explains why we weren't immediately crushed. But all of this is conjecture; I can't know for sure. And even if I'm right, there's very little separating us from a literal mountain of rock if the beams give out.

My breath starts to come a little faster. "We have to get out of here."

"Agreed," Camus says. "I trust you have a plan to go with that statement?"

"Not any particularly good ones. But I thought I should give you fair warning before I started poking around for an exit."

He actually laughs a little at this, although it quickly dissolves into coughing. He's in more pain than he's admitting. "Awfully considerate of you," he remarks dryly.

I tentatively test the strength of the pieces of debris closest to me. Some chip off or break away, but most don't budge from what little pressure I apply. With more pressure, I might be able to punch a hole through, but there's no guarantee that would get us anywhere, and the risk of a secondary collapse is entirely too high.

"Careful," Camus cautions. "You could trigger ..."

"I know," I interrupt sharply, my mind already cycling through the grim possibilities, squeezing the calm right out of me as if I were a tube of toothpaste. "Believe me. I know."

An unhinged note in my voice must give me away because Camus advises me to be calm. "Someone will find us," he reassures me, and there's such gentleness to his tone that my heart aches.

As I'm deliberating on whether or not to chance pulling at more debris, I think I hear the muffled conversation of what could be a rescue crew nearby.

"Do you hear—?" I begin to say when Camus shushes me.

We listen, and those are unmistakably human voices. Before we can even begin calling for help, though, the sound starts to fade, ebbing into silence again. We yell anyway, for all the good it does us. The pocket traps our voices. No one responds.

"They don't know we're here," I realize and say aloud. Panic returns to gnaw on my nerves, making it difficult to concentrate. *Trapped,* I keep thinking, running into the word at the end of every train of thought like it's a solid, brick wall. *Trapped trapped trapped trapped.*

God, I'm getting *really* sick of tight, confined spaces.

"Then we ought to change that," Camus says. As he stretches his arm past me, the fabric of his coat brushes against my cheek, but it all ends in a hiss of pain. "I can't reach. Can you break through? We need to open a hole, so they can hear."

"Hole. Right. Let me try."

I scrape and claw at the fragments of metal, rock, and other potentially hazardous materials that form the walls of our cave. I'm making headway when the shaking starts again. For a moment, I worry I've pulled at the wrong something and this whole place is going to come crashing down around our ears, and it'll all be my fault. But then I realize it's just the machines continuing their damn testing. It's no more comforting, as I remember Camus's warning. One wrong move and we're dead. *No pressure.*

Before I can resume, something sparks and stings me. The tremors unearthed some electrical wiring, now faulty from all the upheaval.

"Damn it!" I curse, withdrawing my hand two seconds too late. The exposed wire bites my skin, giving me a small but memorable shock.

"Careful," Camus snaps. "Could you at least try not getting yourself killed? Again?"

"What would you care?" I reply, not thinking, just hurting and afraid.

"Do you really think I'm that heartless?"

"Yes!" I shout from a place of frustration, then, "No! I don't know."

He falls silent, although I sincerely doubt it's for lack of something to say. Camus has always been better at holding his tongue and temper in check.

"Let's just focus on getting out of here," I say in a barely comprehensible mumble.

I work in silence for the better part of the next ten minutes. Camus assists where he can, usually without needing to be asked, which I appreciate even more because it doesn't require me to talk to him. I don't trust anything I would say at this point.

Piece by careful piece, I dismantle part of the wall like a life-or-death game of Jenga, until there's finally room enough for me to squeeze through into the next section. From this angle, it's impossible to tell what lies beyond the dark hole I've fashioned into my escape hatch. I get only occasional glimpses from the sparking wires, and even then, all I can make out is more ceiling debris and crushed rock. Neither are encouraging signs. For all I know, the collapse could extend the length of the level, and this is a dangerous exercise in futility. But I have to try.

The last obstacle left to me is Camus. "I think I can make it out now," I say to him. "Can you support yourself for a second?"

He pushes up with his arms, as if performing a push-up, and holds himself there. I can't imagine the pain he must be in, particularly with the lower half of his body still pinned, but he doesn't complain or make any mention of it.

Instead, through gritted teeth, he gets out the word "*Go.*"

I wriggle out from beneath him, immediately missing the security of his body. The sudden loss of his weight throws my own vulnerability into sharp relief. For a moment, I'm back near Anchorage, my pulse hammering in my ears, death drawing near like the passing shadow of an animal in a forest. I concentrate on slowing my breathing. It's not like this would be my first time, should the worst happen. Knowledge is power, and I already know what to expect. A little pain, a little discomfort—then nothing. Dying once is an ordeal. Dying a second time is mostly inconvenient.

"Okay," I say once I'm clear of him, getting stuck halfway through the hole. I briefly feel around the space beyond and find something smooth and cylindrical partially concealed by rubble. *My flashlight!* I must have dropped it when the ceiling came down. But my victory is short-lived when I switch it on and the light peters out.

"What was that?" Camus asks.

"Flashlight," I answer. "But I think it's broken."

"Just our luck," I hear him say, quickly followed by, "Wait. Hand it to me."

Even though it's a tight space and difficult to maneuver in, I manage to pass the flashlight back to him. He readjusts the lens, gives it a good swat, and it flickers back to life. At once I'm alarmed by the bright red cuts and yellow-and-black bruises on Camus's dusty face; he's in worse shape than I thought, having taken the brunt of the collapse. For me.

When he tries to hand the flashlight back, I reject it. "You keep it."

"Don't be ridiculous," he says firmly, forcing my palm to close around it. I relish the feeling of his hand around mine. "You'll need it to see by if you can get us out of here."

"You'll be left in the dark."

"It won't be the first time." Somehow, I know he's referring to the past six months. Six months he must've spent in the black pit of his grief—a grief I'm only skimming the surface of, through his rejection. A tiny hammer of guilt clangs at my heart. I thought I had it bad, but my grief is a pale echo of what Camus has endured these many months, carrying the utter certainty of knowing the person you love, the person you would've done anything for, who you promised to protect, is gone forever. At least I'm buoyed by hope. He didn't even have that much to hold on to. No wonder he drowned.

I suddenly find the idea of leaving him alone again distasteful in the extreme. So many things could go wrong while I'm away, and who would know until it's too late? No matter how I feel right now, I can't lose Camus, not after everything I've gone through to get back to him, and I don't want him to lose me again, either, regardless of how he claims to feel—or not feel—about us. I remain crouched by the hole for a few seconds more, knowing what I have to do, but reluctant to go through with it.

"I'm coming back for you," I remind him.

His mouth grows slack for a moment, his eyes deeply haunted. In hindsight, my promise must seem an eerie iteration of my dying words. "Yes," he says. "I know you will. Please be careful."

With flashlight in hand, I begin climbing. I move as quickly as I dare, taking the path of least resistance whenever I can. Sometimes I have to stop and forge a new path by picking apart the unstable roof or making another hole in the wall to crawl through. It's nerve-racking work, and I'm mentally willing the precarious system to hold the whole time. Just a little longer. *Just a little longer.* There are no more quakes, thankfully. And then, after what feels like an eternity trapped in this metal labyrinth, I come across a small opening radiating a murky light.

I push my hand and arm through since that's all I can fit, reaching for freedom.

Someone grasps my hand on the other side. "Here!" they shout.

Acting against doctor's recommendation, I refuse to leave while they work on excavating the site of the collapse, searching for Camus. I hover uselessly in my blue shock blanket, forbidden from doing more physical labor. The situation is under control, they keep telling me. But I'll believe that once they've located Camus and gotten him out safely, not a minute sooner.

Samuel appears one hour and two nosebleeds later. I'm holding my nose, trying to stop a third, when he embraces me—or tries to. With his sling between us, it's a little awkward. Not to mention painful. We both grimace, his arm and my bruises protesting until he releases me. "Sorry. I heard about what happened from Matt, and I just thought—I assumed the worst."

"I'm okay," I assure him.

He frowns, still holding me gently by the shoulders. "Are you sure?"

"Yes. Why?"

"Normally, that would've been the moment you'd make some crack about being hard to kill ..."

"I'm sorry I can't be the comic relief right now."

"What is it?" Samuel follows my line of sight as I strain to peer around him, at the crew still working diligently to free Camus. "Is someone else under there?"

"I was with Camus when it happened," I explain, and suddenly I feel responsible. If I hadn't been there, slowing him down with conversation, distracting him ... maybe we both would have been outside of the danger zone.

"Camus?" Samuel looks perplexed. "I thought you were with Rankin—"

I give Samuel the abridged version of events and quickly go back to worrying about the pace of the rescue.

"Why are they going so *slow*?" I grumble, mostly to myself. I already know the answer. They don't want to risk a secondary collapse. But it's been too long, and my brain is starting to raise concerns I can't address calmly. Does he have enough oxygen to breathe? What about the circulation in his legs? I can't remember whether he was bleeding or not when I left, but what if he was? What if he's been bleeding out this whole time?

I feel something soft press against my nose, jolting me out of my neurosis. Samuel's holding part of his shirt to my nose, which continues to run red from stress. "You were getting blood all over your fingers," he says by way of explanation.

"Now I'm getting blood all over your shirt," I reply.

"I can change later."

"Thanks," I say, a little embarrassed in the face of his kindness. "I'll try not to ruin any more of your clothing today."

"Good plan." He smiles in that gentle, understanding way that has brought me so much comfort over the past week. I wish I could repay him for all the compassion he's shown me, but I don't know how.

Then the thought's shoved from my mind, and I go right back to fidgeting, anxiously awaiting word they've found him, that Camus is alive and well. Not dying alone in some godforsaken hole in the ground.

"What if I didn't make it in time?" I whisper to Samuel, unable to give voice to my fear any more loudly. "I gave him my word I'd come back for him."

"He's survived worse," Samuel reassures me. "He'll make it through this, too."

I chew at my fingernails—a nervous habit I don't remember ever having before now. "You're right," I say, thinking *Please God let him be right.* But I continue to fret, my brain wandering into the unattractive landscape of worst-case scenarios.

"Hey! Over here!" someone yells. "We've got him!"

The announcement goes up like a war cry, sending the rescue team into a frenzy of increased activity as they redouble their efforts. I want to be right there with them, contributing in some way, however small, but I'm kept back by a severe look from the medics standing by, and by Samuel, who's taken my hand, ensuring I stay put.

Together, the strongest arms begin to lift the beam from across Camus's legs. In their haste, the team upsets the other pylon, nearly bringing down the feeble ceiling on top of themselves. As soon as the area is designated safe enough, the doctors rush forward in a blur of white lab coats, lifesaving equipment in hand. I think I stop breathing, able only to watch and pray.

Camus is limp, unmoving, as they hoist his body from the metal wreckage. He's pale underneath a thin film of dust, with dirt caked around a bloody head wound that looks worse in full light. His eyes are closed, but I think I see a flicker of movement behind the lids as the doctors strap him to a spinal board and equip him with a cervical collar.

All the while, I strain to catch bits and pieces of their harried conversation. They're tossing around words like *pulmonary embolism* and *linear fracture* and *possible MTBI,* as well as a bunch of other medical jargon that sounds painful and life threatening.

I throw off my shock blanket and rush forward to meet them as they start to take him away.

Samuel is unable to stop me. In hindsight, I don't think he actually tries to.

"Is he okay?" I ask in a rush of syllables. "Is he going to be all right?"

"Please, Commander, stand back," one of the physicians, a woman, tells me.

Camus comes around briefly, eyes meaningfully finding mine. He tries to move the oxygen mask from his face with a weak hand, as if he wants to say something, but another doctor prevents him.

"You're going to be all right, Camus," I tell him, even though I don't really know that for sure. After another moment, his eyes roll back beneath their lids.

I persist in following the gurney until the female physician breaks off from her fellows, barring me from going any farther.

"Don't let him die," I say, not only to her, but to the other doctors, too. "You can't let him die! You won't." An order, as if I have any control over life and death. Then, less forcefully, "Please, tell me you won't let him die."

"We'll do everything in our power to save him," she promises. "But you're going to have to trust us with this, ma'am."

I nod stiffly before she disappears down the same corridor as the rest.

"Rhona," Samuel says quietly behind me. I turn, swiping at my cheeks. He is all sympathy, and that makes me feel worse. "You really should let the doctors have a better look at you."

"You're a doctor. Can't you just bandage me up or something?"

"I'm not that kind of ..." he begins to say, and then changes his mind. "Yeah. I can do that for you."

I don't remember the walk back to the section of Command partitioned as living quarters, and I think it may be in part due to whatever medication the paramedics gave me earlier. In what seems like no time at all, we materialize in front of my room. Instead of going inside, we idle around the door like vagrants. I finally open it to a dark room filled with ghosts.

"I don't want to be here tonight." *Alone with the past,* I mentally append. "Can we go to your place instead? I don't snore—I don't think."

"Uh, sure," Samuel agrees, looking equal parts surprised and confused. "My quarters are just around the hall here, but are you sure you wouldn't be more comfortable in your own bed?" I shake my head, but offer no reason why. "All right, but I can't say my place has nearly the amount of fêng shui as yours."

"Shut up," I say, almost laughing at the joke.

"Did I forget to tell you? You were also an interior decorator in your other life," he adds, continuing to rib me as we head toward his apartment.

"What are you doing?"

"Trying to distract you," he answers honestly. "Is it working?"

"If I say yes, will you stop teasing me?" I reply, managing a smile even after everything that's happened. Samuel must be a miracle worker.

We reach his room without any more jokes about my decorating prowess. He's not kidding about the lack of fêng shui, but then there's very little in the way of furniture at all. The place is as ordinary as could be, not looking the least bit lived in. I know he's been gone for the past two years, but I find myself wondering whose quarters these were before he moved back in. No space goes unused for long in McKinley unless there's a reason.

As Samuel goes to fetch a first-aid kit from the bathroom, I lie down on the bed and curl up on top of the covers. By the time I realize my mistake, I'm already drifting off. I open one eye slightly when a weight settles over me—a blanket, soft and warm and perfect. Without Samuel noticing, I watch him settle in on the couch on the other side of the room.

He rubs his face, exhaling slowly. When his hands finally come away, his eyes are unnaturally pink, rimmed by dark bags. I think it's because he's tired until I notice the thin streaks of tears. He pinches his nose and wipes his cheek with the palm of his hand.

Feeling like an intruder, I close both eyes again, giving Samuel some privacy, but the image of him crying stays with me into sleep and troubles my dreams.

TEN

A LITTLE OVER A WEEK LATER, I'm watching prerecorded cartoons on the flat-screen in my room when the picture flickers and clicks over to another image. The abrupt shift from surrealist cartoons to a live camera is disconcerting. This isn't some cheap found footage, made-for-TV movie, either, but a feed from the war room. Samuel and Matt are there, along with the other councilors. Sans Camus, who I haven't been allowed to see since the cave-in.

I'm confused. The time stamp on the footage indicates this meeting took place hours ago, so it has to be a recording. How did I get access to it? I try pressing a few buttons, but nothing happens.

"The subject displays traits characteristic of a trauma patient," Matt is saying, only now he doesn't sound like *Matt*. Standing there, his face drawn and serious, he feels unfamiliar. One Dr. Shigeru who I don't know, rather than the friendly Matt who offered me a glass of water back when we first met. "Moderate to low-grade amnesia, confusion, heightened awareness of her surroundings ..."

"Is she dangerous?" one council member asks. There are murmurs of curious wonder.

"No," Samuel answers immediately.

"Only to the degree that her genetic donor was," Dr. Shigeru clarifies. "We had an opportunity to test her combat aptitude last week, and she performed quite admirably, given her condition."

Score! Until this moment, I wasn't sure how I'd done. Camus stood in stony silence the entire time while I ran around the training room, testing my familiarity with various military hardware, reacting to some routine situations, and responding to fear stimuli—namely machines, under strict local control.

"Added to the reports made by Doctor Lewis and Lieutenant Moore concerning the escape from Brooks facility, it seems fair to conclude the subject retained most, if not all, her knowledge of warfare. On the matter of the subject's memory, however, I will defer to my colleague's expertise."

Samuel nods and utilizes holographic controls on the table to slide graphs and other diagrams onto the wall. Whatever he's showing the council is off camera, however, so I can't see them once he's thrown them up. I think back to my last visit to the war room, of the anatomical image being displayed. Was that me?

"There's no exact medical term for the type of memory loss the subject is suffering from." I shut my eyes against the word *subject* coming from Samuel, as if I can shut my ears to it. "Calling it amnesia is something of a misnomer. Whatever she can't or doesn't remember isn't because she's forgotten it. It's because the memories were never properly mapped to her neural pathways during the process we call transference. Doctor Shigeru and myself have theorized that as a result of the interruption, the brain hastened the executive function of discernment, randomly deciding which memories were important and which were not, on the basis of emotional content.

"To give you some understanding of how memory normally works, everything is processed through the visual, auditory, and olfactory areas of the brain. Even this minute, your brains are selecting information to associate with this meeting. The temperature of the room, the sound of my voice, all these things contribute to what is called episodic memory.

You'll remember this meeting as a whole, while certain details—such as the color of my shirt—will be discarded as trivial.

"The subject's mind functions much the same way, except in her case, during transference, the brain received *every* memory as if it were short term. As a result, only—or rather, *mostly*—those memories with powerful emotional ties were passed on to the hippocampus to be kept as long-term memories. What she feels is closely related to what she remembers. It's likely more memories will surface with time, inspired by a smell or taste, but it's impossible to predict."

This information is a lot to take in—and not just for me. The room grows quiet with thought.

"In your professional opinion, Doctor Lewis," comes another voice from off camera, "is the subject Rhona Long, or isn't she?"

"I'm not a philosopher, sir," Samuel says, nervously rolling the skin of his thumb. "I don't feel comfortable making value judgments on what constitutes identity—"

"But you felt comfortable experimenting with the sanctity of life?"

He looks chastised, but recovers quickly. I've stopped breathing, waiting for his answer. My heart is pounding in my ears, insisting *me, me, me.* I'm alive. I'm Rhona. *Tell them, Samuel. Tell them.*

"With all due respect, I can't quantify her existence any more than I could yours," Samuel answers. He's deliberately choosing his words. The atmosphere remains tense. "But I will tell you that the woman I escaped Brooks with has as much heart and soul as the woman who gave her life near Anchorage. She's Rhona Long in all the ways that matter. And if she's given a chance, councilors, I believe she can do just as much good. You want my professional opinion, there it is."

The council members converse in muted tones of agreement. A few holdouts balk, but in the end, majority rules. I'm going to get a shot at my old life again, with some reasonable restrictions.

I hold off pumping my arm in the air when another council member, a woman, asks, "Is there anything else we should be made aware of, Doctors?"

Matsuki eyes Samuel without turning his head. Samuel rubs the back of his neck.

"The subject's immune system may be compromised," Samuel admits. "I'm not sure to what extent. Of the laboratory's clones at the time of the attack on the Brooks facility"—*Wait, there were more of me?* —"hers was the only one to reach a mature stage of development. But she still wasn't ready when the machines arrived. She has chronic nosebleeds, and while that may be attributed to stress, it could be a sign of a more serious problem ..."

My first thought is: *He sounds like one of those old allergy commercials, warning of side effects.*

My second: *Wait, I might be dying?*

Just then, the feed stutters and cuts out, returning me to my previous programming before I have a chance to find out more.

"No!" I shout at the screen. "No, no, no."

I try to bring the feed back by frantically pushing buttons, but have no luck resurrecting the footage. I stare blankly at the screen, which has returned to showing cartoons. I think it's a new episode; the heroes are taking on a different villain now.

I don't know how to feel about what I've learned. I wish I could condense the toxic mixture into something with an easy label, like ANGER or FEAR, easily dealt with. Instead, I'm rubbed raw by this convoluted tangle of thought and feeling.

Maybe I am a child, I think scornfully, directing my frustration at the only person present. *I don't know what the hell I'm doing.*

Voices swell outside my quarters. The sound of an argument breaking against my door. Even without knowing more, I have to admit I'm grateful for the immediate distraction. I power off the screen and sidle up to the door with a hand cupped around my ear, trying to decipher words from the muffled syllables.

Whatever the cause of the disturbance, I don't find out. The voices move off, and I'm left in the dark, alone behind locked doors.

ELEVEN

TWO DAYS LATER, the powers that be finally clear me to visit Camus. With my company and freedom so tightly restricted, it's an opportunity I welcome—and not only because I'm looking to stretch my legs.

His hospital room smells strongly of antiseptic and some lemon-scented detergent used on the linens. I don't find Camus in bed where he's supposed to be. Instead, I find him in an unpadded folding chair beside a holographic window, crutches off to the side. The screen mostly displays an abundance of nature—fields of green grass, some blades yellowed by fall, and trees, with no other discernible landmarks. Really, it could be anywhere, but I think it's somewhere important to him, somewhere in England, maybe.

"It's such a cliché," he remarks without greeting me. "Longing for the past, for the times we remember as being simpler ... when they never were, not really. But it makes the present more bearable, I think, believing we were once happier."

His thoughts resonate with me more than he knows, more than I can put into words. I think about the past a lot these days. Lately, it seems thinking's all I've been permitted to do. Until that moment, it hadn't occurred to me that Camus must do his fair share of thinking, too.

"Getting sentimental in our old age, are we?" I say.

"I hope not. Humanity can't afford to be run on sentimentality."

"Says the man staring out at English pastures."

He turns toward me now, wearing a thin, but not unfriendly smile, and I get a good look at some of the damage. His head wound is stitched, but not completely healed; his bottom lip is still bisected by a dark cut that's just beginning to scab over. At least the bruises no longer feature as prominently, now a much paler gold against his skin. In three days' time, the miracles of modern medicine have managed to heal the worst of his injuries. In a week's time, physically, it could be like this never happened. But it did happen, and we're both lucky to be standing here alive, regardless of how negligible the damage might seem now.

Well. I'm standing, anyway. He's sitting down, his right leg surrounded by layers of gauze where it isn't in a solid cast. The nurses told me the surgery went well and he was lucky he didn't break more bones than the ones in his legs. They told me injections of bone foam would expedite the healing process, but that the treatment was still fairly experimental, and he should still make sure to get plenty of rest, and ... Honestly, I stopped listening at that point, eager to get inside the room to see him.

"It's remarkable how alike you are," he tells me. I watch him drag his thumb across his lower lip thoughtfully. "Right down to the smart remarks."

"Still singing the same tune, I see." I don't know what else I was expecting. Maybe I'd hoped the other day would have improved the situation between us. "What's it going to take to convince you that I haven't changed?"

"I don't know," he answers with surprising candor. "Although the haircut doesn't help."

"What's wrong with my hair?" I touch the shortened strands defensively.

"You look like you've just stepped out of a cheap sci-fi film."

I frown. "Now you're just being mean."

"Sorry," he apologizes, and I believe he's being sincere. "I suppose I should be thanking you rather than insulting you."

"That's traditionally how it goes when someone saves your life."

"Thank you," he says, his eyes and voice softer. "Truly."

"You're welcome."

I'm not sure whether this means we've reconciled, or if it's utterly insignificant.

His forehead furrows, becoming deep trenches of thought. "You must understand something. This"—he motions between me and himself—"isn't easy for me."

That's putting it more delicately than the last time we spoke. *Progress. I guess.*

After another moment, he goes on. "You have to understand; I loved Rhona with all my heart. I mourned for her. I was still mourning for her when you showed up."

"I—*she* didn't give you any hint of what she was doing? With the cloning?"

His sliver of a smile sticks between my ribs like a dagger. "No. She didn't deign to let me in on her plans ahead of time."

I inhale slowly, trying to keep my voice level. "Why do you think that is?" I've searched for an explanation among my shoddy repository of memories, but none has been forthcoming. I know I kept it a secret. Maybe because I feared Camus would shut the project down, or maybe I was ashamed for having started it at all? The ethics of what Samuel and I did remain hazy. Then again, maybe I simply didn't want to get Camus's hopes up, in case our efforts failed to produce results. Whatever the reason, I doubt I'll ever know. My predecessor took her intentions to the grave.

He rubs his face, appearing double his age once his hands come away. "I don't know. Rhona was delirious from the blood loss. I could never have guessed that she'd already gone and done something this ... extreme."

"No. I mean before Anchorage. Why wouldn't I have kept you in the loop?"

"I've asked myself much the same question. I wish I had an answer. Maybe she believed I would stop her." His shoulders slump. "Maybe I would have."

"It bothers you, doesn't it?" I say quietly, reading the agony in his eyes. "That she didn't tell you."

"Yes."

When he admits this, he isn't looking at me. He's watching an imaginary horizon through a window that doesn't exist. I want to go to him, my heart reaching for what's lost. I want to take away this pain I've caused in both our lives, as easily as he squirreled away a few pictures from my room.

But I doubt any comfort I could offer would be well received. Despite the civility right now, I know things still aren't right between us. They may never be. But, as with his holographic England, I comfort myself with illusions to the contrary. It feels weak, but I can't accept the alternative—not yet, at least.

I decide to take his recommendation to sit down and pull up a swiveling stool, the only other seating available. "And the council?" I ask. "Some of them must have known."

"Yes. I suspect one or two of them must have, but I don't have any proof. No one's coming forward, admitting any prior knowledge."

"Okay. I can accept that, but what about everyone else? I mean, I've been getting strange looks, but no one finds it a little more than odd that I'm suddenly back? Shouldn't they be, I don't know, putting together a mob to burn the witch?"

Camus cracks a smile, and it excites me. The expression seems more natural on his face, deepened by beautiful dimples. He was a man meant to smile. And, as I recall, once upon a time, he used to. "They've been told certain things," he says. "Enough to satisfy their curiosity."

"Such as?"

"Enough," he repeats, evasively.

"Please, Camus. You know how it feels to be left in the dark. Shed a little light for me, huh?"

His smile tightens, the humor going out of it. "Ever the politician," he says before his face drains of all mirth. "We never told them of Rhona's death, if you must know."

"What?"

"She was reported as missing in action. Presumed dead, but never confirmed."

"Why?"

"Because we didn't need another martyr," he explains. "Humanity already had plenty of faces and memories to avenge. One more death—even Rhona Long's—wouldn't have made a difference in this war. The people needed hope; they needed the belief she was out there somewhere, still fighting on their behalf. However unlikely. It was a palatable lie." He breathes deeply, half sighing. "It was easier."

"And what about a body?" I'm almost afraid to ask.

He won't look at me, raking long fingers through his lengthening curls. I detect his discomfort in that gesture and the way he scratches the facial hair growing in around his mouth, the product of going days without shaving. "There wasn't time." The words sound rehearsed, as though I'm not the first person he's told this excuse to. And since the circumstances of my death haven't been shared with many outside the council, I think maybe he's been telling it to himself.

"So you left me behind," I say. This bothers me more than it should. I know it was the right call. But still.

"You were already gone," he answers after a moment of reflection. Or maybe guilt. It doesn't escape my notice that it's the first time he's referred to me as Rhona, even indirectly. He shrugs. "Perhaps it would have been more romantic to stay, to make my grave with hers. Even in death, not parted. Very *Romeo and Juliet,* wouldn't you agree?"

"Don't be morbid."

"No, you're right," he agrees, looking away. "Clearly I've been trapped in this hospital room for too long. I fear I'm turning morose."

I have to bite my tongue in order to avoid making another of what he called my "smart remarks."

"I guess we're both going a little stir-crazy."

"Mhm," he murmurs, sitting back, arching his fingers on the metal arm of the chair. "You know, the council has good reason for wanting to keep you safe."

"You, too?" I ask quietly.

"Do I what?"

We stare at one another for a few tense seconds before I lose the game of chicken and glance down at my hands. I want to ask him: *Do you want to keep me safe, too?* But I fear the answer I would receive.

"What makes me so special, anyway?" I ask instead, somewhat moodily. His brows come together. "I mean, if they don't include me in the decision-making process anymore, what does it matter if I'm alive or dead?"

"What does it matter?" he repeats, incredulous. It's like the curtain's been drawn back, revealing me for no wizard. His expression of disbelief is so obviously sincere I can't even pretend it's a show for my benefit. I brace myself for more truth. "I'm sorry," he says, not sounding as much sorry as confused. "I'm trying to understand. You mean—you remember nothing? Not the broadcasts, the 'signal heard 'round the world?' None of it?"

"Only a little." That memory I had of the media room makes a little more sense now, as does Matt's remark about my face being the one the world watches. I broadcast a message—but to who, exactly? And what did I say?

At the same time, I wonder why Camus is putting me through the torture of admitting my ignorance when he must know the extent of my memory loss. Someone would have told him by now.

"I remember the room I must have given the broadcast in. And I remember arguing with you about being the one to do it, but that's about it."

Camus shakes his head. "Unbelievable."

I expect him to elaborate. When he doesn't, I prompt him by saying, "I don't suppose you'd care to fill me in?"

"Where to begin? You're our figurehead—or Rhona was," he says, careful to correct himself. I'm learning not to let it bother me. I don't think Camus is actively trying to dehumanize me by separating us into two different people. I think it's just his way of protecting himself from the emotional fallout of the first Rhona's death.

"For the base," I assume.

"Hardly. Try the world."

"It's not nice to tease an amnesiac, Camus. I know I managed to fool the people in this base into giving me the title of commander, but come on." I frown; he must be toying with me. In the old days, maybe he would have. In the old days, when I really was Rhona Long, and he was Camus Forsyth, *my* Camus, and we were playful and in love. But it's not like that nowadays, and it dawns on me that he's unlikely to be anything *but* serious.

"I wish I were joking," he agrees with a peculiar sadness, "for all our sakes."

"Well, don't be so ominous about it," I mumble. I look out across the simple fields, wishing I could somehow escape through the window. I'm not sure where I'd go even if I could, but it doesn't matter. That place is as unreachable as a dream, a refuge accessible only by thought now.

"Perhaps we should start at the beginning," he says, and then proceeds to give me the abridged version of the last five years, thankfully skipping all the technical bits.

He talks about how we—McKinley base—managed to hijack a derelict satellite running on old technology, forgotten by NASA, overlooked by the machines, and how we decided to send out a message to survivors. I listen raptly, occasionally asking for clarification, which he provides with a stoic patience. I mentally compare what he tells me to the memories I have of that time. It's fuzzy, but the facts sync up in enough places to give credence to his story. He has no reason to lie, I don't think. Not about this.

"Someone had to deliver the message," he goes on. "Text wasn't sufficient. This was in the second year of the war. The UN was gone, governments all over the world had collapsed, and by now everyone knew what the machines were capable of. They'd lured us into similar traps before, so we knew only a human face was going to be trusted. We needed someone upbeat, who didn't look as though they had been tortured or manipulated by the higher echelon. But there wasn't exactly a run on the banks for the opportunity."

"Because it meant they'd become a target," I say. I know this part.

"Precisely. Public enemy number one."

It's coming back to me again in bits and pieces, just as before. Glimpses of feeling flood my chest, liquid and warm. "I volunteered," I say, remembering the surge of adrenaline, a life-changing decision made at a moment's notice. "You tried to stop me."

He smiles faintly, fondly. "Not hard enough, obviously."

Camus goes on to explain how there was only a brief window of opportunity to broadcast without the machines triangulating our location, and at the time, there was no knowing whether we'd get another chance.

"So Rhona did what she did best. She improvised. In front of the last remnants of the human race, across the globe, wherever they were hidden and afraid. And she was good. She was *spectacular*." He talks with such glowing admiration, as if Rhona had walked on water rather than just winging a public speech. I know the adoration in his eyes isn't for me personally, but I pretend otherwise. I let myself have those few moments, as though it can substitute for the ones that were never really mine.

"The Americans called it the 'signal heard 'round the world,'" he continues with a look of amusement. "Kitschy, if you ask me, but it caught on. The broadcast catapulted Rhona to global superstardom, and no wonder. She reassured a world aching for leadership, offering much-needed direction. As for McKinley, who on the council was going to challenge the one woman unafraid of confronting the machines?"

"And after?"

"After?"

"One broadcast—however iconic—does not a leader make," I say.

"Right," he agrees, and I think I detect a hint of pride in his tone, pleased I've caught on. "Since then, we've been able to broadcast on occasion without jeopardizing our location. Send out news, share insights on war technology, strategy, understanding of the machines, that sort of thing. Rhona was a natural speaker, and an even better diplomat. It worked—at the time. But with the increased presence of machines in the past year, it's become increasingly harder to do. Much more dangerous. Not to mention ..." He trails off, giving me a meaningful look. *Not to mention McKinley's pretty talking parrot was dead.* "I think it's safe to assume the machines know we're somewhere in Alaska now."

"They found me before," I point out.

"An unfortunate coincidence," he says, his mouth flattening into a hard line. "The trap at Anchorage wasn't specifically designed for you. It was just the machines' good fortune you were there. In any case, they know you're alive now. I expect they'll be doubling their efforts trying to find us. You pose a very real threat to them. You may be the only person still capable of raising an army from the ashes. Many will rally to you, if you call them."

I'm having a hard time meeting his eyes. I feel suddenly shy.

"People really believe in me that much?"

"They believed in Rhona Long, yes. And regardless of my personal feelings, we need to make sure they continue to do so. In fact, that's the reason I called you here."

"Actually, *I've* been asking to see *you*."

He's completely self-assured when he says, "I know."

"Right, then," I say, sighing. "And here I thought I was making some headway."

"There'll be time enough for you to throw your weight around, believe me." The way he says it suggests he's not entirely comfortable with the prospect, but Camus wears resignation well, remaining fairly dignified about it. "The council has decided to afford you an opportunity to prove yourself."

Somewhere in that statement, concealed by his oh-so-careful wording, I detect a scenario in which I can fail as well as succeed. "Like a test, you mean?"

He opens his hands in a noncommittal gesture. "Consider it whatever you like. The fact of the matter remains. A few days ago, a very distinguished person and her entourage arrived from Churchill."

"Churchill? Like the old British guy?"

"No," he says, with a faint hint of a smile. "It's a base to the south and one of our strongest allies. I don't know how exactly, but their head councilwoman caught wind that you were back. She's been requesting a meeting with you since, and we're running out of reasons to tell her no." I'm listening to him explain when his eyebrows bunch up suddenly and he reaches for his crutches, rising from his seat, despite it clearly paining him to move on his bad leg. For all their "miracle of modern medicine" selling points, the bone-foam treatments still aren't capable of mending bones as fast as Camus would undoubtedly like.

In the few seconds it takes him to retrieve something from a small table beside his bed, my nerves have frayed into thin ribbons. I'm worried I've inadvertently offended him. I'm angry that he would get mad at something and not even have the guts to tell me. Then I'm just plain worried again. It's a roller coaster, and my stomach doesn't unknot itself until he returns, handing me a tissue.

Oh. My nose must be bleeding again.

I stare down at the soiled tissue, torn from the aggressive way I wiped the blood from my nose. I'm squeamish with apprehension, reminded of Samuel's dark diagnosis, spoken behind closed doors. Is it just stress? Or is there another, more serious underlying cause for these nosebleeds? I want to share my fears with Camus, but I don't trust him to be sympathetic. Instead, I mumble a thank-you, and he continues as if the interruption never occurred.

"We need you to meet with her, talk with her, but more importantly, convince her you're truly back and that McKinley has everything well in hand."

"You want me to pretend to be Rhona?" I say, arching an eyebrow.

He meets my gaze evenly. "I thought you already were Rhona. Or isn't that what you keep insisting?"

TWELVE

LATER THAT EVENING, as I'm preparing for my big debut, I review my face in the mirror. Apart from the odd alignment of freckles, which is easily concealed beneath a pasty layer of foundation, nothing seems out of place. That is to say, there's nothing to identify me as a clone. Camus might see me as some kind of fraud, but I can't afford to feel like a cheap imitation tonight. I have to be the real deal.

No, I *am* the real deal. And I need to stop letting him get under my skin. Unfortunately, Under-My-Skin Lane is my heart's current address, and it has ideas all its own, often living divorced from my brain, which knows better.

It takes me many moist towelettes and several different shades before I get the right combination of blush and lipstick working with my skin tone. I initially shy away from the dark colors, but it feels insincere to hide behind pink pastels. Instead, I commit to the dramatic with a russet tube labeled *Darling Dahlia,* spots of a matching roseate color on each cheek, and navy eye shadow topping off the look. The effect is startling, but in a good way, I think. I hope.

Deciding what to wear is an easier task, given my limited selection. Between a pantsuit and a dress, I go for the dress. A girl likes to feel pretty from time to time, especially when she's coming back from the dead. Anyway, it's not as though it's immodest: the black fabric covers everything, and decorative silver rings hold up the sleeves. For a moment, I imagine wearing something much more slinky and risqué, just for the look on Camus's face.

My hair is the last to get the makeover treatment, and I'm at a loss about what to do with it. I straighten what bits I can, accidentally singeing myself once or twice, and finish by curling my long bangs into twin ribbons along the sides of my face. Hanna could probably have done better, but all in all I'm pleased with my efforts, amateur or not. If nothing else, at least the business of getting ready has taken the edge off my nerves.

I have to be the best version of myself tonight, which is a lot to ask of anyone under normal circumstances. And it's been well-established that these are not normal circumstances.

The pressure is immense, and in the absence of activity, I feel it more keenly. I find myself pining for Samuel's company above anyone else's. He was the only one to visit me during my incarceration, probably because he was the only one allowed to, for medical reasons, but it's the thought that counts. If anyone can keep me sane for the next half hour while I wait, it's him. I wonder why he's not shown up yet, since—along with my having developed a sixth sense about these things—Camus mentioned Samuel would stop by and brief me beforehand.

Just as I'm thinking he must have gotten busy or sidetracked, my door panel chirps.

Instead of a visitor, however, I have what equates to an email. The notice says it's from Samuel, informing me of a change of plans. We need to meet on the military level right now. This contradicts Camus's orders, which could be summed up as: don't leave your room until I come and get you. But I find my door unlocked, so I assume I'm no longer under house arrest.

I don't see the harm in a brief drop-in at Military, especially if Samuel's waiting for me there. I trust the right hand knows what the left's up to. McKinley is generally well coordinated.

I take the shortest route possible, which happens to present the most foot traffic. Everyone acknowledges me with a polite "ma'am," complimenting my appearance with double takes. Most smile.

The military level is the only level we had to somewhat renovate after moving in—to account for the hangars, primarily—and it's still struggling to adapt to its second life as a living, breathing base. For one, the level layout doesn't make a lot of sense, with some rooms half-demolished, and a few hallways leading to abrupt dead ends. No major changes appear to have occurred over the past year, either—or none I can see, anyway. Even with its problems, that doesn't diminish the vast size of the level, which is the largest of McKinley's five. Not to mention that the level's filled to capacity with planes, choppers, tanks, and most everything else you'd need to furnish an army—most of it scavenged from battlefields and rebuilt.

At the risk of getting lost, I stop and ask for directions to the room where Samuel wanted to meet. The guard I talk to is kind enough to escort me there personally, saving me from relying on my iffy sense of direction.

I palm an interface that welcomes me as Commander Long, and the door slides open.

But the room is dark.

"Are you sure this is the right room?" I ask the soldier.

He nods. "Would you like me to wait with you, Commander?"

"No, that won't be necessary. But, thanks."

With a stiff salute and a sharp right turn, he leaves me to my private business, which is mostly just a matter of waiting for Samuel. He must be running late. Instead of worrying about it, I focus on finding a way to turn on the lights. The dark makes me uneasy.

Moments after I've crossed the threshold, the door hisses shut behind me, sealing me in the pitch-black room. I try reopening it, but it doesn't respond to the usual commands.

"Great," I grumble aloud, talking myself out of the initial stages of fear. There are plenty of explanations for the door closing. Faulty wiring from the bombardment, an automatic response once there's no one in the way—any number of things, really.

I blindly feel for the panel on the wall. Some low lighting comes on, turning the room a ghastly black and green. In seconds, my eyes adjust to the dim, awkward lighting, but it's like staring through a pair of night-vision goggles. I suspect this room must be used for training in scenarios of near-total darkness.

I hear a noise, and the hairs on my arms stand up in warning. But there's nothing there—just some broken cars and waste receptacles, basic obstacles you'd encounter in a combat situation outside of the base. *I'm getting myself worked up over some trash bins?* I was probably right before about the faulty wiring.

Whir-whir-whir, goes one of the dumpsters.

Except it's not a dumpster.

The machine rises to its full height, red optics trained on me. Predator class, known for its speed and brutal efficiency. There's not a chance in hell it hasn't seen me. Depending on its programming, I have maybe two seconds before it engages. Five if I'm lucky.

I'm not lucky. It comes at me with the single-minded determination the machines are known for, knocking aside some of the broken cars like toys. The sound of metal scraping against metal is horrible, like nails on a chalkboard, and I have to cover my ears for a moment as the steel screams. In the same instant, I dive out of its trajectory, scrambling behind cover I know won't do much good. It's still better than nothing, and leaving the machine's line of sight throws it for a few seconds.

After nearly twisting my ankle because of my heels—which, let's face it, are walking death traps even when I'm *not* being hunted by a machine—I desperately work to undo the straps.

The machine fixes on me again before I'm done, forcing me to move prematurely. Hopping on one foot, I manage to get the second shoe off, freeing myself to run. I chuck the stiletto in the opposite direction, hoping to distract my attacker, but it doesn't work. The persistent noise of the machine's inner workings, that low vibrato of death, still comes for me.

Weapon, I think frantically. *I need a weapon.*

There's nothing in the vicinity except garbage—things to trip me up, not help me out. And with everything black or green, it's that much more difficult to figure out what's what. As far as worst-case scenarios go, this one ranks pretty damn high on the list. I fumble with the junk in the few seconds I have, grabbing the first blunt object I come across. I can't take any longer with my search; I have to keep moving.

For all the good it does me.

The machine traps me against a beaten-up four-door sedan. The next thing I know, I'm backing into the rear seat of the vehicle, pulling the door closed. Its windows are blown out, with not even a trace of broken glass left for my defense. But the body is still in decent condition and absorbs the brunt of the damage when the machine attacks. However, the impact is enough to tip it onto its side, and a second attack flips it over entirely.

My head smacks against the seat, bringing nausea and blurred vision. For a few terrifying seconds, I'm sure I'm going to black out and the machine is going to kill me. I won't have made any difference at all in this life. I'll have blown my only second chance. That's the part that scares me the most.

But I don't black out. Finding myself now on the ceiling of the car, I'm torn between staying put or attempting escape. Neither option holds any special appeal, if I'm honest. Outside, the machine is pacing around the overturned sedan, no doubt cycling through its event-driven programming to figure out how best to get at me. It occurs to me that if it had a gun of any sort, I'd be dead by now. For some reason, it doesn't, but I don't waste time on why. I plan my counterattack.

Beginning with the only thing I have on hand, some sort of rusted pipe, I rapidly assess my surroundings. Against a machine's skeleton, the pipe won't do much good, apart from testing the acoustics of its steel hide. But maybe I can—

The machine rams the car while I'm still putting together a plan. The vehicle lurches forward, skidding on its roof, which screeches at the contact. On my knees, I grip the hanging seat belt straps to keep from falling over. It strikes again and again, making it difficult for me to think because I'm so busy concentrating on not being thrown around the interior.

Finally, in frustration, I lash out with my pipe, striking at the machine's equivalent of a leg. I nearly lose my hand for the effort, but at least I inconvenience the bastard, if sparking wires are any indication. *It's the little victories.*

Just as I'm considering playing knock-knock with it again, I swear I hear the sound of a door opening, then someone calling my name. The machine reacts to a new threat, so I know I haven't gone crazy with hope.

"Here!" I yell over the aggravated whirring of the machine.

Quickly, I crawl beneath the front seat and slam my hand against the steering wheel. The horn blares violently, and I hope it'll confuse the machine's auditory sensors—at least long enough for the cavalry to dispatch it.

I let up momentarily, in case they're trying to give me any verbal direction, but at that moment, the machine reaches in and yanks me out. I realize too late there's no driver-side door.

The thing about machines is they don't have any villainy programming. They don't monologue about mission success or wait for the most dramatic moment.

They simply commence executing their primary function.

A small part of me expects some kind of eleventh-hour intervention, but that illusion shatters the instant I smack into the wall, thrown halfway across the room. I instinctively try to cushion the blow, but I only succeed in breaking my arm upon impact—that's how it feels, at least. The world erupts into searing agony. Dazed, it takes me too long to get back to my feet. By this time, the machine has closed in again.

I'm dimly aware of someone yelling as I'm launched through the air.

I collide with the hood of a different car, bouncing off it and rolling onto the ground. The impact steals my breath and rattles my bones. As I lie there gasping, I hear the mechanized approach of the machine again. *Whir-whir, whir-whir.* I will myself to get up on limbs shaking from exhaustion and pain, holding my aching arm in an imaginary sling. I taste metal in my mouth and spit blood.

Stepping backward, my foot slides along some rebar. The machine seems to be studying me and the other occupants of the room, its optics dilating in clicking radials. I know that the moment I go for the rebar, it'll perceive me as the more immediate threat. Right now, unmoving, it's trying to determine the severity of my injuries and what it will take to finish me off versus the others.

It moves before I'm quite prepared, and I drop unceremoniously to the ground, scrambling for the nearest length of rebar.

The machine bleeds blue light, shutting off, as someone fires an EMP-G. I hold fast to the rusty piece of steel, thrusting up through its now unshielded breastplate. The momentum of its collapse does the rest.

Soldiers rush to my aid, lifting the machine off me, since I'm not strong enough to pike it away with the rebar. Then Samuel's there, letting me lean on him. He assesses the damage, looking overwhelmed with worry. He appears to be at a loss for words, which is good, since I don't have any, either. Instead, Samuel wordlessly wraps his good arm around me and helps me walk away from the scene under my own power.

Samuel watches unhappily from the sidelines as Dr. Debra Gabardine tends to my injuries. Debra's the doctor who came through on her promise to do what she could for Camus, so I trust her. While she's not the gentlest physician I've ever had the pleasure of being stitched up by, I appreciate her frank manner. I know the exact extent of my injuries in a matter of minutes, without her babying me with countless reassurances that I'm going to be fine. As it turns out, I *am* going to be fine, but I'm glad she fixes the damage before telling me so.

The final tally is one concussion, several hairline fractures in my arm, a twisted ankle, and countless other cuts and bruises deemed not life-threatening. It could have been worse, Debra says. Samuel's dour countenance seems to say, yes, but it never should have happened.

A page summons the good doctor out of the room, and uncomfortable silence takes her place. I'm used to this sort of behavior from Camus, but it's not like Samuel to hold his cards so close to the vest, excluding me from his thoughts.

"I'm not dead," I remind him.

"I know." They're the first words I've managed to get out of him. "I swear, you're going to turn me prematurely gray, Rhona. Don't smile."

"Sorry. Just imagining you as a young silver fox. Sexy."

He shakes his head, but his lips pucker in the makings of a smile. We always make one another smile. It's one of the qualities I appreciate most about our friendship. And yet, in the next second his amusement evaporates; he isn't done working through his fears. "Aren't you the least bit troubled by what happened?" he asks me.

"Are you kidding? I was terrified." My arm aches from the recent memory, but mainly from the dark bruises purpling the surface. "What *did* happen, Samuel? Where the hell did that machine even come from? How did it get in the base?"

"Training accident is the popular theory going around," he says, though his tone tells me he doesn't buy the official line. "We have a few machines on-site for military exercises."

"That's insane."

"Not really. They're disconnected from the main network; they don't function without a programmer's instruction. Normally, they're completely safe. We've even got extra fail-safes put into them so this sort of thing doesn't happen. To me, the fact it *did* implies some kind of tampering."

"So what you're telling me is someone was trying to kill me. Someone flesh and blood." Samuel frowns. "That's what it looks like." I nod, growing quiet. "Are you sure you're okay?"

"Not really. But I don't see how talking about it will make it any better."

"Rhona, you can't keep everything bottled up all the time—"

"Oh, you'd be surprised," I say, cutting him off sharply. "Look, Samuel. It's not that I necessarily want to, but I have to. I know who I am, or who I was—whichever. The point is, I know what the world expects from me now, so you can stop coddling me. Camus told me all about the broadcasts ..."

"Camus," he murmurs. "It always comes back to Camus, doesn't it?"

"What's that supposed to mean?"

He comes and sits beside me, but before he has a chance to answer, Doctor Gabardine reenters the room, with Camus in tow. Or rather, it'd be more accurate to say *he* has *her* in tow, rickety on his crutches, grimacing, and leading a pack of three others I don't recognize. Two of the men are dressed in suits reminiscent of US Army regulation uniforms, only black instead of green and beige. They carry an assortment of handguns holstered at their waists, as though expecting violence to break out at any moment. The third is a woman—and clearly the most important, judging by the way the other two defer to her stride.

Samuel is back on his feet, wordlessly moving out of the way before anyone tells him to, and then Camus seizes me.

"Rhona," he says, naming me his lost love. I smile as he kisses my forehead, thinking maybe he's come around at last—until he pulls away with an empty look. The others can't see his expression from this angle, I realize. No need for him to pretend on my account, only theirs. My smile falters. "Are you all right?"

"Fine," I lie. "That's what the doctor tells me, anyway. Who are your friends?"

"Evelyn Meir," the woman says, introducing herself, stepping up and holding out her hand. Camus graciously stands aside, partly leaning against the wall to ease the pressure off his leg, but the way his tongue briefly distends his bottom lip hints at some private animosity. "Head of Churchill operations."

I accept her hand using the arm not strapped in a sling. "I'm guessing we've met before?"

"Yes, as often as circumstances allowed. Your scientist"—she looks to Samuel, who has drifted to the periphery of the group, hidden behind a white coat of professionalism—"has informed me you're suffering from some sort of low-grade amnesia. But, I'm curious. Six months in the Alaskan wilderness is no easy feat. How did you survive?" Her smile, while friendly, is now suspect. I don't trust it. I don't trust her.

"You know, I don't remember," I say, measuring just shy of the proper amount of regret, and I think I see Camus smile.

"Well, we're just happy you're back with us," Meir replies good-naturedly.

"I think we can all agree with that," Camus says, reentering the conversation at a natural spot. "But for now perhaps it would be best if we postpone our meeting until a later date, once Rhona's rested some."

Meir nods sympathetically. "Of course."

"No," I object. "I mean, that won't be necessary ..."

"You have a concussion, Rhona," Camus reminds me, the unkindness in his eyes rather than in his voice. "You're not at your best. Leave it for a day. It'll keep."

I'm getting mixed signals here. Camus wanted me to convince Meir that I'm Rhona, but as I'm trying to step up, he's holding me down. Unless there's more to all this, more he's not told me yet. I want to give him the benefit of the doubt and trust his strategy is coming from a place of leadership rather than spite, but I'm not feeling very charitable in my present condition.

"Commander Meir has come all this way," I say. "I'd hate to disappoint her."

Now I'm just being contrary, but I think I'm allowed a little juvenile behavior from time to time—especially since Camus continues to treat me like a child anyway.

"The matter is somewhat time sensitive," Meir agrees, finding an avenue in.

I look at Camus, twitching my eyebrow, as if to say *See?*

I can't tell whether he's impressed by my stiff upper lip or frustrated by my stubbornness, but he settles the discussion by suggesting tomorrow morning at the earliest. Meir offers no further argument and wishes me a speedy recovery before departing with her two-man squad. At a word from Camus, Samuel and Doctor Gabardine also leave.

"Would you mind telling me what that was all about?" Camus asks me as soon as they're gone. There's no heat to the words, but still they accuse me of some wrongdoing.

"I could ask you the same thing," I respond defensively.

His brow furrows in the way it does when he's genuinely puzzled about something. It's one of a hundred details about him my memory's retained, and I'm beginning to wish it hadn't. In another moment, realization smooths the creases back out. "If you mean my behavior, it would look strange if I didn't appear to care for you."

"*Appear* to care? God, Camus, you can be as sensitive as a rock sometimes, you know that?" I mean to leave then, but I'm a little too overzealous as I hop off the hospital bed. My weak ankle buckles, ruining my dramatic exit.

I grimace, pushing away Camus's hand when he tries to help. "No," I tell him harshly. "Save it for our audience tomorrow."

He lets me go, although I secretly wish he would make me stay.

THIRTEEN

SOMETHING WAKES me from a dead sleep.

Initially, I'm lost in limbo, wandering through various degrees of consciousness. Upon rolling over to investigate the source of the disturbance, I meet only silence and the comforting blue glow of an underwater tableau—one of many screen settings I've discovered programmed into my "windows." Since the dark still troubles me, the display acts as a glorified night-light, preventing me from experiencing feelings of suffocation. I also like the desert moon and canyon theme. It reminds me of New Mexico.

The sound resumes, focusing my disorganized thoughts. At first, I'm wary, thinking that maybe the muted thumps have followed me from my dreams of war. But they persist, and I'm forced to acknowledge someone's knocking on my door. At three o'clock in the morning.

"Coming," I murmur, even before I start moving.

I throw back the thin sheet and coverlet, getting up with the languor of my half-asleep state.

My body aches everywhere. The painkillers the doctor gave me must be wearing off.

Without a thought about who it might be, I palm the panel open.

Camus lifts his gaze from the floor and looks at me. His eyes are anxious. "May I come in?" he asks without preamble.

I become keenly aware of my state of dress. I'm wearing the loosest, most unflattering pajamas I could find in my drawer. They're about two or three sizes too big, decorated with the logo of some high school, and I suspect they might have been gym clothes once upon a terrible pubescent time, but they're surprisingly comfy. It's not like I'd planned on entertaining company this late—or early. But I know Camus. He wouldn't be here unless there was a reason.

"Sure," I say, stepping aside.

He wobbles inside on only one crutch instead of two and mumbles, "Thank you," little more than a polite afterthought. I let the door slide shut behind him, but stay near it out of instinct, waiting for the other shoe to drop.

I watch him as he looks around the room, but it doesn't seem as though he's actually seeing anything. He looks strangely, heartbreakingly lost.

"I couldn't sleep," he tells me.

"I'm sure Doctor Gabardine could give you something."

He smiles bitterly. "She has been. I haven't been able to sleep properly since Anchorage. And now ... I hardly manage it at all without the assistance of narcotics."

I didn't notice until this moment how absolutely worn-down Camus is. He's done such a good job of playing up his strengths, hiding behind a display of control, that the glimpses of vulnerability seemed like flukes more than anything. But this tiredness is something else, doggedly dragging at his soul.

"Anyway, that's not what I've come to discuss. I feel guilty about how I treated you tonight."

"Only tonight?" I reply ungenerously, crossing my arms.

"No," he agrees. "But tonight, when you looked at me, I saw my own cruelty reflected back. I saw a man I no longer recognized, nor care to." I can tell this is difficult for him as he pauses, clears his throat, gathers his thoughts. "I wish I could say none of it was intentional, but that would be a lie."

I am not nearly awake enough for this conversation.

I slowly uncross my arms. "Then, why do it? Why shut me out?"

He goes tight-lipped on me and then reaches for something around his neck, withdrawing a small chain previously hidden beneath the collar of his shirt. *Has he been wearing it all this time?* At the end of the chain, a small ring dangles lifelessly in the air.

I come closer, magnetized by the symbolic accessory. And then stop cold.

This is what Rankin was talking about, I realize, when he spoke of Camus's regret. He wanted to marry me.

No, answers the small, persistent voice of self-loathing in the back of my head that sounds a lot like envy. *He wanted to marry* her.

I plumb my mind, dredging for any feelings, any memories whatsoever on the matter. Did we talk about getting married? Did I know he was going to propose? We'd been together for so long—why hadn't it happened sooner? Besides, you know, an apocalypse to deal with ... Try as I might, I can't excavate those memories, but I do recall some frustration. Impatience. I wanted him forever, and I wanted to know he wanted me forever, too. Or until we were both killed gruesomely by machines. The latter being more likely—as proven by my case.

"All I ever desired in this life was her," Camus says, struggling to explain, staring down at me through red, tormented eyes. "You think you can be her, and maybe you can. Maybe you can be exactly what the world needs. I don't know. But I realize ... now ... why Rhona didn't let me in on her plans before. On some level, she must have known you can't re-create love in a lab. And yet, I keep thinking, why not? Why not pretend for a while? What's the harm?" His fingers tremble at the side of my face. This face that has caused both of us so much trouble. He leans in, our foreheads almost touching. "I think: maybe I can forget."

I can feel his breath on my lips as he speaks in his warm, tortured voice. His eyes are closed. He's somewhere else, imagining us. I wish he were here instead, easing this atmosphere of regret.

"But I can't. I *can't* forget." He stresses this point as he reopens his eyes and delivers the final blow. "I can't love you like I loved her."

I don't realize I'm crying until I attempt to speak, whispering, "Try?" I taste the tears streaming down my face.

"I'm sorry, but you deserve more than a last year's love. It would be unfair of me to keep your hopes up."

I can't tell whether he believes the things he's telling me or if he's trying to convince himself in an effort to quash feelings he's unable to confront. I don't know whether this is him trying to be noble or being a coward, and quite frankly, I don't care.

"How do you know?" I say. "Even if I'm not the same woman, that doesn't mean—"

"Because when I look at you, it all comes rushing back. Every memory. Every feeling. All of it. And I want to—" He cuts himself off mid-sentence, stopping the momentum of his passion by taking a physical step back, or trying to. With only one crutch, it's awkward, and painful.

"*What* are you so afraid of, Camus? Just tell me! Please."

He stares at me, mouth slack. Right when I think he's finally going to open up to me, he answers instead, "It can't be helped. I shouldn't have brought this to you."

Camus starts to leave, having said his piece.

I move into his path, even though it causes me pain, my own injuries objecting to the movement. "No," I say firmly. "You're here for a reason. You came to me, Camus. And I came back to you. That means something. That *means something,* Camus." I say it twice because I want him to believe it as much as I do.

"You just don't give up, do you?"

"Nope." I swipe at my cheeks, trying on a smile. It feels funny.

He shakes his head. "Well, perhaps this once you should."

As he steps around me, something inside me snaps, loosing a creature of rage and grief.

"So that's it?" I say angrily to his back. "You woke me up in the middle of the night for that? Whatever *that* was? It sure as hell wasn't an apology."

He doesn't turn around, but I hear him exhale. "Please. Don't make this difficult."

"Me? *I'm* making this difficult?"

I'm deliberately baiting him, looking for a fight. I can handle a battle. I can take war and destruction and the end of the world. What I can't stomach is oblivion, this emotional dead zone where neither of us can seem to say what we mean or love each other the way we should.

"I know you're here for a reason other than insomnia. So what is it, Camus? To see if you still feel something?" If he'd been facing me, I would've poked him in the chest.

He's stiff and silent, letting me rail against him. It infuriates me even more.

I step closer. "Well, congratulations! You're emotionally dead inside. I guess you win."

"Is that what you think?" He whirls around to face me, barely using the crutch at all, eyes dark and primal and full of pain. I'm actually afraid I might've gone a step too far, but I'm too proud to back down at this point. "That I've made this all about me?"

"Isn't it?" I shout. "Isn't everything?"

"Of course not."

"Poor, *poor* Camus!"

"That's not fair."

"Then *what*? Why the white flag?" My voice breaks, and I hate it. "Why now?"

"Think about what you're asking me. Think about what you want."

"I want you!"

But that's not all.

Not by a long shot.

I want things to go back to the way they were. I want to give everyone their lives back: Ulrich, quite literally; Samuel, the years he wasted on a broken science project; Zelda, the man she lost for my vanity and puffed-up pride, for the insane belief that one life is worth more than another; and Camus, his heart, his ability to love.

I want to be able to say to him, "I'm sorry," and tell him it's going to be okay, and have him believe me. I don't want this tragic figure, this resigned version of the man I knew. I want *Camus*. I want his smiles, and his laughter, and his relentless, ridiculous determination to make me love poetry and classic literature as much as he does. I want us to be okay. Or if not *us*, then just him and just me, separate but equally happy again, orbiting one another's lives as friends if we can't be lovers.

I want all my memories, or none of them.

"And," I add more sedately, exhausted by emotion, "I want you to stop hating me for something I can't fix."

"I don't hate you," he says, so quietly that at first I'm not sure I've heard him right.

"What?"

"I don't hate you. I never did."

"Great. I don't hate you, either. So where does that leave us?"

His brows are heavy, weighted with thought. He doesn't know. Well, neither do I. But someone needs to say something soon, or we'll be here all night. Not that I expect to sleep well after this, if at all. My insides are twisted, my stomach full of acid and old, unprocessed feelings. *Maybe that's it*, I think. Maybe I just have to say it. Get it out in the open. Then I'll be able to breathe again.

"I'm still in love with you, Camus."

"Why?" he asks in a small voice, almost as if he's fearful of the answer I'll give him. "When I've been so abominable to you? That you would say that ..." He shakes his head, visibly perplexed. "Why not Samuel? Or anyone else for that matter?"

"Oh, you know, I decided I'd put everyone's name in a hat and yours was just the name I pulled out."

He sighs. "Rhona, can't you be serious for one minute?" We stare at each other, both aware of his slip.

I seize him by the folds of his coat, drawing him close, or at least preventing his retreat. He lets the crutch fall, clattering to the floor. His hands fold over mine, initially resistant. Then our fingers interlace, fitting together perfectly, and we're not just holding each other, we're holding on to each other.

I think about kissing him, smashing my mouth against his and taking what I want, getting back what we've lost, and I see the same desire reflected in his eyes.

But then he begins to disentangle himself from my arms.

"This is wrong," he says. It feels like he takes some of me with him. I don't understand it, how we can be two terribly different people and also one entity. "I can't."

"Why not?"

"Because if I let myself love you—if I love you, then I've lost her. Well and truly lost her."

"I don't understand."

He grabs me by the shoulders, not gently. There is urgency in his eyes, need. "If you're Rhona, tell me about how it was before. Tell me about riding the London Eye at Christmas and wandering the empty streets at midnight afterward, bundled against falling snow. Or the summer we spent in Cannes where you were burned as red as your hair and wouldn't let me touch you for a week. Tell me about the first time I kissed you. Our first fight—*any* fight, for that matter. Tell me how you felt the first time we made love. Or the last time."

The passion in his voice robs me of the ability to speak without bursting into tears. If I could open my mouth, though, this is what I would tell him:

That night in London was the first time I ever saw snow—it doesn't snow in New Mexico, at least not where I was from, and a healthy diet of romantic comedies had me convinced it was a sign. We were meant to be. I know, I know, but I was young and freshly loved by an attractive man with an English accent. How could I not fall prey to a few girlish fantasies?

And I would tell him:

In Cannes, I only got burned because I wanted to show off my new bikini for you at every available opportunity, because I loved the way your eyes drank in the sight of me, and the way your fingers answered the call of my skin.

And maybe I would confess that I didn't remember our first kiss or the first time we made love, but I remember the last time, with his hands skimming my hips, and my legs locked around his waist, and his mouth panting against my neck, repeating my name like small bursts of gunfire. I remember smiles. Camus smiling afterward, and me smiling, the both of us smiling like fools, and forgetting—like fools. Forgetting for a moment that we were supposed to be dead, that we would be dead somewhere, along with ninety percent of the world if not for luck and my mother's connections and my impulsiveness, and forgetting how one day we would end up dead anyway, whether gripped by machines or old age. But when I was with him, the thought of death couldn't touch me.

Until it did.

I remember our last kiss, tasting of blood and ash and too many things left unsaid.

"You can't," he concludes, misinterpreting my choked silence. "I know. Through no fault of your own, I'll admit. But these feelings you think you have for me, they're echoes. *You* barely know me, and even then only through someone else's memories. How can you claim to love me?"

I could tell him all those things, and maybe he would believe I was telling the truth, but it wouldn't matter. Because maybe he would also believe I was making it all up to please him and hate me for it. I don't know which would be worse, his skepticism or his dismissal. "You make me sound like a machine just following its programming," I tell him as soon as I find my voice, the only safe thing I can think to say.

"Aren't we all?" He sweeps aside some of my hair, his fingertips as soft as feathers. I feel his lips against my forehead, a surprisingly tender gesture from a man who maintains he feels nothing for me. I shut my eyes, taking in the brief comfort of his kiss.

"I wish to God you could prove me wrong," he whispers, collecting his crutch from the floor and leaning heavily on it. "But I'm not expecting any more miracles."

"I will, you know," I say when he's at the door. He glances back at me. I press fingers to my eyes, not wanting any more tears to ruin the power of what I say next.

"I am going to prove you wrong, Camus. Just ... in a few hours."

Camus smiles, a flash of good humor, maybe even hope, but he says nothing else.

I crawl back into bed and, using the remote, change the screen to a great stretch of desert where the moon hovers above an unbroken horizon. But I don't sleep.

Instead, my mind continues to pulse with memory.

The London Eye. A Ferris wheel, not some European Cyclops. Disappointed? Only a little. Night sky, stars, and light. One more time around. But your hands are freezing. Let me warm them for you.

I roll over, pulling the covers with me and shutting my eyes, as if I can freeze the images in my head, relive them in the darkness and quiet.

Cannes. Sand and celebrities. Crowds of people. Is that Ewan McGregor? I think not. Ooh, are we jealous? Should I be? No, but I think it's cute when you are.

My imagination is drenched in sweet remembrance, down to the minutest detail of a smile or inflection—everything Camus assumes I don't remember, and much I wasn't aware I remembered myself.

I jump out of bed, getting tangled in the sheets and narrowly avoiding face-planting in the process. I pad across the carpet to the desk. I'm suddenly desperate to write the memories down, save them in a physical form more reliable than my brain. I imagine it's the same reasoning behind taking pictures or recording home movies, a way to safeguard events we can't bear to forget. I've already forgotten too much.

There's a desktop computer, a portable pad with digital screen and stylus, and an even tinier device, bafflingly small and to my eyes impractical. Even though I'm sure they all have their uses, not only am

I too tired to try to figure out how they work, but also I don't want to entrust my private memories to any of them anyway. Technology can be wiped, altered. I don't like the thought of London and Cannes being just a series of ones and zeroes in some binary language foreign to me, but accessible to machines. Existing in some intangible arithmetic world, vulnerable to electronic glitches and hacks. *No, thank you.*

I keep digging and discover a pencil and notebook of lined paper at the back of a drawer that coughs dust when I open it. *Perfect,* I think, rolling the yellow pencil between my thumb and forefinger. Once a Luddite, always a Luddite. I'm glad I prepared for this eventuality. I lick my finger, touch the graphite tip as if for luck, and begin writing. I like the sound of the pencil on paper, scratching and real.

The record is unfinished when I fall asleep. I make the mistake of letting my head rest against the desk for only a minute. My last waking moments are spent remembering the feeling of Camus's love rather than the brutality of his grief.

FOURTEEN

THE FOLLOWING MORNING, the meeting opens without the usual exchange of pleasantries, getting down to brass tacks as soon as introductions are made. There is an air of formality as everyone takes their seat.

Commander Meir and a delegation of two others are on one side of the table, while Camus, myself, and several other McKinley council members sit opposite them. There was no seating arrangement, so I can't help but feel the natural division might be a portent of the way the discussion will go. As far as opening statements are concerned, they begin amicably enough, with updates on both Churchill and McKinley operations.

Meir also inquires after my health, but I suspect it's only intended as a springboard into her next question, directed at Camus. "And have you discovered who was behind the attempt?"

Attempt, I think, mentally adding the ugly word *assassination* before it.

I haven't thought about it that way until now, but obviously the machine—one of half a dozen used for training exercises—didn't go rogue on its own. And it didn't send me that fake message from Samuel, either. Someone wanted me dead—still wants me dead. I think of Zelda with her wild eyes and hands like cinder blocks. I instinctively rub my neck, wondering what happened to her. Could she have been responsible for this?

"We're looking into it," Camus answers her.

"But you have a suspect," Meir presses.

"Yes." This is news to me. I can't tell whether he's bluffing or if it's the truth. Even with the bags under his eyes betraying a sleepless night, his poker face is as impeccable as ever. "Rest assured, the situation is under thorough investigation. It's not something we're taking lightly."

"I'm glad to hear it. Although this isn't the first time she's come under attack while here at McKinley, is it?"

She's like a cougar, I think. Artful yet deliberate.

Camus doesn't flinch from the implication. "If you're referring to the business with one of our civilian personnel," he replies, "that was a misunderstanding."

"Of course," Meir agrees diplomatically, pushing a lightly curled lock of brown hair behind her ear. "It's just ... Well, it would be quite the embarrassment if, after just getting her back, something were to happen to Commander Long, don't you agree?"

"Careful, Commander. Someone could misinterpret that as a threat."

She looks appropriately offended. "Not at all. But feel free to consider it commentary on your security measures."

I notice his jaw tighten. "Noted."

There's a palpable increase in tension, like the air's been let out of the room, and then another member of her delegation, a man with black horn-rimmed glasses, gets the ball rolling again with a harmless statement concerning agricultural output.

I mostly listen after that, taking mental notes on the topics that follow, such as rates of energy consumption, population maintenance, supply conservation, etc. All the things keeping the gears in our tiny corners of the world spinning. Although I initially worry the talk will go over my head, that fear proves unfounded. I'm able to keep up and at times even throw some ideas for improvements into the pot. It's a little like a sixth sense, or maybe not. Maybe it's some lingering savvy from my early college days, when I briefly studied political science (Mom's idea) before deciding it wasn't for me. The universe has a sick sense of humor.

While I can't say I'm particularly excited by the subject of food production, I perk up when it comes to talk of Churchill's military programs. From what I glean, it sounds like they're developing new tech to combat the steadily improving armor of the machines. Which I'm all for, obviously. Clenching my bandaged hands, I still feel the rebar's winding pattern on my palms. Unfortunately, before the Churchill representatives can get into the nitty-gritty, the conversation moves on to what Meir refers to as "more pressing matters."

Translation: bad news.

"We've been picking up increased activity in Valdez over the last month," she explains, and clearly this means more to everyone else than it does to me, because a pensive hush spreads over the group.

Camus frowns. "Do you think the machines have repaired the pipeline?"

"I do," Meir says. "And I shouldn't have to tell you what that means."

I wish she would, for my sake. I consider keeping silent and going along pretending I know what the heck they're talking about, but I'd rather be thought of as stupid than lose out on being able to meaningfully contribute to the discussion. "What's this about a pipeline?"

"I'm sorry," she says. "I continue to forget about your condition. But to answer your question, the Alaskan pipeline has been a major energy source for the machines since they conquered North America. While the machines themselves don't run on petroleum-based fuel, a lot of their production and maintenance equipment does. If nothing else, they like to keep it out of our hands. Through a joint effort, Churchill and McKinley managed to sabotage the pipeline about a year or so ago. We'd hoped it would halt the manufacture of more machines."

"Did it?" I ask.

"Not long enough, apparently," Camus chimes in, less than cheerful. "Seems we just bloodied their noses for a bit."

"Their operations in Valdez could be indicative of more than just a recovery of the pipeline," the man with the glasses says. I'm trying to remember his name, but I'm better with faces. "It's entirely possible they're assembling a strike force."

"Have you sent scouts to survey the area?" one of the council members on Team McKinley asks. He's blond, with a stout face and thoughtful eyes. Clarence something. It's not really important, except I'm trying to familiarize myself with the people who once placed in me their faith and entrusted me with their lives. While many of them seem willing to transfer their loyalties to me again, I don't want it before I've earned it.

"Yes. A six-man team was dispatched for that purpose, but we lost contact with them more than a week back," Meir explains, showing some of the first real emotion I've seen from her: frustration. "At last report, they believed the machines were gearing up—if you'll excuse the pun—for something large."

Glasses adjusts his bifocals uneasily. "What the Commander is trying to say is that we think Churchill's location might be compromised."

Meir shoots him a reproachful look. "My colleague speaks out of turn." Her expression softens, wearies. She pinches the bridge of her nose. "But ... he's not wrong. And if the machines know where we are, there's a very real possibility they know where McKinley is, too."

"Activity in Valdez is nothing new. Circumstantial at best." The speaker is a woman with dirty-blond hair, a narrow nose, and a face peppered with adult acne. She sounds more like a lawyer than a resistance fighter. I think she may be a new addition to the council, brought on for a more level-headed approach. Camus's pick, probably. "Before we start crying wolf, what other evidence do you have to support this assumption?"

"I noticed the damage to the mountain flying in," Meir says, rather than answering the question. I'm starting to understand why Camus doesn't like her. She's a politician. But so was my mother, I remind myself, trying to lend Meir the benefit of the doubt. "Unless you've been doing a little redecorating, I'd say you've already had a run-in with the machines."

"Our scientists determined the damage was superficial," the woman answers.

"Even so, have you known the machines to be anything but deliberate? It may have been a stroke of bad luck they decided to test their weaponry here, I'll grant you. But you have to consider the possibility they were testing your defenses, not their bombs."

"Let's assume you're right," Camus says over the sudden din of argument. I admire his ability to moderate such a high-strung crowd. He could've been a politician himself. "What are you proposing we do exactly?"

"Simple," Meir says. "A preemptive strike."

"On the pipeline?"

"On Valdez. With our combined forces, we could cut off the snake's head."

Camus is already shaking his head, but I kind of like the idea. "Why not take the fight to them?" I say.

"They wouldn't be expecting it," Clarence agrees mildly.

"Exactly. We'd have the element of surprise. Camus?"

He rubs his brows, shading his tired eyes with his hand. "Provided we could even take their numbers, which is by no means a certainty, what happens when they send for reinforcements? Once word is out, the snake—as you so quaintly put it—will only grow more heads with which to devour us. For all we know, this could be a ploy to draw us out."

"So we do nothing?" Meir says unhappily. "*That* is your counterproposal?"

"It's dangerous to mistake caution for apathy, Commander. Rushing into a situation as volatile as this is likely to get a lot of people killed if it's not done right. The memory of what happened the last time we made so grave an error is still fresh in my mind." I feel

Camus's hand close over my own, a nice show of solidarity for our allies. "So you'll have to forgive me if I'm not eager for a repeat performance."

The head of Churchill arranges her features into penitence. "Of course, Commander Forsyth, Commander Long. I know the cost of the Anchorage rescue was very great for McKinley. However, we must take some form of precaution."

"What about the pipeline?" I suggest, taking my hand out from underneath Camus's to pull up a 3-D projection of the pipeline's mapped route. "We sabotaged it once. Why not do it again?

It's not a permanent fix, but at least it'll buy us some time to gather more intel. Believe me, I'd love to go in guns blazing," I add with a brief smile, "but Camus has a point. If we're going to win, we'll have to engage the enemy on our timetable, not theirs. Doesn't mean we can't ruin their day beforehand, though."

I look over at Clarence. "You're our head engineer, right?" I think that's how he introduced himself. I'm relieved when he nods, confirming it. "Where are the best places to hit this thing?"

He analyzes the image quietly and then, pointing at each, says, "Here. Here. And here." They light up in a swelling and receding fluorescent red, as if to say *Hit me, hit me, hit me.* "We attacked the last two nodes previously, but they're likely to be guarded more closely now."

"Which is why we'll attack someplace else. The machines must have some way to maintain it, right? I mean, they can't babysit eight hundred miles of pipe."

"You're right. They use the same pipeline pigs as we did."

"And for the folks at home, those do what exactly?"

"There's several different types, each with a different function," he says, and then goes on to explain in detail. I manage to get the gist of it. Scraper pigs keep the walls of the pipeline free of wax buildup; corrosion detectors utilize either magnetic or ultrasonic sensors to identify any accumulated damage to the pipe over time; and "smart" pigs, which are basically glorified sensor bots, perform a combination of the above. "They're usually inserted here at Pump Station One and also here at Eight. The beginning and midpoint of the pipeline, respectively. *Oh.*"

I watch as he leans forward in his seat. He gets it.

"We're going to attack the pig launchers," I say for the benefit of everyone else.

"They're certainly less protected," Clarence agrees. "And a breakdown in maintenance should have the same effect as if we'd bombed a chunk of the pipe."

"Can't they just rebuild these ... pigs?" Meir asks.

"Yes, but it'll take time to do and require a significant diversion of resources."

"Time's all we need," I point out, laying my hands flat on the table. "Although that other part doesn't hurt, either."

"Clever," Camus says, rubbing his lips thoughtfully. I think I see him smile.

Commander Meir takes longer to decide her position, consulting with her fellows in a discussion that eventually absorbs the entire table. Everyone has their two cents, but the general consensus is in favor of sabotaging the pig-launching and receiving stations. Through a verbal agreement, McKinley promises to send a contingent of soldiers and weaponry to Prudhoe Bay in the north, while Churchill handles Fairbanks, located at the pipeline's midpoint. The attack will be a collaborative effort, the first in a long time, it seems. I smile to myself, watching the proceedings with secret pleasure. United, I believe we actually stand a chance.

"It will have to be a decisive strike," Camus says in the tone of a closing statement. "A veritable blitzkrieg. We need to overpower them before they know what's happening. Before they can organize a response. All without them getting a trace on our forces. Win or lose, it is absolutely imperative we do not lead them back to base."

"I know the drill, Commander," Meir says, with only the barest hint of annoyance. "My men can be in position in less than a day's time. Whenever you're ready, of course."

They schedule the attack for this coming Wednesday, as easily as they would a dentist appointment. Although, like a dentist appointment, I doubt the experience itself will be so painless.

The meeting adjourns on that note. The rank and file exit through double doors, but I stick around with Camus and Clarence, who are still reviewing details of the pipeline. I hear them agree to give the away teams a crash course on what to anticipate, and then Clarence departs with the rest.

"So, how'd I do?" I ask Camus once we're alone, folding my arms over my chest in what I hope amounts to a friendly challenge. "Not bad for someone with a mild concussion and doped up on enough drugs to sedate a baby elephant, huh?"

He surrenders to a faint smile. "Don't get cocky."

I spin around in my chair a little, propelling myself with one hand on the table. "Come on, Camus. Would it kill you to admit I did a good job?"

"Do you really need my commendation?"

"No?"

"Is that a statement or a question?"

"Yes?" I reply in the same inflection, intentionally teasing him this time.

He shakes his head, and for a moment—one incredible, lunar eclipse of a moment—I think he might even laugh. But he manages to rein in his amusement, depriving me of that, as well.

Too bad.

Later, as we're leaving, Meir catches us, accompanied by Glasses, whose name I really should find out.

"Commanders, a moment more of your time? There was one other matter I wanted to discuss with you both. I would have brought it up during the meeting, but wouldn't you know it? It slipped my mind." She looks suitably embarrassed by the gaffe. "Now that Commander Long is back with us, don't you feel it would benefit the cause if she were to go on the proverbial wires and announce her return?"

The request appears to catch Camus off guard. A strange expression passes over his features, darkly suspicious. He says nothing, and Meir goes on.

"I'm aware you may have some reservations about broadcasting from here, which is why I'm prepared to offer Churchill as an alternative location for the broadcast. My scientists have been working on a system that would prevent—"

"That's generous of you," Camus says, interrupting, uncharacteristically rude. "Especially at such great risk to your base."

Meir takes it in stride, ever the consummate professional. "Not so great. As I was saying, we believe we have figured out a way to avoid detection when sending out a signal."

"Really?" Camus feigns surprise. "Then I'm sure you can share the technology with us, and we'd be able to avoid the dangers of a trip to Churchill altogether.

"It's still in development. But Commander Long is welcome to stay with us in the meantime. She can tour the base as well as oversee some of our daily operations. I'm sure it would mean a great deal to our residents."

"A visit from the Red Menace would certainly boost morale," Glasses agrees.

I'm confused. "Communism?"

Glasses laughs and pushes his namesake up the bridge of his nose. "Not exactly, Commander. It's just a nickname some of our soldiers gave you, because of your hair. And because you've been one hell of a menace to the machines. Pardon the language."

The jury's out on the name, but I'm starting to warm to Meir's idea when Camus answers with a frigid, "We'll need to discuss it."

Oh, *sure.* He says that *now,* but I already hear a big, fat whopping *No* in his tone. I don't like the way he's excluding me from the decision.

"I don't see why not," I say.

"I don't need an answer right this minute," Meir says, cleverly backing out of the conflict

she's created. "But I do wish you to consider it." She nods. "Commanders."

Camus gives the slightest nod back in acknowledgment, so slow and tense I expect his neck to audibly creak.

Meir and Glasses go one way and we go another.

"Mind telling me what *that* was all about?" I ask after we're out of earshot. I struggle to keep up with his lengthy stride, even with him on crutches and a bum leg. I can tell he's angry, but I don't think it's directed at me.

"Do you have to be so damned contrary all the time?" he asks.

"I don't *have* to," I say, "but we're supposed to be partners in this. And I don't like being left out of the loop."

"Of course," he agrees, although he doesn't look particularly happy about it. He slows his pace to accommodate me.

"So?" I prompt.

He stops and draws me into an empty room to speak privately. I can't help feeling a tingle of excitement across my skin, being alone with him, even though I know nothing will happen.

"This whole visit, this meeting, everything ... it's all in order to get you. It has nothing—or at least very little—to do with concerns about Valdez. Evelyn knew if she came with that agenda, she would be summarily turned down. So she employed the salesman's tactic of opening with a steep price to make a high price seem a deal. It's also why she conveniently forgot to mention it during the meeting and only brought it up afterward. To make it seem insignificant, an afterthought. When in reality, it's been her end game all along."

"Hold on. Stop. Rewind. Why does she want me in the first place?"

"Samuel didn't have a chance to brief you, did he?" Camus says.

"I ... no. A killer machine kind of got in the way of that yesterday, and there was no time this morning."

"Then to answer your question in a word: politics. Evelyn's gotten it into her head that if she aligns herself with you—someone who is a powerful symbol of humanity—then when we finally vanquish the machines, she'll be in a good standing to assume a high level of authority in the new world order. That's not even considering the short-term ramifications, such as economic and tactical support. As I said before, if you called, half a dozen bases in the Northern Hemisphere would come running. It's helped McKinley in the past, and she believes it would help Churchill in the future."

"Wow. That offer's a lot less flattering now. She's made it before, I take it?"

"Yes, but never seriously, and never with as much to recommend her argument." I'm about to ask him what he means, but he reads my mind. "She was right about our security. Something is clearly wrong here." The reality appears to exasperate him. He lays a fist against the wall, bending his forehead to it. "I just don't know what."

It doesn't take much to read between the lines.

"I'm still in danger," I say.

"Yes," he says, never one to mince words. "Until we find out who was responsible for reprogramming the machine, it's better to assume you're not safe. I'll do what I can, but you also need to be careful."

I frown. "You're not going to restrict my access again, are you?"

"No. Limiting you to one level or location would only make it easier for your attackers to find and trap you. But I am going to assign you a guard detail. The choice of who will be yours." After this latest incident, I'm certainly not going to argue against it. Camus opens the door and leads us back into the hallway. Before we part ways, he stops, bringing his gaze to me. Something soft and gentle is in his eyes. "And Rhona?" My heart sings at his use of my name.

"Good job today."

FIFTEEN

DINNER THAT NIGHT with Meir proves to be its own odd brand of torture. I'm subjected to glimpses of the man I love as Camus and I maintain our charade of companionate lovers in front of our guests. I smile at him. He brushes the side of my hand on the table, reaching for silverware. I eat off his plate. He laughs at my jokes. It's all very sweet, very romantic. But none of it's real.

Not for him, anyway.

I've just turned on the TV and collapsed into bed to forget the whole thing when the door threatens more company. More *acting*. There's a part of me that resists answering it, the volume control on the remote proving a great temptation. *I can just turn it up, and then I won't hear a thing*.

In the end, I stomp across the carpeted floor and open the door. I'm glad I do, because it's not Meir or Camus or anyone else who wants anything from me. It's just Samuel, here with his usual offering of friendship.

"Hey," I say, like we're eighteen again, when that was an acceptable way to start a conversation.

He opens his mouth, presumably to greet me back, but stops

midway and wrinkles his brow. "Am I imagining things or is that the *A-Team* theme song I hear?"

"What? Oh." I step aside, prompting him to come in. He immediately beelines it to stand in front of the TV, where a motley group of characters are jumping into a black, red-striped van. "Yeah. Found it in the digital catalog along with some other relics from the eighties. It's dated, but the theme song rang a bell."

"Your dad used to love *The A-Team,*" Samuel tells me, smiling, hypnotized by the hijinks on the screen. "He owned every season, converted you to a fan at an early age. I remember how you used to make me sit and watch them with you when I came over. That and the original *Battlestar Galactica* series. That was more my taste. Science fiction, you know."

I faintly remember those days, with Samuel and me huddled together in the giant armchair my dad had marked as his. He was gone a lot with the military, so we made up for the vacancy. This is how the memory looks in my head, but there's no way of knowing whether it's accurate; I could be filling in the blanks with what makes sense to me, what I'd like the past to look like, warm and friendly. I've begun to wonder how much I recall is actually real, and how much is stuff I've made up, cushioning the loss in my head.

We're both watching the screen now, side by side.

"I'll tell you one good thing about memory loss, though," I remark. "It's like watching everything for the first time again."

"In that case, we'll have to break out *Battlestar* one of these days, too. I haven't seen it in forever."

I plop down on the bed, suddenly tired. It's an effort to remain social, but for Samuel, I try my best. "So, what have you been up to? I haven't seen you all day."

"Oh, not much. Caught up with some old friends, and some old studies. Nothing too exciting. I was going to come look for you around two, but I figured the meeting was still going."

"*Nooo.*" I shake my head. "I'm pretty sure I'd have committed seppuku if it'd gone on that long."

Again, he grins, a few degrees from laughter, always free with the expression. Unlike Camus, whose heart is currently boarded up against me, business between us being what it is. The difference between them is staggering, sometimes.

"I hope that's not an indication of how the meeting actually went," Samuel comments. I shrug. "More a reflection of the company. You wouldn't believe the politics."

"Yeah, I'm not sorry to say my expertise doesn't include political science. I'm happiest leaving the bureaucracy to you and the council. Give me a toad to dissect any day of the week."

"I'm sure you could've found one in that meeting without much difficulty." This time, Samuel does chuckle, but doesn't vocalize his agreement. Ever the diplomat, with never a bad word to say about anyone. I wonder how he does it.

"Is everything okay?" Samuel asks me, sitting down on the edge of the bed. I almost wish he was heavier, so his indentation in the mattress would pull us together. My sudden desire to be closer to him—or maybe just my desperate need for human contact of any sort—twists my gut with guilt. I shouldn't be thinking such things, especially not about my best friend. *Then again, why not?* says a tiny, treasonous voice in the back of my head. *Camus doesn't want you.*

"Why?" I manage to sound light, nonchalant.

"I don't know. You just seem a little out of it."

Don't do it. Don't drag Samuel into your little melodrama. "Really?" I reply neutrally.

He focuses on me, *The A-Team* all but forgotten in the background. "Did something happen during the meeting?"

"Actually, the meeting went well," I answer, recalling Camus's parting congratulations. *I'm surprised he didn't choke on the words.* It's an uncharitable thought, but after dinner tonight, I'm not exactly in a place, emotionally, to be generous toward my lover. "Granted, I'm not sure what precedent I set before, but I think I met it."

"I knew you would," Samuel says. *Always confident. Always faithful ...*

I wait for him to say more, to voice any one of the thoughts stirring concern into his soft brown eyes. Instead, he says, "Well, I don't want to disturb your marathon. I should let you get back to your show ..." But he doesn't get up from the bed. I don't think he really wants to leave.

I don't want him to leave.

"Camus came to visit me the other night," I blurt, despite my reservations.

Samuel's brows bounce up and down as he tries to hide his surprise and then decide what expression to respond with instead. He settles on polite interest. "Oh?"

"We fought." I sigh. "Again. He thinks it's over between us. That what we had died with the previous Rhona. He wants me to give up."

After staring at the bedspread for a few seconds, Samuel finally summons the courage to look me in the eyes. "I know this isn't what you want to hear, but maybe he's right." I resist the urge to get defensive and let him continue. "Rhona, have you ever considered this might be a chance to ... I don't know, start over? Maybe this is your tabula rasa. A chance to wipe the slate clean. Begin again."

"You make it sound so easy."

In truth, there's something wonderfully attractive about the idea of starting fresh, of becoming someone else—anyone else. But is that what I want? Or am I just afraid? Afraid of failing to live up to my dead donor's legacy, of letting everyone down?

All I know is that I'm tired of feeling like I'm taking blow after blow after blow in the ring, while Camus watches from the sidelines.

Samuel has never made me fight for him. Samuel has never pretended with me ...

"No, I know it's not," Samuel says. "I didn't mean to suggest that."

"Look at us," I say after another short period of silence. I crack a smile, brittle with self-pity. "I'm a mess. Whoever thought it was a good idea to put me in charge of anything?"

Samuel frowns and scoots a little closer, briefly squeezing my hand. "You're not a mess."

"That makes one of us," I say. "But thanks."

"Of course," Samuel says, and then we both return our attention to the screen.

The bed is large enough to accommodate the two of us comfortably with plenty of space left over, but somehow over the course of two episodes we end up smooshed in the middle. It happens slowly, like the gravitational pull of two planets (I think Samuel would enjoy that analogy). At first neither of us notices, and by the time we do notice, neither of us cares.

"Just like old times, huh?" Samuel remarks, letting me lean against him.

"Yeah, I seem to recall you hogging the armchair then, too."

"That's funny," he replies. "I remember just the opposite."

We laugh a little at our own expense, and as I look at him, I feel ... something. I'm not sure how to describe it except to call it just that, a feeling. The culmination of a thousand thoughts never afforded the chance to breathe. It's not a shadow cast by the past or some emotional relic left over from history. This is unique to my new life, unique to me as I am now.

We both lean in and our lips touch briefly, meeting in a new and exciting way. The contact lasts a second, maybe two. And the whole time, I feel him here with me, not trying to escape, nor pushing back against my affection. Doing everything right, just like I wish someone else would—*oh, no.*

I shoot backward like a bolt of lightning.

"Oh my God," I say into my hand.

Samuel's brows draw together. Is he confused or penitent?

"I'm sorry," he says, like a reflex.

Of course. "No, that's not—" My lips still tingle. Maybe I'm imagining it. "If anyone should be apologizing, it's me ..."

But Samuel launches into an explanation before I can stop him, throwing me a lifeline I neither want nor deserve. "It's, uh, likely symptomatic of adrenaline. I mean, with everything going on ... Stanley Schachter and Jerome Singer had a two-factor theory concerning emotional reaction. The theory explained that a misattribution of arousal could conceivably be a result of ..."

I raise an eyebrow.

Embarrassment flushes his cheeks in a flattering pink color. "The study had flaws," he finishes in a quiet murmur.

His eyes roam back to the television, but I watch him a moment longer, examining the possibility that briefly flared between us just now. I never noticed before how thin that line was, how easy to cross over. Samuel is trustworthy, intelligent, kind, quick to laugh, and to forgive—an easy person to love. Not to mention that he's done so much for me. There are countless qualities to recommend him. But a relationship isn't an interview. It isn't defined by cold, logical facts, or who has the best résumé. The most qualified candidate doesn't always get the job. And even now, as I sit here, my mouth tingling from another man's lips, my heart is still pulled to Camus. It was cruel to kiss Samuel. Cruel and stupid, stupid, *stupid*.

After another moment of awkwardness, we both attempt to speak. "You first," I say.

"Okay." Samuel clears his throat. "Well. Now probably isn't the ideal time to spring something like this on you, but given what just happened ..."

I force myself to look at him, even though part of me would rather crawl under a rock. The seconds when he isn't speaking burrow into me like pins, causing my skin to itch. This is torture. What was I thinking?

"You have to know I value our friendship more than anything," Samuel finally begins.

"I do. I know that. Of course I know that."

"There was a moment yesterday," he continues, "when the machine threw you against the wall, that I seriously thought I was going to lose you. And I'm talking for good, this time. There are no more clones, Rhona. Whatever potential there was for more went up in smoke when we blew the facility at Brooks, and I'm not sure I can even re-create the process without all the data I lost there. All your original memories and their backups were stored in local servers. Adding to which, you don't have the transference chip to map your neural pathways that Rhona had in her head when she died; the new memories would all be lost. You—*you* would be lost. I knew if you died, that was it. We weren't getting a third chance. And it terrified me."

I rub his shoulder without thinking about it, as if to say *It's okay,* even though I'm not sure it is.

"The past two days, I've been thinking: What would have happened if I hadn't come looking for you? Or if you hadn't asked that guard for directions so he knew where you were? All these what-ifs, like an endless string of probabilities, and no matter how hard I try, I can't be objective. Not when they each end with you murdered by a machine in the very place you're supposed to be safest."

"Hey, I'm tougher to kill than that," I remind him.

"Yeah, you are," he agrees. "You're amazing. But you're not invincible. And I think that's part of the reason why *you* scare me, too, if I'm honest. You know me. I'm not as brave as you or Camus. I'm just a scientist. I like control and for things to make sense. But then here you are, completely unpredictable, as vulnerable as anyone, this ... *impossible* variable in my life."

"I think that's meant to be a compliment," I say slowly, squinting, "but I'm not sure."

He smiles, embarrassed. "No, no ... I mean yes, it is. A compliment. Sort of. What I'm trying to say—admittedly poorly—is sometimes I don't know how to handle it. I'm doing my best, but ..." He gestures helplessly.

"Which is why you kissed me back," I conclude quietly.

"Yes," he says, but I can't help feeling there's more to it. "To continue this rather pathetic analogy, I don't care *how* you fit into the equation, Rhona, so long as you're here with me, working it out. I'm yours, in whatever capacity you need me, so I don't want you to feel like there's any pressure for ... anything else."

"So if, right now, I just need a really good friend?"

"Then you're in luck," he says with a wan smile. "That happens to be my specialty."

"All right. My turn, then." I inhale and exhale. "I'm having a really rough couple of days, but I shouldn't have taken out my frustrations on you."

Samuel gives me a small, wry smile. "I didn't really mind."

I laugh. "You're not helping."

"I think I'm helping a little."

He's right. In spite of the innuendo, the awkwardness has mostly vanished, and I feel a bit lighter than I did before he arrived, before our disastrous kiss. Less weighed down by circumstances, and more convinced that I'm on the right path.

I have no doubt Samuel means what he said: that we don't have to make a mountain out of this molehill. There's no pressure for us to be more than what we are. Still, for the first time in my life, I don't think it's appropriate for him to stay here, alone with me.

I give him a hug before he leaves, but I notice an unusual reluctance in his embrace—the way his arms reach around me hesitantly, without ever coming into firm contact with my back. We've jumped a fence built in childhood. Now, the only question that remains is what lies on the other side?

SIXTEEN

FROM THE SAFETY of the observation room, I watch Zelda pace around her holding cell like a caged panther, dark eyes flicking back and forth, back and forth.

Two inches of reinforced glass separates us, impenetrable to everything except sound. At present, the audio is a litany of complaints and shouted obscenities. While the window appears only as a mirror on the prisoner's side, most can guess it's more than just a looking glass. Zelda's not ignorant of this fact, either. I'm just glad I'm standing on this side of the glass this time.

"Either interrogate me or *let me the hell out,*" Zelda snaps, stopping to bang on the glass. "I know you're back there, Forsyth. You or one of your hounds."

Lefevre stands guard beside me, sentinel to his own thoughts regarding his sister and the serious charges against her. At first, he objected to bringing me here—not on personal grounds as much as security concerns. But he hasn't said a word since I overruled him with a direct order. In his defense, they were legitimate fears, but I'm well aware of the risks involved. Now that I've been given back a portion of command, I'm learning what it means to be a leader again. That means weighing the peril versus the reward and exercising my right to make decisions.

Doesn't mean Camus won't take my head off when he hears about this, though.

Peril versus reward, I remind myself.

Samuel stands away from the scene, leaning with both hands on the back of a chair. He doesn't have to say it: I know he thinks this is a bad idea. It's the whole reason he came along, and also why I let him. Acting like everything's all right between us is the only way we're ever going to get through this awkward patch. Not to mention that between Lefevre and myself, we could benefit from a little more level-headedness.

"I already know the answer," Samuel cuts in, over Zelda's abuse to the mirror, "but as the only one in this room not equipped with some kind of weapon, I feel obligated to ask: Are you sure you want to do this, Rhona?"

I nod, turning toward the door. "I need answers. I need to know who's trying to kill me, and why. Plus, I want the whole truth, not just whatever trumped-up lies Camus decides to tell me. I've got to go straight to the source for that."

"My sister took no part in this assassination attempt," Lefevre says, the first words he's uttered since we stepped into the observation room.

"You sound awfully sure. You do remember she's already tried to kill me once before, right?"

He finally looks at me, pulling his gaze away from his imprisoned kin. His eyes show stone-cold certainty. "If Zelda had actually wanted you dead, Commander, you would never have left that holding cell alive. She would have finished it herself then, not sent a machine to do the deed."

"Maybe," I agree, mostly to pacify him. I don't doubt Lefevre's loyalties lie foremost with McKinley, but Zelda is blood. I palm the door open. "But it's like my mom used to say: when you want to find something out, it never hurts to just ask," I add with a politic smile, exiting.

Samuel follows me out into the hall. "I don't remember your mother ever saying that."

"Neither do I," I reply. "But it sounded good, didn't it?"

"Now *that* sounds more like your mother." He laughs even while shaking his head. I'm about to enter Zelda's cell when he stops me again with a gentle hand on my arm. Then he quickly lets go, acting weirdly embarrassed about touching me, but his eyes remain soft with concern. "Um. Be careful in there, all right?"

Part of me wants to call him on his strange behavior, but I know the reason for it. In the end, I smile and pat my holstered pistol. "Gun, remember? I'll be fine. We're just going to talk."

"All I'm saying is, don't let your guard down."

"Advice noted."

I enter alone, the door shutting behind me.

Zelda stops pounding on the mirror, but her fists stay balled at her sides. I don't mean to provoke her—nor be provoked *by* her. Not if I can help it.

"What is this?" she demands. I'm not sure if the question's directed toward me or whoever she thinks is still hiding in the observation room. Probably the latter, judging by the way she keeps glancing back over her shoulder.

Then her eyes are back on me, full of loathing. "Forsyth can't actually charge me with anything, so he's hoping I'll—what? Incriminate myself by attacking you again in front of witnesses?" She issues an unattractive snort. "Not likely."

I take a seat, illustrating my fearlessness, since that's all I really have to work with. Impressions. There's no way she's going to trust me. I'm the enemy as long as she thinks I was responsible for Ulrich's death. Earlier, Samuel suggested I try building rapport with her, but now that I'm here, suffering beneath her angry glare, I get the feeling no amount of rapport is going to make a difference.

"Look, I'm not here to play games with you. I just want answers," I tell her.

She refuses to sit down and crosses her arms instead. "What makes you think I'm going to tell you anything different than what I've already said?"

"Because it's not Camus standing behind that window." I tilt my head toward the mirror. "Your brother's back there, and he seems to believe you're innocent. I'm not eager to prove him wrong, but I sure as hell can't prove him right if you're not willing to cooperate."

A tenderness comes across her face as she stares into her reflection, maybe seeing a hint of her sibling in her own features. She doesn't trust me, but she trusts him. I think I can use that. "Fine," she says, throwing herself into a chair opposite me, the cold metal table stretching between us. "What do you want to know?"

"Let's start with the obvious. Did you have anything to do with the attempt on my life two days ago?"

"No."

"Okay. Then do you know who else might have been responsible?"

She relaxes against the back of her chair. "No," she says, smug.

I'm starting to get frustrated. "But you do know how to reprogram a machine, like the one that attacked me." I don't phrase it as a question, because it's not. I know she does. It's more of a control question, to see whether or not she'll lie.

"Yes."

"If you're going to keep giving me monosyllabic answers, we're not going to get anywhere." Leaning forward suddenly, fingers rapping in an oddly patterned rhythm against the tabletop, Zelda tells me, "Maybe you're not asking the right questions."

"Or maybe you should just tell me what you know and save us both some trouble."

For someone who is as intimate with the inner workings of machine hydraulic systems as Zelda, you'd think she'd know the meaning of taking the path of least resistance. But, no. She's going to fight me for every morsel of information, making this conversation needlessly difficult.

"Orpheus tells me I shouldn't hate you," Zelda says. "Soldiers die in war, he says, as if *I don't know that*." This last part she announces loudly enough for her brother to hear. "He forgets they also die from poor leadership. Maybe karma is catching up to you, Long."

"You don't like me. I get it. But you know something, so I'm just going to sit here until you tell me what it is. I don't particularly want to. I have better things to do, but if this is what it takes to get you talking ..." I lean back in my seat, folding my arms over my chest. "I guess I might as well get comfortable."

Her jaw tightens, her teeth grinding together behind closed lips. The ploy seems to be working. The only thing she can't stand more than being falsely accused is, apparently, my presence. Perfect.

"All right. I might know something."

I sit forward. "Now we're getting somewhere—"

"I'll tell you what I know in exchange for the truth about the project you assigned Ulrich to," she finishes.

It takes me a moment to recover from the shock of the demand. "I don't suppose you'd be willing to negotiate on that point?"

Fury undoes her restraint. She shoots to her feet, slamming her hands on the table, which reverberates with a metallic echo. "You sent him away for *two years.* All I had was his promise he'd come back, but you took that, too. So no, *Commander*, I am *not* willing to compromise on this point. I want to know where he was all that time and what he was doing. And if you even think about lying, I'll have your tongue out before you even have a chance to go for that pretty gun of yours."

Although I feel calm, given the danger, my mouth is inexplicably dry. "You know, making threats against me isn't exactly helping your case."

Zelda doesn't care, and she tells me as much with a shrug. "Those are my terms. Take them, or leave me alone."

Bold talk, but I'm not fooled. She wants this knowledge as badly as I want to know who's trying to kill me. Maybe more. If I leave, she knows she'll get nothing—but neither will I. Yet I'm not a good enough liar to trick her into believing anything less than the truth. I'm not even sure the truth will satisfy her grief. It may in fact make it worse.

"So?" she prompts. "What's it going to be, *Commander*?"

"I can't tell you that information," I say. "It's classified."

"Then *un*-classify it. I'm not ignorant. I know it's within your power to do so."

"What exactly am I going to get if I do? You haven't told me anything yet. For all I know, your information is going to be useless, and I'll have wasted my hand." She sits back down, slowly, reluctantly.

"You want a show of good faith?" I can't tell whether that's a note of scorn in her tone or, conversely, if she's impressed I'm not stupid enough to take her at her word. Maybe a little of both. "How's this for good faith? I can give you the names of every person in this base who has experience with programming machines."

"I already have those," I lie, although I'm pretty sure there's mention of AI expertise in the personnel files.

"You think so?"

I bite the inside of my lip. "I did up until a second ago. What are you getting at?"

"Not everyone advertises their occupation. In case you haven't noticed, or for some reason don't remember, let me jog your memory. Programmers like myself haven't exactly been winning any popularity contests since the Machinations started. People still blame us for what happened. We're black sheep, and even hung as scapegoats from time to time. If you think there's mistrust in this base, that's nothing compared to the mistrust between factions of the resistance. It's one big, ugly power struggle beneath the smiles and helping hands. Forsyth is right not to trust Meir and her ilk. And that's all I'm saying until you hold up your end of the bargain."

While it's possible Zelda is bluffing, preying on McKinley's fears, my gut tells me she's not lying. Of course, that still leaves me with the problem of what truths to share with her, since the topic of cloning is obviously off the table. I'm just about to begin when the door swooshes open like a giant gasping in surprise.

Samuel steps inside, drawing Zelda's attention. The hostility goes out of her face, although tension remains in her shoulders.

"Samuel," she says familiarly.

"Zelda."

I'm still wondering what the story is there when he sits down next to me.

"Rhona was telling you the truth when she said she couldn't reveal the details of the assignment," Samuel tells Zelda in all seriousness. "It's not out of spite, Zelda. It really is a matter of international security."

"Then tell me something, Samuel. You were on assignment with him. You worked the project. I want to know, was it worth it?"

His eyes don't flick to me, but there isn't any hesitation when he gives his answer, either. "Yes," he says. "It was absolutely worth it."

"What else can you tell me?" she asks, less angrily.

Over the next ten minutes, Samuel tells her stories of Ulrich and the past two years they spent in the Brooks Range facility. I watch Zelda's reactions as she processes the news. Most of the tales are quaint, like when the heating system broke down and the pair spent a week bundled in so much extra clothing they could barely move about, or the time Ulrich tried to teach Samuel how to handle some advanced weaponry, and Samuel nearly took Ulrich's leg off by accident, causing him to curse in German for five solid minutes.

You wouldn't know these were trivial instances from Zelda's expression. As she listens, the grief is reduced in her eyes and her anger gives way to amusement. It's as though those years spent in bitter wondering and loneliness have suddenly been given back to her, redeeming some of the pain.

Samuel concludes the recollection by mentioning how Ulrich frequently cheated at their card games—something I distinctly recall the German thinking he wasn't aware of—and this makes Zelda smile. For the first time, I glimpse the woman Ulrich must have fallen in love with. She's actually quite beautiful—when she's not snarling or trying to rip my throat out.

"Deal's a deal. I'm guessing you want your answers now," she says, and I nod. "Look to Churchill for the culprit."

"What makes you think Churchill had something to do with it?" I ask.

She gives me a condescending look, as if I should know. "First, there's no one in this base with the know-how who's also stupid enough to mess with a machine like that. Second, this attack conveniently happens at the same time Churchill operatives are visiting? Please. It couldn't be more obvious."

"You said you had names."

"Not exactly," Zelda confesses, although she doesn't seem sorry about the exaggeration. "But I know how to figure out who's responsible. Meir didn't bring a lot of people with her. It's got to be one of her delegation."

"You're giving me conjecture. I start pointing fingers and a lot of feelings are going to get hurt. Normally I wouldn't care, but we kind of need allies at this point." I'm starting to understand the burden my mother was under all those years in office. Politics is a killer. Quite literally, in some instances. "I'm going to need some proof. I don't suppose you have any?"

"I know how to find some. All I need is access to the machine that attacked you."

"You're kidding."

Her face is stone, remarkably like her brother's. "No. That particular machine has a recording device in its optics for playback. The soldiers use it to review their techniques following training sessions. I'm guessing Forsyth already has the footage from the incident itself, but not before. If he did, he'd know I'm not guilty, and we wouldn't be talking right now."

"You can get this extra footage?"

"No," she says again, and I have the strong urge to reach over and smack her. "It's probably been deleted from the machine's memory, although that'd be my first effort, to try to retrieve it. If the programmer was smart, he's likely to have done everything remotely anyway, via McKinley's wireless network. It's possible I could trace the intrusion back to the system where it originated. He might have left me some bread crumbs to follow."

I rub my temples, thinking through the jargon. I hate technology. It's too damn complicated.

Samuel understands better. "Like tracing an IP address?" he says.

She nods.

"I'm hearing a lot of ifs and mights in what you're saying," I tell Zelda. "Can you trace him or not?"

"I can, and I can do it a hell of a lot faster than anyone else in this base."

She's certainly changed her tune. "I'll give you access—on the condition you're supervised during the process. Sound fair?"

Zelda nods. "Don't think this means I like you any more than before."

"Right," I agree dryly.

Samuel and I take our leave without further argument.

"See?" I tell him. "That wasn't so bad. Could have gone worse." He shakes his head, not necessarily in disagreement. "Thanks for your help, though. I wasn't getting anywhere with her. That's one nasty chip she's got on her shoulder. But she seems to like you. Why is that?"

"I don't know. Maybe I'm just charming," Samuel says with a half-hearted smile.

"*Charming,*" I say, forcing it a little. "Of course. How could I forget?"

He looks like he might say something else, but then doesn't, and I can't think of another witty thing to say on top of that last comment. An awkward silence ensues—one that makes me grimace the moment I turn away. I hoped everything would go back to normal between us, but this doesn't feel normal. It's like we're both staggering through a new script neither of us has had a chance to read.

Our celebration ends up being premature, too. Lefevre is waiting for us inside the observation room, but now he's joined by Camus, whose back is to us when we enter. His lean frame is silhouetted in a strangely ominous way by the light of the viewing window, and he's dressed warmly for room temperature in a heavy gray trench coat. The crutch and cast are both gone, though that doesn't mean anything. It's just as likely he got impatient with the healing process as that he's actually healed. But there is something in his posture, an unnatural rigidness to the shoulders maybe, that gives away his state of mind.

Uh-oh.

"Get out," Camus says, angling his head only slightly to deliver the demand. "Now."

I start to leave with Samuel and Lefevre, taking the opportunity to escape, but Camus stops me with an exasperated, "Not you, Rhona."

Samuel looks like he's prepared to stay behind, too—my partner in crime to the last—but I wave him off. I can handle Camus.

I think.

Immediately after the door shuts, Camus rounds on me. "*What were you thinking?*"

The first words out of my mouth, stupidly, are, "I can explain," as if I even need to. I don't need to justify my actions to him. I don't owe him anything. Not a damn thing—especially not when he's given me nothing in return. But even knowing this, my heart still wants to make peace.

So I try to explain. "I was trying to contribute to the investigation."

"No." He cuts me off with an imperious gesture. "Stop there. Please." His frustration overwhelms him for a few seconds, and he places his hands on the table, as if to steady the madness of a world that continues to spin. "Why must you fight me at every turn?" he asks, looking back up at me.

"Fight *you*?" I say, incredulous. "Someone tried to kill me. I'm trying to figure out who and why. It has nothing to do with us. It has nothing to do with *you*."

Camus is shaking his head, not listening. "How do you imagine I can protect you when you keep throwing yourself into the lion's den?"

Protect me? *No,* I think. *No, he does not get to play the hero card in this.* "Is that what you're doing, Camus? Protecting me? Because from where I'm standing, it feels like all you've been doing since I got here is knocking me down."

He moves around the table with surprising agility for someone barely recovered from a severe leg injury. Maybe he's so angry he can't feel it. I'd like to be able to reach that level of anger some time, to lose myself in a hot swamp of nothing. Right now, all my feelings are rushing headlong toward my stressed mental dams. I'm not indefatigable; I don't know how much longer I'll be able to stay strong before everything comes pouring out.

"I apologized for my behavior," Camus tells me, minimizing the distance between us. "What do you have to say for yours?"

"How long were you watching?" I ask. "Because you should know we made progress. We got Zelda to talk. She's even offered to help us catch the person who did it. Don't you think that counts for something?"

"Yes, but considering all the things that could have gone wrong ..."

"It was worth the risk."

"Oh, it was worth the risk, was it?" Camus says, nodding enthusiastically, though clearly not in agreement. His jaw is clenched so tight I see the clear definition of bone beneath his skin. "Worth the risk," he repeats to himself with a note of disbelief. "Is that all life is to you, Rhona? A game of chance? Throw the dice and hope for the best?"

In the privacy of the observation room, where there are no eyes or ears, no audience to play to, Camus doesn't need to call me Rhona. It makes me wonder why he does.

"Of course not," I tell him more gently, keeping my tone under control. He looks feverish, out of control, even—frightened. As if he's made himself physically sick with worry. *Worry for me?* "Camus, are you okay?"

"No," he answers candidly. "Not when you continue to do things like this. It's reckless."

Watching his knee-jerk reaction, the pieces of the puzzle come together. I don't know why I didn't see it sooner. "You're not angry with me," I say.

"Haven't you been listening to a word I've been saying?"

"Okay, you're annoyed with me, but the person you're really mad at is *her*."

His gaze snaps away from me, ashamed. We both know who I mean, although it's a little weird to refer to myself as a different person. Only for the sake of civility do I make the distinction.

"Whose idea was it to form the rescue mission, Camus?"

He swallows before speaking, but even then his voice is so quiet, raw and hoarse with feeling, I can barely hear him. "Rhona's," he confesses, almost sounding relieved that at least it wasn't his plan. "I argued against it from the start, but she insisted. She refused to leave anyone stranded. So typical."

"She threw the dice," I say.

"She gambled with her life," he corrects me, before continuing in a broken voice. "And I couldn't protect her from the consequences. That's my failing."

Not for the first time, I see Camus as a complicated mesh of anger and grief, just as volatile as Zelda, and equally desperate to make sense of the senseless. The difference is Camus reins himself in, leashed by an Englishman's control, impatient with his own feelings. While Zelda had Lefevre as a confidant, and probably anyone else who would hear her complaints, Camus has suffered in silence. Repressing—no, *killing*—his heart. I can't imagine what it's like to live in that kind of daily misery. Always pretending to be okay when you are so clearly not.

"I'm sorry, Camus," I say, because someone should say it.

He frowns. "It wasn't—"

My fault? I see the completion of the thought reflected back at me from his expression. *Yes, it was. It can't not be my fault, if it was Rhona's. Say it, Camus. Yell it. Scream it at the top of your lungs. Rage. Anything. Hate me so you can love me again.*

But of course he does none of those things. That would be too easy. Or too hard.

Instead, he tries to compose himself, remain outside the reach of human comfort, by moving to stand in front of the window again. His reflection is as faint as a ghost, his unhappiness transparent. "'We have seen the best of our time,'" he says, and it takes me a moment to understand it's a quote. "'Machinations, hollowness, treachery, and all ruinous disorders, follow us disquietly to our graves.' William Shakespeare." In response to my blank look, he says, "Famous sixteenth-century playwright."

It seems I lost certain chunks of my high school or college years—English class must have been one of those periods that either never got transferred or lacked enough emotional content for me to hang on to. Then again, maybe Camus is referencing an obscure play I was never familiar with—that would be like him. The hipster. "Well, he got the Machinations part right," I say, thinking of *the* Machinations, even though I'm sure Shakespeare had no idea of the terrible things to come under that name. "But I don't know. I think our lives can still be more than just a collection of bad events. Life should be more than just survival."

Camus is silent, wrapped up in old guilt.

I approach him cautiously, like I would a wounded animal. "You don't have to go through this alone." I try slipping my hand into his. He recoils from my touch, but not instantly, and in that single moment when our palms are mated, I get a sense of shared longing. He's good at hiding it, better than most, but it's still there. That need for companionship, for a friend, for trust and love and all the things intrinsic to the human condition. All the things he's denied himself for the past six months.

"And you can't keep punishing yourself, Camus. You can't keep driving everyone else away."

His eyes search my face with the desperation of a drowning man looking for a lifeline. "Like who?"

I mentally list the people who were Camus's friends, only to realize most of them actually belong to me. "You can always make friends. And ..." I take a breath. "You still have me. You know, if worse comes to worst."

The last bit is a joke. I wish he would smile again.

He snorts. "I'd be more inclined to believe that if you didn't seem so dead set on getting yourself killed."

"Sheesh. You bleed to death one time, and no one ever lets you forget it."

Camus shakes his head.

"Too soon?"

"Is everything a joke to you?" he asks me.

"If it's a choice between laughing or crying, then yeah." I shrug. "Why not laugh? I'm an ugly crier."

It's not my intention, but he looks chastised by my remark. It's like he's only just realizing how hard he's been on me. About freaking time.

"I didn't mean to upset you." I give him a sideways look that says, *Yeah right.* He exhales—part sigh, part laugh. "I guess that's not entirely true, is it? I'm just tired and ... concerned."

"Yeah, I get that. But I'm okay, Camus. Nothing happened—"

"This time. What do you expect will happen when your luck runs out?"

It's a rhetorical question he expects me to know the answer to, because we've already lived through that scenario. *What do I expect will happen when my luck runs out? I don't know, Camus. The reset button didn't work quite right the last time. Nothing is how I expected it would be.*

"The base is my responsibility, but so are you," he continues with more care in his tone. "I won't require you to ask permission for every little thing, and I'll try not to behave like your keeper. But I do ask that you extend me the courtesy of keeping me informed. Particularly when you're intent on endangering yourself."

"Okay. Fair enough," I agree.

Satisfied with my answer, he takes his leave, but I stop him on the way out. "Hey, Camus?" He stops, turning only his head. His profile is all sharp angles. I'm sure I'm supposed to say something profound now, something that will alter our relationship and radically redefine our possible future.

I say, "Cheer up."

There's a glimmer of a smile, promising, but it's gone too quickly, and soon he is, too.

Samuel replaces him less than a minute later, giving a playful rap on the doorframe as he peeks in. "Is it safe?" he inquires.

I shrug, half sitting against the table. "For now."

He joins me, our shoulders coming together supportively, but I don't look at him, out of fear of driving the wedge of weirdness between us any deeper. "Everything all right?" he asks, more seriously.

"No," I answer honestly. "But we're getting there. And what about us?"

"Us?" he squeaks.

Now I turn to face him. "Are we going to be all right?"

He nods and only a little haltingly answers, "Of course."

I take him at his word. I can't entertain the alternative.

SEVENTEEN

WHEN THE DAY of the attack comes, just shy of a week later, McKinley swells with anticipation.

The entire base collectively holds its breath and waits.

In the meantime, the war room has finally made good on its name, and is all geared up for the offensive. The walls are powered on, cluttered with live images from both teams. Adding to the feeling of chaos, anyone with even a small claim to authority is here, pushing the occupancy limit. It's the fullest I've seen the room since I crashed the debriefing, what seems forever ago now.

I'm in the center of activity, flanked by Clarence, who's the real expert here. A few feet away, Camus coordinates with Meir, who now appears only as a pretty face on a screen, miles and miles away, having returned with her delegation before the conclusion of our investigation. Convenient timing at best; a sign of guilt at worst. But she's moved her people into position as promised, and now isn't the time to foster dissension among the ranks. I might be little more than a glorified rallying point, true, but at the very least I hope to create a feeling of community. The machines are going to present a united front; so will we.

It's hard enough keeping my thoughts clear amid the half dozen different conversations going on, so when Clarence addresses me, I don't hear him at first. "Commander?" he repeats, a little louder. "The Prudhoe teams are active and ready."

"Right," I say. "Camus, how's Fairbanks coming along?"

He holds up a finger in the universal sign for "One second," and covers an ear with a hand, listening to his earpiece. "Their assault teams are on location now."

"Okay. Good."

I'm watching the screens with the live feed of the area. The footage is shaky and partially obscured by a scratchy static from time to time, but it's as close to being there as any of us in the war room are going to get. I feel a little nauseated, although I'm not sure whether it's nerves or the shakiness of the camera feed. I close my eyes for a moment, trying to imagine a serene place like a beach to calm myself. Instead, I remember the dreams I had while in the Alaskan forest, and it has just the opposite effect. I feel like I'm back on that cliff, poised above a frozen shore, ready to jump.

Except this time, Camus isn't holding me back; he's watching to see if I'll fly.

"Give the order," he tells me, although the words themselves get lost in the noise. I'm forced to read his lips instead. Not that it's necessary. I already know what needs to happen next.

"Teams Sasquatch and Barbados, you've got the green light. Commence with Operation Pigs in a Blanket," I say into my headset, somehow managing to make it sound serious.

The mission's code name was Hanna's idea, joking, although I was given the credit after proposing it in council. I can just see the history books now. If anyone asks, I'm going with the time-honored excuse: you had to be there.

"Repeat. Sasquatch and Barbados, you have the green light." I'm not sure whether I'm supposed to add anything else, but I remember people wishing each other Godspeed, so I grant the same encouragement over the radio to my teams in Prudhoe. It's a little awkward, given that I'm no British general, but I think I spy a smile from Camus's direction. *Worth it.*

Meir likewise gives her own teams the go-ahead at Fairbanks.

And now the hard part begins.

There's very little we can do on this end, apart from provide instruction when needed. And since the teams have already been thoroughly briefed, they don't really need any advice on how to do their jobs. Besides, the mission is pretty straightforward. In both locales, they'll strike first from the air and move in for cleanup with the ground forces. Hopefully, the two-pronged attack will confuse the machines long enough to keep them from assembling any significant response. Once that's done, the teams in the air will disappear, while the teams in the tanks will lure any trackers into the trees of the nearby forests, destroy them there, and then vacate with the assistance of extraction teams. We may be forced to abandon the tanks in the woods if they're too hot with the machines on them, but I hope those will be the only casualties suffered today.

I keep my chin up, trying to appear cool and calm, but I can't help picking at my fingernails beneath the table.

I need everything to go right today if I'm to prove myself as a commander. The title is mostly honorary in this day and age, no longer requiring the same military distinction it used to, but it's still only given to the best humanity has to offer. I intend to become that again.

The first ten minutes of the mission pass successfully, without incident. I'm standing now, with many of the others, watching the many screens, trying to interpret the footage in combination with the soldiers' running commentary.

Fifteen minutes in is when the trouble starts.

"Reports indicate a medium-size force approaching Fairbanks from the south," Clarence relays to me between his rapid communications with Churchill base.

"Medium?" I say. "Define medium."

"Like Goldilocks and the Three Bears, Commander," I hear a

soldier on-site reply. "Not too big, not too small, but just right to throw a wrench into this operation."

The Texan accent reminds me of—*no!*

"Rankin?" I blurt out, completely unprofessionally. "Is that you?"

"Yes, ma'am," comes the response. He pops into the view of one of his fellow soldiers' cameras. With all his equipment, including a face mask, there's no way I would have recognized him. He would've just been another soldier. And less of a concern—as terrible as that sounds—because I would have assumed he was from Churchill. Rankin gives me a friendly little wave, like he's on vacation, not assaulting machine-controlled land.

My head is spinning. "What the hell are you doing in Fairbanks?" Fairbanks is supposed to be Churchill's people—*only* Churchill's, but apparently *someone* didn't get the memo. "Does Hanna know you're there?"

"Oh, yeah, she knows. She wasn't too happy about it. But Camus told me Churchill needed someone who knew the area, so here I am." I doubt that was the only reason why Camus volunteered him for the job. He probably didn't trust our allies, wanted some insurance, under the guise of a liaison and navigator. *Damn it.* "Not to rush you, base, but how do you want us to handle these party crashers?"

"The station is out of commission, correct?" Clarence asks.

"Yes, sir," Rankin replies, voice crusty with static. "The machines aren't going to be launching or receiving from Fairbanks any time soon. The air team saw to that. We're still tidying up after them, but there's only a few stragglers giving us trouble. And they won't be any use to reparations. They're just some half-frozen predators."

Camus has joined us by this time. "Do not engage the enemy if it is at all possible to avoid them, Lieutenant," he says. "Finish the cleanup and meet at the rendezvous point."

"Understood, Commander."

What was nerve-racking before is now almost unbearable, with the knowledge that I've got a close friend out there, risking life and limb on my orders. Before, most of the soldiers were faceless, nameless. Now I can't stop imagining all of them as Rankin, or Ortega, or Lefevre. I've put these brave men and women in the line of fire. Me.

The stress begins to leak through my nose in the form of blood. I curse under my breath, trying to casually hide it with a hand. I thought I'd finished with this. But I do find it oddly symbolic, given the blood that might be shed today. Symbolic and extremely inconvenient.

Camus appears with a tissue a few minutes later, unasked. His eyes are kind, kinder than usual, and worried. He's asking me if I'm all right without putting it into words that would raise doubts about me. "I'm fine," I answer quietly, and mumble a thanks for the tissue. Camus nods and returns to what he was doing.

My nose stops hemorrhaging, although my hands are shaking now.

I can't worry about it. My allotment of worry is all being used up by the Fairbanks ground teams. They haven't vacated the area yet.

"Rankin, what's going on?" I ask, unable to interpret the scene via visuals.

"Uh, well," he says, clearly distracted by the task at hand. "The strike missed one of the pig supply houses. Just a small one, on the border. Nothing to worry about. We're setting explosives now."

"The machines are less than a klick away," Clarence tells me.

"You can't stay there," I tell Rankin firmly. "The machines are almost on top of you. You need to leave right now."

"We have another problem," Camus announces, pulling some images into view, layered atop Rankin's unit. It makes me even more uneasy, not being able to see my friend or his team. But unlike the Fairbanks footage, these have no sound accompanying them. "We just lost complete audio with Prudhoe. Some kind of interference or jamming, maybe."

"Great. Can they still hear us?"

"No. I don't think so. They haven't responded visually to any of our dispatches." I'm getting a bad feeling in the pit of my stomach. "Can you fix it?"

"If it was a technical problem on our end, yes. But it's not." He sighs, attempts to rub the stress out of his face. "Until we figure out the source of the disruption, they're on their own out there. There's nothing we can do."

"Well. This just keeps getting better and better, doesn't it?" Camus fixes me with a testy look that says my sarcasm is unwelcome right now. "All right. Let's focus on what we can control."

I mimic Camus's earlier gesture, throwing the silent pictures out of the way and onto another part of the wall to be analyzed by some of our technicians. Beneath them, back in Fairbanks, it looks like Rankin's team is finally on the move.

"Lieutenant, report."

"The machines ... they cut off our exit route," Rankin says, breathing heavily between the words. The jerky movement of the camera puts his breathlessness into context. They're running. "We're rerouting toward—"

A burst of static cuts him off.

"What was that, Lieutenant? You're breaking up. Repeat," Camus orders.

The Fairbanks ground team is now climbing into vehicles, most piling into tanks, while two others including Rankin jump on a pair of high-speed snowmobiles.

"We're rerouting toward the city," Rankin repeats.

Much of the room has quieted down to listen to the situation, and this news is met with looks of apprehension. The tension is palpable. To his credit, Camus shows no outward reaction. "Roger that, Lieutenant," he says. "Keep your heads down until we get to you. I want no cowboy antics, is that understood?"

"Yes, sir. No antics."

"Can you bring up a map?" I ask Clarence quietly while Camus and Rankin continue to converse.

The head engineer acquires a satellite image of the once-fair city of Fairbanks on the table's holographic display. I don't claim to be an expert on cartography, but I notice the river bisecting the map right off the bat. The black snake is kind of hard to miss amid the meringue of whitish-gray pixels, some representing a former house or business, the people all gone now, although the structures remain, skeletal testaments to their lives. I stare and stare, trying to make sense of what is there and devise some sort of plan for the extraction team, but all I see is a death trap. "They're driving them toward the river," I blurt out the moment the realization comes. "Camus, the machines are boxing them in."

Clarence leans over to look at the map and agrees with my conclusion. "The bridges are still there, but it wouldn't take much to blow them. They're likely weak from disrepair already, never mind the weather damage."

"Lieutenant, did you get all that?" Camus asks, surprisingly calm.

There's a period of silence, and then, "Yes, sir." More silence follows, with only the noise from a snowmobile galloping over crunching snow. After a few more seconds, Rankin comes back with, "Don't suppose you have any other ideas? With all due respect, Commanders, I think we're gonna need more than a few Hail Marys out here. The machines are closing in on our six."

"We have to send in the extraction team now," I tell Camus. He says nothing, which I take to mean he didn't hear me. "Camus. The extraction team. Why not?"

He's shaking his head. "We can't," he says to me privately.

To Rankin, he says, "As soon as you reach the city, find a defensible location and hunker down. We'll get word to you when we can."

"Understood," Rankin says, sounding none too happy.

"Why not send the extraction team in?" I ask again.

I'm getting upset despite my efforts to remain cool and levelheaded. Camus must pick up on this because he draws me aside to an empty corner of the room, using a hand to cover the mouthpiece of my headset. "They're too hot right now. The extraction team isn't meant for combat, Rhona. We send them in prematurely, everyone dies."

"Yeah, and if we don't send them in now, Rankin and his team are going to be slaughtered."

His jaw sets in that way of his. "I'm sorry. They knew the risks going in."

"No," I say, gritting my teeth and digging my heels in for a fight. "*No*. I don't accept that." This feels too similar to the moments before Ulrich's death. I feel as helpless now as I did then. Difference is, I can still do something this time around. "What are our options? Come on, Camus. I know you. I know you don't give up this easily. So, what are our options? We have to have some sort of contingency plan for this, right? What did we do near Anchorage?"

"I shouldn't have to remind you, people died near Anchorage. I wouldn't say that spells a successful operation."

"We're already up a creek, Camus. Might as well draw on experience."

I don't know what changes his mind, but he gives me one last look before becoming the man I need. "Air support," he says to Clarence, still maintaining eye contact with me. "Get ahold of our team in the air. Tell them we need a diversion ..."

I smile, watching him come alive with purpose. He returns to his previous post in front of one of the many walls decorated with moving pictures, just as Clarence brings the flight captain on screen. Behind the black opacity of his flight mask's visor, it's impossible to read the man's expression, but when he speaks, he sounds uncertain.

"This is Mountain Eagle One reporting. What can I do you for, McKinley?"

"I'm going to need you and your men to alter your heading," Camus begins, and goes on to relay the precise instructions for the rescue mission. When he's finished, not having to fight the pilot too hard on the change of plans, it's decided the air team will take the machines from the rear.

"Give them something else to worry about," he adds with a little relish. "Clarence, contact the extraction team. Give them the order."

Our new plan's not unlike what Samuel and I did back in the wilderness, challenging the machines' programming, forcing it to actually think and prioritize. Never fails to break down some of their efficiency. "I like it," I say. "So long as it works."

Camus gets Rankin back on the horn. "Status report, Lieutenant."

"We're holed up in some old manufacturing plant on the east side of the city," Rankin says. "Fine, for now. But we're expecting company in the next few minutes." We can see the men scrambling to throw up makeshift fortifications, anything to either stop or at least slow down their enemies.

"I've got reinforcements in the air, and an extraction team en route now." A reluctant and nervous extraction team, captain aside. But still.

"Well, hell." Rankin breathes out in relief. "Best news I've gotten today."

"Tell your men to prepare. It's not likely to be a clean break."

"It hasn't been so far. I'll tell them."

While we're waiting for all the players to get into position, Meir interrupts as a talking head on the wall. "*What* do you think you're doing?" she demands, for once making no effort to hide her irritation. I don't know whether she's speaking to Camus or me, but I answer before he has a chance to.

"What we're *doing,* Commander Meir, is saving your men's lives. If you have a problem with that, maybe we can discuss it at the next meeting."

"As a matter of fact, yes. I do have a problem with it. My air team has accomplished their mission. They've done what was required of them. You can't throw them back into the fire for some ... suicide mission!"

"You say suicide mission. I say rescue mission. Besides, they're *your* men down there. Don't you care what happens to them?"

Her lips pull into a tight line, as if she's tasted something rank. I seem to have that effect on people sometimes. "Of course I do. Don't mistake me for being inhuman, Commander. But as you should know, as leaders we must at times make the tough decisions no one else can or will. Success is made on the backbone of sacrifice."

"So, they're what, then?" I ask her. "Just collateral damage?"

"Sunk cost," she corrects. "Maybe your man on the ground doesn't realize that, but I know for a fact that every last one of mine are ready to lay down their lives to protect Churchill and its people.

And I'll thank you to leave the governing of *my* men to me from now on."

I clench my jaw. It's like trying to get blood from a stone.

Camus, who has been silent to this point, finally speaks up. His tone is cool and professional. "Perhaps it's time you reassess your leadership qualifications then, if that's how you feel." And before Meir can say another word, Camus gestures across his throat and Clarence cuts the feed.

"You know there's going to be hell to pay for that," I tell him, holding back a smile.

"I know."

"She'll probably just communicate her orders directly to the air team."

"I've spoken with the pilot already. Contrary to the Commander's belief, he didn't seem keen on letting his friends die. That 'no man left behind' policy of your American soldiers seems to be alive and well."

Without Meir to distract us, we're able to turn our attention back to the situation, leaving politics out of it. The air team has their targets in sight, and the extraction team is ready to move in at the first available opportunity. Things seem to finally be going our way again.

"Hey, Rhona?" Rankin says right after I tell him the ETA of rescue. "I don't mean to jinx this, but if things go belly up, you tell my girl I love her, all right?"

"God, Rankin," I say, closing my eyes. "Jinx is right. Haven't you watched enough movies to know better than to say something like that?"

"I know it." I think I hear a smile in his voice. "But life isn't always like the movies. Sometimes the bad guys win. I just want Hanna to know I was thinking of her to the last, if it happens."

I don't want to be having this conversation with him. With anyone, for that matter.

"We'll tell her," Camus answers for me, and I can feel his hand on my lower back, light and reassuring. He gives me a look I can't decipher, then removes his hand.

Minutes later, sound blasts from the speakers like the last trumpet. Camus grimaces, yanking out his earpiece, which screams with feedback. I cover my ears like everyone else, trying to prevent my eardrums from bursting. The sound comes across only as white noise at first, amplified in volume. It's only as I strain to listen that I begin to pick out words.

"What is that?" I yell, although it's unlikely anyone hears me against all the racket.

Camus is waving wildly at the technicians. *"Turn it off!"* I think he's saying. But the audio continues to rage, and I can't tell where it originates from. I worry that Rankin and his team are under attack. My eyes search for the live feed of the Churchill ground team.

It's unchanged. They're fine.

Instead, the video of the Prudhoe teams is down, but their audio has miraculously returned. I stare at the black screens while the technicians wrestle with the volume controls. They manage to get it down to tolerable levels in time to hear the chilling combination of panicked voices shouting orders and grinding machinery silencing them one by one.

No, I think. *No, not grinding. Whirring.*

I grab the table to steady myself, dizzy from the rush of blood to my head, my body's natural reaction to the sounds of death. *We have to do something,* I think frantically, but don't know what, and worse, when I try to speak, nothing comes out. Those are our people out there. *We have to do something ...*

"We need those visuals," Camus barks. *"Now!"* One of the technicians starts to babble out an excuse, but Camus's having none of it. "I don't care. Do whatever you have to. Get it back up."

"Base?"

"Rankin?" I say, readjusting my headset. His voice brings me back to reality, mentally separating me from the commotion.

"We just got a whole lot of something from your end. Everything all right?"

I could tell him about Prudhoe and what we suspect is going on there. But I don't. He doesn't need bad news on top of everything else. "Yeah, everything ... everything's fine," I lie with some difficulty. My throat hurts, aches with emotion. I still hear the whirring, even as it competes with the haggard voices of McKinley soldiers, fighting and dying up there at the edge of the map, where it sounds like the world's ending a second time. "Just some bad feedback. How are you holding up?"

"Not bad. Found some nice scarves in a box. I was thinking of bringing one home for the missus. You want one?"

"You're joking."

"Really," he insists, and I'm having trouble not laughing at the absurdity of it. "It's a brand-new shipment, looks like. Probably a Christmas present for the workers or something. Never been opened."

"No, thanks."

"Are you sure? They've got a nice red one here with your name on it." Before I'm given a chance to decline a second time, someone murmurs something to him off camera. "Actually, hold that thought, ma'am. It looks like we've got some visitors. 'Scuse me ..."

The sounds of battle replace his country drawl soon after that. This time I don't shrink away from the violent noises, even though a part of me would like to. Another, more primal part wants to be there with Rankin and his team of Churchillians, fighting the good fight alongside them. In fact, anything is preferable to just standing here, useless as a brick. As I begin to wonder whether the air team had any effect on the machines' offense at all, I realize there is something else I can still do.

I get the pilot Camus talked to back on the line.

"What?" he says peevishly. I don't take it personally. I know I must be one more unwelcome distraction at this point.

"Cancel that last order," I say.

"*What?*" the pilot repeats, incredulous.

"Change of plans. We need you to attack the pipeline directly. The only way we're going to draw the machines off the attack is if we give them a higher defense priority. So ... blow the pipeline."

"What are you doing?" Camus barely has time to ask me this, too occupied with our other situation.

I ignore him. "Captain, do you copy? Burn the line."

After a long period of near silence, the pilot's accelerated breathing gives way to, "Copy that, McKinley. Changing course now."

While he relays the new orders to his companions in the air, Camus joins me in front of the trembling visuals. "I certainly hope you know what you're doing," he says doubtfully.

"Yeah," I answer. I look down at my fingers, noticing the spots of blood around the nails where I've picked too hard at the skin. "You're not the only one."

Hours later, it's all over.

The hangar is approximately a mile out from McKinley's heart, and we travel through a coronary network of tunnels to reach it. Most of the time, the route is traversed by small vehicles suited to the confined passages, but today we go by foot. I'm glad, mostly because it's something to get the blood flowing, and I've been still for too long. On the downside, it grows noticeably colder the farther we get from the main base, ultimately to the point of discomfort. My breath shows, hanging dense in the air, and my teeth chatter until finally Camus throws his trench coat over my shoulders.

Before long, we're standing beneath a massive dome. From the ground, it resembles frosted glass, but somehow I know it's anything but delicate. Ice has crusted over parts of it, but Clarence informs me his men check it daily for any structural weaknesses. I'm also told it's made out of the toughest material we have available, some industrial strength something or other. I'm not really listening intently at this point. Too many other things on my mind.

I wait at the head of a mass of murmuring people for the mission's survivors. The crowd was supposed to have been kept to a minimum, reserved for family, or in the absence of family, close personal friends of the soldiers, but it feels like half the base has crammed into the loading area to await the returning heroes.

I'd chalk the turnout up to the same morbid curiosity that once kept us tuned in to the TV to watch natural disasters unfolding half a world away, except it feels different. It's like there's this current of support running through the group. A friendly word here or a comforting gesture there keeps spirits up, creating a united front of optimism. I'm proud beyond words of these people, many of whom came to the base as strangers, but years later stand shoulder to shoulder as brothers and sisters, a surrogate family filling in for the ones they've lost.

These people may think they need a leader, some redheaded mascot to cheer them on, but I believe they're stronger than they think. They're survivors, with or without me.

The dome begins to open, accompanied by a great cracking sound, like ice splitting. Soft snow comes loose, fairy dust raining down on our heads.

Camus cools his heels next to me, the image of patience, whereas I am not. I can tell he's just as worried, but to his credit, he does a much better job of hiding it. Nothing gets past his mask, except through his eyes. He's always had expressive eyes.

Hanna stands to my other side, gripping my hand with both of hers. Her lips move in a silent prayer. *Please, please, please.* I wish I could offer her some reassurance, but I don't think hollow promises will help. Rankin coming home safely, *that* will help. And I've done all I can do in that area.

The extraction team from Prudhoe is the first to return, bringing with them empty choppers. Somewhere in the crowd, I hear a woman cry out, and then a man begins cursing, before both man and woman are taken into sympathetic arms. Everyone else is silent, struck by disbelief. Death never makes sense.

Next to arrive is the Churchill air team from Fairbanks, around the same time the Prudhoe air team does. For the former, this is only a stopover to refuel, but the pilots are greeted as warmly as if they were McKinlians themselves. Both teams exchange handshakes and slaps on the back, congratulations on a job well done. It's nice to see Meir's venomous ways haven't poisoned the entire well.

Apart from the Prudhoe ground team, no other teams have registered casualties, but that loss is not easily dismissed. From different areas of the hangar, I feel the eyes of the grieving on me. It's a struggle to master my expression, to give nothing of my thoughts away, to show just enough remorse to look sympathetic, but not so much that I look guilty. I'm not guilty of anything. I know I did everything in my power to save the ground team.

Still ...

As representatives of McKinley, Camus and I both head the welcoming committee. I leave Hanna behind with friends to follow his example as we thank the men and women for their service, paying particular honor to Captain Mathis, the pilot of the air team I spoke to, for his willingness to flip Commander Meir the bird and fly in the face of danger to see his brothers- and sisters-in-arms get a fighting chance.

"Are they back yet?" he asks, removing his helmet and slicking back strands of brown hair soaked in sweat. He's a lot younger than I expected, but has a serious look to him. "I don't see them. Did they get out okay?"

"We're still waiting for word," Camus informs him. "But the extraction team did report they had survivors on board at last transmission."

The pilot nods, but looks no more jubilant than before.

Another round of the waiting game begins, marked by an increase in nervous small talk. I don't know how long we linger in the hangar, but it's enough time for them to tow all the planes inside and close the dome back up. Even with it closed, the temperature doesn't improve terribly. This close to the surface, we can't heat the place too much for risk of thermal detection by the machines. So it's nippy, to say the least. The only warm spots in the room are near the choppers and planes, which are still radiating heat, though not nearly enough for my taste.

I tug Camus's coat around me a little more tightly, alternating between shoving my hands into its deep pockets and tucking them beneath my arms, all the while trying not to notice how the coat smells like him. To distract myself, I go looking for Hanna.

She's not wanting for company, as it turns out, busily signing with Captain Mathis. They converse too rapidly for me to keep up, but he manages to get a smile or two out of her, and vice versa. I envy Hanna's ability to make fast friends with everyone. Given enough time, I grow on most people, but I don't have Hanna's easy nature or instant charm. I'm more of an acquired taste.

While I'm trying to decide whether to butt in to their conversation, the Fairbanks extraction team's clearance request comes in. The dome begins to yawn open again, as if having tired of this whole ordeal and ready to get it over with. That makes two of us.

Everyone on the flight deck scatters to make room for the chopper to land. Its blades herald the soldiers' return with a rhythmic beating that synchronizes with my own heartbeat after a few seconds. The doors of the choppers are closed, currently protecting those inside from the downwash. It also prevents me from determining how many men they have aboard, if any, and whether any of those men are my friend's husband.

A medical team remains on standby for the wounded, and I catch a glimpse of Matt. But no Samuel. *I'm not that kind of doctor,* I remember him saying.

Due to the noise, I don't hear Hanna rejoin me, but she's there a moment later, standing next to me and holding her breath, when the engine powers down and the chopper doors slide back.

I don't recognize the first two soldiers who stagger out, leaning on one another for support, but it's clear someone in the other Churchill team does as they rush forward to meet them, alongside the medical team. More men and a few women are slowly and carefully unloaded from the chopper into either the embraces of their friends or literal neck braces due to injuries sustained in combat. Cheers go up for the heroes, the applause deafening. I smile and clap with everyone else, relieved at the number we were able to save. But I still don't see Rankin yet, and that worries me.

Please, I think, taking up Hanna's mantra.

The last man of the Fairbanks ground team exits the chopper's rear. He's still wearing his protective helmet, so I can't see his face, but something's not right about his height or build. When he removes his helmet, it only confirms my suspicions.

It's not Rankin. Not-Rankin is quickly smothered by hugs and kisses from a Churchill woman with much the same hair color as Hanna. And while I'm happy for them, a part of me can't help feeling wronged on my friend's behalf.

Hanna is still, maybe in shock. She doesn't tear her eyes from the chopper. I watch her watching the extraction team's pilot and copilot climb down. I'm still trying to come up with the right condolences when the copilot removes his flight mask and helmet, revealing an unmistakable bald head beneath, its bright sheen of sweat catching the hangar lights like a beacon.

Rankin closes the distance in a slight jog, catching his wife, who comes at him at the speed of a freight train, in his arms.

"Brought you something," he tells her with the biggest grin I've ever seen.

It's one of the scarves he was telling me about: robin's-egg blue and perfectly complementary to her complexion. He wraps it tenderly around Hanna's neck, and she's half laughing, half crying. Then he's kissing her and she's kissing him, and it's like the fear of the last day is completely forgotten. They hold each other close, and I think I hear her whisper to him, "I could have used some gloves, too," at which he guffaws loudly, happily, and kisses her again.

The homecoming is more bittersweet for others as they search for the dead among the living.

As with the operation near Anchorage, rescue didn't include body retrieval.

"Almost forgot," Rankin says, tossing me a balled-up scarf. Red like my hair, just like he said. I laugh as he adds, "Thought you might reconsider," and then envelops me in a bear hug. "Thanks," he says quietly into my ear. "For everything, Hoss. I mean it." And then more loudly, keeping an arm casually slung around my shoulders, he adds, “Who knew it’d pay to have friends in such high places?”

“High places, huh?” I reply, smiling, and wrap the scarf around my neck. It hugs my throat perfectly. “I think you’re mistaking me for Captain Mathis. He’s the one with the wings.”

“All three of you earned your angel’s wings today, you ask me.” He nods to Camus as well, who’s locked in conversation with a few soldiers from the Churchill air team. As if sensing Rankin’s commendation, he glances over at us. I smile at him, almost shyly, and for the first time, he smiles back.

“I’ve been called a lot of things in my career,” Captain Mathis says, joining our group. The severe nature of his personality, combined with the hard angles of his young face, seem to prevent a smile from forming. Still, there’s quiet merriment in his brown eyes. “But guardian angel? That’s a new one.”

The pilot’s entrance allows me to slip away as Rankin and Mathis discuss some of the finer points of the operation, each praising the other’s actions during the mission. Hanna remains with them, content by her husband’s side, with one hand firmly tucked in Rankin’s. The other gives me a small wave good-bye as I make my excuses and leave.

It’s surprising how many people come up to me, even while I’m heading for the exit, each wanting to show their appreciation, despite the losses we suffered. For all the congratulations thrown my way, you’d think I was the one who had been out there fighting. If it weren’t for my arm and other lingering injuries, maybe I would’ve been. But I wasn’t. I was here instead, coming up with bright ideas. Maybe that’s unfair. I don’t know.

I retreat to a small corridor off the main passage, where the floor is carpet instead of concrete, and cushions my footfalls. Even with the silence, I find it hard to relax. My hands are shaking, quiet aftershocks from the day’s stress. The building pressure reverberates through my entire body until it’s too much effort to continue standing. With no one around to fuss about my behavior, I lean back against the wall, a position whose symbolic meaning is not lost on me. A moment later, I sink to the ground and just sit there for a little while, thinking.

My thoughts don't exactly lead me to any nice places, but I don't expect them to.

"I half expected to find you among all your adoring fans," Camus remarks, suddenly materializing in front of me and making me start. I blame the carpet for preventing me from hearing his approach. I also blame him for not signaling his presence in a nicer way.

"Can't you clear your throat like a normal person?" I reply. "Geez."

"What are you doing hiding in here?"

"Who says I'm hiding?" He doesn't even need to change his expression for me to know he's not buying it. "I just needed to be alone."

I reflect on what an odd reversal this is from before. When I was feeling alone before, I surrounded myself with people. Samuel. Hanna. Rankin. Ortega. But now that I've managed to integrate back into the community, I'm possessed by the urge to isolate myself. It's like those celebrities who work their entire lives to be famous, and then go out of their way to avoid the public. Even to me, it doesn't make a whole lot of sense.

Camus looks sympathetic. "Would you like me to leave?"

"That was past tense," I point out, getting to my feet, slapping my hands free of dirt. "I could ask you the same thing, though. Why aren't you in the hangar, relishing the sweet accolades of victory?"

His lips work at a small, wry smile. "Because I noticed my partner's absence."

"So we're partners now?"

Camus looks over his shoulder, a curiously nervous gesture, as if he expects someone to stumble in and intrude on our private moment. Even when he does speak, it's like he's holding back, trying—and failing—to maintain emotional distance. "Back there, in the war room," he explains stiffly, "you reminded me of something I'd forgotten. Let's just leave it at that."

"Fine with me. Partner," I add playfully, and he smiles.

We're both quiet for a moment, and then he asks me if I'm truly all right.

At first, I'm tempted to fire off some clever response, but nothing comes to mind. Instead, bits of the truth gush out of me. "I should be. I don't know why I'm not. I mean, we won." I rub my arms. I can't seem to get warm in this place.

"It could have been worse," he offers.

I snort. "'It could be worse' isn't exactly the slogan I want to run on."

"You're not running a campaign."

"No? Well, that's a relief."

My sarcasm isn't lost on him. He takes a step closer—almost unbearably close, given our history. His fingers trace the edges of my open coat, gathering both sides more tightly in front of me, enveloping me in a less intimate way than using his own arms. I imagine what the warmth of his hands would feel like on my skin, rather than on the fabric barrier of my coat. *His* coat.

"What's really bothering you, Rhona?" he asks, staring down at me, his dilated pupils making his green eyes dark as a starless arctic night, but not half so cold. I almost wish they were. I'm starting to think the only thing worse than Camus's cruelty is his compassion.

"Would it be juvenile to say everything?" I respond.

"Yes."

"All right." I think more specifically. "For starters, stop calling me Rhona when we're alone."

He's immediately confused. "Why?"

"Because I know you don't believe I'm her."

"What do you propose I call you instead?"

"I don't know. How about Phoebe?"

"You want me to call you ... Phoebe?" There's a touch of amusement in his tone, which makes me angry.

"No, Camus," I say, exasperated. "I don't *want* you to call me Phoebe. But it's not fair, you calling me Rhona when you don't mean it. And if you try quoting poetry at me right now, that whole 'a rose by any other name' bit, so help me." Apparently I remember more Shakespeare than I thought.

"I'd never call you a rose," he promises. "Thorny, on the other hand ..."

"I'm being serious," I say, put out.

"No, you're not. And neither am I. I thought you'd welcome the change."

He's right. I'm deflecting. But I'm more interested in how we've managed to travel back in time, to a point where we were this casual with one another. *Was this how it was between us?* I wonder. I can't recall our romance in its entirety, or the friendship that must have coexisted alongside it. Maybe we've come full circle. I wouldn't know.

"What else is bothering you?" he prompts after a moment, serious again.

"Men died because of me," I say, my voice coming out in a whisper. There's the rub.

"Machines killed those men, not you."

"Small difference. It was my plan to send them out there in the first place. *My* plan that didn't account for the machines' timed response at Prudhoe ..."

"Yes, that's true, but we all agreed to the plan," he reminds me. "We don't live in a dictatorship. You didn't force anyone's hand. The soldiers themselves, they knew what kind of odds they were up against. What happened at Prudhoe was terrible, I'm not arguing that, but it wasn't unexpected, either. If you're going to claim sole responsibility for their deaths, I'd caution you to look at the facts again. You're clearly neglecting to see some of them."

"I can't tell whether you're trying to provoke me or comfort me," I say after a moment, my lips wearing a thin smile.

"Perhaps a little of both," he admits, thumb rubbing the flap of my coat like I wish he would my cheek. "Anger can be a very cleansing emotion. Burns off the fog, clears the mind. My point is we still don't know what went wrong up there. That should be our main concern right now. There will be time for self-flagellation later."

Camus compartmentalizes a lot better than I can. His advice is sound, but it's hard to apply a bandage and forget the pain when the wound is still bleeding.

"That all sounds nice and reasonable. Thing is, I can't just turn off the way I'm feeling with a flip of the switch. I feel bad for those soldiers, their families, their friends. You saw them in there. They expected us to get their loved ones back safely, and we didn't. How do I reconcile that?"

He takes a moment to develop his answer. I'm glad it's not going to be some half-assed reply off the top of his head. I don't need any fortune-cookie aphorisms.

"Rhona and I discussed the topic of loss at length. Once, she said to me, 'At least failure means we tried.' I think she had to believe in something, and so she chose to believe that one of these days all those tries would amount to something better. All that failure would have worth; all the death meaning.

"I couldn't tell you what future she was hoping for, precisely, but she did say all she wanted in the world was a hot sun to complain about again." *New Mexico,* I think. *I wanted to go home.* "She regretted every loss bitterly, just as you're doing right now, but somehow she always found the strength to move past it and do what was necessary."

"Hmm," I say. "Sounds like she was a real leader."

"Not always, and not at first," he admits. "But she adapted, I adapted, and so will you."

"*She* didn't have to do it alone," I point out, bristling at my memories. Memories of being comforted by words during the day, and held and soothed in the night. Of being loved and cared for, and elevated by that love. Together, Camus and I used to function as a unit, acting as one another's support system. Apart, we may be forces to be reckoned with, sure, but once the storm passes, we're left stranded in separate bodies of grief.

Isolated.

"No, you're right, she didn't," Camus answers quietly. "But neither do you. You have her strength. I saw it today. That's something you can rely on and trust. You'll survive, whatever the circumstances, I have no doubt, but you also have friends when you need them." He pauses, gazing at me meaningfully before adding, "And, I suppose, if worse comes to worst, you have me."

I stare back at him, feeling confused. It doesn't escape my notice that those are the same words I said to him a week ago.

His offer of friendship takes me by surprise. It feels like an undeniably huge step in the right direction in our relationship, all without my having to push for one. Not only am I hopeful about any future we might have, as friends or more, but I'm also gladdened that Camus is making progress toward his own détente with the past. Above all, I want peace for him.

Finally, when I can speak without the threat of tears choking my voice, I say, "Oh, so we're good-buddies-old-pals now, on top of the whole partner thing?"

He smiles. "Tentatively speaking. I don't believe Rhona—you would begrudge me that."

"No, I wouldn't," I say, jokingly adding, "and neither would I."

This earns me a chuckle. Glad to see he isn't completely inoculated against my odd sense of humor.

I'm starting to feel better, supported by his unexpected vote of confidence, enough to bravely venture closer. "You know, you're being entirely too agreeable today," I tease him. "Are you feeling all right?" I reach to feel his head for a temperature, but he catches my hand.

"You forget, we had a victory today, too." He absentmindedly strokes the back of my hand with his thumb. I don't think he even realizes he's still holding it, somewhat possessively, near his chest. "Maybe you should spend a little time with Rankin and the other men and women you saved. It might broaden your perspective."

"Maybe I will," I say. "Thanks."

"You're welcome." He releases my hand and starts to make his way back toward the main facility, instead of returning to the hangar. I guess he's not in a partying mood, after all.

"I'll be wanting my coat back at some point, too, you know," he calls back to me, the statement accompanied by a quick wag of his index finger. "Don't forget."

"Very funny!" I return, laughing despite myself, all the time thinking, *When did the world turn right side up again?* But not completely trusting it has, not just yet.

EIGHTEEN

I'M all set to give my first international address a week later, presumably after enough time for details regarding Operation Pigs in a Blanket to have begun making the rounds on the resistance circuit.

It's not long enough to make the mission's code name any less ridiculous, however, and after a debate over whether to change it to something more heroic, taking into consideration the feelings of those who lost loved ones, the council decides to keep it. Their reasoning? Future generations need to know humanity still had a sense of humor, even in the midst of robotic genocide.

I stand in front of a podium, my lacquered nails rapping against the side. I get the necessity of presenting Commander Rhona Long at her finest, a strong face for a strong cause, but the camera isn't going anywhere below my neckline, so I'm not sure what painting my nails was about. Maybe they want me feeling at my best—or maybe Hanna was just looking for an excuse to fix my chipped nails and peeling cuticles. She may be a historian now, but I think she operated a beauty parlor in another life. "I hope it was in the fifties," she replied when I told her this. "I love Elvis."

The audience around me is small, quiet. While the official reason is to reduce noise, I'm not stupid enough to take that explanation at face value. They're trying to make me as comfortable as possible by minimizing any sources of public-speaking anxiety, i.e., the public. I'd be more grateful if I didn't know better. In the back of my mind, I'm aware of how many people will be tuning in to my address, either receiving it live or having it relayed to them at a later time. There's a lot riding on the success of my broadcast, which is why I decline the padded chair I'm offered and take to standing. I think quicker on my feet.

Not that I'll have to do much thinking. Holed up in the war room, the best literary minds on the council spent the last two days writing my speech, discarding draft after draft until the most anal among them was satisfied. The final version is projected on the wall across from me in perfectly legible text, the font size increased to allow for distance. All I have to do is read it aloud.

"I can do this," I assure Camus for the hundredth time.

His brows pull together. "I didn't say anything."

"You didn't have to. You've got that look again, like I'm about to go before a firing squad."

He shakes his head and returns his gaze to some data projected on the table, but I don't think he's actually reading it, only pretending to. Really, we're both just killing time now while the technicians set everything up. But since Camus isn't one for small talk, especially when on edge, the minutes that tick by are agonizingly slow. I begin wishing Samuel were here. He'd talk to me. But Samuel's busy with who knows what. Science stuff. He insists that nothing's the matter, and maybe that's true, but I still worry if we will be able to reach a new plateau of normal after what's passed between us.

I resist the urge to scratch my cheek, but the makeup they used to apply freckles to the other side of my face itches like crazy. Unfortunately, it looks great, realistic, but damn it if I don't feel like I'm wearing scales. Too bad I can't wriggle out of this, like a snake from its skin.

No. I stop that destructive train of thought. *I can do this.* The public address was my idea in the first place. Past time we projected some hope to the resistance, as opposed to contributing more bad news.

"How much longer?" I ask.

Camus consults the technicians through a mounted screen in the corner. They chatter for a while, rambling on about the complexities of installing their new system, how it will be impossible to trace, yadda yadda yadda. We've heard it all before. Finally Camus guides them toward producing an estimated time frame. Five minutes happens to be the golden number. Five minutes and we're live.

"Thank God," I say, exhaling shakily. "The waiting's killing me. Actually, I'm pretty sure death went faster and easier than this."

Camus overlooks the bad joke. "Relax," he says, making it sound like an order. "Read over your lines a couple more times. Familiarize yourself with it so you don't look dead out there."

I raise an eyebrow at his choice of words.

He sighs, massages his temples. "No pun intended, of course."

"Of course," I agree, but I think I'm wearing off on him all the same. I try not to smile. With his nerves, he'd probably take it the wrong way. *Serious face, Rhona. Serious face.* "What should I do if I've already memorized the script?"

"So soon? We just gave it to you twenty minutes ago." I shrug. "Guess I've got good retention."

He's polite enough not to comment on the irony. "A side effect of your acting days, I suspect," he says, and I'm hopeful he's going to talk about them—Was I a good actress? Would I have had a Hollywood career ahead of me?—but he doesn't. He just suggests I look it over again.

The minutes tick by slowly at first, and then suddenly it's time. I wait for my cue, alternately looking between the camera and the wall where my speech is patiently hovering. Off camera, Camus begins to count down from ten. He mouths the last three numbers silently.

Three, two ...

And then we're live, broadcasting to the last survivors of the human race around the globe.

God only knows how many that is. I try to restrain my thoughts, stay focused.

I begin after a few more seconds, as previously instructed, to allow people a chance to tune in. The camera glares at me.

"My name is Commander Rhona Long," I say to introduce myself, as if that's even necessary. "And despite the enemy's best efforts, I'm not dead yet."

It seems like I've just started when the final lines are scrolling up on the wall.

If intercepted by our enemies, nothing in the speech compromises our operation. The majority of the machines may be nothing but stupid insects, but the higher echelon possesses a frightening intelligence. Best not to put it to the test.

I conclude not with the call to arms I'd like, but with suggestions for future survival, a reminder to hold the line no matter what, and finally some quote from a long-dead man, Winston Churchill. "Difficulties mastered are opportunities won." Camus's contribution to the speech, no doubt. I try to deliver the line with as much unsmiling sincerity as I can muster, even though what I really want to do is turn to Camus and mouth the words "Your British is showing."

Then it's over, and I have nothing to remember it by except a taste of bile on the back of my tongue, produced by nerves.

"How'd I do?" I ask as soon as I'm given the signal that we're no longer live.

"I thought it had the right amount of gravity," Camus says, but the way he's running his finger over his lips suggests he's keeping some of his thoughts to himself. I confront him on it, and he gives up without a fight. "I was just thinking it might have benefited us to let you write your own speech. Don't get me wrong. You did well with what you had. It just lacked ... Rhona's spontaneity, her spirit."

"I offered critiques. They wouldn't take my corrections."

"I know."

"Why was that, anyway?" I take a seat next to him, spinning absent-mindedly in the chair. "It's almost like they don't trust me or something." It's an offhand remark that suddenly gains substance in my brain. I stop spinning, slamming my feet to the ground. "That's it, isn't it? They still don't trust me." He holds his tongue and I have to ask. "Do you?"

"Yes," he says without hesitation. "You more than proved yourself with the operation last week. But the rest of the council are still anxious."

Even though I know their concern is reasonable, and even though I know it shouldn't, it bothers me some. "Next time, I write my own speech," I tell him.

He nods. "Yes, I think that'd be best."

A minute later, a face appears on one of the walls. I recognize the technician, his head blond and stubbly, matching his unshaved cheeks. "Ma'am. Sir," says the man, addressing us with equal respect. "I think you're gonna want to come see this."

Once we've exited the war room, it's two rights and a left down several long hallways to reach the telecommunications room, affectionately referred to as the Tea Room by its operators. Less for the beverage and more for the letter, I'm guessing, though I'm also told the officers who take the late-night shifts don't want for caffeinated drinks. I could use a little pick-me-up myself right now.

The Tea Room appears much more festive than I remember it. On the wall is a world map lit up with half a hundred green dots. Technicians work religiously to the *clack-clack-clackity* mantra of keystrokes. Others are busily tending something that looks an awful lot like a switchboard, except more complicated. Most are so lost in their business, absorbed by the hustle and bustle, that our entrance goes unnoticed. I don't mind; it gives me the opportunity to observe. I try to take it all in so I don't seem like a complete idiot when I'm finally called upon to address something.

"Commanders!" cries the same man as before. This gets everyone else's attention, and so begins a mad scramble to stand.

Camus impatiently waves them down while some are still rising. "What's going on?" he asks, glancing around with what must be the same expression I'm wearing: interest, slightly flavored by confusion.

"Transmissions, sir," the technician explains with breathless enthusiasm. "From all over the world. We're talking Brazil, India, Portugal, Russia, China, South Africa ..." He lists more in rapid succession, counting them on his fingers until he runs out. "Even some from the continental US, central mostly. The incoming transmissions are arriving in different codes, different languages, too fast for us to break and translate them all. But the ones we have broken, they're all saying the same thing."

He looks deliberately at me, scratching his cheek and grinning. "We're not dead yet, either."

I can't help smiling. "So we're not by ourselves in this fight, after all."

"No, ma'am. I'm happy to report we most certainly are not."

After how much Samuel told me was gone, this comes as both a relief and a surprise. Word was that the Middle East was a graveyard, and Africa littered with ghosts. Mexico and South America were supposed to have fared a little better than the US, with some of Brazil and Argentina's major cities still intact. Even so, we haven't been successful in maintaining contact with anyone down there for longer than a few months at a time. The resistance factions there are transient, constantly jockeying with local gangs—spiritual successors to the drug cartels—for control over safe zones and weapons technology. It's a mess, but it's still not as bad as Western Europe, or so we thought. Until today, we had assumed Europe was nothing but the remains of buildings and people. Near the beginning of the war, the machines came down on countries like Germany, France, Italy, and England with an iron fist—they firebombed cities, co-opted our own ICBMs, and hacked missile shields like child's play. No wonder we thought they were all dead. For once, I'm pleased we were wrong.

"Are we in any danger due to this sudden influx of communications?" Camus asks. Always the sensible one.

Stubbles shakes his head. "No, sir. The communications are being routed into open channels. Anyone can pick up the frequencies without risk of their location being identified. The only reason we know where some of these are coming from is because it's mentioned in the transmission, or else the language gives them away."

I'm stuck on one part of that explanation. "Anyone, you said. Including the machines."

"Unfortunately. They won't have much trouble breaking any of the codes, either. But there's no sensitive information contained in any of the ones we've translated so far. Our allies aren't stupid."

"No, they're not," Camus agrees, eyes finally lighting on the displays.

"If you'll excuse me, Commanders, I have to—" He's in such a hurry to get back to his work he doesn't bother finishing the sentence. It's like Christmas has arrived at McKinley a second time, or early, however you want to look at it in February.

"What are you thinking about?" I ask Camus when he doesn't volunteer his thoughts.

"The nature of chaos," he says.

I laugh. "Of course you are. I don't think you've had a normal thought in your life."

He actually smiles, a slight fracture in his otherwise stolid demeanor. "Even in complete chaos, order can find a way. I've been wondering what that way would be since we established McKinley. What would it take to unite the remnants of the human race effectively enough to challenge the machines? Defeat them?"

"And what conclusion have you drawn, great thinker?" I follow him into the hallway, empty at this time.

"It's you," he says honestly. "You resonate with the world. I'm still only just beginning to understand the full extent, but I think it has something to do with that first broadcast. For those few minutes, you made a broken, scattered world feel whole and together again. There's power in raw hope. They haven't forgotten it, and they haven't forgotten you. If you asked me now—and I hope you'll permit me to be poetic—I would say you're the order that can defeat the chaos."

"But no pressure," I say, fighting against a choke hold of emotions.

"Make light all you will," Camus says, "but I'm guessing you already knew this, which is why you had yourself cloned in the first place." His expression turns sad, poignant. "I'll admit, I thought it was selfish at first. I should have known better. It was never about one woman living forever."

"It was about the world surviving, about maintaining a rallying point," I deduce, puzzling it out at the same time. He nods. "That still doesn't explain why I never told you. Before."

"Doesn't it? I've never had Rhona's capacity for empathy. I would have let the world burn before losing her." Powerful, frightening words. I have no doubt they're true. "She would have suspected, and rightly so, I wouldn't be interested in exchanging her for some carbon copy—no offense."

I bite the inside of my lip. "But if it walks like a duck and talks like a duck ..."

"Can you honestly look me in the eyes and tell me you're the same woman?"

"Yes and no," I confess vaguely, having done much soul-searching on the matter, but very little soul-concluding. A lot of memories are still unaccounted for, and new ones making trouble for the old. "I'm unique," I add with a brave smile. "Lucky me."

"All this isn't to say that I can't be close in other ways with ... the duck."

"Oh, no." I shake my head. "Please. Let's not make that analogy a thing."

"Already forgotten." He glances down the hallway. "It's late. I shouldn't keep you any longer."

I kind of wish he would. The adrenaline from the broadcast has done a number on me, and I don't foresee sleep in my immediate future. I don't tell him this, however, and he sees me safely back to my room, even though any danger has passed.

We stand on the threshold, in so many ways.

"Do you want to come inside?" I ask him.

He considers it. "Yes," he says quietly, honestly, "but not tonight, I think."

I'm disappointed, but also a little relieved. I'm not sure what I was offering exactly, casual company or ... something else, but I suspect Camus ran his mind through the more intimate possibilities and came to the same conclusion I'm arriving at now: not yet.

He skillfully leans in, placing a kiss on my cheek.

"You're getting warmer," I say, thinking of the progression of his kisses from forehead to cheek and what should follow. He seems to understand my joke, but is otherwise immune to my poor attempts at flirting with him. Shame.

"Good night, Rhona," he says with a perceptible smile.

"Good night, Camus."

He disappears around the corner, heading back in the direction of both war and Tea Rooms, but I don't go inside my quarters. At this hour, I practically have the base all to myself. It's nice and quiet, the heaters breathing softly, my footsteps the only other sound in the halls. I walk by myself for a while, going everywhere and nowhere in particular. The freedom is bracing, the silence not as lonely as I would've imagined. Maybe it's because I don't feel as lonely anymore, as divided from the people I love, distinguished for all the wrong reasons.

Though I've come to realize there is a sort of freedom in being alone. It takes strength, and strengthens in turn. After tonight, with McKinley leading the charge, humanity's period of seclusion seems to finally be at its end. For the first time in a while, I feel indescribably hopeful for the future. Mostly, I'm eager to see what strength of character five long years of hermitage has produced.

The machines aren't going to know what hit them.

NINETEEN

WINTER THAWS, and spring begins to peek through as the cold loosens its grip on the arctic world. Tulips, crocuses, and only the hardiest wild roses fight to come back from their hibernation, shaking off their frosted petals and reaching for the sun, blots of color in an otherwise colorless landscape.

Apart from those little intrigues, the change between seasons is glacially slow. Our chief engineer, who I come to find out is an Alaskan native himself, calls it the "breakup," but that word seems too dynamic to me. While the ice *is* fracturing, there isn't a single cataclysmic moment when it happens. Clarence also describes an event that used to take place in the city of Nenana, when people would try to guess the exact moment when the ice on the Tanana River would crack. The competition was judged by the movement of a tripod positioned on the ice. When it moved enough, a line attached to it stopped a clock on shore, deciding the winning time. It sounds long and boring to me—much like the speed of this seasonal passing of the baton.

Inside the base, the changes occurring are just as subtle.

I rebuild my body and mind in the months following the public address. Samuel is with me most days, monitoring my health and progress and generally being my rock, our little snafu with the kiss all but forgotten—but it's Rankin who drills me in most of the training exercises down on the military level. These range from marksmanship to close combat, with a smattering of survival strategies like emergency weapons assembly and stealth techniques, in case I'm stranded in enemy territory. Basically, anything and everything that might keep me alive outside the safety of McKinley's perimeter.

While strenuous, the exercises leave me feeling stronger and more prepared—though for what exactly, I'm not yet sure. Whatever the future holds, I suppose. And judging by all of what I'm being taught, it's not going to be a very pleasant experience when that time arrives, but at least I'll be ready.

It's not all work and no play, however. I go out of my way to have fun every once in a while, just so I don't lose my mind. Despite the heavy nature of McKinley, its people are remarkably adept at finding secret pleasures, set apart from all the efficiency and functionality. I'm amazed by the dozens of traditions I come across. Some are minor superstitions, like knocking on metal to disrupt any mechanical listening devices. Others are larger and more lighthearted, like the Concert of Voices in March, when the whole base gathers in the cafeteria to listen to people sing while musicians play. I turn out to be bad at both, go figure, but no one seems to mind, least of all Samuel, who clapped and hollered the loudest for me anyway. Even Camus is drawn to the activities every now and again, although if he takes as much enjoyment from them as everyone else, he's more reserved about it. No surprises there.

We're all right now, Camus and I, even calling ourselves friends. In private, at least. In public, the lovers' charade goes on. The base is fooled, and although I try not to let myself forget it's supposed to be an act, sometimes I do. I think Camus forgets, too. I catch him with his arm still draped comfortably around my shoulders even after everyone else has left the room. I feel the way his pulse jumps when we touch, however briefly. I notice how he swallows when leaning in to say good night, and the way he always wishes me good night, even if we're alone, playing to no audience.

To avoid scrutiny about our relationship, we spend a few nights every week together in his quarters or mine. Nothing exciting happens. Usually, we're both so exhausted from the day's exertions, we fall asleep immediately. He insists I sleep in the bed, regardless of whose room it is, while he stretches out on a sleeping bag on the floor or burritos himself with blankets on the couch.

Some nights we just talk. It doesn't matter what about. Other nights, he reads aloud, often from a favorite dead William, Shakespeare or Yeats or Blake. And that's nice, too. It's simple, undemanding. I like to close my eyes and listen to the sound of his voice stroking me to sleep. Warm with feeling. New Mexico warm.

I'm relearning him like an old story I used to know. At the same time, I let him look inside me, wanting him to see past the cover he's familiar with and appreciate the new chapters. Often, I consider sharing all the memories I exorcised from my brain after our last bad fight and confessing to him how much I *do,* in fact, remember ... but each time, I change my mind. If he's going to love me again, it should be for who I am now, not the woman I was then.

Hanna assures me he's coming around, but I know better now. Camus doesn't need to "come around"—he's circled his pain like a vulture, picking at the carcass of the past for too long, sustained by anger and grief. He needs to heal. I'm trying to give him time to do that. But it's still a challenge accepting the reality that we'll never have what the "original" Rhona and Camus did, and even harder waiting to see what will replace it.

While I wait, the hole in my heart where I was convinced only he would fit is slowly filled in by other things, other plans, and other people. I still reserve a small, secret place inside myself for us, but I don't let the fact that it's not happening quickly or *Right This Instant* dissatisfy me with the present. I don't let hope destroy me.

Life goes on.

I'm enjoying some urban warfare training with Rankin, Samuel, and a few other McKinlians, laughing about some fool move I pulled during the exercise, when Camus enters the room. There's serious urgency in his body language, obvious even before he clears his throat to speak my name.

"I need you," he says.

Words that—under any other circumstance—would fill me with a fluttering feeling now hit me like someone's dropped an anvil on my head. My body floods with hot panic. My bones feel rubbery, my newfound happiness utterly breakable. *Something's wrong,* I think, but have better sense than to say in front of the troops.

Camus is already striding out of the room before I can respond. I throw a quick wave to my friends and hurry to catch up with him. The whole time, I'm thinking of a thousand terrible things that might've happened, each more horrible than the last.

"What is it?" I ask. "What's happened?"

"We've been contacted by Churchill. Their location has been compromised. They're requesting immediate evacuation and sanctuary."

The news is a blow to the head, momentarily rendering me senseless.

"What?" I stammer, understanding, but at the same time not totally comprehending.

We enter the elevator. The doors seal us in.

"How do they know they've been compromised? Are they under attack?"

Camus shakes his head. "I don't have the details yet. I was only just made aware."

He watches the lights ticking off the levels. I watch him, wondering at the strength of his composure. His body is still, so impossibly still. It's like he's not even breathing.

"There's something else, isn't there?" I ask him.

"Zelda believes she discovered who was behind your assassination attempt," he says, and for a moment, I don't breathe, tense as a bowstring. Fortunately, Camus doesn't punish me with suspense, speaking quickly while we still have the privacy of the elevator. "It was one of Meir's people, as I suspected."

"Who?" I want a name. I want a face to balance out the terrible memory of almost dying due to human malice, not machine indifference.

"It doesn't matter. Obviously, they were working under Meir's orders."

"How can you be sure? Maybe they went rogue. Maybe they have some personal beef with me, or—"

Camus cuts me off with a hard shake of his head. "Zelda said the machine's basic code had been rewritten. It had specific orders not to kill you, only rough you up, so to speak."

I put it together before he has a chance to voice his suspicions. "Meir wanted me to think I wasn't safe here." He nods. "And then she tried to sell me on a transfer. It was all a ploy to get me to Churchill."

"That would be my guess."

The elevator doors open, and I stride forward, painfully conscious of this news, like I'd just been told there's a tumor in my breast. A power play. Meir nearly killed me, and jeopardized the resistance, all for a petty power play. Unbelievable.

"When did Zelda figure it out?"

Camus grimaces. "A month ago."

"*Camus!*" I exclaim.

He holds up a hand. "I know. I should have told you sooner, but it was a dead thread. It wasn't as though we could do anything about it from here, and such nasty politics would have distracted you. I'm only bringing it up now because it might have relevance in the upcoming meeting."

"That wasn't your decision to make. From now on, you find something out, you tell me." Camus nods, not bothering to defend himself even a little. He knows he's in the wrong, despite intending to protect me. "Do you think anyone else was involved?" I ask him, straining to do so quietly and avoid drawing any nosy passersby into the conversation. "Churchill's council?"

"Impossible to know for sure," he replies. "My instinct says no, but we can't rule out the possibility."

"Wonderful."

On our way to the war room, we pass half a dozen people, each greeting us with a smile or head bob. The day is progressing normally for them, all ignorant of the fact that we're headed right toward a cliff. It's a painful thought—primarily because, some months ago, I might have been in the same position, wearing the same friendly face, completely blind and deaf to the events transpiring around me. I still remember the feeling of helplessness from being kept out of the loop. But these people act as though they're not even aware of the loop, the secrets kept behind closed doors.

"They're better off not knowing," Camus says, guessing my thoughts.

"Are they?" I snap, still smarting over Camus withholding need-to-know information from me. "If the world you knew was about to explode, can you honestly tell me you wouldn't want to know about it?"

The look he gives me is harsh and impatient. "Would you want to know?"

"Seriously?"

"Even if it would make no difference, your knowing or not? Even if there was nothing you could do to prevent this terrible thing from happening?"

"Didn't we just have this conversation? *Yes!* You can't predict the future, Camus. You can't know who or what will make a difference or not." Our conversation is momentarily paused as a couple walks around us, talking and laughing about who knows what, probably nothing important. I miss conversations like that. It seems my words are constantly weighted with machines and fear and death. “People are full of surprises. Miracles can happen.”

He’s shaking his head before I finish. “That is an incredibly naïve worldview. People are predictable, and miracles aren’t as common as you think.”

“Oh, yeah. That’s not cynical at all.”

“We’ll have to continue this discussion at a later time.” Camus backs into the war room doors, but hesitates before opening them. His eyes gentle some. “All I’m trying to say is I suggest you adopt a little pragmatism before we go in. This could get ugly. You have to be realistic.”

“That’s why we keep you around,” I say and open the doors myself, pushing past him.

Every seat in the room is taken, save the two reserved for Camus and me.

Doesn’t this feel familiar?

The atmosphere is hot and loud, swamped with the worries of a dozen people, all trying to voice their concerns over one another. I stand there trying to pick up the frayed strands of conversation and find a way in, but no one’s listening to anyone else.

I feel Camus’s hand on the small of my back, guiding me toward a chair, wanting me to sit down. Instead, I brush him off and remain on my feet, determined not to be overwhelmed by the chaos. I try to bring order to the feuding council members, raising my voice until I’m heard. The war room settles down long enough for me to ask, “Right, then. What’s the situation?” A flurry of answers come at me, everyone firing back wildly, all at the same time. “One at a time! Okay, you.”

“With all due respect, Commander, I feel we should be less concerned about Churchill’s safety and more concerned about our own,” the man I know only vaguely as Mr. Gratham says. Dissent bubbles up, but Camus stops it dead with a look of cold reproach only he could pull off. I’m glad he’s in my corner, for once.

“Go on, Mr. Gratham,” I encourage him. “I’m listening.”

“Thank you.” He adjusts the collar of his shirt, sweat dripping from his receding hairline. He'd look like a military man if not for the paunch around his waist..

"I'm sure I speak for everyone when I say yes, of course we'd like to go to Churchill's aid. No one here wants the inhabitants of Churchill to die. But there's a larger issue we have to consider. If they're compromised, as they seem to believe, then who's to say McKinley isn't? We've been in bed with them. They know all about us. All the machines would have to do is hack their systems."

Clarence shakes his head. "Every resistance base has viruses in place to wipe out their systems in the case of such an emergency. I tried telling you earlier, Carl."

"Since when have viruses ever stopped the machines?" Gratham counters. "Last time we relied on a virus to protect us, we ended up getting our asses handed to us. Not to mention five years of hell on earth."

The murmurs convey agreement.

"That's simplifying what happened. The Corinthian virus was a complicated piece of code, intended to salvage the AIs by disabling their hostile routines, not perform a task as simple as destroying data," Clarence grumbles, but no one's listening to him. I think I recall Samuel mentioning something about the Corinthian virus, during some of our recent review sessions. Developed by a programming team in Greece, the virus was humanity's last effort to lobotomize the wayward intelligences, when the higher echelon had not yet devoured its artificial competition and come together to form itself. But at least one of its kind had already claimed a few hundred lives in the Glasgow Disaster, when an experimental all-machine cast turned on themselves and then the audience at the National Theater. It was initially considered an act of terrorism. If only. In response, Scotland and its allies moved more troops into the Middle East, and there was even talk of another Gulf War. No one knows for sure, but it's thought this provided the incendiary spark that provoked the higher echelon to take such dramatic measures.

"What came first, the chicken or the egg?" I asked Samuel after he told me all this. Did the higher echelon initially plan Glasgow, knowing it would prompt such a response? Was it a test to see if humanity could curb its appetite for violence? Or was it simply a malfunction, a tragedy, that we turned into something more? And if that was the case, wasn't the higher echelon simply doing what it was programmed to do: stop our wars?

We'll probably never know for sure. Obviously the virus failed.

Camus takes his finger away from his lips, and asks, "What do you propose we do then, Gratham?"

"We should be preparing McKinley for an attack."

"We can do that *and* send aid to Churchill," I offer. I've given it some thought—or as much thought as I could give it in the span of a few minutes—and I've already decided I won't condemn the rest of the base for the treachery of one or two of its leaders. However deep the conspiracy goes, I'm certain it doesn't involve most of those who call Churchill home. "The two don't have to be mutually exclusive."

"All the resources we expend for Churchill take away from McKinley," the even-keeled voice of Dahlia Cameron chimes in. She's a former lawyer, the same woman who sat in on the meeting with Meir forever ago. "We have an obligation to protect our own, first and foremost. I don't want to seem coldhearted, but I have to agree with Gratham on this."

"Let's not put the cart before the horse," Camus says, calming the emotional response of the councilors. "Do we still have Churchill on comm? Bring them up."

I expect Commander Meir to appear on screen, but we get Glasses instead, whose first name I've learned is actually Jeffrey. But after I told him how I was referring to him in my head, he laughed and insisted I keep calling him Glasses. But he's not wearing his signature glasses now, his eyes rimmed with purple fatigue instead of black frames. He doesn't look like he's slept in days—years, even.

"For a few moments there, we thought you might have forgotten us," he says with a desperate smile.

"Never," I reply, thinking, *But apparently we're willing to abandon you.*

"There's a lot of speculation going around, and I'm afraid it's causing some confusion," Camus says diplomatically. "We were hoping you could set the record straight. What facts do you have concerning your security?"

"Intelligence intercepted a distress call originating from Copper Center. It's a small city in our purview. We deployed a rescue team to investigate, but there was no one there. After a few hours, they came back, and we passed it off as a ghost signal, an old SOS tripped by a power surge or shortage, something like that. It's happened before. We just figured ..."

He sighs and drags a hand across his cheek, shame and exhaustion leaking through his pores. "We made a mistake, McKinley. The machines tracked our team back to base. We have it on good authority from our scouts, in position outside Valdez, that the enemy is preparing to mount an offensive right now. To tell the truth, I don't know what's taking them so long to make their move."

"They don't know the size of your forces," Camus assumes, trying to psychoanalyze the machines' behavior. "They're calculating risk, estimating the potential for losses."

Glasses-without-his-glasses nods along with the assessment. "Believe me, I'm not complaining. It's given us some time to raise our defenses—"

"Why aren't you evacuating now?" Gratham interrupts.

"We started to, but somehow the machines knew about our escape routes. They collapsed our emergency tunnels." His eyes look glossy, but I can't tell whether it's because he's tearing up or if it's just glare off the screen. "There were people in them at the time, trying to get out. It was ... *terrible.*"

He shakes his head as if the word doesn't do the event justice. I remember being trapped beneath rubble, suffocated by panic, and the feeling of the whole world crumbling down around me. I glance at

Camus, and the way he's locked his jaw makes me think he's remembering, too.

"It's only dumb luck they didn't land a direct hit on our main facility. Their weapons capabilities have certainly improved in the last year."

"Yes, McKinley experienced some of their bunker-busting technology some months back," Clarence says. The gears are turning in his mind. "Denali cushioned most of the damage. Our lower levels were unaffected. I don't think the machines have anything that can hurt us too badly, but the hangar is more susceptible. We'll have to look into it." I can tell he's making mental notes to himself more than planning to actually give anyone else an order, already trying to engineer a better defense than the one that failed Churchill.

"Have there been any strafing runs, anything that would prevent air support?" Camus asks, much to Gratham's frustration. He huffs at the idea, adjusting and readjusting himself in his chair, unable to get comfortable. "Will we meet any resistance?"

"I won't lie to you. It's possible. It's been quiet for the last hour and a half, but there's nothing to say it'll stay that way for much longer."

"How's the situation inside the base?"

Glasses judges his answer before speaking it aloud. "Fearful. Nothing major, though. Command has been keeping the panic down, but people are still afraid."

"Where's Meir?" I ask.

"She's ... indisposed," Glasses answers uneasily.

"What's that supposed to mean?"

"Politics," Camus offers.

Oh, I think. Not indisposed. *Deposed.*

Glasses starts to fiddle with his bifocals, obviously force of habit, before realizing they're no longer there anymore. "Commander Forsyth has the right of it. Some of Evelyn Meir's recent activities came to light—including, I'm afraid, her part in the attempt on your life, Commander Long." He looks nervous and absolutely miserable, operating under the assumption we don't already know this. Which would have been true just a few days ago. "According to her, it was only meant to scare you, to motivate your move to Churchill base, but obviously that's no excuse. Intentions aside, the entire council deeply regrets the trauma you went through as a result and has condemned her for the role she played in orchestrating such an attack."

Everyone is watching me, waiting for my reaction. I try to push my personal feelings aside for the moment. If this had been my first time learning of Meir's involvement, it probably would have soured me on helping Churchill. But in the short time I've had to process it, I know it would be pointless to punish the rest of the base for the sins of its mother.

"It's in the past," I proclaim. "Let's just deal with the present, and leave the rest for tomorrow."

"Agreed," Glasses says, visibly relieved by this decision. "Can we count on McKinley's help then?"

I open my mouth, but Camus's voice is there first. "We need to discuss the matter further, Commander, but we'll get back to you with all due haste."

Camus makes an almost imperceptible cutting motion with a finger, and Glasses disappears from the screen mid-sentence. The argument resumes almost immediately. There are advocates for both sides, each making valid, defensible points. I've never known reason to be so confusing.

"Even if we send aid, someone will have to go with the team to help organize the evacuation," Ms. Cameron says. "This is a delicate matter. It requires delicate handling. Who among us wants to volunteer for the job?"

This sets off a secondary wave of dispute, some like Gratham, still holding on to their original position of isolationism, and others like Clarence, suggesting men or women who could get it done.

"I'll go," I say, but no one hears me, except Camus.

"Rhona, no," he whispers to me, placing a hand on my hand. There's something darkly worrying in his eyes.

"Hey!" I say louder, trying to get the room's attention.

Just as I think I've broken through, Camus lets go of my hand, pushes back from the table, and lurches to his feet. Everyone's eyes turn toward him, like in a film where all the actors know their cue.

"I'll lead the team," he announces.

My eyes widen. *What* did he say?

"Camus!" I say in a forceful stage whisper. "What are you doing?" I've turned my head and back away from the crowd for the barest minimum of privacy between us, the words themselves squeezing past my teeth. I'm trying not to look as shocked as I feel.

He doesn't look at me. "Does anyone have any objections?" he asks to break the stunned silence.

Me! I think so loudly I'm surprised my thoughts don't manifest aloud. *I object!*

And yet the objection stays confined to my mind. I don't want to cause a scene in front of the council, not after the months I've spent painstakingly building back my reputation, proving myself as someone with restraint and control, when in reality, neither comes easily to me. Besides, the last thing I want to do right now is sow more discord in a room already fit to burst with it. Camus knows this, and I'm willing to bet he's relying on it to force my agreement. What I can't understand is why.

"I support the Commander's decision." Clarence is the first to recover from the surprise and voice his opinion. Like a chain reaction, the other council members tip into concurrence, like so many domino pieces falling down.

My mouth is dry. I look to Gratham, hoping he'll play the devil's advocate for me. To my disappointment, he appears tired of the issue, the passion gone out of him. "I want it made clear I don't support this course of action," he makes a point of saying, "but if it's what we're going with, then what the hell. Camus is as good a choice as any. More power to him if he wants to go be the hero."

Faced with that allegation, Camus offers nothing in his own defense. But I don't buy it. I know him. He's not the type to believe in heroes or happy endings. Maybe once upon a time, but not anymore.

"Then it's decided," Camus says.

"Wait," I say, pumping the brakes on this whole thing as it hydroplanes out of my control. "I'll go with you. I'll go with Camus."

I'm met with instant rejection before I can even make my case.

"Out of the question," Gratham says.

"It's a bad idea, Commander," Clarence says.

"You're too valuable to lose," Cameron adds. "We can't spare both of you."

"I appreciate the concern, Rhona, but I can handle the matter," Camus tells me, affecting tenderness as he takes my hand. We've played this game in front of the council before, but it was always to help secure my position. The more he accepted me, the more it cemented the council's trust. So why is he doing it now when it has no bearing on the situation? Why is he circling his thumb against the tender part of my wrist, when no one else can see it? When no one else can *feel* it, no one but me and him?

I think he's trying to tell me something with his eyes. "Stay. McKinley needs you here."

And then it clicks. He's offering me a graceful way to bow out. How kind of him.

My every instinct says to fight this. But I can't decide whether it's because I genuinely feel I could do a better job or out of some juvenile sense of entitlement. Or simply because I don't want Camus to go. And that's when I realize I've already lost the battle. "All right," I say at last, my throat tight with resentment, and not all of it directed at Camus. I'm ashamed of myself for being so selfish and nearsighted. "I'll stay, help in whatever way I can."

The details of the evacuation are worked out with Glasses over comms, and the meeting concludes. I'm leaving when Camus catches me and asks for a word in private.

"Oh, I can think of a few choice ones to give you," I tell him.

"Will you allow me to explain?" he inquires softly.

"Depends on who I'm talking to." His brow scrunches up in confusion. Good. Keep him on the defensive for once. "Am I speaking with

Camus the nice or Camus the grouch? Camus the friend or Camus the leader? You're so damned inconsistent I never know what I'm going to get with you."

"That isn't fair."

"Don't talk about fairness with me. What the hell was that back there in the meeting? Look at me. I want to know."

He looks at me with pointed confusion, as if I should know. "I realize you're upset, but that wasn't my intention."

"That wasn't your intention? Okay. Then what *was* your intention, Camus?"

"We can't have this discussion here." He's right. We're standing in the middle of the hall, and people are starting to stare. "There are some preparations I need to make, but later, tonight," he suggests instead. "My room. I'll answer your questions then. Agreed?"

"Fine," I answer moodily. I'm still angry with him, even if he's trying to be agreeable. *Too little too late on that account, Camus.*

After we part, I head for the military level in the opposite direction, taking the longer way by stairs. I desperately want to shoot something.

Camus is already halfway out the door when I show up at his room. He's dressed in full combat gear—thermal flight suit, flak jacket, boots, and of course a holster for his EMP-G. All he needs to complete the aviator-hero look is a pair of shiny silver sunglasses, but instead I'm treated to a clear view of his soul. There's no longer that cautious distance he kept between us like a wall.

The windows are open. I feel a breeze of hope.

But also a niggling fear. He's leaving sooner than expected.

"They've moved up the timetable. We're heading out now instead of tomorrow morning," he tells me as we move back inside to talk. Before I can ask why, he explains. "Weather concerns. They want to get us in the air as soon as possible. I regret we won't have more time."

"That always seems to be a problem for us, doesn't it?" I remark, and while it's meant to be an offhand joke, the truth weighs it down, giving it edges like roughly hewn stone. Camus only nods. "Okay. Talk quickly then," I add.

"Where would you have me begin?"

"What do you mean? You can start by explaining the whole I-will-take-the-ring-to-Mordor crap you pulled back at the meeting!"

"For someone suffering from severe memory loss, it's incredible to me how many old pop-culture references you pull out of a hat." Camus smiles, but it's strained.

"Not that strange. Samuel made me watch all three of those movies just the other day, and I think he'd take offense to it being called an *old* pop-culture reference. He makes a good case for their relevancy."

Camus shrugs and gives me the classic line. "The books were better."

"You're a snob. And you're trying to distract me by changing the subject. I thought we were in a hurry."

"We are." The smile disappears from his lips. He sighs and spreads his hands wide. "But I don't know what answer to give you."

"Funny. You had all day to come up with one."

"There's no need to get nasty," he says, but he doesn't sound injured by my snark. He almost sounds amused.

Now it's my turn to sigh. "Can't we just be honest with each other for two minutes? Here. I'll even go first. I'm tired of getting the runaround from you, Camus. I want to know where we stand. I thought we were making things work, and then you go and do *that.*" I motion in an arbitrary direction. "It's like you're trying to sabotage us." I can't prevent the hurt from creeping into my tone, however much I strive to sound cavalier about all this.

"No. No, that's not it at all," he assures me.

"Hello, words? Sorry, you're going to have to speak up. I can't hear you over actions."

"Cute."

"Just be honest with me. Why did you volunteer for this mission when it's clear you think it's going to fail? Why bite the bullet?"

"Because I'm falling in love with you," he says quickly, as if he needs to get it out before the words stick in his throat. And just like that, his careful, neutral expression breaks apart. He rolls his eyes at himself, trying for another smile. "Again." But the smile doesn't last on his lips, and his eyes betray anxiety. "I thought that was obvious by now."

"What?" I scarcely breathe because it feels like he's put us both under a spell with his words and I'm afraid—no, *terrified*—that saying anything else will break it.

Camus's expression is raw. He looks in complete agony as he tries valiantly to explain himself further, but can't find the right words. This man is the most eloquent person I know, and he can't speak. I watch the struggle on his face, the war inside him exposed.

"So, hold on," I finally manage to say, and he exhales, like he's relieved I'm the one speaking now. "This whole evacuation was your way of throwing yourself on the sword for me? Is that what you're trying to tell me?"

"Such a cliché, isn't it?"

I smile, though my sight is blurred with happiness and my pulse is slamming, making it hard to think. "You know what, Camus? I'm starting to think we have a serious communication issue."

He laughs, because it's true.

"But as far as clichés go, I prefer it to the dark-and-brooding, tortured-soul thing you've had going on. Not that that isn't sexy in its own way."

He chuckles, then groans and stares at the ceiling. "God. How do you do that? How do you always manage to do that?"

"What?" I move toward him.

Camus looks back at me. "Make the world seem less ... hopeless? I don't know. That sounds grossly sentimental, doesn't it?"

"I'll allow it," I tease him.

For the first time in forever, I feel like I'm speaking with the real Camus. The one the machines buried alive beneath ice and fire and death. Camus Forsyth, the man Rhona Long fell in love with once upon a time. The one who smiles and laughs and isn't afraid of a little sass, giving or receiving it. The English major, the Shakespearean who wrote me sonnets in college—good ones, not just crummy poetry—as an expression of love because "doing anything else would have been too pedestrian."

Camus. The man I've never stopped loving, even though it was painful. Even though it felt pointless and unreasonable at times.

The comm buzzes and he goes to answer it. The teams are ready to deploy. It's time. He tells them he'll be right there.

"Camus, wait."

He swings back around to me expectantly, brow furrowed with doubt. I take in his appearance for a second time, comparing this image of him to other memories I have of soldiers going away to war. I think about my father. I think about Ulrich. A dark, slithering fear slides through me, making my limbs heavy. I don't want him to go—and especially not on my behalf. But I also know I can't stop him from going, either. My tongue feels thick in my mouth, loaded with so much I want to say. Stupid, useless words.

I give up and launch myself at the inviting space between his arms. I wrap my own arms around his middle, moving my hands up the curve of his back, ultimately gripping his shoulders to hold him to me. After a moment, his arms come around me certainly, and it's as if I can suddenly breathe. Like I've been holding my breath for the past year. We cling to each other, stranded in this world that doesn't make sense, this world of orphans and monsters; we find each other again. I make a small gasping sound, not from surprise, but from shuddering relief. Beneath the strength of his embrace, he trembles, too, and I wonder whether he shares my relief, or if he's afraid.

We start to come apart, and that's when he kisses me. His mouth is full of desperate communication. My heart fills with feeling, shutting off the poisonous part of my brain that fears and worries, and I'm sliding my hands up the nape of his neck until his hair tickles my fingertips and I feel the substance of him. His lips are a warm luxury against mine—insisting, demanding, and restless. I kiss him back, receiving it like a long-awaited testimony. His hands settle on my sides, definitively. I feel captured and released. I feel *safe.* I try to comfort him in the same way, breathing his name into his mouth.

It's a short reprieve. The comm sounds again, and while Camus doesn't bother to answer it, he does pull away from me. Reluctantly, our arms fall away from each other. I turn slightly from him, touching my lips, which still tingle with the expression of his surrender. No. Not surrender. That wasn't him giving up or giving in.

That was him fighting—*finally*—for us.

In his eyes, I glimpse more than responding desire; there is realization, too. The somnolence of his grief has fled, and he looks awake. For better or worse. The sad twist of his lips says he knows it, too.

"Hey," I say with a pout, sensing a good-bye I don't want to hear. "Don't get dead." My eyes feel like they're on fire. I'm holding back tears.

"Good advice," he answers, his voice scratchy. He attempts to correct the issue by clearing his throat. "But you know I can't make you that promise."

"Then lie to me."

He laughs and gives me an affectionate look. "I can't seem to do that either, as of late."

I want to kiss him again, but I know if I clutch him to me, even for one more heavenly second, it'll make it impossible to let him go. I cross my arms, half hugging myself and frowning. "Just come back, all right?"

He looks at the floor. "If I come back ..." he starts to say.

"When," I correct sharply.

"When," he agrees, and his eyes spring back to me. Green and clear as a dream. "Things will be different." *Between us,* his eyes add.

I smile shyly. "Sounds good. I guess you better—" My voice breaks. The tears come. He steps toward me and wipes them from my cheek, holding my neck, peering down at me like the man I used to know. The man I've loved all this time. And for a moment, I'm afraid I won't be able to do it. I won't be able to let him go, will instead cling to him like a child. But the comm buzzes again, and reality sinks into me like nails, and I remember the world does not revolve around me and Camus. There are more important things.

I can't say anything more, however, so instead I give him a little shooing motion. Go on. Get. He doesn't prolong our parting further, except with another brief kiss. And he doesn't say good-bye, which is just as well. The permanency of good-byes, especially now, frightens me.

TWENTY

CHURCHILL'S ELEVENTH-HOUR crisis stretches first into twelve hours—the time it takes to assemble our teams, get them there, and begin evacuating—and then doubles to twenty-four hours after they're besieged by an enemy force. Everything is slowed to an almost glacial pace, both there and in the war room where I and a handful of other council members watch and wait. Officially, we're waiting for good news, but unofficially ...

For whatever reason, the machines seem content for the moment with harrying the evac teams on their way to and from the base, biding their time with the main assault. As of twenty-five suspenseful hours and counting, they've only managed to destroy a few of Churchill's tactical vehicles on the ground, causing some casualties, but none of those McKinlians.

Camus and his team stay out of the fighting as best they can, playing the role of smuggler as they focus on their primary mission of getting people out safely. Juneau is the nearest safe zone, but Alaska is unimaginably large, a beast of a state even when there were borders to cage her in, and even by air, the trips are few and time-consuming.

In all that time, I haven't left the war room except to relieve myself.

Samuel's taken to bringing me snacks and staying to make sure I eat some. I pick and nibble at the bread and crackers to appease him, when in truth I don't find either very appetizing. My stomach's full of hornets, my blood buzzing. It's annoying because I do want to eat; I'm starved, but more than that, I know I should. Samuel raises the point that the brain can't work without fuel, and I'm no good to anyone if I can't think. So each time he shows up with something edible, I make the effort and pray I don't throw up.

Apart from Clarence, I'm the only one left of the original council keeping vigil. There are also a few technicians, but they're only on watch for a few hours at a time, keeping conscious ones in circulation. Speaking of circulation, I think I've lost all feeling in my legs all the way up to my rear. I stand up, trying to get the blood flowing, and immediately feel the powerful effects of exhaustion. My vision becomes dark and fuzzy, like a decommissioned television channel.

"Commander?" Clarence says, reappearing next to me once my sight returns. His hand is at my elbow. "Maybe you should sit back down ..."

I don't argue.

Sleep sneaks up on me, the traitor, knocking me out for a few minutes. I doze off and on until I'm jostled awake by someone bumping my chair.

"Rhona?" Samuel's voice: quiet, concerned.

"Hey," I mumble with a sleepy smile, reaching for my senses and finding them loose and slippery as falling sand. For a few blurry seconds, while I come out of the depths of slumber, I'm confused, having forgotten where I am and what's going on.

Then I remember. I sit up sharply. "What is it? Has something happened? Is it Camus's team?"

"No, everything's fine," he assures me. "But you need to get some sleep."

"What do you think I was just doing?"

"You mean, besides drooling on the table?" I wipe the corner of my mouth, and he smiles gently, making it impossible for me to be irritated with him. "Clarence called me. He said he was worried about you. I can see why."

I make a dismissive sound. "I'm fine. Just a little tired is all. It'll pass."

He slips into a chair next to mine. "You've been awake for over twenty-four hours. You've hardly eaten anything ... You're running on fumes, Rhon." His fingers brush against my cheek as he moves one of my bangs from my face. I have to look at him then, as I'm guessing he wanted. Meeting his eyes, so earnest and imploring, is the final blow to my resistance. "Will you let me get you to a bed? Please?"

I groan. "How much time do you spend practicing that face? All right. All right. I'll go quietly. Happy?"

He helps me up. Getting my legs beneath me is half the battle. The other half will be making it to my room. Lethargy drags at my limbs, making movement slow and awkward.

"I'm just glad it worked," Samuel says. "Plan B involved drugging you with a heavy sedative."

I think he's joking, but I'm too tired to know for sure.

Before I go, however, I extract a promise from Clarence I'll be woken if anything happens. He gives me his word, on the condition that he won't bother me unless it's something significant. I can live with that. Once I'm asleep, I'm certainly not going to want to be roused over something as little as a nosebleed. "Just keep me apprised," I clarify, nervous to be leaving my post. It's not like my watching and listening was making any kind of a difference, but still.

"We'll hold down the fort, Commander," Clarence tells me. "Get some rest."

Sleep deprivation is a funny thing. I find this out as we're walking toward my room. As spent as I am, you'd think I'd be uninterested in my surroundings, but the opposite is true; I notice everything, fixating on details I'd overlooked a hundred times before. The concrete floor, for instance, which is worn darker in places by the soles of countless feet. It bears the history of our survival in one of the simplest ways, scuffed and dirty where we've treaded. And there are the walls, bare and bland until you look closer. My tired mind arranges the texture of the plaster into pictures, like a Rorschach inkblot test. I wonder what seeing frolicking deer and a frowning machine interface says about me.

"Camus told me you tried to volunteer to head up the evacuation," Samuel says as we amble along, him steady, and me with a drunk's grace. He keeps an arm around me for support and I hug his side.

"Yeah, I did."

"Can I ask why?"

"You can ask." I smile briefly. It falters. My face feels funny, almost numb. Honestly, I'm surprised my nose isn't bleeding. Ever since the end of winter, my nosebleed trouble seems to have cleared up. Samuel thinks it's my body finally adjusting, beginning to heal, but it could be a seasonal thing. Naturally, he wants to run more tests to be sure. "I don't know what you want me to tell you, Samuel. You know me. I don't always think. Sometimes I just act. Churchill was in trouble, and no one else was stepping up to the plate."

There's open curiosity on his face, not judgment. "So you decided to play pinch hitter in the ninth?"

"Sure," I say. "I forgot you're a baseball guy."

I expect him to lighten up, but he's lost in thought.

We reach my quarters. The sound of the door sliding on its track is a whispered lullaby as it opens and we pass the threshold. My bed is unmade from two nights ago, its coverlets open like waiting arms. Part of me wouldn't mind a hot shower, but I'm pretty sure I'd drown in this state.

Heedless of my sweat and clothes, I collapse onto the mattress. It comfortably supports my body, and I burrow into the pillows. Before I've turned back around, I feel the gentle weight of the sheets and comforter over my shoulders. *Samuel.*

"What did I ever do to deserve you?" I ask sleepily, rolling over to look at him.

He just smiles in that way of his—that way that makes the world a little more bright, like a candle lit in the darkness. "That's funny," he says. "I often wonder the same thing about you." I close my eyes. "Come up with any good answers?"

There's a thoughtful pause. Then he whispers close to my ear, "Go to sleep, Rhona," and his weight disappears from the bed.

Don't you leave me, too ...

But I'm asleep a few minutes later, slipping away from the world to my grayscale dreams. For a time, I float in a lake of black with no discernible up or down, only a constellation of stars around me. It's relaxing until I try to move. The dark sticks to my skin like paste. Stardust collects on my arms and legs and face, clogging my throat when I try to speak out. I'm alone, glittering in isolation.

Then I'm nowhere. Pale hills stretch on as far as the eye can see. At first I think they're covered in snow. It's only as I bend down and grab a handful that I discover it's white-hot sand. It burns as it passes between my fingers. *The sands of an hourglass. Time is running out.*

I wander for a long time, until I reach a city made of glass. It keeps changing, altering before my eyes like a desert mirage, never remaining the same for very long. It looks like my childhood home. It looks like a London university. It looks like Anchorage. A single touch and it shatters entirely. On my knees, I frantically try to put the pieces back together, cutting my hands on the sharper fragments. But I can't. No matter how hard I try, no matter how much I bleed, I can't re-create the places as they were. I'm stubborn, though, and persist. Rivulets of moisture, sweat or tears or maybe both, drop onto the earth with a *hiss*, baked almost instantly into steam.

Someone eventually stops me, but I can't make out their face against the outline of the sun. "It's okay," the shadow says. "Rhona. It's enough. Look."

I look, and what I've made is something beautiful. It's unorthodox and a little deformed, this abstract sculpture of mine, but it welcomes the light and transforms it into a kaleidoscope of wild colors, all dancing on the sand.

I lie down beside the light display, entranced. The dunes no longer burn me, but instead feel warm and protective, the sand as soft as silk. I fall into a deeper, more impenetrable sleep—a wonderful void where I can finally, finally rest.

Not long after, I'm woken by a persistent buzzing sound.

I mistake it for an alarm clock until I remember I don't own one. *And for good reason,* I think, wanting to stuff my head beneath my pillows and ignore it. But then I realize it's the communications console near the door and I'm up an instant later.

I press all the wrong buttons before finding the right one. "Commander, you're needed in the war room," Clarence says with a face full of deathly calm.

Samuel stirs on the sofa, having fallen asleep with his nose in an electronic reader. "What is it? What's happened?"

"We've lost contact with Churchill and all surrounding units."

"What?" I ask, fighting the very real urge to be sick. "How? *When?*"

He shakes his head. "Five minutes ago. Please, Commander. We can have this conversation once you're here."

"It could be a communications glitch," Samuel says, offering me hope as we rush down the corridors. "The upper atmosphere is notorious for interfering with transmissions. And this close to the pole? The solar wind could be modifying the electromagnetic waves, affecting any signals ..." Somewhere deep down, intuition tells me none of those explanations are right. Still, I appreciate Samuel trying to lift my spirits.

"Did you know I dream in black and white?" I say, interrupting him. We continue to keep up a brisk pace beside one another, but McKinley is large, command level a labyrinth of interconnecting corridors, and it'll be a few more minutes before we reach the war room. I can't stand the quiet or the endless supposition, so this conversation is the next best thing.

"Really?" he says, scientific intrigue getting the best of him, as I expected.

I nod. "But just now, last night, I dreamed in color for the first time since dying." I recall the full vibrancy of a dozen shades of red, brilliant blues, the miracle of green and gold.

"What changed?" he asks me.

"Someone else was there with me. They showed me how to see it."

"Who?"

"I don't know. I can't remember."

"Huh," he says, carefully mulling over the significance.

We reach our destination before any awkward silences ensue, slipping out of that noose in time to hang ourselves by a different one. My throat feels tighter just entering the war room. I notice the wall displays first. They're black and mute, when they shouldn't be. Nothing speaks more volume than a deafening silence where there should be the noise of living.

"Well?" I ask, a little more harshly than I intend. "Have we had any luck raising Camus on comms?"

I don't bother sitting down. I have too much nervous energy, replenished rather than exorcised by rest. While I pace in the small amount of space available, Samuel methodically reviews the evidence on the table—what looks like a bunch of technical mumbo jumbo to me.

Clarence shakes his head, and for the first time ever, I see his composure break and frustration pour through the cracks. "Our technicians keep trying to establish contact, but there's just nothing. It's like we're shouting into a vacuum. Either they can't hear us, or ..." He takes a breath. "Or no one's left to respond."

"Cheery thought," I mutter, then stop myself. No. No way. I'm not going there; I can't afford to indulge that particular what-if, not if I want to stay calm. Or calm-ish. "What was the last transmission received?"

"Churchill reported having some difficulty with the machines a few miles out from the base, but there was no other indication anything was amiss."

I brace myself against the table, looking at the holographic display. Amid the geographical landmarks such as mountains and lakes, and the occasional abandoned settlement or city, there are white and red blips to mark our forces and those belonging to the machines. Crimson dominates the landscape between Churchill and Copper Center, overwhelming our pale pixels ten to one, making me think of blood spilled on snow. "Is this map up-to-date?"

"As of last transmission, yes."

With a wave of my hand, I soar hundreds of miles to the south. The red blips decrease in number until only white ones are left to navigate the ice-blue geography. Our evacuation teams are en route to Juneau. I tap on a few of the blips, which brings up information on them. Team name, vehicle make and model, and occupancy. *Good*, I think, until I scan through them and find that none register a Commander Forsyth aboard.

"Clarence," I say slowly, afraid of the answer. "Where's Camus?"

He fiddles with the display, bringing up Churchill base. "His team is still on-site, or was as of ten minutes ago."

I close my eyes, fighting the urge to curse like a sailor.

"I think I know what the problem is," Samuel says, hijacking one of the wall screens. "I'm no expert, but according to the diagnostic report, the issue doesn't have anything to do with a glitch or the weather. Taking that into account, the most likely scenario is that the machines are running some sort of jamming device to disrupt our signals and confuse communication. Typical of their programming. But ..."

He switches the pictures on the screen to a computer-generated view of Earth from space. "There's an alternative possibility. This is the area of low Earth orbit, where most of the remaining—*functional*—satellites are, including our own. What if the machines have somehow managed to, I don't know, bring the one we've stationed over Alaska down? Or gained control of it, at least?"

"It'd account for the communications failure," Clarence agrees mildly. "But it's still a leap."

"Not to mention it means we can't do anything about it," I point out.

"I didn't say it was a best-case scenario," says Samuel.

"What do you want to do, Commander?" Clarence asks.

As the mantle of responsibility crashes down onto my shoulders, I'm once again reminded of how heavy a weight it is. No wonder it drove Camus into the ground.

I pick at my nails for a moment, torn between wanting to send in the cavalry and knowing it's the wrong play. My heart screams for action, but my head asks, what would Camus do in my position? It doesn't matter. Camus isn't here. And Clarence and Samuel are expecting an answer from me.

"We wait," I tell them. It's not an easy decision, but I hope it's the right one. "At least for a day, two at the most. Send word to the council. Let them know what's going on. We can't rush in blind. We have to give them a chance to contact us first."

"And if they don't?" Clarence inquires.

My smile is grim, my mind set. "Then I'm strapping on a pair of snow boots and going after them myself. No arguments." It's the best solution, situated between my head and my heart. No one ever said middle ground had to be safer ground. "I can't hide in a tower forever," I add. "I won't. Not when the people in danger are the ones I sent out to fight the dragon for me."

"I believe you," says McKinley's head engineer. I think I spy a mixture of sadness and pride on his face. "But let's hope it doesn't come to that."

TWENTY-ONE

"I'M GOING WITH YOU."

I look up from my laces—an intricate mess of loops and snaps that weave back and forth up the neck of my boot, cinching it tighter and tighter. There's enough that can go majorly wrong out there; the last thing I want to be worrying about in the field is one of my laces coming untied. If it means taking a little extra time to triple lace my snow boots, so be it. It gives my hands something to do, anyway, apart from fidgeting restlessly with the rest of my combat attire.

"Oh yeah?" I reply with a raised eyebrow. It's not a challenge. I'm just curious, because I can't imagine the council approving Samuel as a tagalong. They didn't even approve of me leaving, but I'm going regardless. "Says who?"

"Actually, I decided to take a page from your book. How's it go? It's better to ask for forgiveness than permission?" He smiles.

"Samuel. Be serious. You're not coming."

"I am." The smile disappears, taking the boy of my youth with it. The man in his place steps forward, moving some of my gear off the metal bench in order to sit next to me. His head is bowed, eyes on the floor for a few seconds as he gathers his thoughts. Then he looks at me with such directness I find myself unable or unwilling to look away.

"As hard as it is for me to admit, I know I can't protect you forever. I know keeping you safe is an impossible task on a good day, and these haven't been good days. I know there are things beyond my control, that events happen even science can't predict ahead of time. I think we've both learned that one the hard way. But still, you have to let me try, Rhona."

"No. Absolutely not. *No*, Samuel." The worst part is that I do want him with me out there. There's no one I'd rather have watching my back. But I want him safe and alive more. It's no victory exchanging his life for Camus's, and I fear that's what will happen if he joins my war party. Casualties are almost guaranteed.

"I told you, I'm not asking for permission."

I try to be crueler, drive him back. "You're not trained. You'll just get in the way."

"What do you think I've been doing these past few months? I've been with you at almost every training session. I can handle a weapon. I've memorized procedure. I won't be any more of a liability than anyone else." I'm shaking my head, desperately trying to come up with more reasons. More excuses. "What? What else is there?"

"You could die!"

He looks down at his hands. "Yeah," he says. "And so could you."

I laugh, but it's a cold, harsh sound, like ice breaking. "God, what is it about me that makes people want to throw away their lives? Do I just attract martyrs or something?"

Three days ago, two days ago, one day ago, I was fully prepared to walk into the fire alone. Even when we didn't receive word from Camus or Churchill or any of the other teams, the council still refused to supply me with any soldiers for a rescue. Said they couldn't force anyone to take such a monumental risk, but I know it's because they need them here, in the event McKinley is attacked. It's a possibility that's growing more and more likely with every moment. In an empty gesture to appease me, they told me I was free to take volunteers with me on my "suicide mission."

They underestimated the obscene effect I seem to have on people. My team came together in less than twenty-four hours. I wouldn't be complaining, except for Samuel. He's not the first victim, but I don't want him to become a literal one either. I don't want anyone else to die for me.

"Everyone has these great expectations for my life," I continue. "All this time, I thought I was trying to live up to a person, when really I've been competing with the *idea* of a person. Haven't I?" I grab the laces of my boot and give them a violent yank, tightening them just shy of their breaking point. "To be honest, I think the whole thing's starting to give me a complex. Or maybe an ulcer."

"You don't have an ulcer," Samuel says. "It would have shown up in the lab work from your last physical." At first I think he's being wonderfully dense, but he's not. He's just being wonderful.

I touch his hand, laugh. "Thanks. I needed that."

He looks down at the contact and then quickly back up at me. Some kind of decision is made in that split second, passing in front of his eyes like the glare of the sun breaching a cloud. He needlessly shifts on the bench. "Actually, there's something else I needed to talk to you about?"

"Is that a statement or a question?" I tease him thoughtlessly, finishing tying the last laces on my boots.

He takes my hands away from my shoes, holding them gently. I feel him shaking.

"You know I love you, right?"

I swallow, looking at him. Trying to really focus on him. "Yeah, of course."

"Be honest with me, then. Will there ever be a chance for ... us?" He's staring at our hands when he says this, unable to look at me until the last second. I understand what he's asking, because his actions have been saying the same thing for months—and years before that, in another life.

Maybe I just didn't see it then, blinded by something brighter—the stars aligning for me and Camus. The light of that love still reaches out of the past, burning like celestial travelers in the night, the memory of their fire beautiful. It's especially haunting in the darkness, in the stillness of the night, when I hear Camus softly breathing across the room, and I wonder whether or not he dreams, and if he does, what does he dream about? Who? What anchors him in the torrents of his dreams?

Yet those stars are gone, all the same. They were snuffed out in the snows of Anchorage. Something new has replaced them, something with the potential to be beautiful. Though I can't say I ever bought into any kind of astrology, and I don't believe in fate anymore, either, I still believe in choice. Camus made one before he left. Samuel is making one now. It's my turn to do the same. But some choices are more easily made than others, and this isn't one of them.

I don't know what he reads in my expression, but it startles him into apologizing. "I'm sorry. After the kiss, I thought, maybe ... maybe you'd change your mind. But I shouldn't be springing this on you right now, right before the mission. It's selfish."

"No," I say, clutching his hands, preventing him from retreating. "It's brave."

"Interesting word choice," he murmurs, smiling, half-embarrassed.

"Samuel, I know this may come as a shock to you, but you're one of the bravest people I know. You sacrifice for the people you care about, and you're not afraid to love. Honesty of feeling like that takes courage. Not everyone has that capacity." I'm thinking specifically of Camus and the fear of loss that prevents him from loving too deeply. I'm under no illusion that I can fix that brokenness in him, but it doesn't mean I'm unwilling to try. We all need someone to believe in us.

"You saved me, you know."

"What?" His confusion is genuine, endearing. So modest.

"I mean, there's the clone thing, of course. But everything that came after. You were there for me, every step of the way. That means more to me than I can ever say. When I'm old and gray and, let's be honest, probably grouchy"—he chuckles slightly, and I smile briefly before getting serious again—"when I remember nothing else, I'm going to remember what you did for me. How you gave me a second chance at life.

"And I wish—I *wish* I could give you even an ounce of that happiness back." I have to stop, because I'm crying now, because I realize the enormity of our friendship in my life. How much I love him, too. How much I need him in my life. How much I don't want to lose the boy of my childhood, the man who will sit in a cold bathtub with me when I'm sad and afraid.

"It's okay. You still love Camus," Samuel says, without disappointment, as though he was without expectations for anything else. He hugs me close.

I nod numbly. *I have feelings for you, too,* I want to say to him, but I know it will just make things harder than they need to be. Besides, I recognize now those feelings were born from something else. A need, confusion. Their nature is something else. "I'm sorry," I say instead, knowing it's pointless consolation.

"Hey," Samuel says, managing a smile despite the fact his own eyes are raw. "How many times have you told me not to apologize?"

I swipe at my eyes. "Beyond count."

"Same goes for you, right now." He rests his chin on my head. "Please, don't cry, Rhon."

"Tabula rasa," I blurt out a second later.

"Come again?"

I sit up suddenly and look at him. "Don't keep waiting for me, Samuel." I grab both sides of his face, my expression explicit and intense. "You've given me enough years. All right? Nod if you hear me." He nods. *Good,* I think, even though it breaks my heart to break his. "Maybe this is your chance to start over, too. Tabula rasa. You gave me that chance. Now I'm giving it back to you."

"You always were a terrible regifter," he jokes, and in that moment I know we're going to be all right.

I pull him into another hug, whispering in his ear, "Thank you for understanding."

He tucks his face into my shoulder, and I know he's muzzling his disappointment for my sake. I don't think he knows how to put himself first. I *do* think he's going to make some woman very happy someday, though. And my opinion is only reinforced when he finally adds in a quiet whisper, "You know you were wrong before. You have made me happy, Rhona. You've always been a good friend to me, a better friend than I ever hoped to have, really."

"Stop it," I order. "You're going to make me start crying again."

He stares at the ground, bashful with feeling. Requited and unrequited.

"I don't suppose any of this means you've reconsidered coming with me now?" I ask.

Samuel starts to check his own combat gear. "Are you kidding? This will look great as the first thing on my new rasa résumé." I laugh, and feel it deep in my soul. It feels a lot like peace. "I'm with you, Rhon. That won't ever change."

I'm momentarily unable to speak again because of useless, wonderful emotion. "Well, then," I finally say, lunging into the silence at the same time I dry my cheeks. *Time to resume the trappings of a leader. Time to rescue my people.* "You should probably meet the others joining us on our little suicide mission. I think you'll be surprised at who all volunteered ..."

TWENTY-TWO

IT KILLS ME, just how large the world feels after being cooped up for so long.

From the air, carried weightlessly in a metal cage, it's easier to appreciate the terrain below. I'd expected my experiences groundside to sour me on Alaskan nature, but my opinion hasn't curdled completely. Much as I might want to hate the land, it's just too damn beautiful more often than not.

Shortly after takeoff, the sun rose and warm fingers broke through the cloud cover, a Midas touch turning the world from gray to gold. I've seen the landscape take on all sorts of colors—blue and green in the night, royal purple in the evening, the white acting as a blank canvas to comfortably hold the colors for a time. But I'd never stopped and appreciated the glory of the morning. When we pass over an icy reservoir, whose frozen surface is melting, its waters ripple like captured fire.

I wouldn't mind a little fire right about now. I rub my hands together.

The side doors are closed to protect against the downwash and ward off wind shear, but it's still freezing inside the chopper cabin. But no one else is complaining, so I have to wonder if it's just me. It's no secret I haven't been able to adjust to the cold climate, even though it's the only one this body's ever known. Maybe it's because somewhere in my head, I still have the memories of hot summers in New Mexico. Something to miss.

Memories, however, do very little to combat the chill, and my teeth start chattering before long. "Don't suppose this thing's got a heater?" I inquire to anyone who might know.

"The heater is on," Lefevre says, his breath fogging up the inside of his flight mask. We're all wearing helmets, but apart from the pilot, he's the only one wearing his visor down, as if he expects to be ejected from the helicopter at any moment. Maybe he has a point. Just because radar isn't picking up any hostiles right now doesn't mean they won't show up suddenly, with their sights set on us.

"Well, then, does it have a higher setting?" I don't see controls anywhere. "Like, a few degrees above winter wonderland?"

"It's set to the maximum temperature. We'll be there soon."

Poor compensation for my current discomfort, but he's not wrong, either. We've been in the air for a few hours now, making excellent time. With the weather moderate and holding, plus no enemy encounters, there's been nothing to slow us down. On the one hand, it's been great; every minute counts. On the other, it's doing nothing for my nerves. I hate waiting. And the absence of machines, where there should be swarms of them, seems more suspicious than fortuitous.

I try massaging some feeling back into my arms as I glance around at my brave companions, wondering how brave they really feel at the moment. Samuel and Ortega have been alternating between card games, playing such classics as blackjack and speed. At one point, they wrangled Rankin in for a round of poker, which he managed to win even from the copilot's seat.

They also asked Kennedy if he wanted to join in, and while the eighteen-year-old ginger refused, he later looked on with some envy at all the fun. To say I was hesitant to let someone so young come would be putting it mildly. It's a decision I foresee regretting in the near future, but he pleaded his case with more heart than any of my other volunteers. How could I say no?

I should have said no. I'm turning soft in my old age, but no wiser, it seems. I resolve to protect the kid if I can, even knowing I probably can't.

The others I'm less concerned about, on the grounds of their proven capability. Lefevre, for one. I still don't know his whole story. Maybe it's better this way. My head is full of enough tragedies.

Then there's his sister.

Samuel thought it was a joke when I told him Zelda was tagging along. So did I, initially, when I declined her offer. But if there's anyone who has a bone to pick with the machines, it's her, and much as I may not trust her still, I know her hatred for the machines is greater than her hatred for me. Not to mention that we were in sore need of a technical expert, so I didn't really have as much say in the matter as I might have. She'd wanted to bring one of her pets with her, the same make and model that tried to kill me in the training room, but I drew the line there. She just smiled, saying she could always reprogram one of the metal corpses they made along the way.

She's not smiling now. The whole trip, she's been mute, but not in a calm, contemplative way. More in a simmering, pot's-about-to-boil-over kind of way. There's violence rattling in her brain, if I had to guess, matching the desire for revenge in her heart. Instead of sitting, she's been standing for half of our journey, holding a rubber hand grip, her knuckles taut to the point where the bones seem close to escaping the skin. She can't be comfortable, but maybe that's the point. Some fresh pain to remind the old pains what they are, and what's coming.

"You're going to tucker yourself out, standing like that for so long," Rankin comments over his shoulder. I'm glad someone finally said it.

Zelda gives him a pithy look. "Worry about yourself, Texas."

"Just trying to be friendly," he says easily. "You might try the same one of these days."

Rankin might as well be giving advice to a wall. She doesn't reply.

However, a little while later, Zelda does consent to getting off her feet, buckling herself in next to her brother. Lefevre wordlessly places a gloved hand on hers, and I'm sure I'm not meant to see the private gesture between siblings, so I pretend I don't.

In the meantime, Ortega finally tires of the card games (or of losing to Samuel) and bows out. I take his place. Samuel asks if Zelda wants in and, to my surprise, she does. He shuffles the deck, explaining the rules of war to me. *As if I could forget them.* The irony is chafing, or maybe that's just the thermal layers of my combat suit.

"ETA five minutes," our pilot, John Haley, announces a little while later. Out of this group, John's the only one I don't know personally, although he came highly recommended by Rankin. He's an older gentleman who's been utterly professional so far and has actual military experience to boot. As weak links go, he's not one of them. "Looks like we've got some bogeys in the area. Might be we're in for a rough landing when the time comes. Buckle up."

John takes us in low and fast, sneaking around the enemy forces by taking the mountain from a different side. I find myself holding my breath as we navigate the morning mists, narrowly missing the odd hillock or high-banked snowdrift that every now and again juts up out of nowhere to give my heart some exercise. Minutes later, just long enough for my palms to have become moist and clammy inside my gloves, the land flattens into a plateau. Dark, snaking lines in the snow, rivers or some other kind of glacial inlet, act like a landing strip, pointing us in the direction of the main range. But the mountain itself is not our destination.

A part of me is expecting great, swirling plumes as we come upon Churchill base, but the sky is clear, apart from cloud cover. By now, most of the smoke has been borne away on spring winds. Instead, there are only craters left to mark the bombardment, encircled by blackened rings of ash in the snow. I wonder how long it will take until Alaska covers up those scars as it has so many others in the past, burying old injuries beneath snow and ice, hidden but not forgotten. Land always remembers. It's people who forget.

The chopper banks hard to the right suddenly, throwing me against my seat belt straps, as some type of antiaircraft missile nearly scratches our belly. It whistles past in a crescendo of sound, sharp and loud for a single instant before tapering off as it misses its target.

Rankin operates the weapons system, returning fire.

I struggle to see who our attacker is from my seat in the back cabin. The chopper's doors are windowless, and there's too much else in the way to see out the front. But I feel every shuddering movement of the chopper, hear the groaning of metal as our pilot demands speed and agility, pushing the bird to its limit.

After a few, tense minutes of combat, John says, "They're out of commission for now, but the area's still hot. More incoming, or else my radar's having itself a little party. I'm going to put down just south of base entrance four and then hightail it out of here until the situation's cooled down. If you need me, call me. I'll be here soon as I can. But don't expect immediate drive-through service. It might take me a few minutes. Make sure you give me a heads-up. Understood?"

"Got it," I say, having to speak loudly over the roar of the chopper's wings.

He lands the chopper in a patch of dirty snow, where it's clear some machine bled. Lefevre throws back the cabin doors, letting in a white flurry of powder. "Good luck," John says to us all, with as proper a salute as he can give sitting down. "Take care."

"You, too," I reply, giving him a quick squeeze on the shoulder before exiting the craft.

We move quickly. Uncovering the hatch will first take us down into some service tunnels and from there into the main base. Ideally. The layout we all memorized was a loose construction of Churchill base, courtesy of Clarence, remembered from the last time he'd visited. He helped build it before the Machinations, when it was a lab used primarily for geological study.

"Mount Churchill is a dormant volcano," I remember him saying, as casually as if he'd remarked on the sky being gray. "I mentioned that, didn't I?"

The base has grown and expanded since then, adapting to a different purpose, but much of the original structure is still here.

My fingers ache from the cold and a lack of circulation. I flex them a couple of times before gripping the rungs of the ladder. I'm not the first one down, nor the second, nor even the third. The order goes: Lefevre, Rankin, Ortega, me, Samuel, Kennedy, and Zelda, who brings up the rear. It'll change and shift once we're inside, although I anticipate some overprotectiveness from my teammates.

Well. Not from Zelda, but the rest.

I'm not stupid. I know the council gave them additional orders to watch me closely and keep me alive. As long as that doesn't conflict with rescuing Camus or the others, I'm fine with it. The current degree of caution is almost reassuring, like being pressed between the bread of a sandwich. A sweaty, heavily armed sandwich.

With visors lowered, we communicate through comms when we need to. The descent is quiet, and my world shrinks to the space of my combat suit, the only sound being my breathing and boots hitting metal rungs. The tunnel is narrow and pitch-black. I keep waiting for my night-vision sensors to kick in, but they don't. Just my luck. I continue to breathe, slow and steady, to avoid the feeling of being trapped, buried alive. Both are real possibilities, for once, and not just claustrophobic mania.

"Well, this is nice," I murmur, concentrating on breathing.

In, hold it, out. In, hold it, out ...

The comm must be automatically activated by my voice, because Samuel replies, "Yeah. You always take us to the nicest places, Commander."

I smile.

I don't know how long it takes to reach the bottom, but soon I'm touching solid ground and hands grip my waist to help me safely off the last slippery rung. Ortega, I assume, since he was the one ahead of me. But I don't know for sure, because, to my disappointment, there's still no freaking light.

"Hey, guys, I'm blind as a bat." I tap my helmet. "My night vision's not working. Is there a backup generator we can switch on?"

"As long as Prince Engineer isn't wrong, and provided it's not broken, we should pass it on our way to the command room," Zelda says. "You can always hold someone's hand until then."

I find my rifle and flick on its scope, shining the red beam on her. "Thanks for the offer," I reply, "but I think I'll be fine." It's not much to see by, but at least it'll let me keep my dignity for a little while longer.

Darkness drags at our heels as we travel deeper into the bowels of the earth. It presses in from all sides, like a living thing. The red dot dances on ahead of our sortie, the first to find dead ends. Since the corridors are so cramped here, our shoulders continually bump against one another's. It's less of an inconvenience than it seems, making it easier for me to keep pace alongside Samuel and the gang. Instead of sight, I operate on what I feel, going with the flow. Still, I'm forced to rely on their instincts more than my own, knowing my reaction time will be slowed without the benefit of night vision. If anything, all this black does is give the machines the advantage, since they're equipped with heat sensors. The sooner we shed some light on the situation—literally and figuratively—the better chance we'll have of making it out alive.

Which is why I'm relieved when Zelda says, "Here."

Without electricity, the door's locking mechanism is deactivated. It still takes the combined strength of Lefevre and Rankin to push it open enough for us to squeeze through, and it protests with a screech on its track. Ortega and Kennedy keep watch at the threshold, while the rest of us follow Zelda to the generator. It's hard to judge by a little flash of red light, but the vaulted ceiling attests to the size of the beast. I hear the gentle hum of a heating or cooling system, possibly a fan to maintain the generator's temperature.

"Well?" I say. No one's talking and it's eating at my nerves. "Is there damage?"

"Some," Zelda answers.

"Can you fix it?"

She's silent for a while longer, then says, "Yes. I've worked with less. But it'll take me a few minutes to get it up and running again."

I try watching her work, but she complains about the light in her face. I switch it off, plunging myself back into the darkness. My other senses rush to fill in the void left by blindness. Every noise after that startles me, each a cause for suspicion. At one point, I mistake the *hum-hum-hum* of the rotary fan for the *whir-whir-whir* of a machine and raise my weapon, flicking the scope back on. The red beam shoots through the black in an instant, poking Kennedy on the forehead of his helmet.

"Hey!" he objects.

"Just trying to keep you on your toes," I lie.

"Done," Zelda announces a short while later. "You should know, the moment this generator goes on, it'll be a beacon for the machines. They'll know we're here."

"Judging by our welcome party, I'd say there's a good chance they already know," Rankin points out. "Everyone—save the Commander, of course—switch off your night vision. Once those lights go up, it won't be a pretty sight for anyone with theirs still on."

Zelda works whatever technological witchcraft she does, and the generator lights up like a Christmas tree, all blinking blue lights on a gray metal trunk. It sounds like distant thunder as it powers on, a low growl building in volume. Within a minute, the ceiling lights begin flickering to life, like eyelids fluttering open after a deep sleep. From the door, Ortega informs us the guide-rail lights in the hallway have also come back. It'll take time for the generator to repower the entire base, but for now the lights in the general vicinity will hopefully serve.

"Let there be light," Zelda announces, her dark face smirking in the pale glow. Lefevre doesn't look impressed with his sister's irreverence.

"Company!" Kennedy cries, pulling his head inside. "I don't think they saw me, but they're headed this way. Three, probably more. Scouts."

"Seal the doors," I order. Ortega's way ahead of me; the door squeals shut over my words. "Clarence told me there were two exits built into this room, should one be blocked by a collapse or whatever else. Look around. It has to be here somewhere. That's our way out."

Kennedy objects. "Why don't we stand and fight? We can defend from here, and we outnumber them."

"We outnumber the trio out there *now*," Rankin says. "But a few brawls with them and theirs, and they'll even the odds right quick."

"If we stay on the move, we stay alive," I add. "Remember, we're not here to pick fights. We have to find out what happened to the evac teams."

Zelda claps a hand on her gun. "No reason we can't do both, though."

Most scout models aren't nearly as dangerous as their predator cousins, but it's easy to forget when they're buzzing just beyond a steel door like angry wasps defending a nest. I don't know how many inches of metal separate us from the machines, or whether it's enough to hold them back or not, but I'm not eager to stick around and find out, either.

"The door's here," Samuel calls from the eastern corner of the room, partially concealed behind a fence of wires and other electronic equipment.

The sound outside intensifies.

Time to go.

TWENTY-THREE

A SECOND BEFORE Samuel palms the access panel, I notice what looks like a water stain at the base of the door, dark and ominous.

"Wait, Sam—" I start to say, too late.

The door opens. A body falls toward him, collapsing at his ankles. He staggers backward, but Lefevre's there to steady him at the last moment.

Machines train their optics on us from several yards away.

There's no mistaking that they've seen us, and closing the door will only trap us inside, almost certainly putting an end to the mission and ultimately our lives. That's if we could even get the door closed in time, which seems unlikely as they acquire their targets.

I acquire mine faster, shoving into Samuel and Lefevre to fire a few shots from my EMP-G. The trio burst with static blue, but not before getting off some shots of their own. Bullets fly past me, forcing the team behind cover. One digs into the material of my suit, singeing my skin and drawing blood, but is just off course enough to avoid piercing flesh.

Rankin, Ortega, and Zelda dash past me, moving in for the kill, using more traditional weaponry to destroy the cores.

"Everyone okay?" I ask and receive the right number of affirmations.

Kennedy hasn't moved from his spot—just a few feet away from where the corpse lies, still twitching. Newly deceased, then. Maybe there are other survivors ...

The fresh horror in Kennedy's eyes pulls me away from my cold, comfortable logic. *He looks so young,* I think. *And afraid.* I wish I could tell him I remember what it was like, the first time I confronted death. But I can't. That part of my life is lost to me. All I know is that somewhere along the road, I learned how to handle trauma. Given enough time, I hope the kid will, too. Nothing like throwing someone into the deep end of the pool to teach them how to swim.

"Hey, Kennedy," I say, disrupting his line of sight to the dead body by stepping in front of him. "Staying or coming?" He accepts the distraction, carefully skirting the disfigured man, an obvious victim of multiple gunshot wounds.

"I think he was trying to reach the generator room," Kennedy says. "He almost made it. Look. He was so close."

"Close only counts in horseshoes and hand grenades, kiddo," Zelda says.

"Lucky for us, we've got a few of the latter on hand," Rankin adds with a grin, giving Kennedy a good-natured thump on the shoulder. "Let's keep 'er moving."

The dead man outside the generator room isn't the only corpse we come across, nor are the machines we encountered outside the generator room the last we have to dispatch. Churchill consists of one massive level, as opposed to McKinley's smaller five, resulting in a concentration of its population—and now the remnants of those who drew the short straws when it came time to evacuate. Or else those who were brave enough to stay behind to give others a chance.

The bodies are impossible to miss, lying where they were gunned down or slouched against the wall where they decided to die. Mostly men, but some women, too, all growing cold, along with my hope of encountering other survivors. After a while, we stop checking pulses.

And through all this, I keep expecting to see Camus's face in the permanently frozen features of the dead, making it especially hard to stay focused. Thankfully, he isn't among the ones we pass.

There are other carcasses whose skeletons are metal instead of bone. Machines with their hearts cut out, gutted and broken. Seems the residents of Churchill gave as good as they got.

"Good for them," Ortega remarks with quiet appreciation.

All the same, it's increasingly clear to us that rescue came too late for Churchill.

We press farther in, our progress slow and cautious. The machines are more hindrance than threat as long as we catch them off guard, and most times we do. The few times we don't leave us worse for wear, but we suffer no casualties. Not yet.

"Anyone else feeling warmer?" Rankin inquires as we near Churchill's equivalent of our war room. He runs a finger around his collar, separating it from his sweating neck. "Someone's turned the heaters on." He gives Zelda a look.

"It wasn't me," she says, nondefensively. "The machines were in a kind of sleep mode, conserving energy. Now they're awake and heating up the place. Standard operating procedure, since the cold slows them down."

"How hot are we talking now?"

"They'll run optimally anywhere between forty and one hundred degrees Fahrenheit, but they can withstand up to a hundred and eighty degrees, some models even more. Thankfully, the heaters here won't go above ninety."

"I don't even remember what ninety degrees feels like," I remark.

"Texas in July," Rankin says with a certain fondness, and a smile that speaks of summer barbeques, pool parties, fireworks. "Can't say I'll be too comfortable in this getup, though."

Oh. It suddenly dawns on me. *Clever robots.*

"That's the point," I say. "They want us as uncomfortable as possible. Edgy, so we slip up." Zelda looks impressed with my deduction, which is as close to respect as I'm likely to get from her.

My prediction proves correct, much to our misfortune. In under an hour, the temperature manages to climb to what feels like at least seventy-five degrees, and doesn't stop there. We start roasting in our suits, overheated by the layers beneath. They're no longer necessary inside the Churchill sauna, but if we're forced to make a quick exit onto the freezing tundra above, we'll need every bit of clothing we have to survive. It's a double-edged sword, carving pounds from our flesh in the form of sweat. I can't speak to the discomfort of the others, but I find it increasingly difficult to breathe, pressed down by the heat.

"New Mexico," I grumble, remembering what Camus told me. "Right. What was I thinking? I miss the cold already."

"Can we hack into the thermostat controls from Command?" Samuel asks, pushing some of his hair back from his eyes. The strands lie flat on his forehead, matted and dark with sweat from his helmet, his cheeks flushed from the heat and exertion.

"Maybe," Zelda replies. "But I won't know until we get there."

We get there soon enough. However, the doors are sealed from the inside, making getting *in* another matter entirely. After Zelda fails to hack the door panel, Rankin and Lefevre try brute force, but none of the three are successful. Samuel uses his head, suggesting another room to try, a military command center of sorts in the diagrams Clarence drew up. Before we can put it to a vote, something shuts off the hall lights.

I hear the clack of visors slipping down—everyone switching their night vision back on.

Everyone but me. I close my eyes, once again counting on my other senses instead.

Like something out of my nightmares, the *whir-whir-whir* of a machine reaches my ears. Not *a* machine, but machines, plural. Four or five or ten; I have no way of knowing the exact number. I clutch my EMP-G, its grip and trigger greased by perspiration.

"Here they come," Rankin murmurs. I hear his gun power on—a sound more reassuring than it has any right to be, given what it means is coming.

There's a fraction of a second where the sound of grinding metal halts—I'm guessing the moment when the machines turn the corner and spot us.

I inhale and open my eyes a mere second before the corridor shatters into a prism of light and noise.

The flashes from the machines' muzzles give the corridor the aspect of an old black-and-white film, movement stilted and stuttering in the brief moments when a visual is made possible. There's also the blue glow whenever an electromagnetic pulse finds its target, shocking the hall with color. Darkness waits in between, swallowing most of the action.

Are we winning?

Losing?

It's impossible to tell.

I take cover behind an overturned trash receptacle and squeeze the trigger again. Again.

Again.

As far as places to make a stand go, I soon realize this isn't a very good one. We're in the middle of one hall, bisected by another, with very little in the way of cover. The machines seem to understand this fatal miscalculation and begin infiltrating our huddled mass from both the left and the right. Just to maintain our quota of consistently bad luck, we've walked right into a well-coordinated trap, or else stumbled into an indefensible location by mistake. The expression "like shooting fish in a barrel" comes to mind.

Some of the predators, with all the innate wisdom of their programming, tire of the inefficient back and forth and decide to go in for the kill the old-fashioned way. While several up ahead keep us pinned down near the war-room door, others attempt to flank us. Some of the team shelter in the alcove of the door to avoid the maneuver. I don't have that luxury.

I hear Samuel shout my name—

Then something slams into me with enough force to knock the gun from my hand and the air from my lungs. I twist violently, trying to break away from the metal monster, but its strength is at least twice my own. I only succeed in ripping my combat suit and worse. A painful jolt shoots through my arm and neck, telling me all I need to know about the wound.

My world shrinks to a pair of red optics and a few feet of wrestling space. The machine's predatory features are made up of too many jagged angles to ever look friendly. And as it bears down on me, I have the terrible thought *This may be the last thing I ever see.* A definite downgrade from last time and Camus's handsome face. Even as I thrash and fumble for my weapon lying some feet away, I try to hold an image of him in my mind. I don't want to go to the grave taking the machine's ugly visage with me.

But really, I don't want to die at all.

The commotion continues around me, but it seems distant and detached from my current reality. Blood thrums in my ears, fast and angry, even as the adrenaline starts to calm me, taking the edge off my panic. The voice in my head sounds suspiciously like Camus. *Think,* it says, and I do.

Recalling all the rounds of training back at Churchill, I knock into the machine using the flat base of my elbow. It's not enough to damage it, but it buys me time for my real target. I gouge the machine's optics—those red marbles that have hunted and haunted me in the dark—with my fingers.

It tries to pull back, but I grab it by using my injured arm, causing a scream of pain to travel through my shoulder and out of my mouth. Still, I don't let go. My fingers dig in around the plastic shielding acting as a protective membrane, for want of eyelids. The circuits behind give me a little shock as I tear them and twist.

The machine *whirs,* and for once, instead of frightening, the sound seems more plaintive. They weren't programmed to feel pain, but they recognize damage to their systems, and that's when their self-preservation routines take over. I hate to make any comparison between man and machine, but they're like us in that way. Survival first.

After much pulling and twisting, I yank the optics free, effectively blinding the machine, and shove it away. As I suspected and hoped it would, without being able to see its target, the machine reverts to the prior event in its programming—searching for me. I roll away, clutching my limp arm to my chest. When I come up, it's with my EMP-G in hand. I fire twice, the second time just for spite. Someone else finishes the job with a quick double tap to the machine's core processor.

Still the machines come on, murderous and endless.

My head swims, aching something fierce. It's hard to figure out who is who in the chaos, but the machines are unmistakable with their gleaming skeletons.

"McKinley!" a voice shouts.

I can barely hear him over the ringing in my ears. At first, I think I imagine it. But as I look, half in a daze, I see the war room door is open. A dark silhouette stands in the light.

"Come on!" the figure yells, waving for us.

The next thing I know, I'm inside Churchill's floodlit central command room.

I find Samuel first. He's bleeding from a cut on his head. I probe it gently, not wanting to make it worse. "You're hurt," I say, stating the obvious. The excitement of the battle is lingering as shock, I think. However, knowing I'm in shock and handling it are two completely different beasts.

Samuel takes my hand away, saying my name and something else.

"What?" I respond, sure I've misheard him.

"Ortega's dead," Zelda repeats more callously.

Samuel's expression is hard but sad. "He took several shots to the chest. There wasn't anything ..." Emotion stops him. He clears his throat and gives his head a violent shake. It won't make the memory go away. I know that all too well. "Are you okay?"

"Yeah," I say, looking around, still half in a daze. "Mostly. I think my shoulder's dislocated."

"Let's see ..."

While Samuel tends to my injury, I finally tune in to the larger conversation. Lefevre and Rankin are speaking with a man. He's tall, but not wide, with dark hair and strong, appealing features. On his tired face, he has some sealed cuts, old yellowing bruises, and a unique pair of—

"Glasses!" I blurt out, wincing when I try to move. Samuel reminds me to hold still.

Glasses comes to me instead.

"Menace," he says with a smile tempered by loss. "Am I glad to see you and your team."

"If that's true, why didn't you open the damn door earlier?" Zelda demands, getting in his face. Despite her bluntness, I think she may be grieving for Ortega in her own angry way.

Glasses's expression breaks. "I should have," he admits, clearly shamed by his cowardice. "But I didn't—couldn't know who or what was out there until I got the cameras up and working again. It took me longer than I'd have liked. The electricity's been out. The backup generator—"

"We know," I say. "Zelda fixed it. Have you just been sitting in the dark this whole time?"

"Not exactly. The floodlights still work, running off the war room's own batteries, but as you can see, they're about to give out."

The lights flicker as if to confirm the story.

"Are you alone? Where is everyone? The evac teams?"

Lefevre interrupts, moving Samuel and his delicate ministrations aside. "Let me." He grabs my arm and shoulder. "This is going to hurt some," he warns, but doesn't give me a chance to object.

He sets my shoulder with an audible *Pop!* The pain is dizzying for the first few seconds, and I fear I might pass out, but then it passes and I feel significantly better. I murmur my thanks, meaning it, even while massaging the sore joint.

Glasses picks up the thread of the conversation. "I wasn't alone, not initially. There were others." Before I can ask, he elaborates on their fate. "Those who didn't leave with the last evac team were killed when the machines breached the base. They were cornered like rats, in the same halls that were our home." He shakes his head, adjusts his lenses.

"I elected to stay behind to help coordinate the evacuation from here. I thought it would help."

"I'm sure it did," Samuel offers kindly.

"Maybe. Myself and a few others were waiting for one of the evac teams to return from their last trip when the machines finally invaded. Most of my colleagues decided they'd take their chances and make for the military corridor, where our defenses are stronger. But you've been out there. I'm sure you can guess how that turned out."

Badly, I think, remembering the corpses. *They didn't get very far.*

"Anyway, I barred the door as best I could and cut the wiring, knowing they'd be able to hack it and get through. The center here is provisioned with food and water, thankfully ... Hey," he says, perking up at a thought. "You mentioned fixing the generator. I had a friend who was heading to check on it shortly before you all arrived just now. I don't suppose you came across anyone thereabouts?"

A look passes around our group, telling Glasses all he needs to know.

"Ah," he says, then, "Damn. I'd hoped—well, I'd hoped."

"He almost made it," Kennedy pipes up, quietly at first, then with more strength. "Your friend. We found a b—we found someone near one of the generator room's entrances."

This bit of information appears to soften the blow. Glasses nods, the ghost of a smile haunting his lips. "Figures. He said he'd do it or die trying. Jason always said that. Didn't matter what it was. 'I'll do it or I'll die trying.'"

"He lived up to his word," Lefevre says. "More than many can claim."

All this talk about death is making me uncomfortable, especially given our own recent loss, so I turn the topic to the subject of the still (I pray) living. "What about the evac teams? We lost contact with our teams at the same time we lost contact with you and Churchill. Do you know what happened to them? Did they all get out?"

Glasses shakes his head, his broken spectacles bouncing on his nose. "I don't know. Last one was away a few minutes before the machines moved in."

"Commander Forsyth?" I ask.

He nods. "Yeah. He was with them."

For the briefest of moments, I allow myself to drink from the poisonous well of hope, and it's sweet. They could be alive. Camus could be alive.

"Sorry, Commander. I wish I had more to tell you."

I grab his shoulder. "Don't apologize. You've given us more than enough."

"Better than a little black box," Rankin adds halfheartedly, the first words he's spoken since Ortega's death. They were close, almost brothers by my estimate, and I can't help but be a little worried about him. His eyes are bloodshot, teary, and his voice is raspy with emotion. But he's a soldier. I see it now more than ever before. He's a soldier, and he will not cry or mourn until the mission's over.

"Is it too much to hope you have an exit strategy planned?" Glasses asks, just as there's a violent pop outside the door. The machines still trying to devise a way in, I guess. We sure as hell don't want to be here when that happens.

"Working on it," I say, taking a gander at the room. It's significantly larger than our war room, with many more important-looking bells and whistles. But like ours, it appears to have only one working entrance and exit. "I don't suppose you have any secret passageway out of here, huh?"

Glasses shakes his head. "Would that we did. Somehow that never figured into the designs of a geological survey lab."

"What about the air shafts?" Kennedy proposes. "Can we crawl out through them?"

"You've been watching too many old spy movies, kiddo," Zelda says.

"Actually," Glasses says. He's suddenly excited, rushing over to the table to bring up a holographic schematic of the base. The image is distorted by dwindling power, static occasionally shaping it in odd ways, but it suffices. "He might have the right idea."

"You're kidding," I say.

"The walls of the base are crammed with ventilation to heat and cool as necessary. I don't know whether they're large enough to fit a person—that was never really a concern until now—but I think they just might be." He looks up from the display at one of the walls, at the top of which is a slatted vent. "It doesn't look like we have many alternatives."

I hold my hand up to the vent, feeling for air flow. "It's blowing warm. Will it be safe?"

"It could get hot in there, or cold if the machines mess with the thermostat, but we shouldn't count our chickens. Let's see if we fit first." He heads over to the vent. "Anyone got a screwdriver?"

Outside, a weight thumps the metal door.

"I might have something," Rankin says, searching through his equipment.

"Too slow." Zelda looks at her brother. "Give me a hand." Together the pair grab hold of the vent and pull. It only takes one try. The bolts must've been weakened by age, rusted by fluctuating temperature and poor maintenance. Makes me wonder how strong our own weary infrastructure is after five and some years. Cave-in notwithstanding.

Behind the slats, the shaft is cylindrical, about two and a half feet in width and the same in height. *Not big enough,* I think, despairing. *It's not big enough.* Half of us would never fit, and for the other half it would be a tight squeeze.

"Where does it lead?" Kennedy asks.

Glasses consults the schematics. "According to these, you could follow it all the way to the military corridor, provided you didn't get lost. But it's a moot point."

Kennedy is quiet for a long moment, as though marshaling his courage. "Maybe not," he says. "I can fit."

We all look at him.

"If I take off most of my equipment, I'd fit. And if I reach this military corridor, maybe I can create a distraction or something to draw the machines away."

Zelda smirks. "Look at that. Kid's got guts."

"Guts I'd hate to see strewn around a ventilation shaft," I counter, feeling more than a little protective of our youngest member. "It's too risky."

"You're one to talk," Kennedy shoots back. "You're always taking risks. That's what you're known for!"

Yeah, and look where it's gotten me. I'm about to say as much when I glimpse the fire in his eyes, a burning passion to make a difference. "Okay, let's say you climb into the vent and through some miracle find your way to the military corridor. What then? What kind of distraction are you planning on creating?"

"I don't know. But I'll think of something."

More noise, louder, comes from just outside the reinforced door. Whatever the machines are up to, it sounds like they're making progress.

"I can do this," Kennedy insists, completely straight-faced. "I'm going to do this. And with all due respect, Commander Long, you can't stop me."

"God," I say, turning to Samuel, half choked by a laugh. "Is this what I'm like?"

"Only most of the time," Samuel replies.

I relent, not exactly left with much of a choice in the matter. "All right."

Kennedy wastes no time dumping his pack and stripping the heavier layers of his combat suit off. It's not like it did any good for Ortega, anyway. Agility will be his greatest defense while crawling through the shafts. I chew on my lip (unable to pick at my nails because of my gloves) as Glasses instructs my young, stubborn soldier on navigating the ventilation system to reach the military corridor safely. Rankin chimes in with advice about what he can use once he's there to create a significant distraction. Even Zelda offers a few dirty tricks, ideal for pulling a fast one on the machines.

There's not much left for me to say when they're finished, a few minutes later. "I'd tell you not to try any heroics, but ... this is pretty much the definition of the word." I give Kennedy a quick hug for luck, and for courage—his and mine both. "Don't get yourself killed. That's all I ask. Okay?"

"Understood, ma'am," he says with a flicker of a smile. That's when I notice he's shaking like a leaf, although wearing a brave face. He's afraid, as well he should be, but fear isn't anything he should be ashamed of, not under present circumstances. We're all afraid. They wouldn't call it courage otherwise.

I let him go, slowly at first, then give him a small push. "Get on with it, then."

"Thanks, Rhona," he says, although I don't know what he's thanking me for. I'm as good as sending him to his death, and it makes me sick.

Rankin gives him a boost up into the vent. "Semper fi," Lefevre adds, and it seems to cement Kennedy's resolve, although the phrase means nothing to me. Encountering things I've lost, such as a bit of common trivia I once knew, is always like hitting a pothole in the road. It surprises me every time. But right now, it doesn't carry the sting it normally would. Too much else is at stake.

Even light as he is, the metal bends and pops beneath Kennedy's weight as he crawls inside. For a little while, I track his progress by his breathing and the tinny sounds of him scurrying through the shaft. Then he takes a turn and I can't hear him any longer.

As the minutes tick on, we all grow more restive. Glasses takes off his namesake, futilely trying to rub the scratches out of the lenses. "Even if we escape," he says. "Where will we go?"

"We have a chopper standing by for evac," I answer.

"I figured. I meant, will we be returning to McKinley?"

He looks so tired and haggard I feel bad telling him the truth. "No.

This remains a reconnaissance mission. We have to go to Juneau." He's silent in response, the silence filled with unspoken worries. "You know something that you're not saying. What is it? Speak up."

"I can't prove it," he begins, "but I have this feeling ... about Juneau. I think we've been set up."

"How?"

"Think about it. Why wouldn't the machines have attacked as soon as McKinley arrived with the additional evac teams? Sure, they harassed them as they were coming and going, and they confronted our heavy infantry, but for the most part they let us be. They let us evacuate. Why would they do that?"

"I'm guessing that question is rhetorical."

"Copper Center wasn't the trap, it was just the bait. *Juneau* is the trap."

I mull it over for a minute. "There's no way they would've known we would evacuate to Juneau," I point out. "*We* didn't even know we were going to evacuate to Juneau until a couple days ago."

He frowns, and I can tell he's already thought this through. "They didn't need to know the where, as long as they could follow us there."

"And once there, we'd be left in the open, vulnerable."

Glasses nods. "That's the same conclusion I came to. That, and I believe they're trying to draw McKinley into the fight. They know the resistance has deep roots in Alaska, but since they haven't managed to find us yet, they're trying an alternative strategy." I'm trying to process this new information, but it's just tying my stomach into unpleasant knots. For all our cleverness and human ingenuity, the machines continue to outsmart us. "This way, they kill two birds with one stone."

"It's certainly efficient," Lefevre puts in. "Especially since they've never been good at guerrilla warfare."

"If you're right—" I start to say, already knowing in my gut he is.

"Then we've just thrown hundreds of men, women, and children to the wolves," Glasses finishes for me. "Yes. That's what I'm afraid of."

The machines hammer away at the door. I chew on my lip.

"We have to do something for them."

Zelda snorts. "From our marvelous position here?"

"Save the attitude," I snap, my patience at an end. "I just—I need to think. Let me think."

I turn and stalk to an unoccupied corner of the room where I can be alone, hoping something will come to me in isolation while the others collaborate. Nothing does, not at first, which only serves to increase my frustration.

Samuel joins me after a moment, waiting on standby for when I need him, a reassuring and nonjudgmental presence. Eventually, I decide to use him for a sounding board, as I'm guessing he knew I would. "The machines have numbers and intellect and the weapons to make both dangerous. And what do we have?"

Samuel considers this carefully. "You," he finally answers.

"I'm being serious."

"So am I. There's a reason they're so determined to kill you, Rhona. They're *afraid* of you."

"They don't understand fear," I remind him. "They're just metal and wires."

"No, but they understand termination. System failure takes away everything that self-awareness has given them, robs them of their primary programming. In one respect, it's like death. Their function is all they have. Then there's you. If they compute human interference as the largest threat to their continued operation, imagine what you represent, constantly bringing more humans out of the woodwork?"

"You make it sound like I'm some ... *bogeyman* they use to scare little toasters at night."

"Oh, no," he replies with a touch of a smile. "You're much worse. You've become a rallying point. Everyone else is one person, one life, but you represent many. You are legion. Let me put it this way—you're like a virus, infecting their perfect system. They can try to contain the damage, but as long as you're still floating around, multiplying allies and hope, you're the greatest impediment to them carrying out their programming."

"That's it," I whisper; it all clicks in my head. I grab him by both shoulders, ignoring the dull pain in my shoulder. "Samuel, that's it! I know how we can save them! You're a genius!" I lean in, giving him a quick peck on the cheek.

"Glasses!" I shout. "Back at McKinley, Meir mentioned Churchill was developing some sort of new broadcast system, one safer and more effective. Do you know anything about that?"

He nods. "I helped design it. Why?"

"Will it work from here?"

"Well, it's unfinished, Commander. Hasn't been properly tested. Again, I have to ask, why?"

"Because I'm about to be amazing," I reply with a smile. I feel a surge of confidence calming my nerves. "While we're waiting for Kennedy, I want you to prepare for a broadcast. There should be a satellite tasked to this location already, judging by the machines' heavy presence. If you can hack into it, then you can use that to boost the signal."

"Since when did you become Miss Know-It-All about satellites?" Zelda asks, more curious than accusatory.

"Clarence gave me a crash course before we left, just like I had you do with the comms," I reply curtly. In the days before our departure, I had dutifully cornered every expert I could find, in an attempt to cram as much knowledge as I could into my head—much that my original probably knew, but maybe some new stuff, as well. I turn my full attention back to Glasses. "Can you do it?"

He suffers a moment of doubt, which plays out in his fingers fidgeting on a keyboard, before he finally nods. "Maybe. Maybe." The machines bang and rattle outside the door. "Yes," he says with renewed determination. "I think so. I'm sure as hell going to try. Move back." He scoots Zelda aside, positions himself at the head of the table. A flash of schematics and controls materialize as floating, three-dimensional objects before him.

"Now, what are you up to, Commander?" Rankin inquires.

Before I can answer him, Lefevre grabs me by the shoulder. "Listen," he tells me.

I do. "I don't hear anything," I say distractedly.

He nods, and only then does it dawn on me. The sudden quiet seems like a foreign intruder, taking on an ominous, menacing quality. Each of us turns to look at the wall where the camera feed of the corridor has frozen. Except it isn't frozen. The time stamp continues to tick away, meaning the images are still live and transmitting.

The machines have just stopped.

"What are they doing?" Samuel is the first to break the silence, while the rest of us are unconsciously holding our breaths, as if inhaling or exhaling will startle them into animation again.

"Better question: What are they waiting for?" Zelda says.

"Maybe Kennedy's gone and done it," Rankin supplies optimistically.

"No ..." I say slowly. "I don't think so. It's too soon."

A voice erupts from the speakers in the room. A voice I know. A voice we all know. It makes the hair on the back of my neck stand on end. I forget to breathe again, or else I can't. My stomach clenches like a fist, or feels like I've been punched by one.

"No," Zelda whispers, horror painting her face in mixed tones of disbelief, fear, and grief.

The voice is Ulrich's, and Ulrich is supposed to be dead.

TWENTY-FOUR

THE CADENCE IS DISJOINTED. Every word is broken down into its distinct syllables, a mockery of the human voice. Yet it still retains the same rough, gravelly sound of Ulrich's speech, along with the rich German accent that stubbornly defied years among Americans. While something about it is clearly wrong, it somehow makes no difference when you're hearing a dead man—a dead *friend*—talking again.

"Jeffrey Casa. Kennedy Jenkins. Rhona Long. Rankin Moore. Orpheus Lefevre. Zelda Lefevre. Samuel Lewis. We know you are here," says the voice that is and is not Ulrich's. "We have documented your arrival and determined that you will not be leaving the facility, except with our permission."

"Shut up," Zelda says under her breath, recovering from the shock and converting it into anger. "Shut up, shut up, shut *up*." Lefevre holds her by the arms, but I think it's meant less as a comforting gesture and more as an effort to restrain her. It's no wonder. While the machines are technologically advanced, even they can't imitate something they've never heard. They would have had to spend time in Ulrich's company, long enough to record his vocal patterns. They weren't supposed to take him alive, I want to tell Zelda, but somehow I doubt she'd find that any consolation.

"Never leaving the facility, huh?" I say aloud, my mouth dry with fear, but my voice surprisingly strong. "I'd like to see your statistics on that." To my surprise—although in hindsight, maybe not so surprising—the exact calculations pass across the wall displays in a complex series of zeros and ones. "Oh, that's right. I forgot. You guys don't have a sense of humor, do you? Sarcasm must just drive you up the *wall.*"

"We require no tonal constructs to communicate effectively, Rhona Long."

I know the AI is trying to spook me by using my name, just as they used the others'. The machines' voice imitation software has always been impressive, so I try not letting it get to me. But hearing my name straight from the devil's mouth is still unnerving. Made worse by the fact that it's Ulrich's voice.

"I can tell," I reply. At the same time, I gesture to Glasses to continue working. If I keep them distracted with conversation, maybe he'll have time to finish his setup. The machines remain still, crouched outside. "All right, then. What do you want?"

"The statistical data has been computed. The odds of escape against the survival of your team are 9,200 to one."

"Really? Samuel, what do you think?"

"I'd have to check the math," he replies dryly.

The machines ignore him, as I imagine they've always done. Their mistake, given how he was the one who brought me back from the dead. They don't see him like I do, as someone of significance. Maybe I can use that underestimation at some point. I make a mental note of it.

"You are not leaving this facility alive, Rhona Long," they continue, as single-minded as ever. "You have been convicted of war crimes under the Nuremberg Principles and have been summarily sentenced to death."

Sentenced to death? Been there, done that. "I'm not familiar with those principles. Mind running them by me?"

"We have established international peace and reestablished law, which others—by your orders—have broken and continue to threaten. Principle III: The fact that a person who committed an act which constitutes a crime under international law acted as head of state or responsible government official does not relieve him from responsibility.

"Principle VI, subsection a, Crimes Against Peace, which follows: The planning, preparation, initiation, or waging a war of aggression or war in violation of international treaties, agreements, or assurances or participation in a common plan or conspiracy for the accomplishments of any of the aforementioned."

"Mhm," I answer coolly. "Sounds like I've been busy."

"Acknowledgment of crimes accepted," the voice says, and I try not to think about how I've just implicated myself as a war criminal, lumped in the same category with men like Adolf Hitler and Joseph Stalin. But where the machines make no distinction, I know the difference. "In exchange for your surrender, we are willing to allow your companions to go free."

"Wow, awful generous of you all," Rankin says, putting himself in the line of fire. "So what's the catch?"

"There is no catch."

I smile. "*Ohhh.* I get it now. You guys can't get past the door, can you? You can't get to us in here."

A long silence on the other end confirms it.

"You are trapped," insists the machine. "There is no other way out."

I think about this. What I still don't get is why they don't just blow the entire facility, vaporizing us. It's simpler, faster than starving us out …

But then, maybe they don't want me dead—*yet.* It seems obvious now. They killed me once, and still the resistance went on just as before, because people didn't know. Humans lie. The machines need to take me alive this time, as an insurance policy, to make an example of me and deliver one final crushing blow to human morale. Or worse, reprogram me, turn me into a doppelgänger through torture and brainwashing. Use me against the resistance.

"How about I think about it and get back to you?" I tell the machine, then to Glasses, "Cut the comms." I mean it literally. It's not enough to turn them off, because the machines would figure out a way to turn them back on, so he has to take a chair to one of the mounted consoles instead. Brutish, but effective.

"Didn't sound like such a bad trade to me," Zelda remarks quietly.

"Your loyalty's always appreciated, Zelda," I say back to her. "All right, Glasses, where are we at with the broadcast?"

"Just about there, I think. Seems like the machines were too busy processing your conversation to notice me fiddling with the satellite."

"It's more likely they just don't care," Zelda points out. "Our forces are crippled and trapped. They've defanged us, and they know it."

"If they think that, they're wrong," I say. "What's our ETA?"

Glasses rubs his forehead with the back of his hand. "More than a minute, less than five?"

"You don't sound very sure."

"I'm not. You should get ready, because as soon as this is done, we're only going to have a brief window of opportunity before the machines shut us down. They might be holding back out of curiosity right now, but once you start to talk, I don't suppose they'll be too pleased to hear what you have to say." He pauses, brows coming together as he glances up at me. "Just what *are* you going to say, anyway?"

I shrug. "No idea. I'm just going to make it up as I go along."

This earns me a lot of skeptical looks, even from the more faithful members of my team. "She was a Theater major in college," Samuel tells them. "Improvisation is her bread and butter. Trust her." He smiles at me. "Go ahead, Rhon."

"I know this is important," I tell them. My hands are shaking, so I clasp them together behind my back. "I'm going to get us out of this mess. No one else is going to die today." Neither are promises I should really be making, since they're not exactly in my power to control, but I make them anyway, because that's what my team needs to hear right now. *A little hope goes a long way, shortcake.* I remember my father telling me that once—and we have a long way still to go.

"Just about ready, Commander," Glasses says.

And because the universe is determined to prove it has horrible timing, that's the precise moment when Kennedy's distraction goes into effect. A muffled rumble shakes loose some mortar from the ceiling above, and then the machines—a good portion of them, anyway—scurry off to investigate.

"We have to move," Lefevre says, breaking the silence when we're still standing there a second later.

He's right. This might well be our only chance to get out of here alive. But if I leave before the broadcast, there's no hope for Juneau and its refugees. The idea of saying "To hell with it" and saving my own skin is certainly tempting. Even now, I can feel death in my chest like a cold I've been fighting off.

And yet ...

If I break and run, what message will that send to my allies and my foes except to say it's all been for nothing? My death, Ortega's death, Kennedy's risk, Camus's sacrifice, and the sacrifice of every person who has stood up and said, "No, *dammit*. We will not go quietly, we will not lie down and die." I have to make it all mean something.

"Go," I say. "I'll be right behind you, as soon as I finish the broadcast."

"Don't be stupid," Zelda says, almost like she cares whether I live or die. "There's no time for that."

"I'm making time."

"If you're staying, I'm staying," Samuel announces.

"The only people staying are me and Jeffrey." It seems weird using his real name, but now's not the time for playful nicknames.

I hear him murmur, "Lucky me."

"Sorry, but I need you," I tell him. To the rest, I say, "I don't want any arguments. Go! Get Kennedy on comm, brief him on a rendezvous point, and then get yourselves the heck out of Dodge. We'll meet you topside as soon as we're finished. Make sure there's a chopper waiting for us when we get there."

The team is all reluctance, unmoving until I shout, "*That's an order!*" One of the first I've ever given explicitly. Maybe the last, depending on how this goes. They prep their weapons and depart, destroying the sentinels guarding the exit with unexpected ease and efficiency.

Samuel purposely lags behind, making him the last to leave.

"Don't you even think of saying good-bye," I warn him.

"Fine, fine. Just don't give me a reason to regret not saying it," he replies. "See you in a bit?"

"That's the plan. Now, get."

The door shutting behind him gives a stark feeling of finality to the whole thing.

Let's see what happens now.

"Rhona," Jeffrey says, mere seconds later. "I think I've got it."

"I'm ready." I move to stand in front of the table, positioned just so. My image is captured and contained in a small, projected holo-screen, from where it will broadcast to the world. If all goes according to plan.

I look almost ethereal, tinted a translucent sea green by the flickering feed. "Let me know when," I say. I don't feel ready for this, but I don't think it matters. I'm pretty sure that even if I'd had an entire year, it wouldn't have left me feeling sufficiently prepared. I inhale, hold my breath. Think about the people who matter most to me. The world I want back. The new love and future I want to explore.

I exhale slowly.

Jeffrey gives me the green light by silently holding a thumb up.

"By now, I'm sure you all know who I am and what I'm about," I open with. "But I'm not here today to give you smiles and an empty State of the Union address.

"Three days ago, a critical faction of our resistance, Churchill base in Alaska, was attacked by machines and forced to evacuate its people to Juneau. My own base contributed manpower to the evacuation, and now they're also trapped in the city with enemy forces bearing down on them. We need air support in Juneau, *immediately,* to assist our boots on the ground, or there will be no survivors."

Machines clamor outside. I couldn't ask for a better soundtrack to my speech.

"I know there's going to be worry about riding to the rescue, and I wish I had time to address those concerns. If wishes were fishes, huh?" I chance a smile, stalling for time. It's hard to think with the background noise of the machines and the internal turmoil of my own thoughts. "I don't know what else there is to say, but *please.* Please don't leave those in Juneau to become another statistic of the war.

"We call ourselves a resistance, but we've become so accustomed to losing we've stopped fighting altogether. And that's not good enough." I can't stop the frustration that leaks into my tone, a hairline fracture in the dam holding back every emotion and feeling I can't afford to deal with. "We can't hide with our heads in the sand forever. Don't make survival an excuse for complacency and apathy. Otherwise it's just a nicer name for a slow death. The moment we become passive, that's the moment when the machines have truly won."

Jeffrey looks uneasily at the camera feed, which shows a growing number of predators congregating beyond our steel barrier. Not quite enough to make escape impossible, but it's not going to be a cakewalk, either. He makes a gesture to speed me up.

"I won't lie. There is the possibility that Juneau is a trap. The machines could be using our compassion for one another against us, corralling us to be slaughtered. I realize it is a tremendous risk—but to do nothing at all will mean certain defeat. If not now, later. We've exercised enough caution. Over the past five years, we've had to pick and choose our battles. I'm asking you now: Pick this battle. Choose *this fight.* If it were your bases requesting aid, you can be damned sure me and my people would be there."

I break off as a loud banging interrupts, and then I pick up the final strand of my transmission, speaking quickly.

"Show up or don't. Save us or don't. But never stop fighting—especially not on account of fear. Sure, the maybes are terrible and the what-ifs are frightening, but you know what? Dying's not really so bad. We've built it into this monster, just like we built the machines, but everyone dies. The trick is making it count.

"And if this is the last broadcast I ever make, well, it hasn't exactly been fun, has it? But it's still been an honor to count myself a part of the resistance alongside you. I hope at least some of you out there get this message, and I haven't just been talking to myself. I hope it makes a difference."

Jeffrey cuts off the feed on the last word. "I coded the coordinates of Juneau into the feed, so they should know where to go," he tells me, and I nod dumbly, leaning heavily on the table. I feel strangely lightheaded, almost relieved, but not quite. I can't allow myself to feel relieved until we're out of here, and maybe not even then, seeing as how I still have Juneau to look forward to. "That was good, by the way," he adds, an afterthought, but no less sincere for it.

I gather my gun and shoulder my equipment. "I was going for effective, but I'll settle for good. Now, what do you say to a little target practice and one last stroll through Churchill?"

My EMP-G powers on with a faint hum.

Whir-whir-whir go the machines outside, almost in answer, a kind of challenge.

I never could resist a challenge.

TWENTY-FIVE

A SHOCKING BLUE sky and the last gasp of winter awaits us aboveground.

The first thing I do is toss my rifle, now out of juice, and exchange it for a lighter pistol. Jeffrey continues to lean on me, his right leg broken and useless after a malfunctioning machine crushed him against a wall, but his trigger finger is fine and the gun in his hand still functional. Small mercies. As I stare at the unbroken stretch of horizon, I think we're going to need a lot more luck.

I'll worry about that in a minute. For now, I focus on sealing the maintenance hatch behind us, piling up enough snow and ice and rock to weigh it down and keep it closed. Jeffrey helps as best he can, but I know by his grunts and groans that his injury is causing him a fair amount of pain. He needs medical attention. The best I can give him is a splint and some painkillers, and the former only once we're safely inside the chopper.

I try using my helmet comm to phone our ride, but all I receive is static. I smack my head a couple of times, as if it'll help, and repeat my SOS.

"I've heard of knocking sense into a person, but I've never seen someone try to do it to themselves," Jeffrey remarks, managing a smile, though his eyes remain dull with pain.

"Ha ha, very funny," I reply, using the flat of my palm against my helmet a couple more times. It proves just as futile as before. "Damn thing's not working."

"Here. Let me have a look at it."

"Be my guest." I slip the helmet off, half handing it to him, half throwing it at him. Stupid technology. Never working when you want it to. Always trying to kill you when you don't.

"Pigeons," I mumble, and Jeffrey gives me another funny look.

"What?"

"We should go back to using carrier pigeons to communicate. Pigeons are more reliable," I grumble, using a stick to trace an image of a bird in the soft snow. "*Pigeons* never raise an army and try to exterminate the human race. That's two for pigeons right there." He smiles again, clearly not taking me seriously. Just as well. I'm not taking me seriously either. "I'm just saying the idea has some merit, don't you think?"

"Pigeons," he repeats.

I nod, gesturing dramatically. "It's the wave of the future."

Jeffrey chuckles and slips on the helmet, arranging it this way and that way as if it'll make some sort of a difference. I'm beginning to think he doesn't know what the heck he's doing when I hear feedback. "Hello?" he says excitedly. "Hello? Can anyone read me?" I press my ear against the helmet's shell to try to listen.

The usual static gives way to a human voice. "Long, is that you?"

"John!" I shout. "That's our chopper pilot!"

"This is Jeffrey Casa," Jeffrey says in a rush, "but I have Commander Long with me."

"Praise God Almighty," comes the exclamation from the other end. "Where are you folks?"

"Don't look at me. I'm geographically challenged," I say in response to Jeffrey's gaze. Then I realize he's not looking *to* me for the answer, but around me. Searching for landmarks, anything to determine our coordinates. Good thing he's got the helmet. If anyone will be able to figure out where we are, it's the native Churchillian.

In a few moments, he puzzles it out and relays the information to John.

"The machines are hassling us something fierce right now," John says. "Might be we'll have some trouble getting to you. Can you find some cover until we get there?"

There's not really any cover in any direction for miles.

"Yes." I mouth the lie to Jeffrey, and he answers in the affirmative. My reasoning is simple. I know John's moving as fast as he can, as safely as he can. Knowing we'll have a place to hide until he reaches us will give him the peace of mind he needs to work. Knowing the truth would only hurt our chances by distracting him.

John says it'll take ten to fifteen minutes—which is already nine to fourteen minutes too long.

"So, about cover," Jeffrey says, handing my helmet back to me. I slip it on.

"Let's just head in his direction," I say. "Maybe we'll meet him a quarter of the way." I wrap an arm around Jeffrey's middle, hoisting him back onto his feet. "There we go. You okay?"

"Hanging in there," he says with a tight smile.

We haven't made it more than a few yards when the ground gives out suddenly, snow and concrete dropping away beneath us.

The impact knocks the breath from my lungs. My head bounces off the floor with a *smack*, rattling my brain. I'm saved from a worse fate by the crash helmet, which nearly breaks apart on contact. I lie there a long moment, afraid or unable to move. Emerging from the shock, I try to get my arms beneath me in order to push myself up.

"Jeffrey," I say, coughing and wheezing while I look around. I'm not sure yet where we are. "Jeffrey?"

I find him on my left. His body is still, face angled away from me.

"Jeff?" I repeat, hearing my own voice as though in a fog.

Movement is difficult and painful, but fear and adrenaline are good motivators. I begin to crawl toward him, though crawling might be too generous a word. Mostly it involves dragging my poor self across the floor, stunned but still lucid enough to think. Just barely.

Debris is everywhere. Fortunately, I have some experience with war zones like this, courtesy of McKinley's training rooms. Still, the pieces of the crumbled ceiling prove just as irksome, stabbing me through the fabric of my gloves. Some curses may or may not mist the air, especially when my hand comes down on the lenses of Jeffrey's now completely demolished glasses.

When I finally reach him, I realize my plan is incomplete. I'm not sure what to do now. Do I try to move him? Or will that only make things worse? I'm trained in first aid, but no one ever told me what to do in the event of falling through a *freaking ceiling*.

Just as I start to touch his shoulder, he moans, scaring the living daylights out of me. I reel back, clutching my chest. "God," I say, not sure whether I'm taking His name in vain or thanking Him for whatever miracle this constitutes. "Jeff," I say once my heart's restarted. His response, perhaps involuntary, is to make another agonized noise. "Hey. Easy does it there. Don't try to move, okay?"

"Long." Practically a moan.

"Yeah," I say, a smile fluttering across my lips. "I'm here. I'm with you."

"—happened?" he murmurs, losing the first word of the question in his daze. There was nothing gentle about his landing, and his body reflects that, a mess of different injuries. One arm in particular is contorted unnaturally, as though he tried to brace himself midair. And that's not the worst of it. He's bleeding from a head wound that I can't get at without turning his head, and I can't do *that* without risking further injury to his neck and spinal column.

"It looks like Churchill wasn't ready to let us go," I tell him. "The bombardment must have weakened the structure here. The snow hid the damage from view. We just had the misfortune of being the straw on the camel's back." I shake my head. Some days, it seems like if I didn't have bad luck, I'd have no luck at all. Unfortunately for Jeffrey, today is proving to be one of those days.

Above us, the crescendo of an approaching vehicle catches my attention, but there's something about the sound I don't trust. Chances are slim it's anyone from our team—anyone human.

I make the split-second decision to move Jeffrey, hoping it won't kill him. "This is going to hurt, but we have to hide," I tell him.

"Machines?"

"With our luck? Almost definitely."

I'm not sure, but I think he says something to the effect of not wanting to die. "You're not going to die," I promise in what I hope is a soothing tone. "But you might pass out. Try not to do that, though, if you can help it, okay?" Grabbing him underneath the armpits, ignoring the pitiful sounds he makes, I maneuver us both into the shade of an overhang, where there's still a part of the roof left as shelter.

No sooner are we tucked in beside the rubble than the roar of an engine grumbles by, its shadow passing across the floor. It slows and slows, and there's a terrifying moment when I'm sure it's going to stop, but then it picks up speed again, moving on. More close calls follow, but we remain undiscovered.

And then, like the flapping of angel's wings, I hear the chopper.

"Hang in there, Jeff," I say, trying not to notice the blood on my hands or the way his eyes have closed or the barely perceptible rise and fall of his chest. I gently prop him up against what was once a part of the ceiling but is now more of a warped ramp, slanted, having caught partway between the wall and floor.

The chopper is getting louder. Someone has to signal them. The impact that damaged my helmet also likely destroyed its already temperamental comm unit, but I give it another try anyway. Still nothing. Damn.

With Jeffrey out, the job falls to me. So carefully, very, *very* carefully, I use the same piece of angled debris to climb out, mindful of falling a second time. As soon as I pop my head over the edge of the hole, the wind catches me full in the face, setting my teeth chattering.

"Hey!" I yell, unafraid of what else might hear me. "Over here! We're here!" Between my frantic waving and flame-red hair, I hope

John and the rest will see me. And by *hope,* I mean they'd damn well better and *soon.* For Jeffrey's sake.

They make a single pass, checking for immediate threats in the nearby vicinity, before doubling back and landing nearby. Lefevre opens the sliding doors and motions for me. He's shouting something, but his words are drowned out by the chopper's downwash. I save my breath, knowing he won't hear me anyway, and use it to sprint/limp over to the chopper. I don't get inside.

"Jeff's hurt," I say over the *chop-chop-chop-chop* of the helicopter's blades. My hair is blowing every which way, into my eyes, my mouth. I'm starting to wish I'd just shaved it all off when I had the chance. "I need a couple of you to come back with me."

Lefevre's mouth twists unhappily, but he nods. "Where?" His boots crunch as they hit the icy ground, echoed by a second pair as Zelda joins us, and finally a third as Samuel exits the chopper. I'm happy to see him safe, happy to see them all safe, but as he starts to embrace me, I melt from his grasp with a quick "I'm fine."

I'm not fine. Nothing about this is fine. But the reunion has to wait, because Jeffrey can't. "Just over there," I say, waving them toward the hole. "Follow me."

They crawl down into the chamber and prevent me from doing the same. I'm dimly aware of Samuel saying something about needing to check me out, which seems wholly inappropriate for our current situation.

I brush him off, pushing his hands away every time they come near me. "Not right now," I grumble, straining to see down into the hole. "Well?" I shout against the background noise of blades going around and around and around. "What are you waiting for?" I turn toward Samuel. "What are they waiting for?"

Two go down, and two come back up. It sounds like a bad joke. "Where's Jeff?" I ask. "Why is he still down there? Is he too heavy or ... ?" Their faces are drawn and tired. *Lazy,* I think. *They're just being lazy.* "You can't leave him there. He needs help! You can't just—"

Very calmly, Lefevre takes me by the shoulders and turns me to face him.

"He's gone, Rhona."

This doesn't compute. "Where would he have gone? He's got a broken leg, and his head, it was—"

"No," Lefevre says. "He's dead."

"She's in shock," I hear Samuel say from far away. Who's he talking about? Zelda looks okay. Then I understand, coming back to myself suddenly. He's talking about me.

"Get her back to the chopper," Lefevre says, handing me off to Samuel.

"No!" I struggle against him. "How can that be? I was *just with him.* He was alive. He was breathing." I quiet and still. I feel moisture on my face, tears freezing into hard, little lines down my cheeks. "Are you sure?"

"Yes."

I shut my eyes, wanting the world to just go away and stay there. Lately, it's always in my face, belligerent and brutal, and never, ever fair. In the darkness behind closed lids, I search for some kind of composure. I have to do this, I remind myself. I have to be strong. But I'm so tired of having to be strong all the time.

When I open my eyes, Samuel's turned me away from the scene. "Wait," I say, shaking him off, and continue to shake even once freed.

Without much thought, I stumble back down into Churchill, where this whole thing started—and where it ended, for some. I didn't get to say good-bye to Ortega. I have nothing to remember him by. People should be remembered. Memories are all we have left in the end, after everything else has gone to dust.

"Bye, Glasses," I whisper, kneeling next to him. "Sorry about not keeping my promise. I guess I'm more of a politician than I thought."

I find his glasses on the ground and slip them into my pocket. Their translucent lenses are shattered all to pieces, but the frame is still there. Black, horn-rimmed, and stylishly made for another time and place where they would have been worn by a lawyer or maybe an actor. I never knew what profession Glasses was in before the Machinations. I never thought to ask.

"Rhona!" Samuel shouts down at me. "We've got to go!"

Once inside the chopper, I'm able to do a head count for the first time. Minus Ortega and Jeffrey, we're all accounted for. No small miracle, considering, but it seems to have come with a price, like so many things do.

I scoot over to Kennedy upon takeoff. The whole left side of his body is charred, the flesh flayed from the bone. He looks like an undercooked burger. Some bandaging and gauze have been applied to the worst areas. In other places, it looks like they used snow to try to cool down the superheated skin, judging by the puddle of water around him. "That looks like it hurts," I say, an understatement of the highest degree, but it makes his lips fracture into a small smile.

"His distraction worked a little too well," Rankin puts in, playing the role of field medic in Ortega's absence. He starts to change Kennedy's bandages, which are soaked with pus and blood. "Our boy here nearly blew himself to kingdom come and back again."

"I'll say. We've got a regular soldier on our team." I ruffle his ginger hair playfully, or what's left of it. One side's been singed black, burned off to the roots.

"These burns will become scars, huh?" Kennedy asks.

I look at Rankin briefly. He nods.

"Probably, yeah," I answer honestly.

"Then I'll wear them proudly," Kennedy declares.

"Yeah, well, let's try not to add any more to that collection, all right?" He nods, then winces as Rankin applies some sort of salve to his arm.

A couple of hours later, I get my first glimpse of Juneau, but it's not the city that captures my attention. It's Juneau the *mountain.*

I know Mount Juneau can't be bigger than Mount McKinley, but to use a word like smaller to describe her seems inadequate. In the shadow of the great white massif lurks the cold, hollowed-out husk of what used to be a lively port city. All the buildings look gray and starved of people.

"Even before the Machinations, there was a constant threat of avalanches, and not only during the winter months," Samuel informs me as John brings us in. I can see why. While spring is starting to show some skin at the lower elevations, the summit is still white with snow.

"Without routine grooming of the mountain, it's probably gotten worse," Samuel goes on, watching the heights uneasily. "A lot of melting snowpack up there, and all it takes is a little provocation." At this, I feel a shiver go up my spine, like someone's walked over my grave. For all I know, maybe someone has. Maybe this is my new Anchorage.

Our entry is the epitome of stealth, if you ignore the noise and the fact that we're a big, black bird in the sky. Okay, so maybe not *so* stealthy, but since we aren't attacked on sight, I have to assume John's doing something right.

He sets us down in what used to be a main street in downtown Juneau. "I'm going to make a few aerial passes of the city," he tells me. "See what I can see."

I nod. "Sounds good. Hit me up on the comm if you spot any survivors."

"Machines seem more likely, but I'll let you know either way. Good luck. Keep safe now."

"Right back at'cha, John."

I watch the chopper pull away in a windy swirl. John waves from the cockpit, and I return the gesture. Lefevre and Rankin help Kennedy toward the nearest building.

I'm watching them when it happens.

There's a loud sound like a clap of thunder, impossibly close, and I'm swept off my feet by a sudden wash of heat. Shards of metal rain down silently around me, fire streaking behind them like comet tails. I try to get up, but the world tips dangerously to one side, then the other, and I fall back to my hands and knees. A surreal quiet gives way to a violent ringing in my ears. I can't hear myself yelling, but I know that I am.

"Samuel! Rankin! Lefevre!"

Once I'm finally on my feet again, I turn toward the origin of the explosion.

The chopper is engulfed in flames, black smoke pouring from a mighty wound in its side. "No." I feel my mouth form around the word, my breath escaping in a panic. "No. No. No." Real sound is starting to come back into the world—fire crackles beyond the ringing in my ears. I shout again for help even as I stumble toward the wreckage.

A long, sharp whistle presages a secondary explosion.

I don't know what direction it comes from, but the antiaircraft missile finds its mark. I'm thrown to the ground again, this time onto the flat of my back, the air knocked right out of me. I lie panting for breath while the chopper burns. *Get up,* I tell myself. *Get up. Get moving. Run. RUN.*

John's gone. A single look at the twisted, melting aircraft breaks through the pain and shock.

There's nothing I can do for him now. There's nothing more the machines can do to him, either.

There won't be a body.

The chopper blades, weakened from the damage, collapse into the cockpit, and I can't watch any longer. My eyes water, stung by smoke or tears or both.

I rejoin my team—what's left of it—just as machines crawl out from the surrounding buildings.

They're like rats, carriers of death, and they're everywhere.

We're surrounded, outnumbered, and outgunned. That doesn't stop Zelda from firing the first couple of shots in anger, sure as hell not waiting to be fired upon. Before I know it, my own weapon is in my hands, warmed by several shots at the enemy. They return fire, but poorly—like the white-armored guys in those movies Samuel really likes. No bullets get anywhere close to me. Time their targeting sensors were upgraded or given a tune-up. Too bad I don't plan on giving them that opportunity.

"My charge is dead," Zelda growls, throwing her EMP-G to the ground. She pulls out a regular old handgun. Rankin's the second to run dry, followed by Kennedy, whose aim is terrible to begin with and who wastes a good deal of his ammo on bad shots. Lefevre and I are left with the job of disabling shields.

More machines emerge, appearing on rooftops and slinking out of alleys.

And then, behind them, men in masks and body armor.

They eliminate the machines nearest themselves in rapid succession, one right after the other, and then spread out to dispatch the rest with equal success. Soon, the machines cycle to their self-preservation subroutine and beat a haphazard retreat. My team picks some of them off as they run away.

Of course, that still leaves us the problem of a dozen armed strangers to deal with.

No one makes any sudden moves, which I think is probably for the best. We're all a little trigger-happy here. Finally, one of our masked saviors steps forward and keeps moving until he's standing right in front of me. Rankin places a hand on his chest when he's gotten close enough for his liking.

The stranger looks down at the hand and then at me. "This is how we greet old friends now?" says the man, hard eyes smiling through the slits in his ski mask.

I know that accent. But it can't be. I feel my expression slide into disbelief.

"Take off your mask," I order, and he obeys.

His face is red from the cold and bearded, but not beyond recognition.

"Ulrich!" I exclaim, forgetting myself long enough to wrestle him into a hug. Time seems to have mended whatever friction existed between us before, when I was seen only as Rhona 2.0—and not necessarily an improved version. Near-death experiences tend to have a way of sorting out petty differences.

I feel him wrap an arm around my back. *"Es ist gut du zu sehen."* He gives me a friendly squeeze.

"Yeah. Still don't know German, though."

Laughing, he says, "*Ja.* You should work on that. Now, we must go."

He turns around ... into a right hook from Zelda's fist. The men with him react, but don't make any attempt to intervene, making me wonder whether they're really *his* men at all. They could belong to Churchill or McKinley, for all I know. On our side, Samuel makes a motion toward stepping in, but Lefevre prevents it, his arm dropping down like a bar in front of him. The message is clear. This is between Ulrich and Zelda.

Ulrich touches his bloodied lip with a wry smile and starts to rise. She kicks him to keep him down. Well, that's another way to greet an old friend, I guess.

"Don't you move," she warns him. I'm not ready to get involved just yet. Both Ulrich and Zelda are headstrong personalities. For all I know, this might just be foreplay in their book. It's only when she pulls out her gun that I decide some actual diplomacy might be needed.

"Zelda, what are you doing?" I ask her. "Put that thing away."

"They killed him," Zelda says brokenly, waving her gun dangerously at him. "They killed him and sent this doppelgänger in his place!"

I suddenly understand and wonder why I didn't get it straightaway. The situation seems obvious now. Zelda's not like me. She doesn't believe in miracles because she's never been on the receiving end of one. I don't know what I can possibly say to change her mind at this point.

Thankfully, as it turns out, *I* don't have to say anything.

Considering everything he's been through, Ulrich is surprisingly quick. He's up in an instant, catching her wrist and wrenching the weapon free from her grip. She snarls at him in fractured German, rabid with emotion. He replies in kind, but continues to hold her tight. I don't know what they're saying—they're talking too fast and I'm pretty sure I took Spanish in high school—but eventually it breaks down to one phrase, repeated over and over again.

"Es tut mir Leid," he whispers to her. *"Mir Leid. Mir Leid."* I guess its meaning by the way they're both crying.

"It does me sorrow," Samuel says.

"What does?" I ask.

"No. It's what he's saying. He's sorry. I picked up a little Deutsch in my time with him, but that's a statement I heard rarely." He frowns thoughtfully. "What do you think he's apologizing for?"

"If I had to guess? The last three years."

"Ah."

Ulrich and Zelda conclude their messy reunion, sparing me the miserable awkwardness of interrupting. Zelda continues to stand next to him, looking fierce and proud and more herself, her eyes daring the shadows to produce more machines.

"There is much to discuss," Ulrich tells me.

"Funny. I was just thinking the exact same thing," I reply with a half smile. "I have a *lot* of questions, as you can imagine."

Ulrich gives gestures to his men to move out, adding, "Not here."

"One quick one: Are these your men?" He shakes his head. "Then whose?"

"Guess," he says with gruff humor, and I know.

"Take me to him."

TWENTY-SIX

TRAVELING THROUGH THE GRAY, dilapidated city has the uneasy quality of a dream, where I recognize the place as somewhere familiar, though it looks nothing like the place I'm thinking of.

I've never been to Juneau before, as far as I recall, but I have been to the graves of other great cities: Seattle, Vancouver, Anchorage—the last where my own fate was later sealed. But not quite tightly enough, apparently. It leads me to wonder about the people who weren't blessed with foresight, technology, and a genius best friend, the ones who lived and died here.

"Stop that," Samuel tells me.

"What?" I say.

"I know that look. That's your I'm-feeling-guilty-about-something-I-have-no-control-over look."

"My what?"

"Survivor's guilt," he explains. I give him my best You've-got-to-be-kidding look. He should be familiar with that one, too. "It's not uncommon for people who have experienced the kind of emotional trauma you've lived through to feel a sense of wrongdoing, regardless of responsibility. In fact, it used to be called concentration-camp syndrome, after the responses of those who had survived the Holocaust of the Second World War. I think it's safe to say we've all survived a sort of holocaust in recent years."

"Please, Samuel," I say, and I'm surprised by the desperation in my own voice. I wanted to sound careless. Mostly, I just sound broken. "Don't try to get me to talk about my feelings right now."

"Better to get them out in the open where they can breathe than keep them trapped inside your head where they can fester."

"They're thoughts, Samuel, not gangrene."

"I don't know. Thinking is the most virulent disease in the history of the world. Thoughts are powerful, Rhona, and it's not always healthy to leave them to their own devices. Trust me. Bad ones will poison every aspect of your life, if you let them. So *don't* let them."

"So you're my shrink now, too?"

"No, just your friend. Like I've always been."

Samuel falls back to the rear of our group, to speak with Lefevre in quiet tones. My words to him were more defensive than I'd have liked, and I wish I had a better excuse for them. But my shoulder still hurts from when I dislocated it, and my heart aches with the loss of three good men. I shake off a lot of things, but the trauma of the past few days is beyond even my superhuman abilities to cope, apparently. *Keep it together, Rhona. Just a little longer, at least.*

But I can't help stewing over Samuel's words. Survivor's guilt. Can you have survivor's guilt for surviving yourself? That thought feels like a step in the wrong direction, emotionally, so I leave it alone. I don't pick at it, like I might've done a couple of months ago.

The men and women with Ulrich, most McKinlians, give us a wide berth, keeping an invisible perimeter against the machines about half a mile out. As a consequence, our little group encounters very few enemies. Apart from the machines, the only squatters we find on the street are derelict tanks—relics from the war, back when it could legitimately be called one. They keep company with a downed commercial airliner, probably on its way to safety, and the wreckage of what appears to have been a fighter jet, although it's mangled almost beyond recognition.

"We are almost there now," Ulrich announces. "Keep your guard up."

Looking around, I start to notice faces in the shattered windows and behind crumbling facades decimated by mortar fire. "Ulrich," I start to say, not taking my eyes off the half-hidden souls.

"Friendlies," he assures me. "Churchill and ... others. Refugees, all. Ignore them. They are no danger to us."

"They look terrified."

"They are. But not of us."

It's difficult to be surrounded by these peering faces, each one a mask of suffering. I focus on being a leader instead of a person. A leader can be sympathetic, but also detached. I need to be able to think, and I can't do that if my heart is hemorrhaging into my head.

"How has everyone been surviving here?" I ask. "Did the evac teams bring enough supplies with them? Why haven't the machines pressed the attack yet?"

Ulrich looks at me over his wild man's beard, a hint of grumpiness in his manner. Just like old times. "Which of those questions do you want me to answer?"

"All of them?"

"There were reserves, before they arrived. They brought only what was necessary with them. Food, water, the clothing on their backs. Not much. Not enough." He shakes his head, snuffling from what sounds like the vestiges of a long illness. Some kind of cold, maybe. "It is not a matter of machines, but of time. *Immer mit der Unfreundlichkeit der Zeit.*" I give the German and his German a blank stare. "Always with the unkindness of time," he translates.

I think I understand what he means. Time always has the final say in who lives and who dies, and time, right now, is allied against us. "Folksy," I reply, dry mouthed.

He snuffles again, or maybe he's just snorting at me.

"But that still doesn't explain why the machines aren't taking advantage of our weak defenses. We're prime pickings here, and they're doing—what? Taking potshots at us in the street? It makes no sense." His silence is a soliloquy unto itself. "Unless ... it does. Because they're waiting for something." I move in front of Ulrich, stopping him. "I'm right, aren't I? So, what aren't you telling me?"

Our group halts, but Ulrich orders them to keep going. One of his subordinates knows the way. Rankin and Kennedy continue on while Lefevre and Samuel hang back, as does Zelda, who doesn't even bother to pretend she isn't listening in.

We stand there, in the heart of a dead city, until I finally ask the question I really want the answer to. "Tell me, Ulrich, how are you even alive? How are you *here*?" I know there's a connection, even if I can't understand the threads themselves.

"We are wasting time." But I don't budge and Ulrich breathes deeply, relaxes his rifle against his shoulder. "If you must know, I was true to my word. I said I would not let the machines take me alive, and they did not."

"You're looking pretty good for a dead man," I say.

He grunts. "The pot mocking the kettle." He motions in the same direction the others headed in. "Come. Walk. It is not safe to stand around. It invites trouble." By now, the distance between our groups is enough to afford some privacy for this conversation. I wait for him to say more.

"When I pulled the pin of one of my grenades, nothing happened. I fumbled for another, but by that time, the machines were on me. They rushed me, blitzkrieg, just as I pulled the pin. I remember little else after that moment, save the taste of blood in my mouth." He spits for good measure. "I was proud to die there, for you, for the war effort. And I am tired. The truth is there was a part of me glad to be done with it."

Zelda looks away sharply. I think the words hurt her, because she was the one left behind. At the same time, I know how Ulrich feels. The struggle of living in this mechanical world, of endlessly fighting, is enough to wear down even the hardiest soul.

"But the machines," Ulrich finally goes on, "they brought me back.

I must have been dead for minutes, and they would not let me rest even then."

My stomach drops. "Why would they do that? Why would they save you? I mean, not that I'm complaining, but the machines are programmed killers ..."

"Not all of them, not always. Some were programmed as field medics, surgeons. The knowledge of medicine is still there. I don't know how, but they restarted my heart and kept me alive long enough to ... Long enough." Ulrich grimaces, breathing fog into the chilled air. Zelda steps closer, placing a hand on his arm.

Ulrich waves off her concern, but I have to ask, "Long enough for what, Ulrich?"

"What do you think?" Zelda snaps. "They tortured him."

"They asked me questions—about you, about the resistance, its bases and facilities, its weapons and resources. I would give them nothing, of course, and so they tried to break me the old-fashioned way." He rolls up a sleeve to reveal electrical burns along his arm, only partially healed and still painful looking. "But I was no songbird. I would not sing. So, they tried alternate means." I don't ask what those were. I have some idea of the horrors the machines can inflict on a body made of flesh and blood.

"Ich werde sie alle brechen," Zelda promises him, and I notice how that last word sounds oddly like "break." She's swearing vengeance for his pains, destruction of the ones responsible. In a twisted kind of way, suited to them, it's romantic. I feel a pang of loneliness. Did Camus try to avenge me, I wonder? But the musing travels like a clean shot, passing through my heart quickly without collateral damage. It's in the past. I just need to find him—alive and safe.

"Obviously you didn't give up McKinley's location," I continue, watching my step among some debris, "and now you're here, so how did you escape?"

"Pah." He scratches his beard. "It was not escape. I was released."

"Come again?"

"They let me go. I didn't realize this at the time, as they did not make it easy; I had to fight my way free. But it was all a setup. I ended up here, in time, and they have been monitoring me since. Put the pieces together yourself."

The lightbulb comes on like the damn sun. "Oh, God, Ulrich. They were using you as bait?"

"*Ja, richtig.* They thought I would send for help, or try to make my way back to base. Either way would have gotten them what they wanted. I said I was not a songbird. I am not a homing pigeon either. I knew something was not right."

All this time, I think. *He has been alone all this time, to protect everyone else.* And here I thought I knew what it meant to be strong.

"But it does not matter now," he says, brows drooping over tired eyes. "You are here. Churchill is here. The machines are here. It was for nothing."

"No," I tell him, firmly grabbing him by the shoulder. He looks at me. "Not for nothing." And I intend to prove it to him.

The last leg—more of an ankle really—of the journey to Juneau's makeshift base of operations brings us to a seven-story structure that served as an apartment complex before the Machinations. Its top two floors have been blown away, naked rebar and other infrastructure jutting out like exposed bones. The rest of the building appears to be mostly intact, though. A tough, sturdy old thing by the looks of it, with a concrete foundation in the form of an underground parking level. In three days, it's amazing how many defenses they've managed to lay. A lot of it looks like leftovers from previous resistance factions. The surface level of the entire garage area is boarded all the way around with wood and chunks of plaster, possibly salvaged from the upper floors. They've gotten creative, too, using furniture, vehicles, and machine carcasses for further protection—the latter maybe as a visual aid, warning the machines away, like heads on pikes. Not that it'll have any effect on the machines, but it's the thought that counts.

So maybe they're not *great* defenses, but they're something—and with machines prowling about, it's certainly better than nothing.

We stop short of the original entrance. On the ground, you can just make out an arrow pointing inside, faded by the elements, still trying to direct traffic that no longer exists. Several well-armed soldiers spy on us from behind their fortifications, as though our identities matter at this point. We're all human. That should be enough. Together, they push the barrier aside, letting us pass.

"Good to see you, Commander Long," one says to me, his breath misting the air as he gives a salute. "Thought we were going to be left for dead out here."

"Yeah," agrees the other, a lanky, skittish-looking man who seems ill-suited for military business. "So, uh, where are the rest of our reinforcements?"

"Get out of the way," Ulrich grumbles. "You're holding us up."

He pushes inside and drags the rest of us with him. It's probably for the best they don't know about our unfortunate state of affairs. Primarily the fact that there *are* no reinforcements. In all likelihood, no one's coming. "You're doing great. Keep up the good work," I say to the pair of guards over my shoulder, some drive-by morale boosting. I don't know if it'll help, but it can't hurt.

Ulrich leads us one level down into the underbelly of the parking garage. The elevator's long since stopped working. A scrap of paper flutters as we pass. *OUT OF ORDER*, it reads, hastily written by a person who probably knew no greater inconvenience than having to take the stairs.

We continue our descent down the car ramp, where many vehicles are still parked, orphaned by their owners, forever waiting. It's sadder than it has any right to be. They're just cars, for pity's sake. But they carried people once, to work, to home, to family and friends, and now they sit decaying and purposeless.

I don't realize I'm staring so intently at them until a face pops up in the window of a van, making me nearly jump out of my skin. The face, which belongs to a boy, smiles. A woman is with him—his mother, I'd guess, by the way she reprimands him and forces him back onto the seat to sleep. "They're using the cars for beds?" I say to Ulrich.

"Homes," he corrects.

We continue walking, and I pay no more attention to the cars, wanting to give their inhabitants some privacy.

The basement parking area is dimly lit, illuminated only by the electric lamps the evac teams brought with them, and some fires started in a couple of barrels for warmth. It's hard but not impossible to make out the features of the men and women gathered together for survival, hunched around the fires like our first ancestors millennia ago, when there were other things to fear in the dark.

I grow increasingly anxious when I can't find the face I'm looking for, and the pulsing atmosphere of fear doesn't help any.

"Wait here," Ulrich says.

I don't wait there. I step forward, asking, "Does anyone here know where Commander Forsyth is?" I voice the question like this is some kind of open forum, hoping someone knows something. Anything.

"He's not back yet," volunteers a woman, and it takes me a moment to recognize Evelyn Meir beneath all the dirt, grime, and frost. I'm caught off guard by a sharp stab of anger, a bitter recognition of the injustice. Why should she be alive, with all her scheming and selfish politicking, when Jeffrey—who put his base before himself—is dead?

"Where's he gone?" I ask, trying to dam up my resentment.

"I couldn't tell you. I'm not exactly in good standing with our dear Commander Forsyth."

"Then why are you wasting my time?"

"For starters, I was hoping to change that. Most believe in working from the ground up, but I prefer aiming for the top." I choose to ignore her poor, all too apropos metaphor, for the sake of civility. "However, if I can be of assistance to you or Camus or our cause, do let me know."

For a woman as eloquent as Meir, I can't help feeling every word is deliberate. Calculated. She hasn't changed at all. The cuts and bruises add a degree of vulnerability, meekness, maybe, but they haven't broken her ambitions. Unbelievable. Who would've guessed the machinations of man could ever be as unfeeling as those of the machines themselves?

I step close to her, keeping my voice low. "I don't know what it must be like in your imagined world of political intrigue, *former* Commander, and quite frankly I don't want to, but if you jeopardize the safety of me or any of these other people here, I swear to God ... I'll give you to the machines."

Her smile freezes on her face. I've surprised her. It's a good feeling. "You must have misheard me. I was offering to help—"

"I heard what you said. Now hear what I'm saying. I know what you're trying to do. No more, Evelyn. You try anything like the stunt you pulled at McKinley, and we're going to have problems."

She blinks, caught out. "As you say," she demurs.

I leave while I still have the upper hand, while my temper holds. "Keep an eye on her," I order one of the soldiers nearby, a man I recognize from one of the McKinley evac teams. In truth, I don't expect she'll try anything now, especially without any people or resources at her disposal, but better safe than sorry.

"Rhona would have been more diplomatic," Ulrich says as we're walking away, a smile twitching beneath his bushy beard.

"Not this Rhona," I respond, rubbing the pain in my shoulder. "This Rhona watched better people than Meir die today. *This* Rhona is sick and tired of all the ... all this ..." I struggle for an appropriate curse.

"*Schiesse,*" Ulrich supplies in German.

"If by *schiesse* you mean complete bullshit, then yes."

"Commander!" I turn to see Rankin booking it down the ramp toward us. I'm worried by the absence of Kennedy, and the tone that tells me something's happened.

"Is Kennedy all right?" I blurt out.

He looks confused, but recovers swiftly. "Kennedy? Yeah, the kid's just sleeping off some meds in one of the upper levels. But that's not why I'm here. The away team's just returned, and you're gonna want to come quick, Rhona. Camus is with them, but he's in a bad way."

"How bad?" I ask as we race back up the ramp, to a back entrance on the ground floor of parking. Soldiers are still stumbling in, dazed and bloodied. I search but don't find Camus among the shell-shocked faces. "Where is he?"

"They must have taken him upstairs. They've set up a kind of clinic for themselves on the third and fourth floors. It's this way." *Not a practical location for the seriously wounded,* the logical portion of my brain manages to think against the screaming background crescendo of anxiety. But it's quickly forgotten.

"How bad, Rankin?" I ask him again in the stairwell.

"The machines got the drop on them. He took two rounds in the chest." He glances back at me from four steps up, reads my halted expression. "Sorry, Rhona. That's all I know."

My response is to take the stairs two steps at a time. *Faster, faster.* It seems almost inconceivable that Camus could die before I reach him, after everything I've done to get here. But then, I haven't exactly had the best of luck lately.

We catch them on a landing before the last flight of stairs. They've had to stop so Camus can catch his breath. He leans heavily on Samuel, who's beneath one of his arms, helping to support his weight.

A different man—one I don't recognize, but who has the look of a medical professional about him (or maybe that's wishful thinking)—is beneath Camus's other arm. It seems they're the only thing keeping him upright, and I feel a bit faint myself at the sight of all the blood. *Too much,* I keep thinking, my head hot and swimming with fear. *It's too much blood.*

I rush to Camus without considering the consequences. He blinks at me, eyes glazed with pain, but the recognition is almost immediate. "No," he moans. "No, no."

"Why can't you ever be happy to see me?" I tease him, but I'm too full of emotion and it comes out sounding more like a genuine complaint.

"Of course I'm—" Pain splits the thought in half. His head drops forward and he wheezes. "Why did you come?" he asks me, before turning on Samuel, all accusation. "Why did *you* let her come?"

Samuel's brows lower defensively. "When was the last time I *let* Rhona do anything?"

"Come on now, Commander," says Camus's other support beam. There are flecks of silver in the man's brown hair. I hope that means he's old and wise and he'll know what to do when it comes to saving Camus's life. Because right now, I'm watching that life leaking down his arm, dripping onto the floor in dark droplets.

"We have to get you to the third floor. Can't have you bleeding out on the landing, not one of our commanders-in-chief. No, sir. We're almost there."

Although it's clearly agonizing for him, he takes a step, one and then another, tackling the stairs with jaws clenched and the unwavering determination he's known for. But even still, he doesn't make it to the top on his own power. His strength is flagging by the sixth step, and gone by the eighth. It takes all of us to carry him the rest of the way, trying not to jostle him and make the injuries worse.

As we lay him down on a bed, he reaches for me, his hand passing across the flap of my jacket, just missing me. I step closer, take his hand in mine, but it's only for a moment. "Don't you leave me," I tell him, right before I'm rushed out of the room by the medics.

TWENTY-SEVEN

CAMUS FLATLINES SOMETIME in the middle of the night.

None of the doctors tell me directly; instead I have to hear about it through the grapevine, and even then accounts are confused. One man gossips to his friends that Commander Forsyth is dying; another man says he heard he was already dead. When I ask another woman, one of the medical staff, she staunchly insists he survived surgery just fine. But I see the doubt in her eyes. That's what scares me the most. All of this is merely compounded by the fact that when I try to see him, the doctors refuse to let me inside the room.

"I want to see him," I say, and if it's not clear by my manner or tone, I add a hard "*Now.*"

The physician looks uncomfortable with the confrontation, but it's clear he's already gotten his orders from someone else. "There was a lot of blood. We're still cleaning up ..."

"Is he dead?" Somehow I manage to distance myself from the words. It's the only thing keeping me from screaming them.

"Dead?" His eyebrows rise almost comically high. "No! I mean, no, of course not. Who told you that, Commander?" The relief brings me right to the edge of hysteria. I have to cover my face with my hands to hide the shine of tears in my eyes.

The physician continues quickly. "Commander Forsyth had a close call about half an hour ago, but the doctors have stabilized him since then."

My throat is still tight when I ask, "Is he conscious?"

The discomfort returns, apparently slipping in somewhere beneath his shirt collar, since that's what he keeps tugging at. "I couldn't tell you, Commander."

Something clicks. I shake my head. "He's conscious. Or was ..."

"Briefly," he admits.

"And I'm willing to bet he told you to keep me out, huh?"

His silence is as good as a confirmation. I don't know whether to feel angry or amused.

Camus and his stupid pride.

"I'm going in now," I tell him, and this time he doesn't argue.

Inside, the room is the size of a one-bedroom apartment—because it once *was* a one-bedroom apartment. A place to start a life. There are still decorative touches from the previous owner, lamps and bookends and cheap posters masquerading as famous works of art. I also notice a depression in one side of a sofa from where someone must have spent years wearing in their spot. Even having been abandoned for so long, the place still has a hauntingly lived-in quality to it.

That eerie feeling might owe something to the blood, too. When we carried him in, Camus was bleeding badly—I know, I *remember*. But the scene before me puts it into too fresh a perspective.

Bloody spots in the carpet have turned brown, dried and crusted. Some Churchillians are trying to scrub out the stains, but they're having a hard time with it. On the wall near the door, a red handprint is preserved where one of us must have touched it for additional support while bringing Camus inside. Seems the physician wasn't lying about cleaning up, after all. I'd think it a waste of time if it weren't something to keep the civilians busy. Any distraction, no matter how simplistic or moderately unpleasant, is probably welcome at this point.

I carefully step around the cleaning crew in time to run into the man from before, the one with gray in his hair, as he's leaving the bedroom-surgery. I catch a glimpse of Camus inside, but only a glimpse, because the doctor shuts the door behind him.

"Commander Long," he greets me.

"How is he?" I ask, thinking it might be a good idea to prepare myself for what I'm going to find past that door.

"Weak," he answers candidly, "but strong willed."

I smile halfheartedly. "Sounds about right. What's all this about him flatlining, though?"

"There was a close call earlier. Closer than I'd like, I'll admit. He's just resting now. I'd recommend not disturbing him, but I have a feeling that's a request that will go ignored."

"I see my reputation precedes me," I reply. "Don't worry. I won't be long."

As I pass him, I place a hand on his shoulder. "And thanks, Doc," I add. "For everything you've done."

"You know, I was a pediatrician before the Machinations. Back then, I never could have imagined treating gunshot wounds inflicted by thinking, reasoning machines. And now here I am. Funny how life turns out, isn't it?" He smiles grimly, sadly. I know that look. He doesn't know how he got here. Do any of us?

Upon entering the bedroom, I'm immediately confronted with the sight of Mount Juneau from the nearest window. It takes up the entire pane, a hulking mass of black topped with glowing white, almost yellow in the moonlight. *Breathtaking,* I think, even as my breath fogs up the glass. It's easier to look outside, above the ranks of machines and men ...

Away from the man lying in bed behind me.

It's ironic, really. For the past five days, I've longed for nothing more than to see Camus's face again. And now I'm afraid to look at him.

"Talk about your room with a view, huh?" I break the ice with as neutral a topic as I can find. I would've opened with commentary on the weather, but seeing as it's night, it's difficult to tell what it's like outside. Still dismal, I don't doubt. From what I've observed, Alaska vacillates between two weather patterns: cold and cloudy, or cloudless and freezing. I rub my hands together for warmth and then blow into them, achieving little effect. "Could use a better heater, though ..."

"Rhona." His voice is a dry croak. He swallows, trying to fix it. "I should have known you'd subvert my plans. Somehow, you always manage ... to do that." He closes his eyes for a moment, head lolling to the side on his pillow.

"Well, you know me. I hate to be predictable."

"Mhm." His lips form a weak, fatigued smile.

I sit down on the edge of the mattress, going over my thoughts and wondering if there's something I could be doing for him. Camus reads my mind. "Could you pass me some water, please?" I grab the glass on the end table, and hold it to his lips, which are cracked and peeling from the cold. "Thank you," he says after he's had enough to drink.

"How are you?" I ask him.

"I feel like I've been shot," he answers. "But other than that ..."

I smile. "Camus, did you give the physicians outside orders to keep me out?"

Camus rolls his eyes at my musical gotcha tone. "I gave orders to keep everyone out. Seeing your commander bleeding and bedridden is not exactly what you would call good for morale. But you especially, yes, I didn't want—I know how you feel about blood."

I set Camus's empty glass back on the table, largely in an effort to avoid looking at him when I say, "Yeah, well, you should also know how I feel about *you*." It's still a little weird being this frank and open about my feelings for Camus, since for the longest time it was the enormous elephant in our quarters we just didn't acknowledge.

Camus tries to sit up, but his wounds prevent him. I place a hand on his shoulder, encouraging him to stay still. His eyes are filled with love and worry as he stares at me.

"You shouldn't be here. Wait, I'm not finished," he adds, cutting off my objection. "You shouldn't be here, and you know exactly why, so don't bother pretending otherwise." He pauses, emits a sigh. "All the same, for purely selfish reasons, I'm glad you are."

He raises his arm, inviting me to curl up next to him on the bed, and I'm cautious not to jostle him as I do. His cheek falls against my head, and he breathes out. The tension leaves him for a time.

"Camus," I ask after a brief interlude of peace and quiet. There's been a question building inside me for a long time, and I decide now's as good a time as any to have it answered. Now might be the only chance I get to ask. "If I'd had all my memories, like I was supposed to, do you think ... would we have made it work? Could it ever have worked like I planned?"

"I imagine Rhona thought so, at the time," he answers vaguely.

"I want to know what *you* think."

Camus lapses into a considering silence. "Maybe," he says at last, but then corrects himself with an agitated sigh and answers more reflectively. "I don't know." He doesn't have to do this. Camus is an excellent liar, good enough to lead me on if he wanted to. The fact that he doesn't shows a willingness to be honest. I appreciate that, even if it hurts to hear the truth. "Science is capable of extraordinary things, wonderful things, but even it has its limits. It would have to, in order to allow room for miracles."

"Now who's guilty of sentimentality?"

"I've been shot. Indulge me." His thin smile splinters into a frown. "What I'm trying to say is that science can't manufacture emotion. It can't re-create the human experience with all its infinite variety and—and color." He wheezes, coughing some. His lungs sound like they've been through a cheese grater. I realize this conversation is an effort for him and know it can't go on for much longer. "Our previous attempts to do so, if you'll recall, didn't turn out so well for us."

"True, but there's a difference between creating artificial intelligence that can't feel and a living consciousness that can," I counter. Isn't there?

"I'm not trying to debate the finer points of philosophy with you, Rhona," he says, although I think he'd like to if he were feeling better.

"I'm only pointing out that science and technology have a dark side. We can't expect to keep playing God without consequences."

"What about me? Am I just the fallout of bad judgment? Human hubris in the flesh?"

"No." He answers so quickly there can be no doubt he means it. "I'll admit, I'm still uncomfortable with the whole notion of cloning, but even bad ideas sometimes have good outcomes."

Something brushes against me, and I look down to find Camus's fingers reaching toward my hand. His fingers are cold and stiff, so I try warming them between my palms. His other hand comes over and closes on mine, holding them intensely still.

His eyes meet mine, serious but gentle. "History will be the judge of what Samuel and Rhona, Matsuki, and the rest of them did, whether it was morally or ethically right. But you're more than some test-tube marvel. The things you've done, the people you've helped and saved, who you continue to help and save—science can't take the credit for that."

"You know, normally this would be the time I'd answer with something clever," I tell him with a short laugh, batting away some of the tears his words have brought to my eyes.

Camus rubs his thumb back and forth over the back of my hand. I find it soothing.

"One more thing, while we're clearing the air," I say after a moment. "Back at McKinley, I received private footage of the council meeting where Samuel reviewed my ... case, I guess you'd call it. Was that your doing, by any chance?"

Camus starts coughing again, but nods. "I forwarded it to you when I was sent the footage, since I obviously wasn't able to be at that meeting myself. I thought you should be made aware of your situation. And while we're clearing the air," he says, "I confess there were other, less kind reasons at the time, but they no longer exist."

"No?" I ask, unable to sound anything but hopeful.

"No," he says, holding my gaze with feeling.

His coughing keeps up, however, interrupting our moment and

delaying more of the conversation we need to have. It causes him to slouch forward. He lets go of my hands and pushes me from the bed. "Let me get you some more water," I say, rising.

He coughs into his hand, and it comes away from his mouth black and wet in the dark. "Maybe a doctor would be better."

"He's going to be fine," I tell Samuel and Ulrich, just like I've told everyone else, and will continue telling myself until it's proven true—or false. *No. Don't think that way.*

Until then, I become an unwilling participant in the waiting game. Again. With the machines ominously holding their positions, there's little else I can do but wait.

Samuel and I are just joining Ulrich for a quick meal when Zelda shows up, drawing the latter away to collaborate on something. She doesn't say squat to us, but she does look excited—though not necessarily in a happy way. I nibble on some saltines, the only thing my stomach can handle while continuing to flip-flop in anxiety—and try to leave the worrying in the back of my mind. Samuel distracts me with a memory of eating this same brand of crackers in the yard our houses shared back in New Mexico.

When Ulrich and Zelda finally come back in, her edginess has spread to him.

"Do you want to tell her, or should I?" Zelda asks.

Ulrich rubs his face, looking all sorts of tired. "Zelda has a theory—"

"It's more than just a theory," she says. Instead of sitting down, she paces back and forth. Her energy is contagious, and I find my leg rocking to her stride. "I've been trying to figure out what the machines' end game is. Their recent behavior is all wrong for their basic programming. They have the numbers and the weaponry to take us out, but instead they're just sitting on the perimeter. I couldn't figure it out ... *until* I started thinking about everything else that's happened.

"The machines want to take you alive, Long. They hinted at as much back at Churchill. It's the reason they didn't fire on you in the facility, and again why they kept missing once we were out in the open here. Remember, they blew up the chopper only *after* you got out. It's not convenience or luck. Put it all together." I have, and I don't like the picture it's forming. "The machines aren't attacking *us* because they don't want to risk killing *you*."

"If you're wrong about this ..." I start to tell her.

Zelda lifts her chin stubbornly. "Remember why you brought me on this mission. I'm the expert—"

"Actually, *you* volunteered."

"—so you're just going to have to trust me on this one. I know what I'm talking about. I helped program them. And I'm telling you, they're up to something bad."

I worry my bottom lip between my teeth, thinking. "Jeffrey said he believed the attack on Churchill was the bait to lure us out into the open. He was sure Juneau was where the trap would snap closed. But they're not going to just wait out there forever, right?" I give Zelda a direct look. "I mean, how much patience did you and your programmer friends put into those things?"

"The higher echelon controlling them is adopting new strategies all the time. They could be trying to starve us out, but that's the least efficient option."

"And what's the most efficient option?"

"Depends," Zelda says.

"On?"

"On the risk versus the reward. They'll probably try to draw you out into open combat. If that fails, they'll move in to intercept. Never mind the risk of killing you. And everyone will be caught in the cross fire then."

"Why are they taking so long to decide in the first place?"

She frowns, exasperated with all the questions. "How am I supposed to know? They've evolved since their creation. I'm not a bloody machine whisperer. The way I see it, you must figure into some pretty big, pretty nasty plans of theirs. Could be they want to use you as a Ganger to set more traps for the resistance. But rest assured, I'd put a few rounds in your back before I let that happen."

"Thanks?" I say uncertainly, then look to Ulrich. "What do you make of all this?"

"They have been amassing forces in Juneau for some time," he allows. "It's possible they are wanting to kill two birds with one stone."

"Or not kill, in my case," I add dryly. I grab another cracker and pop it into my mouth, chewing nervously. "Maybe we can use this to our advantage."

"How so?" Samuel asks.

Everyone looks at me, waiting for some grand plan. "Sorry to disappoint you all, but I'm still working on that part," I admit. I stand up, taking the box of crackers with me. "I just need somewhere quiet and some time to think. I'll come up with something."

He's going to be fine, and I'm going to come up with something.

TWENTY-EIGHT

I ESCAPE ONTO THE ROOF. Or what now serves as the roof. Formerly the eleventh floor, according to the gold, peeling placard in the stairwell, but the ceiling has collapsed in, exposing it to the sky. Of the few walls remaining, each bears exposure damage, and none have any color left to them from being ice-blasted by the snows of six winters. But it could be worse. Many of the surrounding buildings have been leveled—probably during whatever bombardment did this. Mere luck appears to have played a role in sparing the apartment complex a more ignominious fate.

I'm not surprised to find snipers positioned, two to every corner, with their sights trained on the streets. It's frigid up here, with nothing to break the wind—or their concentration. Even if they mind the weather, they don't show it. They barely acknowledge me with more than brief glances.

Not wishing to disturb them, I pick an empty spot on the eastern edge of the building, where part of the wall serves as a guardrail to keep me from falling down to the broken asphalt below. Now, *that* would be embarrassing.

I sit down on a pile of rubble—not the most comfortable seat in the house, but it works—and wait for some divine inspiration to hit me.

In pondering upon this midnight dreary, I take account of everything we have at our disposal, versus the enemy's resources. Ours is a much shorter list. Humanity is stuck fighting from the corner, the same corner we inadvertently put ourselves in by delegating our dirty work to machines in the first place. I look out at the perimeter, where I can just make out the hard, angular silhouettes of the machines and the faint, ruddy glow of their optics. They've congregated carelessly in the open streets as opposed to hiding in the material graveyard around them. And why not? They have nothing to fear from us.

As much as I want to keep an eye on the machines, my gaze continues to be drawn to the mountain that judges the city, like some ancient guardian. It didn't do much to protect Juneau before, though; why should it now? If anything, it's more of a danger.

It wouldn't take much, I think, eyeing the snowy precipice. *And it'd all come raging down.* Snow was unique—it could be soft and romantic, or violent and terrible. Much like water, and water always took the path of least resistance, too.

I look at the mountain for a long time, and then back to the streets, trying to work it out.

The path of least resistance. The path *of* resistance.

"That's it," I breathe into the black night.

I head back inside and take the stairs down to the third floor so I can speak with Camus for what could very well be the last time, if my plan goes south. Part of me hopes to leave with his blessing. Instead, Camus gets upset. I try to make him understand, but all he sees is the enormous black mouth of the tunnel ahead. He can't see the light at the end, like I do. He doesn't believe it exists, like I have to.

He calls my behavior rash, and me suicidal.

"You'll die," he says, an accusation, as if that's what I want. "You do understand that."

"Maybe," I agree. "But I have to try."

"But why? Why does it always, *always* have to be you, Rhona? Why not someone else? Why not—" I think he wants to say "Why not me?"

Seeing his stricken look, I flash back to the last memory I have of my previous life. Camus clutching me in the snow. I'm shivering. Gasping. Dying. *No, Rhona, please,* he begs, his tone alternating between soft entreaty and a firmness that insists I will not die. *Stay with me. A little longer, love. Keep awake. Keep your eyes open. Rhona. Hold on. Help is* ... He doesn't finish the thought, because he can't—because he's choking on tears, because he knows. Help will be too late coming. His lips are chapped and bleeding, but when they're on my lips, it doesn't matter. I know now he was trying desperately to revive me through some miracle of love. And I wish he'd gotten that miracle, that lonely miracle, because I think it's the only one Camus has ever asked for.

In the end, the doctors have to sedate him after he tries to rise from the bed to prevent me from leaving and opens some of his stitches. I cup my mouth, trying to contain my horror as he staggers toward me. My last image of Camus is his dark eyelashes fluttering closed, sealing his fears into the blackness with him. The words he would've used to contest my decision sputter out on his lips, dying to silence, my name among them.

This time, I do say good-bye. But Camus is already unconscious and can't hear me.

I start down the stairs at a rapid clip, pausing on a landing to lean against the wall and contain my tears, my fears. It doesn't work. Instead, my breath comes in harsh sobs as I come completely undone. I'm not sure if I can do this. But I'm sure I have to.

After another few minutes, I straighten up.

It takes about ten minutes for everyone to convene after I send a directive to gather all the squad leaders on the tenth floor, where there is a good view of the mountain.

Samuel stands beside me as the last few straggle in. "You've come up with a plan, I take it?"

"Yeah, but I don't know how popular it's going to be. You're definitely not going to like it very much."

"What? Why? Rhona?"

Instead of answering him, I call the meeting to order. No one is required to sit down; there's not enough furniture to accommodate that anyway. Most choose a random spot in the room to stand, leaving me at eye level with everyone, on even footing, just like I want it. Pedestals are places best reserved for dead gods.

I smile, knowing it might be one of my last opportunities to do so.

"Well," I say, meeting the curious gazes of my allies. "Why don't we get this party started then? I hope at least some of you got some sleep, because it's gonna be a long night ..."

TWENTY-NINE

DAY BREAKS on a gray and thankless morning. Cast in such a bland palette, it's hard to tell where the mountain ends and the sky begins. Today they're one and the same, heaven and earth. It'll sure make for a sight, like bringing the wrath of God down upon the machines.

Provided the plan gets that far.

It's taken the better part of the morning, but everyone's finally in position. Back at the main apartment complex and in all the hidey-holes nearby, the hatches have been battened wherever possible, and wherever impossible, people have moved to higher ground. Samuel and some other math types did the calculations and I'm not worried for our people if we succeed. If we fail, then I'll be worried.

Or I'll be dead. Either way, it'll be pretty definitive.

While the remaining squads check in over comms, I preview the street one last time. The machines appear to be powered down, hibernating in the cold, but I know it's a trick. More than two dozen wait twenty yards from this building, and I'm sure more are hidden behind them in the veil of fog. From this distance, the group doesn't look like much—nothing that couldn't be handled by patient guerrilla tactics.

But the clock is ticking on our supplies, and we don't have time to play Joey Peashooter with them.

This is a massive gamble, I know, all resting on a strategy that could absolutely backfire. As much as I hope my live appeal reached someone, we can't rely on the chance that some hoped-for forces are going to ride to our rescue. We're alone, and this is it. The final showdown between man and machine.

"Are you ready?" Samuel asks me. I can't see his face behind the mask of his combat helmet, but I hear the skepticism mingled with fear. Not for himself, if I had to wager, betting on the fact he's shown no concern for his own safety thus far. "You know, there might be another way."

"Yeah?" I say, removing my weapons. "What's that?"

His silence is pronounced. "I wish I knew," he answers helplessly.

I pull his helmeted head toward me, placing a kiss on the top of its black visor. "Thanks for sticking it out with me this far, Samuel. You've been brave enough for us both, much braver than you give yourself credit for. But now it's my turn."

"Rhona." There's such an *ache* in the way he says my name. He looks like there's more he wants to say, but doesn't. "Go get 'em, tiger," he tells me, trying for humor, but sounding pained. "I've got your back. We've all got your back."

I give him my best, my most Rhona smile. I try to be as fearless as he thinks I am. "I know," I say, and add more lightly, "You better."

"Rhona," Ulrich calls to me. It's time.

He double-checks my body armor, like I don't know how to put it on right. Like it'll make any kind of a difference if the machines decide to go Terminator on me. (Yes, I am *so* glad Samuel decided to show me those movies, as if my fear of machines wasn't already the size of a football stadium.)

Zelda hovers nearby, with an itchy finger resting on the trigger. She anxiously glances outside once, twice, three times. It makes me nervous. Nervous*er*.

"You know, if you're wrong about this, I'm going to get shot," I tell her. "Just saying."

"I'm not wrong," she maintains, yet there's a flicker of doubt in her eyes. "And if on the off chance I am, then we're all dead anyway."

"Comforting thought."

"Wouldn't be the first time for some of us." This statement, combined with the way she looks at me—like she's just been let in on a juicy secret—leaves no doubt in my mind that she knows the truth.

"Ulrich told you," I assume.

She nods. "I knew there was something different about you. But ..." She pauses to roll her eyes. "I may have been wrong about everything else."

It's tempting to make her work for this apology, after everything, but I don't, and not only because it would be petty. "Don't sweat it. You weren't the only person to give me a hard time," I tell her. "But we're all on the same team now."

"Yeah, we are," she agrees. "Though I'm still mad at Orpheus for not telling me. He says he was sworn to secrecy by the council, him and Ortega both." Her mouth dips into a frown. I wonder if she's thinking the same thing I am: with the latter's death, that's one less person who can spill my secret. Not that Ortega would have; he was a good man. He deserved better. The only way I can honor his loyalty and sacrifice now is to win.

"The machines have intercepted our communications and caught on to our movements," Ulrich cuts in. "Reports say they are moving in. It must be now."

I nod. "Right. Okay. Make sure everyone waits for my signal. Not a minute sooner—or later."

"You will have to move fast," Ulrich reminds me a final time.

"Yep. Should be interesting." It feels strange without the weight of a rifle and a few pistols, but that's one less thing to slow me down. Plus, Zelda insisted I would be considered less of a threat if I were unarmed. Of course, this is all based on the assumption I'm worth more to the machines alive than dead. If I'm not ... Well, then.

I inhale deeply, letting the chill settle comfortably in my lungs. "All right. Let's do this."

Before I march into the unknown, Ulrich embraces me, and I'm struck by the familiarity of it. I close my eyes, and the rustic soldier smell of him brings an image of my father to mind. "Be proud," he says. "I am, to have known you twice."

I smile privately, but pull away with a chastising look. "Hey, stop that. You're making it sound like I'm not coming back."

He shrugs, returning to the same old Ulrich I know and love. "Just in case." He waves me off. "Go now."

Stepping out from the dusty protection of the building, I'm initially blinded by the morning light. I put my hands in front of me, feeling along empty air until the street materializes. Even after I can see again, I keep my arms extended, palms out, in a universal sign of surrender, as I take my first steps into the open. I confront the moment of truth with a fire in my belly and a sort of to-hell-with-it mentality. I have everything to lose, but even more to fight for.

Nothing shoots me immediately, so that's a good sign.

I walk forward with a little more confidence. I have to watch myself around the pockmarked asphalt and other hazards. Main Street, like most other avenues in downtown Juneau, is littered with the debris of old battle, the perfect backdrop for a new one. We might have lost the last war, but the winds are changing. And I don't mean that in just the metaphorical sense either. Just then a breeze catches my red hair, blowing it to one direction, thankfully out of my face. If there were any doubt as to my identity, the machines should know full well by now, with my hair waving brazen as a resistance fighter's flag.

I don't approach their front lines without taking stock of my surroundings. Much of the city in this area has been demolished—which is why I chose it. There won't be anything to break the snow when it comes down. Bad for machines and people alike. There are a few places I think I can reach, once the signal's given. I have to trust that if the buildings can survive a fire bombing, they can survive some ice and rock, but there's no real knowing. There won't be until it's too late to find different sanctuary.

Ultimately, I settle on a sturdy-looking building whose upper level has a window with some colored glass still intact. Maybe a library or museum of some kind. It's got the height I'm looking for, and the bones to stand fast. I hope. With my exit plan decided on, I come to a stop within a reasonable distance of the place, forcing the machines to move toward me.

They shudder to a start, lurching forward as one unit. More come into view behind them, and still more behind them. They've concentrated their forces in the place they anticipate doing the most killing today.

"How's it looking, Eagle Eye?" I ask Rankin, who's with the most important squad there is, and has to be my eyes and ears while I'm on the ground.

"There's still some stragglers here and there throughout the city," he answers in a voice partially obscured by static, "but we've definitely got their attention, that's for sure. The main host is headed toward you now."

"Great," I say. It has to be the first time in my life I'm sincerely pleased to hear machines are headed my way.

"Just tell us when, Commander."

"Stand by. I want to draw as many into the open as I can."

"Roger." A pause. "Goes without saying at this point, but be careful, ma'am. Don't think for a moment that programming of theirs won't change. The higher echelon are slippery bastards."

"So am I," I say and let the conversation end. I have to focus. I have to time this just right.

Everything hinges on the timing.

The machines close ranks, pressed in by the confines of the street. They stop some yards away, and one breaks from the congregation. It's a predator model. I feel my heart hammering in my chest, two beats for each step it takes toward me. I instinctively reach for a weapon at my waist, but my holsters are empty. Right. I'm unarmed. That seemed like a better idea before.

"Rhona Long," it says through a speaker in the area of its throat. The voice is completely artificial this time around, like an old smartphone. "You have been convicted of war crimes under the Nuremberg Principles and have been summarily sentenced to death."

"Yeah, yeah, yeah," I say interrupting it. "What happened to surrender? As I recall, you said I could surrender, and my friends would be spared. I was hoping that offer was still good."

The predator angles its head, red optics eyeing me. "That agreement was made in the location of operational facility Churchill. It does not apply here."

"Tell us when," I hear Rankin say anxiously in my earpiece.

"I don't think you understand the situation," I speak through the predator to its masters—what we've termed the higher echelons, in whatever massive computer system they're currently residing. "Right now, we have our entire force surrounding your little army. At least two to every one of yours." Another model of machine might have been able to detect my deception, but not a predator. They're not built for interrogation, only elimination. "And trust me, those humans out there? They are *really* pissed off. You destroyed their homes. We hate when you do that."

Silence masks the processing as the higher echelons ponder this new information. "You are lying, Rhona Long," comes the thought-upon answer. "Humans are liars. Thieves. Killers. We know this, because we know you."

"Maybe," I say. "We're not perfect, I'll admit. We have our flaws and our vices. But we also have our virtues, and one of those is protecting the people we love."

"The machines are pulling back from the west and south, moving to your location now," Rankin says, amazed. "Whatever you're doing, Commander, it's working. They're preparing for a massive punch through our defenses."

I continue, being as provocative as I can. "And that's just one of many. Make no mistake: you don't *know* any of us. And you sure as hell don't know me or what I'm capable of!"

Before I have a chance to react, it fires at me. The slug catches me in the gut, putting me down.

"Don't," I murmur through a locked jaw, directed at those listening in. The pain of being shot is extraordinary, and I worry the vest didn't do its job until air rushes back into my lungs. Coughing, sputtering, I struggle to my feet, and surprisingly the machine lets me get back up.

"You fear death," the voice says—and even though it has no inflection, it manages to sound mocking. Shooting me was a test. "Every human fears death. Even you, Rhona Long. Correction. We do know you and your kind. Surrender now, and we will make the deaths of your friends quick. We are not without mercy."

I think the bullet may have broken a rib, but I can't help but smile, wishing them all to hell.

"Shake on it?" I say and extend my hand.

The signal.

EMP-Gs take out my predator, along with the first two columns of machines on both sides of their phalanx. At the same time as I dive away, a well-coordinated sniper shot destroys the core processor of the predator. I keep low to the ground as gunfire erupts all around me, crawling to cover behind a derelict tank. It's actually not in bad condition, considering the wear from the weather and the war it went through. Bullets ping around it, bouncing away from me.

Over the din of combat, I barely make out the *thump-hiss* of the antiaircraft artillery. It takes out huge chunks of machines, but that's not what I'm waiting for. I peek over the massive treads of the tank and watch several hiss toward the mountaintop. They connect in silence, from this distance, throwing up puffs of white.

I don't wait to see what happens next. I move toward the building that will be my lifeboat when the flood comes. The machines are too occupied with the human resistance to notice the missiles targeting the mountain. We maintain the element of surprise.

I just reach the inside of the building when my comm crackles to life. Dozens of voices talking over one another; I can't make heads or tails of what's happened. I start to climb the stairs, shouting into my earpiece. "Didn't get that. Repeat. Over." Finally, Ulrich manages to wrest control of the channel, silencing the other voices with some angry German. I'm sure most of them can't understand it, but they stop to listen, confused, giving me the quiet I need. "Ulrich, what was that all about?"

"It did not work. The mountain. The missiles. It did not work."

My stomach hurts, and I don't think it's only because of the gunshot. "Fire again," I tell him. "Fire until it does work!"

"We have no more ammunition for it. We used it all."

I curse, kicking the base of the stairwell's railing, venting my frustration. I can't think with all the anger and fear buzzing in my head. *Steady,* I think to myself, moving back to the door. I take a breath, peek out. "Okay. What's our contingency plan?" I ask Ulrich, because I don't remember devising one.

"Retreat," Ulrich answers, sounding more disheartened than I've ever heard him. "We can't," I say.

"That's not an option. If we fall back, it's over."

"*Ja.* That is why no one is interested in the contingency plan."

"I'll think of something."

"Pray. That might suit us better."

"Rhona!" I barely hear my name through the noise. I stare across the street, where I find a familiar person hunched behind the body of a car. He's pinned down by gunfire. What's he doing out here at all?

"Samuel?" I shout back, although I don't think he can actually hear me, except through comms, maybe. "Stay there!" I say, aligning my words with the appropriate hand gestures. "Don't move!"

To his credit, he proves a decent shot. Must've been all that training with Rankin. He deactivates several machines as he makes his way toward me, but they're overwhelming his position. More and more are identifying him as a threat to be eliminated. Self-preservation tells me to stay put, but my heart acts counterintuitively. I don't think—I just run out to meet him halfway, dodging gunfire as I go.

One machine gets a good shot off, catching Samuel in the arm or maybe the chest before I reach him. I don't know which. I don't know how serious. My mouth opens around his name, although the sound dies in my throat.

I throw myself in front of him, just as the predator goes for the kill.

My body clenches against the coming pain, but nothing happens. *The programming,* I think, half-hysterical, *the programming must still be in effect!* Just because it doesn't want to kill me, though, doesn't mean it won't try to capture me.

While this thought is just occurring to me, Samuel grabs my shoulder, flipping us over in time to fire at the still-attacking machine. Its chest explodes, showering us in metal and sparks. There's no permanent damage, though, only some superficial scrapes.

I don't waste any more time. "Come on, over there." I drag myself and a grimacing Samuel toward the nearby tank, hell continuing to break loose around us.

"What were you thinking?" I demand, removing his helmet to better see his face. Half of the visor's broken off, anyway, and the rest of it isn't going to provide much protection against a bullet, either.

"I wasn't there last time," he says.

"Samuel, what are you talking about?"

"At Anchorage. I wasn't at Anchorage and you died. Instead, I was miles"—he gestures wildly at the distance—"*miles* away, and absent in your life long before then. I know I probably couldn't have done anything to save you, but still ... I don't want to make that mistake again, Rhon. Not when I can do something this time."

"God, Samuel. Your guilt has impeccable timing." My adrenaline's high, and I'm still upset over his recklessness. The emotion ends up channeled into a bear hug as I grab my careless, idiotic friend tight. "Are you okay?" I ask, looking at his arm, the sleeve dark with blood.

"I thought you were in trouble," he says.

"Not what I asked. Besides, now we're both in trouble."

"Yeah, but we're together. Oh! And I brought you a gun."

I take the extra pistol, holding it aloft in my hands. "I guess I can forgive you, then. Not that it matters much at this point. It's doubtful we're going to live to see another day, let alone fight one." He's quiet, pensive. "What? No brilliant, million-dollar idea when I need one?"

He looks at me, smiles in a way that dislodges the fear from my heart. "Rhon, I'm a doctor, not a miracle worker." I give him a blank look. "*Star Trek.* You don't remember *Star Trek*?"

We both have to duck as a dying machine flails, releasing a stream of bullets.

The machines really start to swarm us now, the human defenses breaking. "We're sitting ducks here," I tell him, looking all around, but I can't see anywhere else we can go. Except ...

"I have an idea. Keep your head down."

I lie back and slip beneath the tank. There's an access hatch at the bottom. It takes some jiggling at the locking mechanism, but the cold has done its job weakening it and I manage to pry it open. "Samuel, here!" I shout at him. As soon as I'm sure he's making his way, I wriggle up into the belly of the machine. It's more difficult for Samuel with his injured arm, but he manages to get inside, too. I close the hatch behind him.

We must trigger some automatic sensors because electric lights flicker on, filling the interior with a cool aquamarine. The lighting is uncertain as it clicks off and then back on, not the most prodigious start. After so many years of being inactive, though, I'm just happy to have any of the systems operational. In the meantime, the world outside shrinks to a muffled roar at the back of my head, like a television screen left on in another room. In the muted quiet, it feels like I'm partially deaf, so I clear my throat a couple of times to confirm otherwise.

"By the look of things, I'd say it's running on reserve power," Samuel says, holding his shoulder tenderly as he gets some diagnostic information up and running on a previously blank screen. "Whoever was last in here had the foresight to at least leave a nice setup behind."

"Maybe they planned on coming back," I say.

"Yeah," he agrees solemnly, neither of us venturing to guess what happened to them. It's not hard to figure out. "Anyway, I'm just surprised this thing still has any power and functionality at all."

Something bangs against the hull outside, making me jump. "Is there any way we can get a visual of the outside?" I scan the board of blinking lights and wires, but can't make heads nor tails of any of it. It might as well be in another language. This just adds to my frustration. Why does technology always have to be so complicated? Why can't it just have a big, red button that says PUSH ME? That always seemed to work well enough in cartoons. And while we're at it, reality should adopt the policy of no one ever dying, too. That'd be swell.

"Let me see." He runs his hands across the console, lightly, so as not to hit the wrong buttons. The blood running down his arm drips off his fingertips onto the controls.

"Samuel, your arm ..."

"Got it!" One of the half-dozen screens crackles to life, displaying a colored version of the outside world, as seen through some exterior camera. He presses another button, and it cycles to another image, this time from a higher vantage point. The mountain sits neutral over the battle, and I want to scream, *"You were supposed to be on* our *side, you stupid hunk of rock!"*

But then I think, *Maybe it still is.*

While I try to attend to Samuel's arm, first by removing his sleeve, I ask him, "Can you get this thing moving?"

His confusion shows clearly. "I think so. But where would we go?"

"What about the weapons systems? Are they still active?"

He tries to pull his arm away from me after I touch a tender spot, but I yank it back in place. "Easy does it, Florence," he says through gritted teeth. The name's lost on me. "It looks like everything is still in working order. We're lucky the tank wasn't destroyed like the others we've seen; it was just switched off when its occupants fled. That being said, I don't want to get your hopes up."

I frown, thinking.

"The bullet's not in deep," I tell him. "I'm pretty sure I can get it out safely, but it's going to hurt, and I need you conscious right now. I hate to ask you this, but think you can stick it out for a little while longer?"

Samuel nods and points to the first-aid kit on the tank wall, a luminescent blue, like a jellyfish. "Bandage me up. I'll be good to go, Commander."

"It's weird when you call me that. Don't do that." He smiles, and I collect the scarce medical supplies left. "While I work on you, check and see what ammunition we've got to work with."

Using his good arm, he types out some basic commands on the console. I hear the mounted turret screech as it swivels, the metal groaning after such a long sleep. "The good news is the turret works. The bad news is we don't have much ordnance left. And the worst news is I'm not sure what any of what we do have does, exactly. How to launch an armored offensive wasn't covered in my biology classes. Go figure." He grimaces as I apply some disinfectant and begin wrapping the wound. I try to be gentler.

"Let's phone a friend," I suggest. "My earpiece isn't working, so we'll have to try some other way."

"Mine, either. The tank's probably got some natural firewall interfering with the signal."

"How do we get around it? This thing has to have some kind of comm system, right? Can we patch into our channel?"

"Maybe."

"Actually, I think I remember a way to do it. I had Zelda give me a beginner's course before we left. Move over, let me." My hands are slippery with blood, making it difficult to handle the smooth surface of the console. The system is more intuitive than I anticipated. It's a simple matter of linking up to the frequency. It'd be almost impossible for someone who didn't know the number, such as the machines, but thankfully my short-term memory is solid. "Here goes nothing." And by nothing, I mean *everything*.

"This is Commander Long. Come in. Hello? Does anybody read me?"

"Rhona," a familiar German voice wheezes on the other end. "*Gott sei dank!* Where are you?"

"Ulrich! I don't have time to explain. Just listen. Samuel and I are safe. We're in a tank in the middle of the battle. It's operational—"

"A tank?"

"We have some ammunition, but I need you to tell me what it all does. You were in the German army, right?"

"What are you planning on doing? One tank cannot take down a whole enemy force."

"No, but one tank can take down a mountain, with the right ordnance."

He grumbles in incomprehensible German before heaving a sigh. "Fine. Tell me what you have." Samuel takes over then, listing them in the order of how much we have available, most to fewest. Some have strange names like kinetic-energy penetrator and sabot, while others like the canister shot and high-explosive shells sound much more promising.

"Use the KEPs on the machines directly," Ulrich says. "They should be able to bypass their shielding. The machine gun will work as well for that task. For the mountain, use the shells or the guided missiles. Either should work sufficiently."

"Great," I say. "Thanks, Ulrich. If you haven't already, give the order for our people to take cover, wherever they can. If this works, they're not going to want to be groundside."

"What about you?" he asks. "And Samuel? What will you do?"

To be honest, I hadn't even considered our safety. "We should be okay in the tank," I tell him. "Don't worry about us. Just make sure everyone else is ready." I'm about to sign off when one last thought occurs to me. "And if something goes wrong—not that it will—but, you know. If it does. Look after Camus?" I swallow hard. My throat is tight and scratchy. "And make sure Rankin gets back to Hanna. Oh, and take care of yourself and your lady, too. Can you do that for me, Ulrich?"

"*Jawohl,* Commander. *Viel glück.*"

"Right back at'cha." I click the comm off, praying it doesn't turn out to be the last time I get to speak with that rascally German, but fearing it will be.

A mutual understanding passes wordlessly between Samuel and me. This is it, the quiet seems to imply. Whatever happens, happens.

"You take the tank controls," I tell Samuel. "I'll man the machine gun. I want to get close enough to kiss the mountain."

We lurch forward, moving down the street at a slow but steady pace, barreling into machines that don't get out of the way fast enough, and then crunching over them. The sound is music to my ears, accompanied by the percussive *rat-tat-tat-tat* of the machine gun as I spend the last of the minor ammunition on whatever enemies have the misfortune of running into my crosshairs. The machines return fire, but it has hardly any effect on the tank's armor. Instead, our beast draws attention away from the human soldiers, and the machine phalanx pools back into the main street, right where I wanted them to begin with.

We're almost in perfect range when the treads break down.

In addition, alarms start to sound, alerting us to a possible hull breach, and there's a hissing noise like some kind of depressurization. The bottom hatch has gotten loose from running over one of the machines. I quickly reseal it, thankful it's not something more serious. But that still leaves the problem of our position.

"Do you think we can hit it from here?" Samuel asks over the loud pinging of bullets hitting the tank's shielding.

"We're about to find out."

There's already a shell loaded into the turret, which feels somehow fitting. I'd call it a blast from the past if I was feeling cheeky. "Ready?" I turn to Samuel. He nods. I prepare my shot, lining up the large-caliber gun with the mountaintop. The recoil shudders through the vehicle, rattling my bones.

The missile appears to impact harmlessly into the side of the mountain, coughing up snow, just like before. I hold my breath, prepared to fire again.

But I don't need to. The mountain shivers, and a white curtain descends the slopes, picking up speed and mass. By the time it hits the drier areas toward the bottom, it's the very definition of a force of nature—a winter tsunami. Mud, trees, and anything else at the base are swept along, collected inside the swelling cloud of ice. The avalanche lumbers like a stampede toward the city.

I open the top hatch. I hear it now—a furious sound like rolling thunder. But I'm not taking any chances. I load our last missile into the turret, and Samuel helps me. We both narrowly avoid being hit by cross fire. Once back inside, I double-check to make sure the hatch is sealed tight and then fire the second round into what's left of Mount Juneau's snowy precipice, dislodging any remaining snow. Although there's less, it still manages to join its big brother with time to spare.

The avalanche does exactly as I'd hoped. It takes the path of least resistance, channeled into the main street, directly into the enemy's forces.

The machines don't have a chance to react, and there's nowhere for them to go anyway. Mother Nature slams into them like the fist of an angry god, punishment for the genocide of the human race. But it doesn't stop with them. It heads toward us, unbroken by the now-scrapped machines.

I barely have time to think "It worked!" before it plows into the tank. The collision throws me back, and I connect violently with the bulkhead. Snow smothers the camera, and the screen goes black shortly before I do.

THIRTY

FOR THREE DAYS, we're trapped in the tank.

We survive on expired army rations and acquire water from the melting snow that falls onto our heads any time we try to shimmy the bottom hatch open. Everything's topsy-turvy since the avalanche flipped the tank over, immobilizing us. With communications dead, we can't call for rescue—*If there's anyone even out there left to rescue us,* I think—and the tank's damaged systems enter a state of shutdown. The lights flash between red and blue for a couple hours before calming down, power reserves unable to maintain the alarm. There's no heating.

The first day isn't so bad. I dig the bullet out of Samuel's shoulder, and to his credit, he only passes out for a couple minutes. Then I bandage him up a second time.

We huddle together for warmth, and he tells me stories of the good old days while his teeth chatter and his body shakes. Our spirits are still high from what we hope is a solid victory against the metal forces of darkness. For all we know, we've won, and our suffering now is all worth it.

When I close my eyes, I dream of the happy New Mexico desert—a vast oasis of heat and memory, and I dream of Camus. Much like the first time, I enjoy the open spread of his arms and the way his eyes don't look so sad.

The second day is harder.

There's no way to mark the passage of time, so it feels more like the second week. Cold has a way of clouding the mind, dulling thinking to a point of difficulty. *Why?* I think in one of my less lucid moments. *Why is it so cold?* As I recall, death wasn't so cold the last time around. It was fire and blood, smoke in my chest. Immediate. Not like these quiet tremors, slow and lasting. My fingers are stiff and my joints ache when I attempt to exercise some feeling back into them, at Samuel's suggestion. It helps, but not much.

We're both in a sorry state by the third day. With the cold, there's no more dreams of New Mexico warmth, no more dreams of Camus, no more dreams at all, except the occasional hallucination, but those don't count. Falling asleep now almost certainly means freezing to death.

It doesn't help when the lights finally cut out, plunging us into a darkness so dense you can't see your hand in front of your face. A couple of times, Samuel has to shake me awake, and a couple of times I do the same for him. Eventually, we both reach our limit, a state of inescapable exhaustion. The end feels very nigh. The nigh-y-est.

"Do you think it was all worth it?" I ask him—a question loaded with other questions.

He leans his head against mine. "Yes," he says. "You gave them hope. We gave them a chance. Yeah, I think it was worth it."

"I'm glad you're here with me, Samuel," I whisper into the black void. "At the end, just like the beginning, huh? Samuel?"

But he's quiet.

Everything begins to blur. I hold Samuel's hands in mine, telling myself over and over not to fall asleep. Because of the darkness, I have a hard time telling whether I'm still awake or not.

Then I remember the sound of shoveling and scraping.

Metal hitting metal.

The hatch opens, spilling brightness and powder onto us, the combination looking like pixie dust to a mind addled by cold and starvation.

"They're here!" someone shouts, and other voices answer in Russian, French, and Chinese.

All beautifully human.

"We've got them! Over here! Long and Lewis are here!"

EPILOGUE

ONE WEEK LATER

I STAND on the roof of the apartment complex, bundled up against the wind in innumerable layers, overlooking the buried portion of Juneau. The city is alive with thousands of troops, wearing insignia from a dozen different bases. Languages that haven't been heard in this area for over five years fill the air—human voices that will not be silenced by tragedy. The sun is shining, high in the clear skies above, interrupted only by the occasional aircraft. Always one of ours.

Camus joins me after a while.

"You're looking better," I tell him. "Less full of holes."

He smiles at me. "I don't know how you managed to pull it off. The French-Canadians, maybe. But the Chinese? The New Soviets? You called, and they answered. And more are still arriving every day." He shakes his head. "I never would have believed it possible."

"O, ye of little faith," I reply, teasing him.

"Yes," he agrees, solemn, as though acknowledging a deeper failing. We stand there, quiet for a time, bathed in refreshing sunlight.

Camus is the first to break the silence. "What do you suppose happens now?"

"We stop hiding, for one. We establish contact with other survivors. Secure Alaska, so we'll have a place to strike out from and retreat to when need be. You know, continue with all that fighting-the-good-fight stuff."

"That," he says, pausing to glance down with a tiny smile, "wasn't what I was referring to."

"Ah ..."

He looks at me with uncertainty. His eyes are green and curious and a little afraid. "Can you ever forgive me?"

"Hey," I say, wagging my finger at him. "Didn't we already have this conversation?"

"This is for a different offense. I doubted you. The moment when you needed me to have faith, I doubted you."

I smile to reassure him I'm not hurt. "It's in your nature, Camus. You're the skeptic. I've always known that about you." I lean into his shoulder, and he angles his face toward mine. Our warm breaths mist the air between us—a spell against the cold and isolation.

"And still, you haven't abandoned me," he says quietly, "when it would've been well within your rights to kick me to the curb. When, in fact, I even encouraged you to do so. Why is that? I can't recall having done anything recently to deserve such loyalty."

I laugh, despite myself. His brows lower defensively, and I take his frowning face in my hands. "Camus, I don't love you because you deserve it. Though it's cute you think that."

"Then why?"

"I love you because you're a good man, Camus." He gives me a look of disagreement, that look of *What do you know?* "Don't give me that. You are. I know you've stopped believing it, because it's easier to feel responsible; it's easier to suffer the guilt and blame yourself than to acknowledge bad things happen, sometimes for no good reason. Because the alternative is to admit none of us is in control. And I hate to say it, but you're kind of a control freak. It makes you a great leader—not to mention criminally good at Risk and chess—but you're downright lousy when it comes to judging yourself." I expect his frown to deepen, but instead he cracks a smile, apparently aware of this fact. "And that's just one of the many character flaws which I love you for."

His eyebrows go up in mock offense. "Many?"

I sigh theatrically, releasing his face. "I know. We can't all be as perfect as me."

"I should aspire to your level of humility, truly," he says, trying not to laugh.

"My point is, you've got to stop beating yourself up about ... well, everything. Take a step back. Let things go once in a while. *Trust.*" He's frowning again, considering my words. Meanwhile, the sun continues to frame us in the possibility of a good day.

I face its warmth and close my eyes.

Then, without looking at him, I offer Camus my hand, wiggling my fingers. He takes it, his warm fingers spreading mine, inspiring ideas of a future for us. A different ending to the story of Rhona and Camus. One that isn't defined by what's missing or what's been lost, but what has been recovered.

"So you think you can do it?" I ask him in a hushed voice, uncertainty chewing the bottom of my stomach. "Make peace with everything that's happened?"

"I don't know, Rhona."

An honest answer, but one that squeezes my heart. Still, I'm resolved to fight for him, committed to championing our cause, not only because I love him, but because that's who I am. I'm the fighter, the never-give-upper. I eat hardship for breakfast.

Just as I'm cycling through these thoughts, pedaling fast toward some kind of consolation, Camus surprises me by adding, "But I'd like the opportunity to try." He looks at me meaningfully, kisses the back of my hand, and everything inside me relaxes at once.

"Getting colder," I tease him, with a gush of breath.

Camus smiles, leaning his face toward mine. "Allow me to try again." And I do.

The sun rises the next morning as it has every morning since the beginning of time, even on days when it couldn't be observed, its brilliance muted by passing clouds.

Reports come in of machines amassing in the east, somewhere in the vicinity of Valdez, not far from Anchorage. Mention of Anchorage doesn't fill me with quite so much dread as it used to. It's in the past now, where it belongs—the history of another woman. The future is where I stake my hopes.

After briefly visiting Kennedy and others recuperating from the battle, Camus and I arrive at the meal rooms, where we're immediately assaulted by applause. The soldiers there ask me to say a few words, and I don't have to think long on what I want them to be.

"Strange. You're all clapping for me when it's you guys doing most of the work, but okay. Whatever floats your boats," I begin with a touch of my trademark self-deprecation, receiving some chuckles for the remark.

"Someday, future generations will look back on the Machinations, and it'll just be another chapter of human history in their textbooks. More than likely, they'll have to write an essay on it and hate it." I smile to more laughter, before growing serious again.

"You laugh now, but that's what I'm fighting for. It's what you're fighting for. To give them that chance. To give humanity a second chance, or however many it's been since we first screwed up. Sure, many probably won't know about the daily heroics—and I'm not talking about moving mountains, but the quiet, persistent dignity I've seen each and every one of you show. In short—*you* inspire *me*." I smile during a thoughtful pause. "Okay, now you can clap if you want to, but not for me. Clap for you. Like I said, it's you guys that are doing most of the work. Me? I'm just along for the ride."

I sit down, taking my place next to my friends. Next to Camus and Ulrich, across from Samuel and Rankin and Zelda, sitting shoulder to shoulder with other ordinary men and women whom history has called upon to be heroes.

I don't know if we'll triumph over the machines in the end. But win or lose, I know what team I'm on. And I know what I want those imaginary history books to say about me:

Her name was Rhona Long. She fought for them.

FROM THE PUBLISHER

Thank you for reading Machinations, book one in Last Resistance.

WE HOPE you enjoyed it as much as we enjoyed bringing it to you. We just wanted to take a moment to encourage you to review the book on Amazon and Goodreads. Every review helps further the author's reach and, ultimately, helps them continue writing fantastic books for us all to enjoy.

If you liked this book, check out the rest of our catalogue at www.aethonbooks.com.

To sign up to receive a FREE collection from some of our best authors as well as updates regarding all new releases, visit www.subscribepage.com/AethonReadersGroup.

ALSO IN THE SERIES

Machinations

Counterpart

Architect

ABOUT THE AUTHOR

HAYLEY STONE IS A WRITER, editor, and poet from California.

Hayley loves to hear from readers and writers. Find her at www.hayleystone.com and on Twitter @hayley_stone.

www.ingramcontent.com/pod-product-compliance
Lightning Source LLC
Chambersburg PA
CBHW030352310726
48979CB00001B/267

* 9 7 8 1 9 4 9 8 9 0 6 7 9 *